Praise for *Island*

"I was consumed by the savage mysteries of Cameron's harsh and haunting fantasy world. A story of love and loss as searing as the desert heat."
—Diana Peterfreund, author of *For Darkness Shows the Stars*

"Harrowing and heartfelt. The intricately realized world of *Island of Exiles* crackles with harsh magic and gripping suspense."
—A.R. Kahler, author of The Runebinder Chronicles series

"*Island of Exiles* is imaginative, bold, and as electrifying as a Shiara storm."
—Lori M. Lee, author of *Gates of Thread and Stone* and *The Infinite*

"A beautifully wrought fantasy filled with magic, rebellion, and romance, plus a strong, butt-kicking heroine to root for!"
—Lea Nolan, *USA Today* bestselling author of *Conjure*, *Allure*, and *Illusion*

"Erica Cameron's *Island of Exiles* is a remarkable achievement: a fantasy world so richly imagined, so finely detailed, and so strikingly original, even the most incredible elements feel totally real. The energy of the desosa will tingle along your skin as you race through this amazing book, and at journey's end, you'll long for the sequel so you can immerse yourself once more in the mysteries of Itagami!"
—Joshua David Bellin, author of the Survival Colony series

"*Island of Exiles* has everything I've been looking for in a fantasy— powerful characters, magical powers that make me itch with envy, and a spoken language that is as intrinsic to the story as it is beautiful."
—Amber Lough, author of *The Fire Wish* and *The Blind Wish*

Also by Erica Cameron

SEA OF STRANGERS

THE RYOGAN CHRONICLES

ERICA CAMERON

Entangled Publishing, LLC
2614 South Timberline Road
Suite 109
Fort Collins, CO 80525

Entangled Teen is an imprint of Entangled Publishing, LLC.

Visit our website at www.entangledpublishing.com.

Edited by Kate Brauning
Cover design by Anna Croswell
Interior design by Toni Kerr

ISBN: 978-1-63375-828-5
Ebook ISBN: 9-781-63375-829-2

Manufactured in the United States of America

First Edition December 2017

10 9 8 7 6 5 4 3 2 1

entangled teen
an imprint of Entangled Publishing LLC

*For Liza Wiemer, who offered me hope when
I needed it and who never lost faith.*

CAST OF CHARACTERS

AHTA – a Ryogan child living in the Mysora Mountains with eir mother Dai-Usho; ey/em

ANDA – Khya and Yorri's blood-mother and a kaigo councilmember; rikinhisu mage; she/her

CHIO HEINANSUTO – Tsua's husband, Varan's brother, and one of the original twelve immortals; dyuniji mage; he/him

DAITSA – former second-in-command of Tyrroh's squad; dyuniji mage; deceased; she/her

DAI-USHO – Ryogan woman who lives in the Mysora Mountains with her child Ahta; she/her

ETARO – member of Tyrroh's squad and currently platonically partnered with Rai; rikinhisu mage; ey/em

KAZU – commander of the Ryogan ship that carries Tyrroh's squad to Ryogo; he/him

KHYA – member of Tyrroh's squad, Yorri's older sister, and Tessen's current partner; fykina mage; she/her

LO'A – Osshi's friend and the voice of a hanaeuu we'la maninaio caravan; she/her

MIARI – member of Tyrroh's squad and currently partnered with Nairo and Wehli; ishiji mage; she/her

NATANI – member of Tyrroh's squad; zoikyo mage; he/him

NAIRO – member of Tyrroh's squad and currently partnered with Miari and Wehli; kasaiji mage; he/him

NEEVA – Tessen's blood-mother and a kaigo councilmember; rusosa mage; she/her

ONO – Khya and Yorri's blood-father and a kaigo councilmember; oraku mage; he/him

OSSHI SHAGAKUSA – Ryogan historian who sailed to Shiara looking for proof of the bobasu's existence; he/him

RAI – member of Tyrroh's squad and currently platonically partnered with Etaro; kasaiji mage; she/her

RYZO – former second-in-command of Tyrroh's squad who remained on Shiara; hishingu mage; he/him

SANII – Yorri's sumai partner and the one who discovered the truth about Yorri; hyari and tusenkei mage; ey/em

SUZU – a leader of Sagen sy Itagami and one of the original twelve immortals; sykina mage; she/her

TESSEN – a member of Tyrroh's squad and Khya's current partner; basaku mage; he/him

TSUA – Chio's wife and one of the original twelve immortals; rikinhisu mage; she/her

TYRROH – the leader of Khya's squad; oraku mage; he/him

Varan Heinansuto – leader of Sagen sy Itagami and one of the original twelve immortals; ishiji mage; he/him

Wehli – member of Tyrroh's squad and currently partnered with Miari and Nairo; ryacho mage; he/him

Yorri – Khya's brother, Sanii's sumai partner, and a born immortal; kynacho mage; he/him

Zonna – Chio and Tsua's son and a born immortal; hishingu mage; he/him

A glossary of terminology is included at the end of the book.

...and although few firsthand accounts of the discovery have survived, most of the earliest records, made a decade after the bobasu and their proselytes are believed to have been cast from Ryogo, are consistent. The conclusions drawn from these documents are that Varan Heinansuto did, in fact, exist, and that the brief time he held sway over Ryogo—and the Great War he instigated—was the darkest time in Ryogo since the schism itself...

...then, on the fifth day of the ninth moon in the three-thousand two-hundred eleventh year after the schism, a great streak of fire burned across the sky and a wave taller than the Kaisubeh tower of Po'umi crashed over the southeastern shores. On that day, the Kaisubeh proved—as they had with the schism of the lands and the raising of the kemberu, the impassable mistveil that enshrouds the land on which Pratel and his army were imprisoned—that they hear and answer the prayers of their followers when that help is both needed and deserved. The black rock they hurled down from the heavens was spotted by a vessel far out to sea, and large pieces were brought home.

Despite the damage its arrival caused to the southern shores of Ryogo, and although it would take another five years for that discovery to be made, the Kaijuko stones proved to be our salvation. And the discovery came just in time to avert utter ruin.

—Excerpts from *The Banishment of the Bobasu: A History of The Great War*, written by Osshi Shagakusa and published in 3738 A.S.

CHAPTER ONE

The ship rocks violently, wind and rain lashing the deck. Tessen and I grab the rope stretched along the center of the deck to keep from sliding to the edge and over. Straight into the dark, angry ocean.

Lightning streaks across the sky, making the three red sails glow as if on fire. For an instant, the world is thrown into stark relief.

The wave cresting several feet above the ship.

The Ryogan crew fighting through wind and rain to keep us upright.

The purple-black storm clouds obscuring almost the entire sky. Almost.

It's been impossibly long since this storm started chasing us. Maybe five days and nights of the twelve or so since we fled Shiara; it's hard to tell without being able to see the sky. Our first sign of hope is what Tessen spotted through the small window of our room on the lower deck. It could save us, get us out of the gale winds and the drenching rain, but only if we can find Osshi or the ship's commander before the storm cracks the vessel in half and drowns us all.

Tessen and I haul ourselves along the deck, scanning for Osshi and Taikan-yi Kazu. The rain is too thick. Without the flash of lightning, I can barely see the rope in my hands. Hopefully, Tessen's vision isn't as hobbled by the storm as mine.

Someone is shouting; the words are lost in the wind, drowned in the crash of a wave slamming into the ship and washing over the deck.

A hand grabs my elbow. The unexpected touch sends an unpleasant shock up my arm. I don't dare shake it off, not without risking my balance.

"Get below, Khya!" Osshi's small eyes are wide, but his square jaw is set and determined. "You can do nothing here. Go!"

"Look! There!" With the hand not gripping the rope, I point to the horizon, to the thin strip of bright blue. It's almost invisible at this distance. His gaze follows my finger, squinting into the driving rain.

"Thank the Kaisubeh." He sags with relief, but the drop of his shoulders only lasts a heartbeat. We've still got to make it there. He pushes me toward the lower deck. "Go! I'll tell Kazu if he doesn't already know."

There's little chance he knows. Taikan-yi Kazu, the commanding officer, is probably too busy steering the ship through the massive waves and making sure the storm doesn't overturn us. I'll be shocked if *any* of the crew have noticed the tiny strip of sky yet. Tessen only did because he's a basaku, and his senses are far stronger and more discerning than anyone else's.

Tessen tugs on my wrist, pulling me toward the safety of the lower deck. And he's right; there's nothing else we can do here.

I follow him, holding the rope tight. The rough fibers scratch my palms. I grip harder. That abrasion means I'm attached to the deck. Not even my magic will save me if I fall into the ocean.

I can't swim.

Tessen reaches the door first. A flash of lightning illuminates the straining muscles under his soaked tunic. The wind must be holding it shut. It shouldn't be this hard for him to open. Yanking myself closer, I wrap my left arm around the rough rope and grab the handle of the door with my right. For a breath, it doesn't budge. Then the wind shifts. It's enough for us to haul the door open and rush inside. A gust slams it closed behind us.

The walls of the ship aren't nearly thick enough to eliminate the howling wind or the waves crashing against the hull, but for a moment, the world sounds silent.

Then Tessen's pained, and poorly stifled, groans register.

I check him for injuries; there aren't any, but the trip obviously wiped him out. "You shouldn't have come with me."

He grunts. Was that supposed to be a word? Maybe, but it looks like he might throw up again if he tries to repeat it.

The rise and fall of the normal sea he handled fine, but the extreme dips and climbs of the storm-tossed waves coated his terra-cotta skin with a sheen of sickly sweat and seemed to turn his stomach upside down. Probably because he's a basaku. He hasn't been able to eat much since the storm started, he's been achy for days, and it seems like the trip took all the energy he had left.

I put my hand out, waiting for him to take it. I expect the rain to have chilled his skin, but his hand is cold even against my rain-cooled skin. Worryingly so. I urge him forward, trying to ignore the ominous creaks and groans that echo through the hull with each wave.

How can any structure not reinforced by magic survive this assault?

The ship tilts. I stumble and lose my hold on Tessen. My shoulder slams against the wall of the narrow hallway. From the thump and groan behind me, Tessen lost his footing, too.

Bellows and blood. It's not a long walk between this deck and our room one level below, but it takes us several minutes. We collect close to a dozen new bruises on the way. Tessen stops twice, heaving even though there's nothing in his stomach left to lose. I stay with him, one hand pressed to his back and the other braced against the wall.

"I know I promised…we'd steal a ship to get back—" He closes his mouth, breathing deeply through his nose. "Back to Shiara, but…we might have to steal a crew…too. I don't think I'll be much use…running the ship."

"You were fine before the storm." I rub circles on his back, trying not to think about how true his worries are. Or how we would ever have survived this trip without Kazu's crew. Or how we'll do it when we make the trip back. Or how long it'll be before that happens.

He rests his head against the wall. "And with our luck… there'd be nothing but storms."

"With our luck, it would be—*will* be—exactly like that." I move my hand to Tessen's arm, pushing all of those thoughts away as much as I can. We have other problems to face first. "Let's get you sitting before I have to drag you the rest of the way."

Tessen pushes himself off the wall. Our rooms are spread throughout this level, the andofume in one, Osshi and Tyrroh in the next, and Miari, Wehli, Nairo, and Natani sharing a third. I haven't seen anyone but Osshi since the storm started. I should check on them, especially since we have to pass the other rooms to reach the one Tessen and I have been sharing with Rai, Etaro, and Sanii. No. Later. Once we're dry and the ship stops trying to kill us.

"Please tell me they're taking us toward the end of this," Rai says with a groan as soon as Tessen and I enter. Though her stomach isn't faring as badly as Tessen's, she's not exactly enjoying this new way of traveling.

"We pointed them to it, but they'll only be able to head that way if the wind lets them." I hover over Tessen as he eases himself down to the floor, mostly to make sure he doesn't collapse, then I sit against the wall next to him.

It's warmer in here, the enclosed space containing everyone's body heat, but I'm soaking wet and the air is so much colder than I'm used to. I shiver; Tessen does, too. When Rai notices, she shakes her head. "No. Can't. Don't have the energy for fire. Change before you both catch a chill and die."

"We won't die from a chill." But she's right. I should've dried off better before I sat down.

"I might." Tessen lifts one of his arms as though thinking about taking off his sopping wet tunic, then drops his hand back to his lap. "Dying would probably hurt less than this."

"No one is dying. There's been enough of that already." Sanii unpacks clothing from our bags and holds out the pieces of cloth. Etaro—who hasn't seemed affected by the storm at all—uses eir magic to float them across the room and make them hover just slightly out of my reach. I strip Tessen and myself out of our soaked clothes and get us both into the dry ones.

The ship rolls again. Tessen's head smacks against the wall. I fall forward, my hands landing on Tessen's chest. Sanii almost tumbles off the low table ey'd been sitting on. Etaro and Rai slide a few feet before they can brace themselves.

"I *hate* that." Sanii moans when the ship rights itself once more.

"Oh really?" Sarcasm practically bleeds from Rai's voice. "I'm sure the Miriseh will call the whole plan off, then."

"We don't know this has anything to do with the Miriseh," Etaro says.

Rai glares, but it's Sanii who says, "We don't know it doesn't, either."

It's an argument we've already beaten to death, especially since the storm hit, but they keep coming back to it. I can't blame them. If talking about whether the Miriseh could create a storm and send it after us would give us an answer, I'd bludgeon the conversation again, too.

But we can't know for sure. We didn't know the truth when we were on the same island—in the same city, even—as the immortal leaders we spent our lives serving. How can we possibly know anything more now that hundreds of miles separate us from them?

Tessen's hand lands on my knee, flopped there without any of his usual grace. I bite back a smile at his pitiful expression and move in front of him, placing his upturned hands on my thighs and applying pressure to the points below his wrist. Our healer Zonna eased Tessen's agony until Kazu's crew started collecting injuries more life-threatening than an upset stomach. Pressure point relief is a poor substitute for magic, but it'll have to be enough. I'm no hishingu. My wards may be able to keep someone from getting hurt, but it can't do a thing to help anyone who's already in pain.

"We were supposed to see land today." Sanii's looking out the small window, eir narrow face tense as ey peers into darkness broken only by lightning. Most of us have to duck or bend to look out the window; ey's so short it's at a perfect height for em. "Or yesterday, if it's past midnight."

"Who can tell?" Etaro stares at the small black stones dancing in midair above eir palm, some of the few we took off Imaku, the barren, black island that was once my brother's prison.

No. My chest tightens, and I press my thumbs deeper into Tessen's skin. I can't think about that place until I have some idea how long it'll be before I can try to rescue Yorri.

Try. Again. For a third time.

"Horizon was...too bright," Tessen manages to say. "Not night. Midday, maybe."

"We could still find land today." Etaro bit eir full bottom lip, eir concave cheeks sucking in deeper. The words are hopeful. Eir expression isn't.

"Do you really want to get there?" Rai asks something I've been thinking, but haven't said.

We're headed to Ryogo—a land I believed I'd only see in death—and it isn't going to look or feel anything like I expected. The realization has hit me in bits and pieces over the past two weeks, like sporadic grains of sand at the beginning of a dust storm. And like those small strikes, it's become more uncomfortable—nearly unbearable—the longer it goes on. The closer we get to the real Ryogo.

"Even with what we stole from Itagami, we'll run out of food soon." Sanii doesn't look away from the window. "Either we find land or we starve."

I look at the empty plate sitting on the floor in the corner of the room. A few hours ago, those of us who could stomach food shared a meal smaller than what *one* of us ate back home; Sagen sy Itagami's kitchens only ever rationed us during the worst of desert droughts. The city where the clan we abandoned lives. Where Yorri is hidden. Where we thought we'd remain our whole lives.

Until Osshi hauled me out of the ocean, I didn't know anywhere but Shiara existed. Even now, even knowing there *has* to be another land, it's hard to convince myself we won't either fall off the side of the world or find ourselves facing the mountains of Shiara's southern shore. Yorri was the only person I knew who had guessed there might be something beyond our island.

Tessen's fingertips lightly brush my forearm. Even through the cloth of my long-sleeved tunic, I can feel his body heat and the softness of the gesture. The ridiculous boy is reading my emotions again.

"Stop it." I don't bother whispering. The room is barely big enough for us all to sit without touching, so everyone will hear, even with the storm in the background. "You've got enough to worry about without adding me."

"I'm always...worried about you." He swallows hard when the ship shudders, but a little of the strain has eased from his wide-set, narrow eyes. Maybe the pressure points are helping. "When I stop paying attention, you...go and do something ridiculous. Like trying to take on the bobasu alone."

"She wasn't ever alone in that." Sanii turns to glare at Tessen.

"Yes, but it's the *Miriseh*, Sanii," Etaro says, not unkindly. "Khya's wards may be able to hold against them for a while, but unless you're as invulnerable as they are—"

"You might as well offer your throat for them to cut." Rai, as always, goes straight for the point Etaro was circling. "It'd be less painful than fighting."

Sanii opens eir mouth. I hold my breath, waiting to see if ey will finally mention eir strange magic. The secret was fine at first—ey didn't know or trust my squad—but it's been almost two weeks now.

I almost laugh with relief when Sanii extends eir arm and stares challengingly at Rai. "I'm not as helpless as you think."

Eir hand, and for the first time *just* eir hand, begins to glow. The light, initially a faint white glow over eir beige-brown skin, grows brighter until it's so strong I have to look away. I turn to Rai, waiting for her reaction.

"Huh. Well, the Miriseh—bobasu—whatever." Rai waves off the mistake. "They definitely didn't know you can do *that*."

"What *is* that?" Etaro leans in, eir narrow face alight. The ship pitches. We all brace—and Tessen and Rai grunt—but when we level out, Etaro reaches out again, hovering over Sanii's hand without touching. "There's no heat."

"It's light, not fire," I say before I can stop myself.

"You— No. Right." Annoyance sparks in Rai's round eyes. "Of course you knew, and of course you didn't tell us."

I don't need the warning tap of Tessen's fingers on the inside of my wrist. This time, I let Sanii answer for emself.

"It wasn't Khya's secret to tell." Sanii's light vanishes. "I asked her to keep quiet, and because she takes her promises seriously, she did until I was ready to trust you."

"Trust us to what?" Etaro asks.

Sanii turns back to the window. "To not look at me like you're scared."

"Of what?" Rai asks, scoffing. "Light?"

"Something different," Sanii says.

"Different isn't scary, it's weird." The ship dips. We all brace. Rai grimaces, but quickly starts speaking again, as though she's desperate for the distraction. "Besides, it's *light*. What's there to be scared of?"

Sanii glances at her, shrugs, and looks back to the storm. It's not the whole story, but the sumai ey managed to create with my brother is a special, private thing. Forging a soulbond should've been impossible for anyone but one of the Miriseh, according to what they taught us about magic, and it can only be performed once. The second time a soul splits, it's a deathblow. So the light isn't Sanii's whole story, but what ey's hiding won't hurt them.

The ship tilts hard. I slap my hands on the wall over Tessen's head to keep from crashing into him. Someone above us screams. The ship's creaking groans are suddenly deafening.

"Oh no." Tessen's horror-wide eyes are fixed on the ceiling. "Wards, Khya!"

I tense, my heart pounding as I create an invisible energy shield around everyone. Less than a second before the small window shatters.

Water pours in. Sanii screams. I clench my fists and push my ward back to the wall of the ship, shoving as much water as I can back into the ocean. And watching at least one of our bags go with it.

Bless whatever piece of luck or fate made me a fykina mage instead of sykina—if my shields could only protect against magic, we'd be dead now.

Closing my eyes, I mentally feel for my wardstones, the power-filled crystals I use as anchors. When we fled Shiara, I hid them all over the ship in case Varan chased us across the ocean. This isn't how I planned on using them, but I can't shield a ship as large as a building without them.

Vicious storms over-excite the desosa. The elemental energy created and used by everything in the world fuels magic, and it can make a mage more powerful—if they're capable of using it. Attempting it when the desosa is this chaotic, though, is dangerous. Life threatening. Most mages don't survive it.

I've done it before, though. More than once.

Pulling in as much of the desosa as I can without turning my brain to charcoal, I activate the hidden wardstones. My ward stretches, growing from each stone in a snap until the sections meet and merge. The connections spark like fire in my mind; each enhances my awareness of the ship. I can feel exactly what's trying to break through. And where.

My heart pounds. My head buzzes. My hands shake. "The hull is broken. A deck below us. Water's trying to break in."

"That's mostly supplies, right?" Etaro looks down. "Is anyone hurt?"

"How should I know?" I snarl. Another wave tilts the ship beyond what the hull can bear. Another too-loud groan of wood and metal as the only thing holding us above the water tries to shatter.

The weight of the waves against my wards is immense. Keeping the water out without squashing one of the crew between my wards and the hull is so hard it hurts. Chest aching and lungs burning, I try to breathe normally instead of panting for air. My vision is fuzzy on the edges and my brain buzzes. I've never tried to make my wards impervious to water while allowing people through. I can't hold this balance for long, either. There's another option, but…

I've always used my wards to either protect or to trap. Using them to reinforce a non-magical barrier? I don't know if it's possible. None of my training taught me how to merge magic with something solid; usually I use it to shove physical things out of the way.

Remembering how I tweaked my wards when we escaped from Imaku, I imagine I'm shaping them like a blacksmith shapes metal. I press my shield toward the hull, pushing water out of cracks and broken windows until the wards meet wood. Keeping the water in the ocean is like trying to carry the weight of a dozen people. It should be impossible—it's too much pressure for one person to bear—but I will *not* let this beat us. I promised I'd go back for Yorri and, bellows and blood, I am not going to break my vow.

I suck in more of the desosa and focus. Molding my magic, I fit it within the cracks and seams and joints of the wooden ship. Overhead and under, I create a dome to protect us from the worst swells.

We're still tossed heedlessly, but now my wards take the

beating. *I* take the beating. I'm being compressed, the water and the wind and the rain and the sky and the desosa and the fury of the storm all pressing closer, as though it's becoming a solid thing trying to crush me to dust. The force of it builds. Sound fades. Pain shoots between my clogged ears every time I clench my jaw. Someone puts his hand on my shoulder; I can barely feel it.

Holding my breath, I count to ten. I have to let go of my wards. Just for a moment. Have to. The pressure is too much and it's going to—

Everything stops.

The ship lurches and then rights itself, gently rocking with the small swells of a calm sea. Wind that's been a constant noise in the background for days dies away. The pressure of the waves against the hull vanishes so fast I almost collapse without the weight as a counterbalance.

"Oh, thank the M—" Tessen bites off the word.

Thank the Miriseh.

Miriseh bless it.

Save us, Miriseh.

The oaths are automatic—phrases we've used and believed our entire lives. I've said them more than once since we left Itagami. It's only been twelve days or so, if I'm right about how long we've been lost in the storm. Compared to the seventeen previous years, it's nothing, but I've gotten angry at myself every time their name brushes my lips. I can almost see the same thoughts passing through Tessen's mind now.

On Shiara, they are the Miriseh, the immortals.

In Ryogo, they're called the bobasu, the exiles.

Tsua, Chio, and Zonna named themselves the andofume, those denied death.

Whatever the word, it means the same thing, and when we land, there isn't much of a chance any Ryogans will see us as anything but the descendants of monsters, ones that, for them, fell into legend centuries ago.

That's assuming we get there alive.

The storm has quieted, but below the waterline there's more than enough pressure to test my wards. I can hold the ocean out for a while, but even with the wardstones as an anchor, a while might not be much longer.

"I need to check with Osshi and Kazu." I swallow and stand, trying to still my shaking hands. "They need to know where the worst damage is."

Tessen watches, his full lips pursed. It's likely he wants to come, but his skin is beaded with sweat, and his gray eyes are glassy. If he tries to get up, I'll push him down and *make* him rest. Now that the ship has stopped rocking so violently, he might be able to sleep.

"I'll go with you." Etaro stands and crosses the room. "I can help with repairs."

A little of the frustration eases out of Tessen's face.

Oh. He still thinks I don't know when or how to ask for help.

I may take too many risks, but I'm not a fool. The crew could use Etaro's help. Ey's a rikinhisu, and eir power is our second-best chance at quickly patching the damage. Tsua is the first, but the andofumes' door is open and the room is empty, so all of them are probably already helping. Before we hit the stairs, I check on Miari and the others; thankfully, the only damage is a few bruises and scrapes, some lost supplies, and a puddle of water on the floor.

Despite how it felt belowdeck, the world is far from calm. The sky is obscured by storm clouds, and the brine-laden wind bellows over the ship hard enough to force us to lean into it to walk. The roll of the sea is why it felt so quiet below. The high, crashing waves we faced during the worst of the storm are gone. It's become a rhythmic slap that's eerily steady.

No, not eerie. Good. We need quiet and calm so we can make repairs. But the suddenness of it is still unnerving.

Osshi and Taikan-yi Kazu are easy to find; both surveying the deck from the front platform. Every few seconds, Kazu shouts orders, his sharp gaze scanning his ship and crew.

"That storm wasn't natural," Kazu says as we close in, his gaze fixed on the southern horizon, which is a solid line of dark clouds and flashing lightning. "This ship should've been able to weather a storm. It has before."

"It fared worse than you know." I tell him what happened and point him toward the holes that, if not patched before I fall straight into a dead sleep, will sink the ship. Kazu gives me a wary glance, but he shifts his crew to those repairs. Etaro offers to assist, and Kazu agrees. Kazu clearly isn't going to turn away a useful tool just because he doesn't like it.

"That was *you*, Khya?" Osshi waves his hand overhead, his expression pinched. "The water rose over our heads but didn't touch us, and the wind—"

"Yes. The ship was breaking apart, Osshi. I *had* to use my wards."

He closes his eyes, shuddering. "Kaisubeh forgive us."

I saved your life. Biting my tongue is harder every time I see him react like this to magic.

On Shiara, Tsua created a bridge for us to cross a ravine, magically lifting wide, flat stones and holding them in midair for us to walk over. I'd thought Osshi's collapse when his feet hit solid land was from a fear of heights, but it's become clear his fear is of magic, of anything more than the most basic usage. *Because the Kaisubeh forbid it* is the only explanation he's given.

"I'm grateful, Khya," Kazu says. "I don't think the ship would've survived without you. And without Etaro and Tsua, this work would take twice as long."

Osshi has been teaching us Ryogan—the spoken and written language—since we left Shiara. Their tongue is similar to Itagamin, which helps, but sometimes it's a struggle to mentally sort through my three languages—Itagamin, Denhitran, and now Ryogan—before speaking.

"We're on this ship, too, Kazu." I smile, hoping it looks more genuine than it feels. I can't tell if he trusts us, especially since he hasn't done anything to stop the fearful whispers of his crew, but I ignore my own nerves and try to reassure his with a joke. "It wouldn't be smart of us to let the ship crack, would it? I can't swim."

Kazu smiles, but a shout from across the deck pulls his attention away before he answers. I watch him walk away, anxiety condensing in my stomach.

The men on this ship—and, oddly, his crew is *only* men— saw where we came from. They know a little of why we needed to flee Shiara and saw the kind of power we're running from— that we're trying to protect *their* homeland from—yet they still don't trust us. Except for Osshi and Kazu, the Ryogans have mostly kept themselves apart, watching us with wariness if not stark fear.

Tsua and Chio have warned us that peoples' fear will only be worse on Ryogo, but it could, they think, help us.

To kill Varan, we have to figure out how he made himself immortal, and if we want to know that, we have to head to the mountains beyond Uraita, the village where Varan and Chio were born. Centuries ago, Chio followed his brother into the mountains, to a spot where Varan liked to hide things he didn't want anyone else to find. Including, we hope, information on his hunt for immortality.

The andofume's theory is that none of our goals should be hard to meet when so few people in Ryogo are warriors.

Even fewer are mages. They can't fight us. Most of them will be afraid to try.

It's good, I remind myself, facing the northwestern horizon. Ryogo is out there somewhere, and it's hiding what I need to free my brother and unravel the bobasu's plan. Varan's secrets are either well guarded or long destroyed, but the Ryogans can't plan for everything.

Lucky for us, magic is one thing they won't see coming.

CHAPTER TWO

Overnight, the solid line of land slowly grows thicker on the horizon, but only Tessen and Tyrroh can see anything other than flickering lights and the solidity of something that isn't water. At dawn, the sun—its light almost as soft as the glow of a cooking fire—reveals the land I once thought the Miriseh were the keepers of.

Varan and the others have lied about almost everything, but maybe not Ryogo.

Spread out before us is a vast, lush land, greener than I've ever seen. No amount of rain would ever transform our desert island into land as fertile and verdant as this. It's all somehow soft, too. The mountains rising high above the coast don't have bare rock or ragged points and edges; their curves and slopes are covered with green that, from a distance, looks like it would be soft as a niora fur mat.

"Is that supposed to be a wall?" Sanii points north of where I've been looking. As I run my thumb along the red cord around my wrist, I follow eir gaze.

"If it was once, it isn't anymore." The massive pieces of

stone standing upright on the coast might be taller than Itagami's walls, but there are massive gaps between them. "I have a hard time believing that ever protected anyone."

"Wait," Osshi says as he joins us. "You'll see when we get closer."

Soon, I do see. It's not a broken wall, it's a row of enormous statues, a line of stone people. Fourteen of them.

"The Kaisubeh Zohogasha. The guardians." Osshi touches his three middle fingers to his forehead, his chest, and then his lips, almost like a salute. "They were erected a decade after the bobasu's exile. The seven facing the ocean shield Ryogo, and the seven facing land bless it. There are Zohogasha sets along the entire coast, but these were the first. Intended to watch the bobasu's prison and guard against their return."

"They're not stopping us." I tilt my head to glance at him. "I don't think they work."

He nods, his expression more solemn than I expected. "Symbols rarely do."

I watch his face carefully. "Still no word from your friend?"

"We're too far away from Po'umi. The garakyu only reaches for five miles." Although his hand falls to the belt pouch where he keeps the clear sphere he can use to send messages, he doesn't take it out. "I only hope they'll know how much trouble I need to be prepared for."

"Will your leaders really kill you on sight?" Sanii sounds skeptical.

"That's the worst possibility. I'm still hoping no one figured out where I went." Osshi takes a deep breath, pulling his attention back to us instead of his homeland. I glance at the cord on my wrist and try not to think about mine. "If they don't know I went hunting for proof of the bobasu, no one will be looking for me, but...I don't think that'll happen."

"It doesn't matter. Your people dying is the only thing

I'm worried about, if my squad meets a Ryogan one." They fear magic and only a small, specific class of their citizens are weapons-trained. So far there's little I've heard about Ryogo that scares me. "Worry more about your friends and our way in than what will happen when—"

Osshi jolts, then both hands drop to the pouch. My heart skips a beat when he nearly fumbles the palm-sized globe into the water. Recovering quickly, he steps away from the railing to speak the spell that brings up a swirl of color in the clear sphere. "Bless the Kaisubeh am I glad to see your face, Iwakari-tan."

"Don't be happy yet." I can't see Iwakari, but his voice is clear. And breathless. And shaky. A quick glance at Sanii, and I know ey's noticed, too—something is wrong. He warns, "Flee, Osshi. It might not be too late if you head back to sea right now."

"What happened?" Osshi brings the orb closer to his face. "Where's—"

"Arrested. And I will be, too, if I can't stay ahead of the tyatsu."

Osshi's eyes go wide and white. "Go to my father! He'll—"

"You think the tyatsu didn't grab him *first*?" Scorn and anger fills Iwakari's voice. "You didn't think at all before leaving on this Kaisubeh-cursed trip of yours, did you? Of course you didn't! Answers before everything else, right, Osshi-sei?"

Bellows and blood. I spot Tessen coming up from the lower deck, and I whistle him closer. We're going to need a new plan. Because of course we are. It's been too many moons since a plan I've helped make has actually worked.

Osshi doesn't speak. It doesn't even look like he's breathing. Iwakari, though, takes an audible breath. "Forget it. I promised you and your father I'd help, so I am. By telling you to stay away from Po'umi and every other port on the east coast. If anyone spots Kazu's ship, the tyatsu will be on you as soon as you land. Just tell me one thing, Osshi."

"What?" His voice is thick.

"Was it worth the voyage?"

Osshi nods. "In ways you won't believe until you see for yourself." Abruptly, he straightens, his gaze focused intently on the globe. "Remember the place I took you to last summer? When you got drunk and slept a whole day?"

"You're bringing that up *now*?"

"Do you remember how to get there or not?" Iwakari must nod, because the set of Osshi's shoulders relaxes. "Head there. I'll meet you. I'll protect you from it all, I promise."

"Your father and most of your friends have been arrested, and you're being chased by the tyatsu, and you're still chasing children's stories?" Iwakari scoffs. "Not this time, Osshi. You're on your own. Just don't get yourself killed, or your father will never forgive me."

And then the garakyu's colors are gone, leaving Osshi staring at nothing.

Small mouth pressed thin, he puts it away, his eyes fixed on the deck of the ship. "I need to talk to Kazu."

Tessen, Sanii, and I watch him walk off. His first steps are slow. Then each one is faster until he's almost running to the rear platform of the ship. To the west, Po'umi is coming into view. It should have been the end of our journey, but now we're veering away from it, running back out to sea.

The golden-bright haze of early morning has intensified. The light's glare doesn't come close to the desert sun, but it's enough. Ships fill the protected harbor, some smaller than the one that carried us here but many larger. All of them have sails in bright colors: blues, greens, whites, yellows, and intricate multicolored patterns.

On land, buildings spread in all directions, rising with

the slightly sloped landscape. Po'umi is packed right up to the base of a steeper hill that climbs several hundred feet up from sea level—a seemingly unguarded hill that'd be the perfect spot from which to attack the town. All of it is almost impossibly colorful, and I can see everything from the water because Po'umi has no walls.

How can they protect themselves without a wall? Maybe they really do expect those statues to protect them. My squad alone could take over the city in an afternoon if we wanted.

"We needed to head north already, didn't we?" Tessen asks as we stare at the shore. "That's where Chio's old village is."

Sanii nods. "And as much as you and Rai hate traveling by water, it'll be faster than trying to run there."

"I hate traveling by water in *storms*," Tessen corrects.

I glance at the door to the lower deck. Despite what I told Osshi about the outcome of a fight between his people and mine, reality is bringing doubts with it. "We need to fill in Tyrroh and the andofume. They're looking for Osshi now, which means we're more likely to be spotted and stopped if he's with us."

"They'll *try* to stop us." Sanii looks up at us, eir dark eyes defiant.

"And either they'll somehow succeed, or we'll be hunted the whole time we're here, and they'll only have to follow the trail of bodies to find us."

Tessen laughs. "As if Rai would leave anything more than ash behind."

"But even the best warriors and the strongest mages can be overwhelmed by superior numbers, and that's just *one* of their cities." I wave my hand toward Po'umi. "The Ryogans could easily overwhelm us if we gave them a reason to try."

Neither of them has a response for that.

When we leave the main deck to look for our commanding

officer and the andofume, my thumb traces the cord around my wrist again. One of them had better be able to come up with a new plan for infiltrating Ryogo. Otherwise, we'll have to take our chances against greater numbers. Just heading out to sea and staying there like Iwakari wanted Osshi to do isn't an option. There's no rot-ridden way I'm leaving Ryogo without the answers I need to save Yorri and kill the man who took him from me.

We stay ahead of the storms and away from the shore for days. A week. Ten days. Two weeks.

The rainwater we collected during the storm ensured we had plenty to drink, but we were running dangerously low on food back when we were closing in on Po'umi. Our rush north means we can't stop for more. Only the fish we catch keep us from starving.

The training we couldn't do during the storm begins again. Just not the type we're used to. It's not Tyrroh running us into physical exhaustion with drills and practice, it's Osshi and the andofume making our brains hurt with language and customs and *reading*.

Sanii and I were right about the wall of tiny markings we found in the cave under Sagen sy Itagami—they mean something when someone knows how to decipher them. Osshi and Tsua started teaching us to read before the storms hit, and the calm seas let us go back to that practice.

Learning how to see the meaning behind these marks is more memorization than any of us have done since we were children expected to know the laws of the clan by rote. It's exhausting.

I pick at the knot binding the red niadagu cord around my wrist, one of the dozen we stole from Imaku. Nothing I learn can tell me for sure how to break the four niadagu cords binding my brother to the black rock of that rot-ridden island. He's not on Imaku anymore, but he's still locked to the black stone platform, wherever the bobasu's servants moved it. Where they moved all thirty-nine platforms.

Tsua gave me a theory on breaking the niadagu spell before I tried to rescue Yorri the second time. It's only a theory, though, the only one I have. If it doesn't work, I won't ever be able to free my brother from whatever prison Varan has him in now.

The work is hard and my eyes, fingers, and head hurt by the time we're finished each night, but at least it gives us something to do besides waiting. We're waiting to see if the few Ryogan ships we pass turn to pursue us. We're waiting until we're far enough north to risk nearing land again. We're waiting for Osshi to be within range of another so-called friend who might be able to sneak us into Ryogo undetected.

I hate waiting.

Most of the time when I take a break, I head up to the main deck, needing the open air. I stand at the railing, watching the Ryogan shoreline pass or studying the crew to learn as much as I can—just in case we really do have to steal a ship to make it back to Shiara. Today, Zonna is already in my usual spot, his elbows on the railing and his eyes locked on the green, mountainous horizon.

"So much has changed. This isn't my parents' home anymore," Zonna says softly when I join him. "It's never been mine, no matter how much I imagined it when I was a child. *Uncle* Varan loved to sit me down and tell me everything about Ryogo."

"*Uncle?* Is that a Ryogan word?" We'd been speaking

Itagamin, but even when I search my mind for a translation, I don't know what that means. "I thought they called Varan and the others bobasu here."

Zonna blinks, his focus shifting to my face as understanding dawns. "Right. The *yugadai*. I'd forgotten that, somehow."

"I don't know what *yugadai* means, either." It's not his fault I haven't learned everything about Ryogo. I won't take it out on him. I *won't*, but it's frustrating.

"Chio used to say everything broken on Shiara was a punishment," Zonna says. "Chasing the Kaisubeh was what led Varan to whatever it was that gave him immortality, and he's been running after them ever since. I really don't think they like it."

I really don't think they exist, and I also don't want to give Varan that much credit, but I close my mouth on the words, hoping Zonna will explain with actual answers. Thankfully, he takes a long breath and keeps talking.

"You need permission to have a child in Itagami, right? The pairing has to be approved by the Miriseh?" When I nod, he runs his fingers through his hair, distress clear on his face. "*That's* the yugadai. When Varan and Suzu took control, they spent hundreds of years using Shiara's original inhabitants, his followers, and the bobasu themselves to breed stronger mages and better warriors." He pauses. "Given what Itagamin mages are capable of now, they succeeded."

No, I want to protest. We need permission and the Miriseh's blessing because resources are scarce and keeping the population steady is the only way to survive. They're the only ones who can give us the *ability* to have children in the first place.

"I'm sorry." He watches me carefully. "We weren't sure if we should tell you or not."

No, no, no. But then, why else would Varan not only have to approve the birth, but the parents as well? And why was there such a strict ban on a nyshin or ahdo pairing with someone from the magicless yonin class? And why the bellows would Zonna lie about this?

"We didn't know about it for almost a century. Not until the first Itagamin escaped to Denhitra. She was injured, and when I healed her, I found…" Zonna shakes his head. "From what we've learned since then, Varan has the hishingu mages alter every citizen of Itagami who might be capable of producing a child. They make the changes young—immediately after puberty, we think—making it, well, not impossible, but extrememly hard for conception to happen."

My hand drops to my stomach. My mind buzzes. Someone changed my insides just to make sure I wouldn't have a baby? Not that I wanted one, especially not *now*, not with everything I have to do, but to have the choice made for me… Did I ever have any control over my life, or has it always been an illusion?

"I can reverse it for all of you if you want," he quietly offers.

I'm shaking my head well before I can manage words. "I don't— No. You can ask the others if they want you to…but it's not a good time for anyone to get pregnant." I'm barely able to wrap my mind around the fact that I *can* without the bond blessing from Varan and Suzu. I don't want to think about this right now, so I ask, "What's the yugadai got to do with an uncle?"

Zonna exhales heavily, but doesn't protest my obvious avoidance. "Because of the yugadai, it's rare for any couple to have more than one child, right? You and Yorri were an exception rather than an expectation."

"In more ways than one." Full-blood siblings are uncommon; the only exceptions are usually born from sumai pairs—two people who chose a soulbond, something tying them together beyond death. So, as rare as full siblings are, it's *rarer* for them to be placed in the same nursery. Yorri and I only had the chance to grow up together because of misunderstood directions. And now Zonna is telling me our births were part of a plan, the same revenge plan that Varan's pursuing across an ocean. Followed by an army of intentionally bred warrior-mages.

My mind spins. Memories surface, my attention snagging on one in particular—the nyshin pair who'd wanted to have a child and had been denied. Without a reason. It had been unexpected—almost all nyshin pairs were approved. Lack of detail sparked rumors that tainted both the nyshins' reputation for moons, and it ended a relationship between the two, which had seemed to be heading toward either a life-long partnership or possibly a sumai. Did all that happen because of the bobasu's yugadai?

I press my hand against my abdomen, betrayal and hurt and confusion churning. How do I add this to everything else? I don't even know if this matters now. What is this when compared to Yorri vanishing, the lies about Ryogo, and the deliberate attempts to destroy so much of what I loved about Shiara? Where does this fit between everything else that's happened?

"Varan doesn't want people forming blood-ties because those almost always become more important than the clan as a whole. It was to my parents. Varan blamed their 'desertion' on me. He wasn't entirely wrong, but I was only part of it." Zonna exhales and leans over the water. "If blood-ties were all that mattered to my father, we never would've left Itagami."

"Because Varan is Chio's blood-brother." Tsua and Chio told us that much before we left Shiara. "Which makes him your uncle?"

"The brother of your father is your uncle," Zonna confirms.

"I wonder if I have an uncle." It's a ridiculous question. The answer doesn't matter. If I ever get back to Shiara, no one in Itagami is going to want to talk to me, blood-relative or no, and no matter how often I tell myself I don't care, just *thinking* about being turned away by my clan makes it hard to breathe.

"I don't think we'll ever know for certain." He looks almost apologetic.

I force myself to shrug. "I've lived the first seventeen years of my life without an uncle. I'm sure I can live another seventeen without one."

"I don't doubt that, youngling." Zonna smiles gently, but it turns strained when his eyes lock on something behind me. Tyrroh is approaching, his eyes bright and his steps quick. It makes the ache in my chest ease to see him.

The only good thing about waiting is that, eventually, it ends. And right now, I desperately need the distraction.

After Tyrroh gestures for us to follow him, he leads us to the room he's been sharing with Osshi. Tsua and Chio are already seated at the low table with Osshi, and Osshi is holding his garakyu again.

"What did your friend say?" I ask as Tyrroh, Zonna, and I sit.

"I don't know yet," Osshi says. "We were waiting for you."

Why? I bite the question back. And have to hold back even more questions when Tyrroh leans down and whispers, "Listen closely. No matter what his friend says, we'll need to come up with a plan that has at least a chance of success."

Finding success depends on how you define it. Killing Varan is everyone else's top priority. Sanii and I are the only ones who are more concerned about saving Yorri. But to do the latter, even I can admit we'll probably have to accomplish the former first.

Osshi lifts the garakyu to his lips and murmurs to it. Colors swirl inside as the magic in the sphere connects his sphere to the one his friend has.

"Osshi Shagakusa." The voice is resonant and melodic and carries a faint rasp. "I do not usually find you in this corner of your country."

Tsua and Chio exchange a loaded glance, one I don't understand. Across the table, Zonna seems just as perplexed.

"Maybe not, but I'm extremely glad to find you here, Lo'a." Osshi's smile is strained. "I'm calling in my favor, and it's not a small one."

"Changing your mind after so many years?" Curiosity fills Lo'a's voice, but all she says is, "What do you need?"

"I'm on a ship off the eastern coast—we're just passing the mouth of the Mysora'ka River. I need you to meet us north of there, somewhere secluded and safe, and take us to Uraita."

"You are right. That is no small favor." Wariness has infused Lo'a's voice. "And you said 'we.' How many are traveling with you?"

His gaze jumps to meet Tsua's before he swallows and looks back at the garakyu. "There are fourteen, including me."

"*Aloshaki ki'i olea'o ka lea'i ho'uliopolikia.*" Lo'a's laughter sounds surprised. "Where in this world did you pick up that many people desperate to get to a nowhere village like Uraita?"

"Meet them and see," Osshi presses. "Will you help us, Lo'a?"

"I think so, yes, but I need to talk to my family first. I will call you in an hour with a place to meet if they agree." The garakyu clears, the connection gone.

Tsua and Chio stare at Osshi with offended incredulity on their faces. "Lo'a is hanaeuu we'la maninaio, isn't she?" Tsua asks. "That's why you didn't want to tell us about her before."

"The prejudice against them is ridiculous!" Osshi protests. "There are more lies than truths in what Ryogans know about the hanaeuu we'la maninaio, and historians have proven that more than once."

"Ridiculous?" Chio's eyes harden. "They attack unprovoked! When I was a boy, they raided Tirodo and burned the Kaisubeh tower to the ground."

"That was far from unprovoked. One of Tirodo's Kaiboshi gave them a gift. Of poisoned meat. It was a supposed peace offering that killed half their family." Osshi's voice grows strident. "The truth about the poisoning was buried. No one wanted to admit *we* could be the ones in the wrong."

Chio nor Tsua hold their tongues, and their expressions slowly shift from angry to pensive. Osshi takes a long breath and starts again.

"When I was ten, I saved a hanaeuu we'la maninaio boy from drowning." He runs his fingers through his hair, pushing the long black locks aside. "My father never believed the stories about them, and *their* people believe a life saved creates a heavy debt, so every time they visited Kanaga'ako, they'd bring me a gift. They swore they'd try to grant any favor I asked, but this—" He shakes his head. "If they get us to Uraita, it'll more than clear that debt."

"Will it be any safer or faster than on our own?" Tsua asks cautiously. "They used to be under severe travel restrictions. They were always watched."

"They're warily ignored now," Osshi admits. "I hate it—the way they're treated is unfounded and unfair—but it's useful for us; those beliefs keep everyone else away. Even the tyatsu ignore the hanaeuu we'la maninaio unless they're forced to interact with them."

He never shortens the name of the group. It's an odd habit considering how long the name is. Our city was called

Sagen sy Itagami, but we rarely used more than just Itagami. For some reason, Osshi doesn't do that with the hanaeuu we'la maninaio.

Chio finally nods. "You've gotten us this far. If you trust them, it's enough for me. For now."

"That only matters if Lo'a's family agrees to help us," I add. "She didn't sound sure they would."

But when Osshi's garakyu swirls with color again less than an hour later, Lo'a proves as reliable as Osshi had hoped. She gives us a destination. Osshi heads off to tell Kazu with relief lightening his steps.

Once he's gone, Tyrroh faces the andofume. "How worried do we need to be about his friends?"

"I honestly don't know." Chio rubs his hand over his once-bald head, brushing over the short, newly grown gray-streaked black strands. "My experiences with the hanaeuu are ancient. Anything could've happened in the interim."

"And yet it all feels the same when we hear their name." Tsua looks at Chio with gentle mockery in her half-moon eyes. "So much for age bringing wisdom and patience."

"If they're still treated with caution," Chio says after a moment, "then they'll have little loyalty to Ryogo. That could be good for us."

But Tsua looks worried. "Unless they remember the stories about us as well as Osshi does."

"Don't tell them unless we have to, then." My words draw everyone's eyes. Since they're waiting instead of hushing me, I keep talking. "If they're doing this favor for Osshi, maybe they won't need to know who any of us are beyond his friends. I'm not saying we lie, but we can't regret something that's never been said. And we can always give them the whole story later."

"I was thinking the same thing," Zonna admits. "But there's a risk to keeping the secret, too—hiding something like this won't make us look very trustworthy, so we'd better hope we don't need their help once we reach Uraita. Omitting this for too long might make them decide we're not worth the risk."

Tsua turns toward the room's small window, then she nods. "We'll wait and see what happens when we meet them. Maybe they'll change their minds about helping and this whole discussion will be irrelevant."

"Guess we'll find out soon," Zonna says as he walks out of the room.

And he's right. The meeting place Lo'a gave Osshi is only an hour from where we are. Of course, once I see the place, I start to wonder if Tsua and Chio had been right about the trustworthiness of the hanaeuu we'la maninaio.

"If you weren't with us, would you be able to find a way to climb this?" I ask Osshi as we stand on the beach and look up at the daunting wall of rough, dark stone. The cove has a small beach, but beyond that are sheer cliffs. At least a hundred feet high. Completely encircling the only safe place to anchor the ship and row the smaller boats to shore. Telling Osshi to land here seems like setting him up to fail. Or fall.

Osshi shakes his head. "Even with you, it's hard to believe I can survive this."

"It won't be that bad. Look." Tessen points to the south edge of the beach, but until we get closer, I can't see what he spotted—an incredibly narrow footpath carved into the rock.

It makes the climb easier, but by no means easy. The path nearly disappears at times, barely wide enough for the balls of our feet. My fingers collect scrapes and cuts from how hard I grip the sharp stone. The wind tugs insistently at my clothing as I climb higher.

We can count on Tsua's and Etaro's magic to catch us if we fall—both are powerful enough rikinhisus for that—but they can't fly us all up the cliff. It's too much even for Tsua, especially since she's already mentally hauling up all our bags and weapons. Miari going first does help, though; since she's an ishiji, she can shape the rock as she climbs, leaving us better handholds and footholds in the stone wall. It helps, but not enough to make the climb painless.

Halfway up, my hands ache. Three quarters of the way up, my arms and shoulders burn. By the time we reach the top, Etaro has caught Osshi twice to keep him from tumbling down to the rocky beach a hundred feet below us, and my hands are seconds away from giving out.

I've been on Ryogo for less than an hour, and I already want to go home.

This isn't the smooth, sand-blasted stone of Shiara's desert. This rock *hurts*, even after Miari manipulates the stone. And I thought that the breeze would warm once we landed, but if anything, it's gotten colder.

Zonna stops by each of us, healing whatever injuries we collected. I smile when he approaches me last, hands held out in front of himself with his palms up. I place my hands on his. Instantly, the soothing energy of his magic sinks into my skin, easing the ache in my shoulders and feet and legs and arms, and healing the cuts on my hands. It felt cool on Shiara, like water from a deep spring rushing over sun-burned skin, but now it seems wonderfully warm to me.

"We need you in one piece for what's coming," he says.

I flex my newly healed hands and try not to let his words sting. He didn't mean them to hurt, but they do. Because he's wrong. Before, that might've been true—it was just me, Sanii, and Tessen against the bobasu. Now, I've been knocked back down to youngest in the squad. "The only thing we need me for is wards when something else goes wrong."

Zonna smiles, but says nothing. In part because Tessen has gone stone-still nearby, his narrowed gaze locked west of us.

"They're coming," Tessen warns.

Tyrroh silently signals us to spread out, weaponless, but magic ready. I stand at the center, just behind Osshi, and I reach for the desosa in the air, testing it and getting myself ready in case whoever's coming brings danger with them. The rest of the squad spreads out in a line to either side.

"Khya, do you feel that?" Tessen moves closer, his voice dropping to a whisper. "Focus on the desosa. Do you sense anything different?"

"No." I'm already focusing on it; it seems normal. "But you obviously do. What is it?"

"I have no idea." He looks up at the impossibly tall plants that grow here. They're densely packed, growing close enough to each other to easily hide an army behind them. "Whatever it is, it's almost here."

Moments later, even I can see the shapes of more than a dozen people in the shadows cast by the tall plants. They're dressed brightly, as colorful as the ships' sails we passed in Po'umi's harbor, but the cut of the clothing worn by some of them vaguely resembles Itagami's.

Our pants bind tight from calf to ankle, theirs fall straight from their hips. Our tunics are long-sleeved and reach just above our knees, split on the sides. Their sleeveless tunics only fall to their hips, and the split is down the front instead of the side, exposing their bare chests even though it's so cold I wish I had several more tunics to put on.

Those not wearing the loose pants are wrapped in voluminous folds of cloth that hang from their hips to the ground. The fabric is bright, multicolored, and patterned with tiny, intricate designs. Breastbands, just as colorful, are wrapped around their chests. The few with anything over the wide band are wearing a shorter version of the open-fronted tunic.

In skin and size and shape, they vary as widely as my clan

in Itagami, from warm beige to rich brown, and from as short as Sanii to one who looks taller than Tyrroh. Including all members of the group, it's more revealed skin than I've seen since the last time I bathed in the pool under Itagami. But what keeps my eyes locked on them is the colorful patterns and designs drawn over almost every inch of exposed flesh. Even their faces bear symbols and marks, though mostly surrounding their eyes.

The closer they get, the more I feel what Tessen must have. The desosa flows in lines and ordered swirls around these people, eddying in certain areas but always moving in what seems like an ordained path. When I reach out to pull some to me, it comes, but only when I insist. What have these people done to the desosa? It almost feels trained. Like the energy *likes* obeying them.

Who are these people that they have such power? Osshi didn't mention magic at all, so they must be able to use it without the Ryogans noticing. Somehow, they're working powerful magic under the Ryogans' noses. I look at the cord on my wrist, and I can't help wondering if they might have an answer the Ryogan books haven't given me yet.

"*Alima'hi*, Lo'a." Osshi inclines his head to the woman at the head of the group. Lo'a. "*Ou'a ka lea'i imloa ka'i ia okopo'ono aloshaki ana'anahou.*"

"*Aloshaki naho olea'o wa'heekohu shahala'kai. O'kaoo malohakama ka lea'i le'anohu.*" She smiles, and her voice is exactly as rich as I remember. It's a relief when she switches to Ryogan. "Osshi Shagakusa, my cousin is going to be extremely upset to have missed you."

"And I'm sad he's not here, but it's a relief to see you," Osshi says.

"I can see that. And that you have had hard times recently." She tilts her head in our direction. The others arrayed beside her follow her gaze; none of their faces are nearly as open or warm as hers. "You trust these people?"

"Yes." His answer is unequivocal. "And if you help us, it will wipe out the family debt."

"More than, I think." Her smile fades. "I am worried about what this favor might cost us, honestly. There are rumors that the Ryogan's coastal guard is searching for a traitor."

Osshi stiffens. "I'm no traitor."

No, he's not. He very well might be a savior if we can get what we need in time, but I don't think his people will ever know what he's risking for them. He's putting his standing with his people in jeopardy to protect them, I realize suddenly. Just like we are.

For a long moment, Lo'a and the others with her watch us. The ordered swirls of energy surrounding them reach out, brushing over us like questing fingers, and it takes all my willpower not to snap my wards into place to stop the intrusion. It's worse than bugs skittering across bare skin, but the touch never digs, pulls, or burns, never grows edges, so I let it be.

When it retreats at last, it's a relief.

Lo'a looks toward two of the older members of her group—both with gray and silver-white streaks through their dark hair. The three of them seem to communicate in small gestures and facial quirks, and then Lo'a turns back to us.

"We should go." Lo'a sweeps her arm the way they came. "There are patrols nearby, and the last thing we want is for them to think you anchored here for something more sinister than evading the port tax."

Osshi mumbles his thanks, quickly picking up his bag and following Lo'a, as though he wants to be sure she doesn't have time to press for more details. The rest of us move a few seconds slower, and as I step closer to the towering plants, I look back at the ocean.

Dangerous as that watery expanse was, at least it was familiar. Ahead, I'll be shocked to find even one small thing that reminds me of home. We're putting our lives in the hands of strangers, and all I can do as I follow them into the shadowy growth is hope Osshi's trust isn't misplaced.

It had better not be. Yorri doesn't have time for me to make mistakes.

And neither does Ryogo.

CHAPTER THREE

"This feels like a horrible idea," Rai mutters in Itagamin as we follow Lo'a and her people through the plants. Then she raps her knuckles against one. "And what the bellows are these things?"

"Trees," Tsua responds.

"There are enough of them to hide an army." Etaro peers around as though ey expects one to attack out of the shadows. "How do you know when someone's coming?"

Tsua takes a long, deep breath. "You learn the scents on the wind, and how to listen."

No way it'll be as easy as that, but I'm more worried about Rai's first comment than what the trees may be hiding. "*Is this a horrible idea, Tsua?*"

"Possibly, but not the worst one I've ever heard." Tsua shrugs and steps over a gnarled root. "Chio and I haven't been here in centuries, Zonna hasn't been here ever, and Osshi is a scholar. He doesn't know these forests like the hanaeuu. If we're going to get to Uraita, we need the help of someone who knows this land. The hanaeuu are the only ones offering."

Hanaeuu we'la maninaio, I correct silently.

Tessen raises his hand and signals—motion ahead. Wherever Lo'a is leading us, we're almost there.

The trees thin. There's a clear space ahead. Clear of trees, at least. Large boxes on wheels sit at the edge of the open space. They're each a different color—all of them incredibly bright—and they're covered with intricate designs. Other symbols made of metal and crystal hang from the eaves of the domed roofs, and more marks are etched around the windows and doors.

In the center of the ring of the colorful boxes are people. There are a bunch of odd animals, too. The ones closest to us are horned beasts, their hide tough-looking and mottled gray. Although they snort and toss their heads, they're otherwise placid, not even trying to free themselves from their loose tethers as they chew on leaves pulled from low-hanging branches. They're bigger than the teegras on Shiara, but those vicious scaled cats would tear us to pieces for even thinking about trapping them like this.

"Is that little, brownish-green thing an animal?" Etaro asks.

I don't spot the creature until one of the children scoops it into their arms. Stranger still, the animal doesn't seem to mind; it curls its lithe body into a smaller ball as though it's trying to make it easier for the child to hold it.

"So weird," Rai mutters. "We would *eat* something like that. They're playing with it."

There are several of the small animals scampering around the camp. One, a white one with golden paws and subtle stripes, falls in by Lo'a's side as soon as it sees her. The two people who Lo'a conferred with earlier, smile at the creature, bending down to brush their fingers over its fur as they say something to Lo'a in their flowing language. Once Lo'a responds, they split off toward the main section of the camp.

"You've painted the wagons since the last time I saw you," Osshi comments as we sit near one of the fires.

Wagons. At least I have a name for the boxes now. The designs covering them seemed random at first, but they're definitely not. Certain marks and patterns repeat on almost every surface, though not always in the same order or configuration. The replicated symbols seem almost buried within the swirling, patterned chaos of the larger design. Deciphering it all reminds me of the puzzles Yorri used to make, one shaped piece of metal intertwining with so many others that it's hard to tell one from the rest.

Yorri would love these wagons. He should be here to see them, and it *hurts* that he's not.

I clear my throat and gesture to the camp. "The colors are beautiful."

"Thank you," Lo'a says. "It is almost due to be repainted."

The way her fingers trace a mark on her arm sparks a realization—the main designs on the wagons are also repeated on their skin.

Lo'a notices my scrutiny. Voice dry, she says, "You are staring, *limahi*. Are you not used to seeing skin where you come from?"

"I'm used to seeing a lot more than you're showing, actually. But usually the only thing decorating that skin is battle scars."

She raises her hands, looking down at the patterns as though she's seeing them for the first time.

"They're beautiful," I say before she can take what I said the wrong way. "There's just nothing like it on Shiara."

Lo'a watches me, her golden-brown eyes wary. "I do not know of Shiara."

"And Shiara knows nothing of you." I hold my breath, hoping she'll let the subject drop.

Lo'a's eyebrows rise, but she thankfully says nothing.

Instead, she turns to Osshi. "We should go. I do not know what your secrets are or where your friends are from, but I think it will be better for all of us if we get to Uraita as soon as possible."

"That's all we ask," Osshi insists. "Safe passage. And help getting some books from the Zunoato library. Once we reach Uraita, you can leave us behind with a debt wiped clean."

"Hmm. You make it sound so easy. But I am warning you now, Osshi Shagakusa—if this harms any of my people, your family will be the ones who owe the debt. Do we have a deal?"

Osshi tenses, and then seems to force himself to relax before he answers. "Yes, of course. It's a deal."

Lo'a whistles, a piercing three-tone call. It causes a flurry of motion. Children and small animals are herded into the wagons. The massive horned beasts are led to poles that extend from one end of each wagon, then they're tied to those poles.

It all happens quickly, and everyone knows their role in the process. Their obvious training is comforting. Maybe they really will be able to get us to Chio's village safely.

"Come with me." Lo'a walks off. Osshi follows first, but the rest of us aren't far behind. She heads toward a yellow wagon with patterns painted in white and brown, approaching steps that lead up to the door. It opens outward before she reaches it. Two people jog down, each burdened with bags and boxes. The second one nods to her and says something in their language.

She nods. "Thank you."

I watch the two leave, wondering if anyone but Lo'a speaks or understands Ryogan. No one else has spoken a word of it yet.

Her gesture to the wagon catches my attention. "Fitting you all in here will be tight, but we cannot spare any more space."

As Osshi assures her we'll be fine, Tyrroh says, "Wardstones first, Khya."

"Yes, Nyshin-ma." I jump the three stairs and head inside.

The wall opposite the door has two platforms, the bottom one about a foot wider than the top, and both are covered with mattresses and blankets. Below them are what might be drawers for storage—that's what they were called on Kazu's ship. To the left, immediately past the door, a flat piece of wood is strapped down. Beyond that is a cushioned bench that stretches all the way to the beds.

I take a breath and wish more than ever for Yorri. He'd love a challenge like this, trying to fit fourteen adults plus their gear, weapons, and bags into this limited space. But we don't have Yorri. All we have is me.

"Tessen, pass up the bags." I place wardstones along the wagon walls. "Keep out small weapons and essential items. Everything else has to be stored."

Thankfully, there's more space than I spotted at first, like the empty area inside the bench seat. Hooks drop down from the ceiling, and there I hang the bags and weapons we might want quick access to. It makes stowing our gear quicker than I'd hoped it would be.

Once we're all inside, Lo'a warns, "Brace yourselves. We must travel fast to make the most of the remaining daylight."

She unhooks the steps from the doorway and secures them to the wall. The look she casts Osshi as she closes the door is somewhere between speculation and warning, but she says nothing.

Tessen shakes his head, slipping through the crowded space toward the door. "There must be a way to keep this open. I've spent too much time the last moon in small, dark spaces."

And in a land this strange, it doesn't feel safe to cut off

our best line of sight. Or escape.

"You'd better figure it out fast," Rai tells Tessen from near the window. "Looks like we'll be moving any second."

Thankfully, it's a simple solution—there's a latch on the wagon's exterior wall. Once it's secure, Tessen and I settle onto the floor in the open doorway. The wagon jerks and rolls forward a moment later.

The motion is uncomfortably reminiscent of the ocean, so it's nice to be able to see, hear, and smell Ryogo to remind me we're back on solid land. I lean out, trying to study as much as I can of this place. To help, Osshi and the elder andofume give us names for plants and animals, none of which have counterparts on Shiara. They even explain the hanaeuu we'la maninaio's animals—the large ukaiahana'lona are kept for work, like pulling their wagons, and the small ahoali'lona are companions, cared for and protected the same way human clan members are.

It's all strange, but the farther we travel into Ryogo, the more some things make sense, too. Like how they can build ships and wagons—and probably cities—with wood. On Shiara, only the kicta ever grows as tall as a person, and the shell of that spine-covered plant becomes unusably holey when it's dried out and dying. I can't imagine ever building a boat out of kicta panels or the kindling we collected from the desert's low-growing brush.

Trees, though. There is so much potential locked in trees. More than that, I think trees might be the most beautiful thing I've ever seen.

They soar high above us—some must be over a hundred feet tall. The bases vary in width, some thin enough that I could wrap my arms around them and touch my fingers on the other side, and others so broad that it'd take three of us to completely encircle it. Leaves sprout from branches that spread in every direction, and the sound they make when the wind blows is wonderful. Like the waves crashing against a distant shore. The only thing I don't like is the shade they cast; it drops the temperature too much, and the air is already cold enough.

It's incredible, but the sight is tainted by a single question: What will all this look like if Varan lands in Ryogo? He was willing to kill and deceive and manipulate and destroy everyone on Shiara for the chance to come back here. I can't trick myself into believing he'll be any kinder to the Ryogans than he was to us. It'll be worse. If we fail—if *I* fail—Varan could sweep through this forest with my clan at his back and raze this land until nothing but ash and blood are left.

After an hour, I have to move away from the door; the weight of what might happen is beginning to overwhelm the wonder of seeing Ryogo for myself.

I'm glad for the distraction of the books on magic and history that Lo'a gave us. Some she had on hand, but the rest she sent several of her people to collect as we hurry northwest. When I find one that mentions the niadagu, I pull it aside and read with careful attention, trying to memorize it, a goal that feels impossible when even understanding the words is a struggle.

By the time we stop for the night, my head hurts and I'm so cold my fingers are nearly numb. Before I let myself settle near the warmth of the blaze our two kasaiji are building, however, I walk the outer edge of the hanaeuu we'la maninaio camp and set my wardstones down at regular intervals. Just in case trouble finds us.

Protections set, I sit between Tessen and Rai near the fire and take a deep breath. The scent of the smoke is an aching reminder of home. For most of the year, Itagami smells like smoke, brine, sulphur, sweet kicta, and bitter scrub. I can't identify what the air is carrying here apart from woodsmoke.

"I can't be the only one who thinks the world smells strange," Sanii says. "Nyshin-ma? Tessen? Either of you know what it is?"

Tyrroh shakes his head, and Tessen says, "I don't know what to call anything here. It's *all* strange."

"I seriously don't envy your senses right now, basaku," Rai says.

"Is this what cold smells like?" Miari rubs the tip of her nose. "I don't like the scent any better than I like the temperature."

"Don't worry." Wehli smirks and leans in to press a kiss to her tawny skin. "Nairo and I will keep you warm."

"The smell we can't do anything about," Nairo adds wryly, adding a jet of flames to make it burn hotter.

"It's not the cold." Osshi gestures widely. "It's the trees."

"That's unfortunate." Natani scoots closer to the fire. "I was just starting to like trees."

Tessen taps my knee, nodding toward the main camp when I look at him. "You might want to warn Lo'a not to touch those wardstones."

Following his gaze, I see Lo'a walking the perimeter of the camp with one of the older hanaeuu we'la maninaio, their attention fixed on the wardstones. The others watch Lo'a's progress but don't approach. As I turn back to Tessen, I can't help wondering if the other hanaeuu we'la maninaio are keeping a distance out of respect for the woman who seems to be their leader, or out of wariness of us.

"Worried she'll dump us here and flee if she learns how dangerous those stones are the same way you did?" I ask. The shock of touching my active wardstones had left his short hair standing straight up.

"Any sane person would," he answers wryly.

"Hmm." I stand up. "What does that say about you?"

He tilts his head back far to look up at me. "That you broke my mind a long time ago."

Grinning, I tap his nose and then jog away, reaching Lo'a just before she reaches toward a wardstone. "I don't recommend that."

"I did not plan on touching it." And she doesn't. Neither does the older woman standing beside her, watching silently. Instead, Lo'a carefully moves her hand over and around the stone, feeling the air, or maybe testing the stone the way she tested us earlier. "This is not like anything I have seen before. Would you tell me how it works?"

"If you'd be willing to tell me how you get the desosa to run like a well-trained soldier through those symbols you use."

Her hand freezes, and her eyes snap to meet mine. The older woman cocks her head, her long, gray-streaked hair falling over her shoulder; there's vigilance in her expression that makes me almost certain she understands Ryogan even if she can't, or chooses not to, speak it.

Lo'a glances at the woman, who doesn't seem to offer her any direction. Then Lo'a shakes her head. "I do not know desosa. What is that?"

Thoughtless of me; of course she doesn't. "The closest word I know in Ryogan is sentukei—magic. But desosa is more than that." I circle my hand in the air, trying to encompass everything. "It's the energy of the world. The power in the air and the land and the water."

"You know the *akiloshulo'e kua'ana manano*?" She stands, eyes intensely focused on me. Surprise shows on the elder's face, too. "You can feel it?"

"You can't?" That doesn't make sense. How can they possibly be channeling it this well if they can't feel it?

"No, of course we can." She waves her hand dismissively.

"But in all the lands we have traveled, we have met very few who can. Many deny it exists, but those people do not see our magic at all. Almost no one in Ryogo can sense it."

By now, I feel the attention of the rest of my group. I'm sure a few of them have moved closer to listen, just like several of Lo'a's people are moving in behind her. No one speaks, and Lo'a seems to pay them no attention, so I ignore them, too.

I take a breath and gesture toward my circle of wardstones. "I'd be willing to teach you about my magic if you explained yours."

Although interest is clear in her expression, she doesn't say anything for almost a minute. The elder woman murmurs something in their language, the words so long and flowing I have a hard time determining where one ends and the next starts. When Lo'a speaks again, it's not what I expected to hear. "Do you know how many colors exist?"

"Colors?" I am utterly confused. "Of course not. How could I?"

"Exactly." She gestures around the camp to, I presume, all the colors her people use. "Just here, there are so many it would take a long time to count them. When you combine some colors, you can create something beautiful, like a shade of blue that captures the essence of the sky. Other times the result is less lovely, a murky darkness that reminds people of death."

"What does that have to do with magic?" I ask.

"There are just as many ways to use the *akiloshulo'e kua'ana manano*—what you call desosa—as there are colors in the world," Lo'a explains. "The wrong combinations can be disastrous. Catastrophic, in certain circumstances. Even if it were allowed, teaching you to see magic the way my people do might not work the way either of us intend."

"Or it could give us a useful new tool, something to help us protect our homes." Most of the magical limits I was taught have been proven wrong in the last several moons. It's not in me to believe the *only* possible outcome is bad.

My words seem to make her think…until her gaze flicks up to focus on something over my shoulder.

"Khya." Tessen's words—spoken in Itagamin—are filled with the kind of worry I've learned to pay attention to. "I think I hear something. Can't be sure here, though. Too much noise for me to filter out."

"Go tell Tyrroh, and be careful." We're not like Tsua and Zonna. He can be hurt. "Make sure you take someone with you if you need to go far."

He turns then, a teasing light in his eyes. "Is that an order, Nyshin-pa?"

"I'm not your nyshin-pa." Our squad had two seconds serving directly under Nyshin-ma Tyrroh. Neither of them is here. Ryzo is still on Shiara, left behind, and Daitsa…

"You are, Khya, whether you've officially accepted the position or not." Smiling, he touches my shoulder gently and leaves, stopping to whisper to Tyrroh. Both continue south. In a few seconds, they're lost in the trees.

Lo'a's sharp gaze tracks their departure, and then she beckons to one of her clansmen. The conversation is short but heated; as far as I can tell when the man walks away, she won. Then she demands to know what's happening.

"Tessen thinks someone might be approaching from the south. He and Tyrroh have gone to check, that's all."

"It seems like more than that." Her gaze locks on Osshi. "What have you brought down on us, Osshi Shagakusa? If you are no traitor, why is there so much fear in your eyes to think someone is coming?"

"I'm *not* a traitor."

"To yourself, maybe. But in the Ryogans' eyes?" she challenges.

"I'll explain it all, Lo'a, tell you whatever you want to know, but if the tyatsu really are coming, we need your help." He walks closer, hands outstretched. "If they find me, I think they'll kill me."

She stiffens. Those standing behind her start whispering amongst themselves, hurried gestures sending one of them running toward the main camp. My pulse speeds up to see the fear and anger on so many of their faces. We've barely started this trek and it already feels like we're about to lose the only possible allies we have here.

The conversation stops when Lo'a raises her hand. "The risk to us is enormous. We are tolerated in Ryogo because of the trade we bring them, but the leaders have been trying to banish us for centuries. If they catch us smuggling a *traitor*, that faction might finally win their fight against us."

"Lo'a, I know it's a lot to ask. Too much." Osshi is nearly pleading with her, and he never even looks at the elders. He's treating Lo'a as if she's the only one who makes decisions for this family, as if he's never noticed how often—like now—she looks to one of the elders for opinions, approval, or advice. "All I ask right now is for you to listen to what we've learned and then decide for yourself if carrying us where we need to go is worth the risk."

She opens her mouth. I hold my breath—

And then Tessen's voice cracks through the forest. "Enemy incoming!"

CHAPTER FOUR

Tessen's low warning has immediate effect. Lo'a whistles sharp and loud. Her clan bursts into motion, their specific, focused paths proving what I'd noticed earlier about practice and training. I run with the squad and the andofume to the outer edge of the wagon circle to meet Tessen and Tyrroh.

"How long do we have?" I ask.

"They're about a mile off, southeast." Tessen's gaze is focused in that direction. "They're following the road we used, and there isn't much of a chance they'll miss us if they keep heading this way. And…" He shakes his head, furrows lining his forehead. "It sounds like they know where Kazu landed the ship—at least the general area. Someone was saying that yes, they should stay on this trail because it's the only one fresh enough to be ours unless we're traveling through the treetops."

"Our magic should hide us from prying eyes, especially Ryogan military," Lo'a says. "I cannot guarantee it, though. Some Ryogans are unexpectedly perceptive, and they take any reason they can find to search our wagons for illegal items, so we should assume they will insist on doing that tonight, too."

"I can ward us." After protecting Kazu's ship against the relentless ocean, shielding the circle of wagons shouldn't be a struggle. And I *will* shield them. They're only in danger because they're helping us. "They'll still be able to see us, but they won't be able to touch us."

"They also can't touch us if we make them disappear." Rai's hands spark, fire building in her palms and climbing up her wrists. Several of the hanaeuu we'la maninaio step back, shock in their eyes.

"Wood burns." Etaro slaps Rai's arms down, unconcerned about the flames. "Look what we're surrounded by."

"I can control my fires!" Rai sends up a tornado of sparks.

"No leaving a body trail, remember? Killing them will be worse than giving them stories to tell." Tyrroh's deep voice cuts through the conversation.

"I wish your wards were an actual wall," Etaro says to me, eir sharp features pinched. "Sometimes it feels better to hide behind something solid."

"I'd settle for becoming invisible," I murmur back, my eyes on a child watching the chaos of their camp through their wagon's window, anxious fear clear on their face. I hate that we've brought our problems to them.

Lo'a shakes her head. "We are not invisible. And intention is powerful. The harder someone looks for us, the better chance they have of finding us."

"Can we run?" I ask.

"Even well rested, our beasts are not quick, and we pushed them hard today." Lo'a's full lips pull tight, and I can't tell if there's more anger or fear in her expression.

"And if we run now, it'll be a long time before we can stop." Tyrroh nods toward the southeast. "Tessen, Khya—I want both of you watching the road for their approach. Everyone else spread out in intervals from there."

Tessen moves toward the trees. I begin to follow, but there's a thought circling the back of my mind like a mykyn bird.

"Nyshin-ma, wait, I—" I need a minute to think.

If they see us but can't reach us because of my wards, they'll run and carry stories about the impossible magic the hanaeuu we'la maninaio are suddenly capable of. Which will bring the Ryogans' fury down on Lo'a and her family. If we don't want them to tell stories at all, we'll have to fight and kill them all. Which will only enrage the Ryogan leaders and bring out reinforcements, causing problems for us *and* the hanaeuu we'la maninaio. There's got to be another way. Something…

Oh. Could I…? I turn away from Tyrroh. "Lo'a, what you said earlier, about combining magic?" I move away from my squad to stop in front of the woman. "You agree it's possible, right? Especially if the mages working the magic are both skilled enough to handle the power."

Her fingers move and the power flowing through the channels surrounding her flares, and her gaze flicks toward the elders again. There's doubt in her eyes when she says, "It can be."

She knows about my wardstones, and has felt them herself, but I quickly explain more. "If you showed me which symbols you use to hide your wagons, and helped me channel my wards through your protections, it might be enough to hide us completely, right?"

The motion of Lo'a's fingers stops. The two elders murmur something, and Lo'a's eyes light up. "*Shomaihopa'a sha opai'hoa*, yes. Come with me."

"Nyshin-ma?" I glance at him, waiting for permission to break ranks.

"Go." He waves me off sharply. "I'll have Wehli lay a false trail to lead them off."

I follow Lo'a, and Tessen tries to follow me, but I shake my head. "Stay on watch. They need your eyes."

His lips purse for a moment, but he nods and jogs off, moving toward the position Tyrroh ordered him into. Nearby, Tyrroh finishes giving Wehli his orders, and our kyneeda bolts off to the south, his magic allowing him to push himself so fast he's little more than a blur. Confident he'll find a way to convince our pursuers that we've gone in a different direction, I turn away and run after Lo'a.

With each of her steps, the black fabric with its vibrant green patterns flows and flutters around her legs, and the desosa seems to do the same, drawn to whatever magic she's working.

"This." Lo'a stops at her own wagon and gestures to a symbol in the center of the wall. It's large and surrounded by an intricate design hiding it in plain sight. If I couldn't feel the desosa flowing around and through the symbol, I'd never have known it had a purpose other than decoration.

Then I meet her eyes, and I realize she's waiting for me to make the next move. "I know this was my idea, but I've never tried this before. What do I do?"

Lo'a extends her hand, palm up. Taking a breath, I lay my palm on hers. She adjusts the hold, sliding her hand up until she can grip my forearm. I do the same, loosely closing my fingers around the thick underside of her arm.

"Raise your protections on the camp. Once they are in place, I will try to use your power to strengthen ours." Lo'a tightens her grip on my arm, her eyes boring into mine. "If you resist when I pull on your energy—and it is natural for you to want to resist—it will hurt. At best."

"And at worst?"

"It could kill us both." She lifts one shoulder, almost believably unconcerned.

Is the danger worth the risk? No, that's not the question. What matters is if I'm willing to let a risk hurt my chances of getting the information I need to stop Varan. And to save Yorri.

Swallowing—and hoping that Tessen isn't listening—I nod. "Let's hope it doesn't get that bad."

Lo'a almost smiles. "May the *alua'sa liona'ano shilua'a* bless us."

I take a deep breath, close my eyes, tighten my fingers around Lo'a's arm, and bring up my wards, surrounding the camp with a shield as strong as I can make it.

"Closing in," Miari says nearby, likely a report passed down the line from Tessen.

If this is going to work, it has to work now.

Knowing my energy is going to be siphoned off any second, I reach out to the desosa to draw in more power. Instead of pulling from the channeled energy flowing around us, I stretch as far from the controlled power of the hanaeuu we'la maninaio's magic as I can reach. It feels like climbing a sheer wall and stretching for a handhold, but I hold my breath and extend another inch, grabbing the desosa tight—

Just as something else grabs me.

I gasp, my fingers tightening on Lo'a until I feel the shape of her bones under her skin.

Don't fight. Don't fight. I can't fight. But it's so hard not to when it feels like someone is trying to pull my blood out through my skin.

It's wrong. It *hurts*. This can't be working. This can't be worth it.

But it doesn't matter if it's worth the pain or not, because I've already dived into the ocean, and now I've got to ride the current or drown.

Shifting my focus away from my own magic and onto hers helps. A little. Enough to let me take a breath. I keep narrowing my focus, and the more of it I center on Lo'a, the more the pain recedes to the back of my awareness. It's still there, but it's as though I've stepped away from it. From myself.

All I can see at first is my own power flowing through my body, down my arm, and into Lo'a through the connection we made. And I really can *see* my magic as a moving, working, almost living thing for the first time. I've felt it, and when I created the wardstones for myself, Sanii, and Tessen, I got a sense of color from each of us, saw it in the way the glow of the stones changed when I keyed them to our energy. This is something completely different.

My magic is a light under my skin, pure red with sparkles of bright white that remind me of a crystal in sunlight or the stars winking in the blackness of night. It changes color where our hands join, transforming to a brilliant yellow, and then shifts to a bright, pale green when it travels up Lo'a's arm. The sight almost makes me laugh.

Her comparison between colors and magic was more accurate than she probably knows.

I follow the movement of her magic. It travels beneath her skin, lighting up the designs and brightening their colors. I watch it stream up her arm, eddy in her chest, and then flow out of her even faster than in, moving into the symbol on the wall. The lines glow with magic, the light no longer Lo'a's green, but a pure white that pulses. Each beat spreads the glow outward like I've always pictured my wards working, no longer constrained by the symbols.

The light is like a wall encircling the camp. Protecting it. Hiding it. I focus on thoughts of exactly what it's protecting, using them to push away the reality of my draining energy and my body's ache.

Then the soldiers are here.

From inside the protection, it seems like there's nothing separating us from them. It seems impossible that they won't be able to see us—not when they're less than thirty feet away, and not when I can see *them* perfectly.

Not one of the fifteen tyatsu more than glances in our direction.

Even though they're dressed in gray and black and their clothes are cut in a very different style than ours or the hanaeuu we'la maninaio's, they remind me of an Itagamin squad. They're clearly used to following orders, naturally falling into silent, ordered rows when the person at the head of the line signals for them to halt, and each one wears several weapons—daggers as well as either swords or bows and arrows.

"They stopped here, maybe to rest, but it looks…" The tyatsu guard searches a few more feet down the main road. "It seems like they continued on."

Another nods sharply. "If we push, we might be able to make it to the next town before it's too dark to risk traveling. We'll be able to check in at the station there and see if any new reports have come in."

The two who spoke confer for another moment, their voices too low for me to hear them, and then they begin to move on. But they're moving so slowly. Why does it look like each of their steps takes so long? And why does it feel like the air is leaking out of my lungs?

Time passes—I don't know how much—before the drain begins to slow. Lo'a takes less of my power. Then less. With each gradual decrease, I come back to myself more.

My skin burns like I've been standing naked in a dust

storm. My muscles burn like I've been training for hours without rest. My vision is spotted with pricks of color. My knees buckle.

Lo'a's grip tightens. There's fear in her eyes. Her mouth moves. I don't hear words. She moves closer, her other arm outstretched as if to catch me—

I fall backward into someone else's hold.

"Tessen." I sigh and close my eyes, letting him carry my weight. Of course it's Tessen. If anyone is going to catch me when I fall, it's him.

"That's unusually sweet of you, Khya."

"Didn't say anything." I feel like I'm moving, but I didn't tell my feet to take me anywhere. I don't think they're touching the ground. Carrying… I think Tessen's carrying me.

He laughs softly. "I am."

"You're doing that thing. With the knowing too much." I want to slap his arm, but all I manage to do is turn my head to let my lips find his throat. "Stop it."

He's taking me somewhere, and talking to someone else, but then it feels like I'm falling. Slowly.

"We're just sitting down." Tessen adjusts his hold until he's sitting cross-legged and I'm leaning against his chest. Then he kisses my forehead. "Maybe fighting them off would've been better. We could've done it. Easily. You didn't have to wear yourself out like this."

"But I learned something new. No one on Shiara can do what I did." I murmur the words against his neck because I don't have the energy to lift my head. "And killing them wouldn't have won us friends, Tessen."

A low laugh rumbles through his chest. "You've never collected friends before. Why start now?"

"They have something I need." But now, all I need is sleep.

"Drink something first. You can sleep in a moment."

The water he helps me drink is cool and eases my aching throat. I hadn't noticed the dryness until it began to fade. Tessen eases me onto the lower bed. As I begin to fall to sleep, he traces his fingers down the side of my face and whispers, "Get some rest, Khya."

His words blur with the memory of Lo'a's voice warning me not to resist, so I exhale my breath and let go.

By the time I wake up, it's the next day, the wagons are underway, and only Tessen is sharing the bed with me. He smiles when I open my eyes, and I reach out, brushing my fingers over the curve of his low cheekbones before I lift my head to look for everyone else. They all seem to be either crowded onto the bench, sitting on the floor, or — according to the creak of the wooden platform — on the bed above.

"You didn't need to give up this much space," I tell them.

"Oh, hush, Nyshin-pa," Sanii teases from eir seat on the bench. "I think you earned this one privilege."

"I wish you could've seen what you *did*." Excitement kindles Rai's expression. "Your wards have always been impressive, you ridiculously overpowered fykina, but what you did deserves a new designation entirely."

"They walked right past the camp!" Etaro grins, so gleeful eir narrow eyes almost disappear. "We were standing there, swords drawn, magic ready, preparing for a fight, and the enemy passed us by like we were trees."

I did see, I almost tell them, but I keep silent because everyone has their own version to tell me, and they're all so eager to tell me what they saw. Trying to mesh their memories with mine is hard, especially since, even though I did somehow help us disappear, I don't understand how. But I *need* to understand. Maybe then I'll be able to repeat it.

"There is one thing you should know. The hanaeuu we'la maninaio almost dropped us here and bolted last night," Sanii says once the stories have been told. "But Lo'a and Osshi convinced them to wait until we explained...well, everything."

I glance at Osshi, but he's sitting in the chair as close to the door as he can get. From his stiff posture and pinched expression, I'm guessing he'd probably be a lot farther away from us if he could manage it. Our magic just got stronger and stranger, and now he knows—if he didn't before—that the hanaeuu we'la maninaio have their own power. He was distant and skittish for hours after I warded Kazu's ship. I hope he won't do that again now; we need his help too much.

"We had to go back all the way to Varan's exile. It took hours." Rai sighs, pulling my attention back to her. "I never want to hear so much about my own life ever again."

"But it worked? They're letting us stay?" I assume they are—we're still here, after all—but it's better to be sure.

"For as long as none of them get caught or killed," Etaro says.

"We'll see how long that lasts," Sanii mutters.

Rai shakes her head. "Not long if what's happened in the last few moons is any sign. And our luck hasn't gotten any better here."

Unfortunately, that's all too true. "And they didn't tell you anything about how we worked the magic last night?"

"They don't seem used to admitting they can *do* magic," Sanii says. "Lo'a didn't say much, and the others... I'm honestly not sure if they speak Ryogan."

"They definitely understand it." Tessen looks toward the camp and then at me. "You'll likely have a better chance getting Lo'a to explain than we did."

I hope he's right, but it isn't until we stop for the night that I get the chance to go searching for her.

As I cross the camp, the other hanaeuu we'la maninaio incline their heads, most of them making the same gesture—thumb pressed to their other four fingers, they touch the center of their forehead and then their chest. After last night, I half expected to be treated with fear again, a repeat of Kazu's ship. This feels like respect; it's like I passed some test of theirs.

Lo'a must've expected me to come looking for her, because she doesn't seem surprised when I approach her near the campfire. "I expected you a lot earlier than this."

"And you would've seen me if we hadn't been moving all day." I clear my throat and take another step closer. "I have questions."

"Not surprising, but I am afraid you might be disappointed by my answers. Come with me." She motions for me to follow and walks across the camp, her wide hips swaying with each step. As we pass, the male elder signals something, a gesture that reminds me of the signs my squad uses to silently communicate. Lo'a doesn't appear to respond, but I'm positive she spotted the sign before she leads me to her blue wagon.

Her home is similar to the one we've been borrowing, but symbols are painted on the walls, swaths of fabric hang in front of the two beds to divide the space, and the shelves are packed with jars and boxes and books. The table is folded up and strapped to the wall, but the bench is cleared and one of the chairs is set out. Lo'a sits on the bed, her skirt—pale yellow with borders and patterns in purple and gray—arrayed around her, so I move to take the chair.

"I'm sorry for causing trouble for your family." If anything had happened to them because of us... I already failed Yorri and abandoned my clan. I don't know how much more guilt I can carry before it becomes a weight too heavy to bear.

Her face goes slack for a blink. "Not where I expected you to start, but I appreciate the apology. And…" She sighs and smooths her skirt. "I must admit that I would probably make the same decisions you have. What I told your friends stands, though—I can only help you for as long as my family is not in unreasonable danger."

"I can't ask anything more. And I promise we'll protect your family as if they were clan for as long as we're traveling with you." I hold her gaze, hoping she can see how much I mean what I'm saying. She seems to, because after several breaths her shoulders relax and she nods.

"You look exhausted, Khya. The magic hit me hard, but I underestimated how much you would pour into the work." She leans in, lines of concern around her large, golden-brown eyes. "Are you all right?"

"I feel like I've gone too far again and need another fifteen hours of sleep, but otherwise fine."

"Again?" She relaxes a little, toying with the end of the open purple tunic she's wearing. Everything about them is so colorful. It almost reminds me of the desert animals who used their glaring colors as a distraction. Or a warning. "This is a habit of yours?"

"In recent moons, yes. Usually because there's no other choice."

Her hands stop moving. "Only usually?"

"Tessen is convinced I don't know when to ask for help. And I'm nearly certain he thinks I'm determined to find my own breaking point."

"Sometimes it is good to find that yourself," Lo's says quietly, her expression serious. "Otherwise someone else may do it for you."

"Maybe, but it's like Tessen's waiting for the day I kill myself in the search."

"I can understand that fear. When you began to collapse, I thought I might have to watch you die." She clenches and flexes her hands, then seems to force herself to smile. "I feel better knowing Tessen is there to catch you."

What? How can she know that? Unless I really did babble anything that entered my head last night. "I—well, he is. But the magic… I know it worked, not how."

"Teaching our magic to outsiders is rarely allowed, but you showed me something new and beautiful last night," she says with a soft smile. "You helped discover this, so you should share the knowledge. I consider it paying off a debt."

She does, or her elders do? Either way, these people seem obsessed with debt. I can't understand it. If I kept track of every favor I did for my clanmembers or every time they offered me help, keeping track of the balance would consume me. Although, maybe that's the difference: clan versus outsider. I feel like I owe Osshi and Kazu more than I can repay, after all. Lo'a's fixation on balance might not be as strange as I thought.

"I know your magic is related to the symbols—the desosa seems to move through them." I look up at the silver symbol hanging over us—an intricate combination of half circles and straight lines—and then lower my gaze to the marks covering her skin. "All of them, not just the ones you're actively using."

"You really are incredibly perceptive." Her smile turns secretive as she settles more comfortably on the bed. "Yes, the symbols are critical to how we work with the *akiloshulo'e kua'ana manano*—the energy you call desosa—but what is more important is how one guides the *akiloshulo'e kua'ana manano* through themselves and how well it holds." She runs her thumb over the border of her skirt. "It is like turning individual threads into a patterned cloth."

It sounds similar to what I do with crystals to create

wardstones, a way to lock magic into a particular spot to perform a specific task. I thought it could only be done with the crystals mined on Shiara, but... "What do you use? To paint these on your wagons?"

"Our paint is made from berries and flowers. Roots of plants, sometimes. Bugs of certain types. Clay and stones ground to dust. Anything natural can work, but the materials must fit with the magic you are working."

"What do you mean?"

"Does it seem like a good idea to place fire magic in a piece of wood?" she asks. "In theory, any natural material can work for any magic, but the power will not be the same as when the right mage uses the right materials for the right magic. Do you understand?"

"I think so." Wood wouldn't hold fire for long. Rock wouldn't do well holding water. Both, though, could potentially become a ward-anchor. "Do Ryogans see magic the same way? Osshi doesn't talk about it."

I don't mention what Tsua and Chio have already taught us; their information is more than a little old.

"Chances are he does not know much. Usually, the only Ryogans who know anything about magic are the few allowed to use it." She shakes her head. "And their views barely resemble ours. They use spoken spells, and they compare the relationship between magic and spells to a river and its banks. Created properly, the borders of a river contain water without constraining it, but if those banks are not strong enough, they can crumble and cause a flood."

"If they live in fear of a flood, how can they ever learn what they're capable of?"

"You do not understand the limits placed on mages in Ryogo. Their work is closely watched. The smallest infraction will land them in prison."

"What is prison?" That's not a word Osshi taught us.

"A cage for those who break laws. A way to keep dangerous people away from everyone else." The way she describes it makes me think of Imaku, a bleak, lonely, dark place. "I cannot tell you more than that because I do not know anything about the mage's prison except that it exists. I also cannot tell you more about our magic—anything else is forbidden."

My stomach sinks. There's so much more I need to know.

"But I also cannot stop you from watching." When I blink, she smiles. "You have already proven to be resourceful and intelligent. There is a lot you could learn by observation."

"And you'll allow that?" Because if *I* can learn a lot, then Tessen could learn *everything*.

"Yes. Until it becomes an issue." Then she smirks. "But I will be watching you as well."

"Fair." Especially since it's not something I'm in a position to argue. "Do your people speak Ryogan as well as they understand it? Are we allowed to talk to them?"

"Truly perceptive." A moment of hesitation. A quick glance. A sigh before she says, "I am the voice of my family; bring any questions you have to me."

Although that's not really an answer to either of my questions, it's clearly as much as I'm going to get. I agree, and she relaxes.

"There is one other thing I wanted to talk to you about." Although I nod, it takes Lo'a a few seconds before she says, "You are being hunted."

"We are," I respond. "Well, Osshi is. So far, unless one of Kazu's men reported us, we don't think the Ryogans know we're here."

"Yet you do not seem afraid of the hunters."

"I'm vigilant, but I—" I close my mouth, thinking. "Maybe it's just hard to be scared of hunters who fear magic so much.

I am afraid, just not of the Ryogans. We can beat a squad of them if we need to. Outrun them. What I'm afraid of is what'll happen—to us and to everyone else—if Varan's army gets here before we have a way to stop him. He's been planning this for centuries, Lo'a. He will decimate anything and anyone that tries to stop him now."

I just have to hope—have to keep believing—that he hasn't already decimated Yorri and everyone else I left behind on Shiara.

She nods, her expression somber. "True, but do not discount the threat Ryogans pose. Their wariness is not weakness. This land is rich with resources more than one foreign power would love to control, yet no one has been able to take it from them."

I nod. "We'll keep it in mind, but we're not trying to take anything. This place is too cold for me. I don't know how you can wear so little. I'm sitting here wishing I had more layers."

"Be prepared then," she says as she gets up. "Osshi is taking you even farther north of here, and as the land rises, the temperature drops."

"Wonderful," I mutter as I follow her back outside. It isn't enough that we're trying to reach a village Chio hasn't seen in centuries and find a cache of information that may not even exist anymore while being hunted by Ryogan soldiers, but we have to do it in the cold? "Something to look forward to."

CHAPTER FIVE

anii and I back away from the mouth of the black tunnel, Yorri held between us, unconscious and dragging awkwardly; Sanii is so much shorter.

There's fear in Tessen's eyes when he turns away from that escape. "*Run!*"

But the tunnel is safer. It doesn't end in water. I try to tell Tessen; only meaningless noise escapes.

"Run, Khya! They'll break this rotten rock into a pile of rubble." Sanii pulls on Yorri, which pulls on me. I keep my eyes on the tunnel, but my mind is mired in quicksand. I can't remember what's in that black tunnel that they're so afraid of.

We pass row after row of black platforms; I refuse to look at a single one. I know the people we're leaving here will plague my mind. If they have faces, it'll be worse.

But…I already tried that, didn't I? It didn't work. Couldn't have; even with my eyes closed I can see every face.

"Wards, Khya!" Fear sharpens Sanii's expression. "What are you doing? We need air or we're going to drown out there."

"I don't know how!" What? That's not what I wanted to

say. This moment feels horribly, painfully familiar, but also different. I didn't mean to say that.

"Rot take you, Khya! Remember!" I've never seen em so angry. "I am not leaving Yorri here for *whatever* this is."

"Wait!" My breathing comes hard and too quick. "Stop and let me—"

"Shut up and move!" Tessen shoves us forward. I stumble; only my desperate grip on Yorri keeps me on my feet. "There's no time. Remember or we're dead, Khya."

Think, think, think. I created the wardstones we're wearing, right? I did, but I don't know how. And these are wrong, their glow too dull and the magic the wrong color. It should be red. It feels gray. Wrong. But we're nearing the end of the passage. The crash of waves against rock is getting louder. Louder. Deafeningly loud.

"Now, Khya!" Tessen barks, his voice harsh and furious.

I mentally reach for the wardstones; the magic spillls through the holes in my concentration like sand.

Ten feet away from the edge of the black island.

Five feet. Blood and rot. They're expecting my wards to give us air underwater?

"Khya!" Sanii hisses. "Jump!"

One foot. Sanii leaps, and I leap with em.

Flying above the waves, we're safe from imprisoning rock and devouring water. But only for a moment. Pain shoots up my arm. Water surrounds me, and cold, but I breathe air, not water. I try to reach for Yorri; my left arm won't answer and my right hand closes on nothing. The water is getting through my ward, and Yorri— Where is Yorri?

My head breaks into the air. I see what my failures have done.

A thick red rope around his neck. Matching bonds around his wrists and ankles. His body is arched out over the water. I could save him. All I need is a moment of pure focus. I tried something before; maybe this time it will work.

Lungs burning, I battle the current toward the island. A hand clamps around my left ankle. My body jerks. My concentration breaks. Water pours through my wards. Yorri vanishes, and I get sucked down into the angry, insatiable ocean. The grip tightens and drags me deeper, but I keep reaching for my brother. Reaching for—

"Let her go!"

The hand on my ankle tightens, holding on no matter how hard I scramble to get away. I should be able to—

"She almost kicked me in the head!"

I reach for my wards, pulling in as much power as I can and—

"Let *go*, Natani!"

I'm free. I gasp for breath, trying to sit up. Get away. New hands grip my shoulders. No! I pull in power again, hoping my wards won't fail me this time. If I shove them out from my body hard enough and fast enough—

"It's me, Khya. Breathe. Breathe."

I'll break their hold. I'll break their *arms*.

Suddenly, I'm leaning against someone's chest. "You're okay." A hand rubs circles on my back. Another gently strokes my short hair. Tessen. "You're safe, I promise. You're safe here."

I exhale heavily; the breath shudders through my body and my muscles tremble, but Tessen's warmth takes the edge off my chilled skin. The soft vibration of the desosa around his body, a pattern I know so well now, is even more soothing than the gentle brush of his fingers down the line of my jaw or the firm, protective hold of his other arm. My heart is beating too fast, every thump too loud, but I relax more with each passing second.

I trust Tessen completely. I promised I would, even in moments like this, but blood and rot, I hate needing him so much. He's not like our andofume. Or like the bobasu. Or like Yorri. Tessen can be killed, and he's following me into a mission where failure is so much more likely than success. If I lose him now, after I've let him in this much—

No. Stop. Hold my breath. Count the seconds. Concentrate on the flow of the desosa.

Useless. None of my usual tricks are working. I need something else to think about.

"Where are we?" I ask.

"Close to Uraita," Tessen says. "But it'll be an hour or two until we leave the caravan."

"We're passing a city. Tirodo, I think." Rai is leaning through the window, almost half her body out of the wagon. "Haven't been this close to one yet. It's so…unprotected. Do they really have so few enemies here?"

Curious, I ease off the bed. I pull Rai back just enough to poke my own head out, too. For a second, my head spins, because the city isn't level with us, it's at the bottom of a fifty-foot drop. I close my eyes and take a breath, pushing aside the vertigo and the lingering shakiness from my nightmare. When I open them again, my vision and my head are more stable.

Like Po'umi, Tirodo is filled with closely packed buildings. The colors are different, though; the sharply sloped roofs are mostly black, the buildings' walls are mostly white, and the clothing I see people wearing is in shades of black and brown. There's one spot of color, and it seems out of place.

"What is that?" I point to the red tower rising above any other building.

"The Kaisubeh tower," Tsua says after peeking out. "Every city has one as a tribute."

"What are the Kaisubeh again?" Etaro asks.

"I don't—oh. Right," Tyrroh says. "Kaisubeh. The Ryogans' invisible, all-powerful gods and goddesses."

"Rot-ridden fools," Rai mutters.

I agree, but when Osshi stiffens in his seat by the door, I wish she hadn't said it aloud. He's still not over my display of power with Lo'a, and he takes serious offense when we doubt his pantheon. Even though no one has seen or heard proof of the Kaisubeh's existence in centuries.

According to Osshi's stories, the last time the Kaisubeh bothered themselves with the Ryogans was before the bobasu's exile. Over five hundred years ago. Even that incident—a massive black rock hurtling down from the sky, a rock with properties that proved to be Varan's undoing—was arguable. The Ryogans couldn't prove the rock was sent by the Kaisubeh any more than they could prove it wasn't. Yet they still build towers in their honor.

I step back from the window, letting Etaro and Sanii take my place. I move to sit at the table with Tyrroh and the andofume and look at the maps they've been studying since yesterday. "What have you found?"

"Almost nothing familiar." Chio runs his middle finger over the arc of his thin eyebrow. "I knew things would change, they did even while we lived here, yet it's still surprising to think Uraita has become so unrecognizable."

My stomach tightens. "What about Varan's notes? Will you be able to find them?"

"No" isn't an acceptable answer. The only trail we can follow right now begins with that information. We can't undo something we don't understand, and no way can we defeat Varan if we don't know how to kill him.

"*If* his hiding places haven't been found, and *if* the seal hasn't been broken, and *if* everything is still inside..." Chio huffs and shakes his head.

"Realistically, the chances of this working are low," Tsua finishes.

"Then why are we doing this?" Sanii drops onto the bench next to me.

"Because if Varan's notes *are* there, they could save us more time than I want to think about." I pull the map closer, trying to fix it in my mind. "I'd rather check this first. At least it gives us a place to start and better odds of finding something."

"Bad odds seem to be all we get these days." Tessen sighs. "But at least we're still alive to face them."

Unlike some of the people we left behind. Or lost on our way here.

Ignoring the way my chest aches, I point to the lines on the map north of Uraita and ask what they mean. Ryogo's system of marks and symbols isn't anything like the one we used in Itagami, and we've been studying it in between Osshi and the andofume's lessons on reading, but these in particular are new.

Osshi purses his lips, but then he moves closer and explains about the caves hidden underground and how they're displayed on paper. His words are stiff at first, but he begins to relax the longer he talks. Almost like he forgets he's afraid of us. I'm glad, because his help means that by the time we're a few miles from the border of Uraita, I nearly have this particular section of Ryogo memorized.

Before the caravan stops mid morning, we dress in the Ryogan clothes Lo'a gave us, ones in the same dark colors we saw people in Tirodo wearing. There are multiple layers of thick fabric kept in place with knots that the hanaeuu we'la maninaio taught us how and where to tie. The clothes are warmer, but it's hard to adjust to their restrictions. Especially the boots. When I first put them on a few days ago, it was like relearning how to walk. The warmth almost isn't worth the trouble. Almost.

Lo'a is waiting with a warning when we leave the wagon with our bags and gear once more strapped to our backs. "You have one full day before we leave. We cannot wait here any longer than that."

"I'm grateful you're willing to wait at all." I've somehow become the squad's spokesperson, a counterpoint to Lo'a's position in her family. But despite the time I've spent talking to her, I wasn't sure she'd be willing to help us after Uraita. Especially not when I know now how secretive the hanaeuu we'la maninaio really are and how much helping us could hurt her family.

"Better make the most of your time, then." She nods in the direction of Uraita. "One day. Not an hour more."

Agreeing and saying goodbye, we move through the woods on our own, Tessen and Chio leading. Osshi, we hide in the middle of the group. It's his voyage to hunt down the truth behind the bobasu legend that got him in trouble in Ryogo, so we're all hoping the tyatsu will assume he'd never consider coming here, a place deeply connected to the same legend. We're hoping, but we can't be sure, so we need to be careful. There's a lot of ground to cover before we reach the mountains, and we'll be coming close to Uraita. A moment's inattention is all it'll take for us to get spotted, but it's the best path and the only plan we've got.

If what Chio believes is hidden in the Mysora Mountains is still there, we can't risk being found. If it's *not* here...we still can't risk it.

We don't know the quirks of this landscape well enough to move as quietly as we could on Shiara, so we give up some speed to stay silent. Twice, though, Tessen signals a halt. Each time, we wait in the shadows as several people trudge past, heavy loads on their backs. It slows us down even more, but we make it to the base of the mountains without trouble.

The trees end about a hundred feet up the slope, which means we have to leave their protection to move any higher. Tessen scans the area and points to three separate paths. "Those paths seem the most used."

Chio shakes his head. "Varan didn't use those. It's this way."

We stay in the shadows to follow Chio west. He's muttering to himself and the fingers of his left hand are moving, almost like he's drawing on the air. Finally, a little more than two miles east of the village, Chio touches a stone.

"'Child of the Kaisubeh.'" Chio traces words etched into the stone; they're small and almost hidden. "Varan called us that when we were young, and he marked the path with this phrase. It won't always be easy to see."

"Maybe for you." I tap Tessen on the shoulder, smiling. "Get to work, basaku."

With a smirk, Tessen nods. "Yes, Nyshin-pa."

"Don't," I warn, shaking my head. "Get us where we need to go."

His lips purse, then he steps closer to Chio and follows him away from the trees.

I shouldn't have said anything about the rot-ridden title, but I can't stand it. It burns when the rest of the squad calls me nyshin-pa, but from Tessen it's worse. It's an unearned honor, and it feels like I'm stealing respect that doesn't belong to me. I don't want anything from Tessen that isn't mine.

But what matters now is the mission, so I shove all of that aside.

The path is steep, and so narrow at times we have to squeeze through sideways. Osshi does better on this trek than he did on Shiara or climbing the face of the cliff when we landed on Ryogo, but Etaro and Tsua still have to take turns magically lifting him up with us. Especially since sometimes the old path is gone, erased by time and rockslides; then, the practice of a life on our rocky island becomes useful even though it's hard to climb with boots between my feet and the rocks. Thankfully, every time I slip, someone is there to catch me.

Chio and Tessen find each of Varan's ancient markers, some of them so worn down by wind and rain and time only Tessen can see them. I run my hand over one as I pass, trying to imagine a younger Varan pressing his hand to this same stone and carving these words into it. I can't. Mostly because when I try I can't help wishing Chio had caught up with him back then and smashed his head in with one of these rocks.

The route they lead us along doesn't always move up. Morning turns into afternoon before we reach a valley with a small river. We stop there to drink, eat, and warm our hands near Rai's and Nairo's fire because despite the sun, it's only gotten colder.

"Varan really didn't want anyone finding this, did he?" I say.

"He loved secrets." Chio looks up at the mountain's peak. "I think they made him feel powerful. It's not much farther, though."

We press on, and in the golden light of late afternoon, we reach a level area barely wide enough to fit us all. Chio stops in the center. "Here. This is it."

Most of us stay back, perching on nearby boulders or hovering a ways down the path to make it easier for Chio, Tsua, and Tessen to search the landing.

My patience holds for about ten minutes. "I thought you remembered where he hid this."

"Not even rock is unchanged by time, Khya." Chio points at a large slab of stone, and Tsua lifts it out of the way. "Nothing here is like it was then. Forgive me if I can't walk into the hills and instantly find a magically protected hole that's been here since I was younger than *you*."

I grind my teeth and hold my tongue, but it feels like they have to completely rearrange the rocks surrounding this shelf before Chio finally says, "Thank the Kaisubeh. It's still here."

I jump down and rush toward them. "What can I do?"

They mentioned yesterday that Varan might have set a trap to guard this place, but neither could guess what it might be until we were here. Now, he and Tsua peer into the crevice, murmuring to each other for several minutes.

Finally, they nod and Tsua turns to me. "Create a ward around us, Khya, one that keeps you on the outside. We're going to have to set off the trap."

"That sounds like a really awful idea," Rai mutters from somewhere.

"Would you rather be on this side of the ward?" Tsua doesn't give Rai a chance to respond before she orders, "Now, Khya."

They've each been carrying one of my wardstones since we left Lo'a, so I use those to anchor my magic, creating a dome that spreads around them and sinks down into the stone, my wards digging into the rock to make sure they're completely sealed inside.

"Ready." I take one step back, but stay close, ready to reinforce the barrier. Varan is nothing if not thorough. In both his defenses and his punishments.

Tsua waves her hand over the crevice. There are sounds— metal falling on stone—and then green-gray gas rises from the hole. It pours out like water bursting through a broken dam. It fills the warded space in seconds until it's so dark and thick I can't see anything inside.

But I can hear. Bellows and blood. My stomach drops.

I can hear them trying not to scream.

"Khya. *Khya*." Tessen's eyes are wide and his body tense.

"I think it's eating through them."

"What do you want me to do? Let it out *here*? What do you think that will do to us if it's doing this to them?"

"You hold that ward until they tell you to stop." Zonna appears on my other side, his square face pained. "They knew what they were doing."

"But how do we get them out of it?" Tessen demands.

"You don't." Zonna closes his eyes. "We wait."

Heart racing, I wait. And wait. Wait. Enough time for my pulse to calm. Enough time for my breathing to even. For my knees to ache from pressing against the stone.

Finally, the smoke changes color, becoming more gray than green. Another interminable length of time later, the smoke shifts again, paler and grayer, but only when it's cloud-white does a hand press flat against the ward.

Their skin is bright red. Blistered. Bleeding. They tap their fingers against the ward three times. Then they pull away, but not before I notice one thing: they're healing. The cuts were closing. The redness fading. I keep reminding myself of that as I release the top of the ward and send a new cloud into the sky.

Immediately, Zonna leaps over what remains of my ward. Hands on his parents' skin, his magic pours into them, healing them even faster than their own immortality can. I can feel it even though the smoke is still too thick for me to see anything but shadows and outlines. By the time the smoke clears, their blisters are gone and only redness like a sunburn is left.

I drop the rest of my ward. "Are you okay?"

"I will be if this turns out to be worthwhile." Tsua presses her face against her son's shoulder and shudders.

Thin lips pressed tight, Chio reaches out to run his hand over her hair, but then he pulls away from them both and leans over the crevice. "Tsua, I need you, vanafitia."

Tsua straightens with a tense nod and shifts to kneel

opposite Chio. Zonna, Tessen, and I move back to give them space as Tsua retrieves a stone box. It's embedded with crystals, etched with words I can't read, and it's no longer than my forearm. It doesn't seem worth what they suffered, but what it holds might be.

I shudder, the andofume's screams still echoing between my ears.

What's inside had better be worth that much pain.

G oing down the mountain is a lot easier than going up. We don't have to follow Varan's twisting, unnecessarily complicated route, for one. Still, it's well past midnight by the time we reach level ground. Everyone is freezing, tired, and hungry, but we're alive, we have a box of something Varan thought was worth guarding with a deadly trap, and we have enough time to make it back to Lo'a's camp before she leaves.

Then Chio mutters something and sighs. "We have a choice to make."

"What kind of choice?" I ask.

"We're several miles west of where we started, and this is populated terrain. We have to skirt Uraita to get back." Chio looks toward the lights flickering in the distance. "Do we keep walking now or rest and eat first?"

"If we wait too long, we might not make it before Lo'a leaves," Tsua says.

Tyrroh and Tessen vote for pushing on, but my fingers are going numb and my stomach is hollow with hunger, so I shake my head. "We're too tired and cold. We're more likely to make a mistake if we don't rest first."

Also, if we rest, Tsua and Chio will have a chance to open

Varan's box. They must be itching to break the seal on it at *least* as much as I am. We won't find all the answers we need inside, but that's okay. All I need it to have is the next step toward killing Varan. And freeing Yorri.

Within minutes, Wehli has gathered enough wood and kindling to feed a good fire. As soon as Rai lights the blaze, Tessen and Natani unpack the provisions as we sit in a tight circle around the warmth.

I sit close to Tsua and Chio, and it's hard not to crowd into their space when they place the stone box on the ground between them. They debate if there's a trap inside the box. I watch and listen for a few minutes before I interject. "I don't think he'd have a trap on this *and* the crevice itself. Varan's paranoid, but he's also arrogant. The tunnel to Imaku was only guarded by locked doors and a ward. Beyond that, the way was open."

"That's after centuries of absolute power." Chio holds the box up and Tsua's hands rise. Light like Sanii's gathers in her palm. I blink. I didn't know she could do that. "The only people he had to worry about on Shiara were us."

Tessen walks toward Chio, his hand outstretched. "May I see it?"

Chio hands over the box. As Tessen examines it, I lean in, needing to see the thing we climbed so far for. Then Tessen's gaze meets mine and I scoot closer. "You need my wards or senses?"

"Senses first." He holds out the box. "Wards after. Maybe."

"Hopefully not." I never want to repeat what happened to Tsua and Chio on that mountain, especially not if it's Tessen trapped inside this time. I take a breath and rest my hands on the box. Relief fills my chest, warming me more than the fire. "If there's anything in there set to kill us, I can't feel it."

"There's something," Tessen says slowly, peering at the

box through narrowed eyes. "But it's subtle. It doesn't feel dangerous."

"You're probably sensing the seal." Tsua takes the box back. "And *that*, thankfully, we know how to break."

Tsua floats the box several feet away, and then she says, "*Goa'wa uita*."

Wards ready, I hold my breath and wait for smoke or sparks or *something*. If something goes wrong this time, I will not leave anyone inside the ward to suffer from it. But the top separates from the rest with nothing worse than the scrape of stone, and Tsua floats both pieces back toward us.

"Perfect timing." Natani pokes the cooking meat one more time, the firelight bringing out the red in his terra-cotta skin. "Food's ready."

Etaro and Rai help Natani pass out dinner, but I stay near Tsua and Chio, watching them slowly and carefully pick through the box's contents. The protections on this must've been strong, because everything seems to be intact from what I can tell. There are papers, stones, and a few small pouches, but it's hard to follow Tsua and Chio's conversation about the items. They speak low and quick, and they jump between multiple languages seemingly at random.

Waiting—and attempting to convince myself they'll explain everything later—scrapes against my patience, so instead of continuing to watch them, I take out the book on niadagu spells I stashed in my pack. I haven't learned anything new from the books, but I can't stand being this close to the next step and unable to take it. I have to do *something*, and this is all I have that feels like it'll bring me even a little bit closer to helping Yorri.

Over the past few days I've read the entire book— traveling has given me plenty of time—but now I reread the pages about weaving magic into fabric.

As I read, I run my thumb along the cord around my wrist. I've tried, but I can't bind even a small piece of my magic to it in any lasting way. It's frustrating, especially since I can do it to wardstones. This can't be much different. I just have to take what I already know, combine it with the information on the pages in front of me, and make it work. Looking at the problem like one of the puzzles Yorri used to make helps. There's a single piece I need to pull out or adjust and the whole thing will fall into place. I'll find it eventually if I just keep looking.

But an hour later, when we get ready to leave, every attempt has failed. Even when I only try to make it hold my wards, I fail. Grinding my teeth, I shove the book back into my pack.

"You have time, but it won't matter if we don't figure out how to kill Varan first." Tessen's murmured words slide through my distraction.

"What won't?"

"That." He nods toward my pack. "I know it's important, but being able to break the cords won't do us any good if we can't kill the bobasu."

"You don't know that." A tremor of anger rolls through my body. My fingers clench the strap of my pack. "None of us know what'll happen with Varan, but I *do* know I need this. If I don't know how to break this, I'll never be able to save Yorri."

"I'm not telling you to not save Yorri. I gave up everything to help you find him." His full lips press thin. "All I'm saying is that we need you working on the bigger problem, too."

"Why? There are thirteen other people, Tessen, and *all* of them are working on destroying the bobasu. Why do *I* need to be working on it, too?"

Tessen blinks, an expression flashing across his face that I've never seen him give me before. Like he's reevaluating my intelligence. "Because you're you, Khya. Because somehow you and Sanii are the ones who saw through Varan's tricks and broke through Suzu's defenses. *You* got us here when who knows how many people tried before. Even Tsua and Chio failed, but you succeeded. Now we have a bigger problem, and you're not working on it with us."

"When the andofume need my help, they'll ask. And I'll give it to them. Until then, I'll be working on the problem *no one* else is even looking at."

Only when I say it do I realize I'm reminding myself of that truth as much as I'm reminding him.

Only when he doesn't respond, walking away from the buried campfire instead, do I realize I was waiting for him to tell me I'm right.

CHAPTER SIX

Night is just giving way to the gray of predawn when we erase all signs of our camp. It's just enough light to travel by, but not enough to read. That—and the need to move silently—are the only things keeping me from taking Varan's papers from the andofume to study while we make our way back to the wagons.

An hour later, we pass an expanse of brown, barren land. So much of Ryogo is lush and green, but this is empty and dry. And it *smells*.

"Where is that coming from?" I whisper to Tyrroh, hand covering my nose and mouth. Tessen is ahead of us, and he has a cloth wrapped over his face.

"I'm trying very hard *not* to smell anything right now." Tyrroh shudders. "I don't know what it could be. Nothing on Shiara is this strong or disgusting. It's like rotten meat surrounded by wuhani flowers—and those feces-scented things are bad enough."

Osshi looks back at us, warinesss in his eyes. Then he clears his throat. "Umm, Chio-ti?" Our andofume halt and turn. "There is… I should tell you something."

"What did he call Chio?" I ask Sanii.

"The -ti is one of their ranks." Sanii waves eir hand. "They have more ranks and honors than we do."

Right. Tsua and Chio addressed him as Osshi-tan after they met him on Shiara. Now, as we stop behind him to listen, I wonder what Osshi needs to say that's so important. And why, if it's so important, he hasn't told us before now.

"Originally we weren't going to visit Uraita. I knew we'd pass close, but I didn't— I mean, I likely should've mentioned it, but I didn't know we'd be…" He casts his eyes up, running a hand through his black, shoulder-length hair.

Tsua looks toward the barren land. "They salted the fields, didn't they?"

Oh no. My stomach flips. That would be catastrophic if it happened on Shiara. The entire clan would collapse in less than a year. Thousands would die. How could they do that to this village?

"It was something much worse than salt." Osshi finally meets their eyes. "But they also erased Varan and Chio's family name from history, destroyed every osukiga portrait painted for your ancestors, banned your names from ever being used, and restricted the village's ability to trade—"

"*Enough*." Tsua turns away from the dead land. "Enough, Osshi. We can guess the rest."

Pain etched in their faces, Tsua and Chio stare at each other. I can only imagine the heartache of returning to Itagami only to find it a ruined shade of what I remembered and loved. Bellows, I probably won't have to imagine that feeling for long—there's no way home will be the same place I remember when I see it again. *If* I see it again.

"You could've warned us, Osshi." Chio rubs his hand over his eyes.

"I didn't know how. I wasn't sure you'd want to know. This is how it's been since the bobasu were exiled." Osshi says it almost hesitantly. "Most people don't believe the bobasu legends anymore, but those who live here aren't allowed to forget. They also—" Osshi clears his throat. "You told me you didn't plan on entering the village, so I thought it didn't matter, but in all Ryogo, *this* is where they're most likely to remember your faces."

Tsua mutters a Denhitran curse, and Chio closes his eyes; his sharp nod is the only sign he heard. Anger burns in my stomach, hot and sharp. When Osshi first met Tsua and Chio, he was so excited. He'd been willing to do anything to help, but ever since we escaped he's become more and more closed off. It's a good thing what we were looking for wasn't in the village. Even if we had to pass through Uraita, I'm not sure if he would've told us until it was nearly too late.

"Honestly, Osshi," Chio begins. "Warn us earlier if there's anything we even *might* need to know."

Osshi nods, eyes cast down, but I can't help wondering.

Maybe it's different because, on Shiara, we were his only chance of survival. Now we're in his homeland, and although some of his people may be hunting him, he has friends. Family. People he'd give his life to protect. Even if he's telling the whole truth now, what will he do when he has to either keep one of Ryogo's secrets or help people he was raised to believe were his enemies?

Don't create trouble, I can almost hear my old training master scold. *Shiara provides us with more than enough.*

We're not on Shiara, but it's still something we need to remember. Everything about Ryogo has been trouble so far. If we're going to get back to Shiara in time to stop Varan from leveling Ryogo, I need to avoid making things more complicated.

By the time we reach Uraita, sunlight has broken through the interlaced branches of the trees. It illuminates a place I never could've imagined.

"*This* is where Varan was born?" Rai's skepticism is louder than her words.

I… I really can't blame her. Even with Osshi's warning, this isn't what I was expecting. The buildings are spread out, and all of them are plain, unpainted wood. Few people are outside; their clothes are ragged and too thin for the chill in the air. The streets are nothing more than uneven dirt. It looks and smells like a place on the verge of death.

"This place used to be beautiful." Tsua puts her hand on a tree like she needs it for balance. "We were small, but we always had enough for ourselves. This isn't…"

"The house Varan and I grew up in was there." Chio points toward a large gap between two other buildings.

Statues of Varan, Chio, Tsua, and Suzu stand where the house used to be, each one wrapped in stone chains. They stand on a wide pedestal that raises them several feet off the ground. Words are carved into that base, but I can't read them from here. It doesn't matter; staring at proof of so much feels like trying to breathe on the highest point of a mountain.

I thought I'd already accepted this, that the leaders we grew up idolizing not only as immortals but as gatekeepers to the paradise of Ryogo were neither. But I'm standing in Ryogo, alive, and I'm staring at stone versions of Itagami's two most powerful leaders—who are two of Ryogo's worst criminals.

The lie of who Varan is has never been clearer or more painful than it is right now. My hands shake no matter how I try to make them stop.

"What does it say?" Chio asks Tessen.

Slowly, Tessen reads the inscription. "'By the will of the Kaisubeh, and for the crimes of two sons and two daughters of

Uraita, this village will suffer for a thousand years. Remember the lesson well, for it is the responsibility of all to ensure no child of Uraita or Ryogo ever repeats the mistakes of their ancestors.'"

Tsua closes her eyes. "The so-called mercy of the Chonochi shunkyus at work. I hope all of them are rotting in the blackness of Kaijuko."

I can't help wishing the same on the former ruling family of Ryogo. In Itagami, our law prescribes exactly the opposite: the actions of one cannot, and should not, be paid for by the suffering of many.

Apparently that wasn't a lesson Varan learned from his homeland.

"Is there anything within Uraita worth searching for?" Tyrroh asks. When Chio slowly shakes his head, Tyrroh takes a step east. "Then we should go."

He's right. The longer we're here, the more likely it is we'll be spotted. And I want to get away from the statues and the ruined village.

Swallowing hard, I tear my eyes away from the images of the people who ripped my brother away from me. I run my thumb along the cord on my wrist and look deeper into the trees.

How many lives has Varan destroyed? I've been so focused on what happened to Yorri and the others trapped on Imaku; I never considered what had happened *here*. An entire village is suffering because of him.

There had been a war, too. Varan incited a rebellion, and thousands died in those battles. Several hundred more died in the aftermath. Even after the bobasu were exiled, Varan caused destruction. Dozens died when the ship carrying the bobasu crashed on Shiara, and after that…

Chio and Tsua haven't mentioned much about their

early days on Shiara, and I haven't asked, but Varan must've spent those years taking control of an island that was already inhabited. It couldn't have been clean. Or smooth. Or painless. People must've died. It has to be part of the reason Itagami's been at war with the other Shiaran clans for so long.

How can one person be the source of so much destruction?

The others catch up with me, but none of them talk. Not even Tessen. Maybe I'm not the only one shaken by Uraita.

The silence holds until we approach another dead stretch of land and Etaro mutters, "Ugh. The smell is back."

"It never left, trust me," Tessen says. "And this isn't just a smell. The desosa is different, too. Can you feel it, Khya? Its like, once it leaves the land, it's trying to escape this place as fast as it can."

He's right. I didn't notice earlier because desosa always rises from growing things, but this is too fast. The energy rising out of these fields is moving as though it's being propelled. Like arrows from bows.

"They can't feel the desosa, but they're still messing with it?" I don't understand that.

"Nothing about Ryogan magic makes sense." Tessen reaches out, his fingers brushing my wrist just above the red cord. "Maybe that's why you can't solve your puzzle."

I can't tell if he's taunting, teasing, or serious, so I pretend it's the last and shrug. "Maybe, but I'll figure it out. If Varan can do it, so can I."

"Varan also lied to us for ages." Rai flicks the air next to my cheek. "I'd rather you didn't pick up all of his skills and habits, Nyshin-pa."

I clench my jaw against a protest on the promotion. "You've spent almost every hour of every day with me for weeks now. How can I possibly lie to you about anything?"

"I don't know, but don't you dare take that as a challenge,"

Rai warns, a glint of humor in her large eyes.

"*Tsst!*" Tessen's quick hiss slices through and stops the group. Osshi stumbles forward two steps before realizing why we've halted. Then Tessen curses. "Forget being quiet. Move!"

I run beside him through the trees. "What's wrong?"

"Someone in the village spotted us when we stopped."

"Blood and rot," Sanii mutters as we run.

"It was a tyatsu guard passing through Uraita, and he saw Osshi, not Chio." He pushes faster. "I heard him. He used a garakyu to call for a squad. He saw Osshi isn't alone. If we don't get out before they arrive, someone will figure out who Osshi brought home with him."

Exhaustion weighs me down. Hiking those mountains was a strain after weeks of forced inactivity. Thankfully, I only have to hold on for a little bit longer—we're not too far from the camp.

When we burst into the clearing, it's obvious Lo'a's warning was serious. The camp is packed, and the ukaiahana'lona are being latched to the front of the wagons. More than one of the hanaeuu we'la maninaio look up when we appear, and many seem to brace for trouble.

"I told you not to bring danger back here, Osshi Shagakusa," Lo'a calls.

"Osshi was spotted," Tyrroh calls back. "If you're willing to take us, we'd be grateful. If not, leave here fast."

"My debt to you is paid, Osshi Shagakusa, but…" Lo'a's hands are on her broad hips, and her eyes are on *me*. "Well, Khya is another story."

"I…" She doesn't owe me anything, but we need her help. None of us have slept since the night before last. "Please. At least take us out of their range. Once we're rested, we'll leave if you ask us to."

Her golden-brown eyes are unreadable, but then she nods.

"Thank you." It's the first time I've seen her make a decision without looking to someone else, and I'm grateful. I bow my head as we hurry to our wagon, exhaustion-tinged-relief making me giddy.

We post a watch, and I raise wards around the caravan. Then, as most of the others settle in to get some sleep, Tyrroh, Osshi, Sanii, the andofume, and I gather around the small table with the stone box in the center.

Tsua carefully removes the lid and sets it aside, then she lifts each item and lays it on the table. Five crystals of varying colors. Two leather pouches. Six rolled papers, all discolored and torn at the edges. A circular piece of silver metal with something painted on the surface.

The last item is a book. It's thick and bound with black leather with white writing on the cover, but Tsua opens it too quickly for me to be certain I read the words right. It looked like the symbols Chio pointed out carved into the mountain—child of the Kaisubeh. Tsua seems to be looking for something specific inside, turning pages with cautious speed. Near the end, she stops, her eyes scanning across the page several times in quick succession.

"I was right. It's a susuji." Tsua carefully flattens the page.

Sanii's large eyes widen as ey leans in. "Really?"

"What is that?" I don't remember learning about those.

"A type of potion, which is a completely different way of creating magic," Sanii says.

Chio nods. "Potions combine certain plants and other special elements. Mixed over flames and infused with desosa, those elements create specific effects, like bringing on sleep or erasing memories, and there are names for each type. A susuji is a potion that heals."

I peer at the page Tsua's staring at and try to make sense of what's written there. It's an odd concept, that cooking things like a stew can somehow create magic, but Osshi is nodding and none of the andofume disagree. "So this is how Varan created immortality?"

I hold my breath, hoping we found an answer, *hoping…* until Chio shakes his head.

"It doesn't make sense." Chio taps the table next to the open stone box. "From everything I know about the plants and how he combined them, this should be an incredibly powerful susuji, but I don't see how this could possibly give someone the lifespan we've had."

Blood and rot. I exhale and link my fingers behind my neck. Should've known from moment one. I should've known as soon as Chio had told us about the possibility of finding Varan's notes that it wouldn't be that easy.

I lean in and open my mouth to ask about one of the items listed, but Zonna shakes his head and points toward the crowded beds. "This is their area of experience, not yours. Get some rest now, and we'll give you more details when you don't look like you're about to fall asleep with your eyes open."

No matter how much I want to protest, Zonna's right. It's been too long since I slept, my vision is beginning to blur. I relent, tugging Sanii's sleeve to pull em with me. Reluctantly, ey follows, climbing to the top bed to squeeze in while I slide into the space Tessen saved for me on the lower bed.

"Paradise is a lot colder than I imagined it would be," Tessen murmurs in my ear as he wraps his arm around my waist, pulling me closer to him.

"One more thing Varan lied about. You shouldn't be surprised," I whisper back. "Assume everything he ever told us is a lie until something proves otherwise. That's what I'm doing."

Or trying to do. Sometimes I don't even understand my own beliefs until I'm facing something that shatters them. Like the moment I saw Uraita.

"Right now, all I care about is the cold." His fingers trace patterns on my back; I barely feel them through the layers of cloth. "Will you keep me warm?"

I laugh, surprised and a little pleased, especially since I thought he might still be upset with me about my work on the niadagu spell. "You're ridiculous, Nyshin-ten. If you wanted someone to keep you warm, you should've attached yourself to Rai or Nairo before they found partners."

"Fire burns." Smiling, he nudges the edge of my nose with his own. "You can warm me up fine without it."

"Now?" I raise my eyebrows. "I didn't think you were one for public displays."

"Me neither," Rai mutters behind him without lifting her head or opening her eyes.

Tessen rolls his eyes. "I never mentioned displaying anything." He lifts his chin and presses a kiss to my forehead. "Get some sleep, Khya. I'll keep you warm this time."

"Good." I close my eyes and burrow between his neck and the mattress. "I have a feeling that we'll be stuck in the cold a lot longer than any of us wants to be."

I have absolutely no idea where we are when we wake up, but I hear voices calling out in Ryogan, the squawks and cries of animals, and the familiar sounds of a blacksmith in the distance.

"Are we in a city?" I carefully edge out of the bed. Tessen and Etaro are still sleeping.

"Near one." Rai is at the window, peering out through the small crack between the thick curtains. "Tirodo. We needed supplies."

"Is it a good idea to go where the people looking for us live?" I lean against the wall near Rai and listen to the cacophony outside. "Which should include any city in Ryogo."

Rai shrugs. "That's why we're stuck in here."

At least, since so many are still sleeping, it doesn't feel crowded yet. It will later, but now only Rai, Tsua, Chio, Zonna, and Tyrroh are awake. The elders are sitting at the table, the stone box and its contents spread out between them. Their focus is on the book.

"Hopefully Lo'a still thinks she owes Khya help, because finding the supplies we need won't be easy," Tsua is saying as I sit. "Some of this was hard to find in our day. I can't imagine it's gotten any easier since then."

"We'll have to ask Lo'a once we can leave this wooden cage," Chio says, glaring at the walls. Then he sighs and looks at me. "Or really, *you'll* have to ask Lo'a. Then, once we figure out how to collect this, we need a place safe enough to stay for a while so we can try to recreate the susuji. With or without the hanaeuu."

"I'll ask about both as soon as we stop somewhere else," I promise. But disappointment sits in my stomach like a rock. "You haven't learned anything else since we went to sleep?"

"There's something, but it's not good." Zonna points in a direction I think might be south. "Before she left, Lo'a told us that the storms Kazu sailed us out of are closing in."

Of course. Because for every step forward we take, something else has to push us back. And the storms I'm sure Varan caused are still chasing us. At this point, I don't know if there's anywhere in the world we could go where they won't eventually reach. They're so persistent it's hard to convince myself they're not capable of stalking us like teegras on the hunt.

I'm not afraid of the tyatsu, but thinking about those

persistent, worsening storms is enough to raise bumps on my skin. From the way Zonna's expression shifts, sympathy filling his eyes, I don't think I'm doing a good job keeping those fears off my face.

"How long do we have?" Rai asks as she joins us at the table.

"Two days," Osshi says. "Maybe three. And that kind of a storm here? It'll be extremely hard to get what you need before it's too dangerous to travel."

"It'll cause the same problems for the tyatsu," Tyrroh points out. "If we can get what we need and make it somewhere safe, the storms might help us create a gap between us and them."

There's too much *if* in that, especially when it's easier for things to go wrong than right. And we only landed a week ago, yet we've already had a near-miss with a tyatsu squad and a brush with a scout. At this rate, fighting and killing a squad of Ryogans is going to become unavoidable in days. And every extra hour we have to spend evading them is an hour wasted, one that we could've been using to find a way to save their people and mine.

But I guess all we can really do is plan and prepare. "What are our priorities?"

Tsua and Chio exchange a glance before Chio counts off the points on his fingers. "Materials for the susuji, a safe place to wait out the storms, and distance between us and the tyatsu. In that order."

"But the first will also be the hardest." Tsua taps the book. "I'm not sure how much of this we'll be able to find in one place."

"And splitting up will be more dangerous than it's worth," Tyrroh says.

"You really think Lo'a's people will be willing to find some of this for us?" I ask. "Even dressed like Ryogans, only you three and Osshi can pass for locals, but you either need to stay hidden or"—I look at Zonna—"you barely know more about Ryogo than we do."

"I guess we're lucky Lo'a feels like she owes you a favor or twenty, aren't we?" Tsua smiles, but the expression is so strained I wonder if she's slept at all. "Otherwise I think we'd have to resort to sneaking and stealing to get what we need."

"We should do that for everything," Rai says. "Might save time."

"Let's keep thievery as our backup plan," Chio says dryly. "The point is to *not* draw attention, remember? It'll arouse suspicions fast if a long list of rare plants and magical ingredients suddenly goes missing, and they used to have ways of trapping and disarming mages. I don't know how well those would work on any of us, but I'd rather not find out. The longer we can keep them from learning about our skills with magic the better."

Tsua and Chio unroll a map of northern Ryogo, talking about plants and cities and so many other things that mean almost nothing to me. I stay and listen closely, trying to learn as much as I can about the ingredients we need to find, the places we need to visit, and the susuji we need to recreate.

I push myself to grasp the spells and the concepts of potions, and so it's hard to keep from getting angry at myself when Sanii understands it all so much faster than I do. Ey seems to be absorbing Ryogan magical theory as easily as I understood wards; if ey could master the manipulation of the desosa the same way, ey'd probably have already figured out the secrets of the niadagu cords, too.

Only one of us needs to be able to break Yorri's cords, I remind myself. *If ey can master it before you, fine. Good. Wanting to be the person who frees him is dangerously selfish.*

I repeat the words to myself all night.

They help so much less than I want them to.

CHAPTER
SEVEN

n two days, thanks to several shortcuts almost too narrow and overgrown for the wagons to travel, we manage to collect most of the items on Varan's list. Or the hanaeuu we'la maninaio do. *We* spend almost all our time inside the wagon, waiting. I waste a lot of energy pretending I'm not counting each day, each hour, and each minute we've been away from Shiara or trying to estimate how long it'll be before we can go back.

Thirty-three days since we sailed away from home.

Too long until I see Shiara—or Yorri—again.

Some of the plants and herbs grow wild or on farms, so they're easy to find and use in everything from potions to stews. The rest of it won't be so simple, but at least we have this. And I was right; potions are disturbingly similar to cooking. I crush a dried leaf between my thumb and forefinger, letting the flakes fall back into a bowl. "It's so hard to believe this is magic."

"And what you do seems impossible to the Ryogans." Tsua picks the bowl up and uses a pestle to grind the leaves into dust.

We stopped for rest a couple hours southeast of Atokoredo, the one reachable city where Lo'a thinks we might be able to find the remaining ingredients. The clearing we're in isn't big enough for the caravan, so most of the wagons are spread along the path in either direction. Only our wagon, Lo'a's, and two others surround the campfires. Thankfully, her people don't seem to begrudge us the precedence. Especially not now.

Two days ago, to stave off the tedium of waiting, Natani, Wehli, Miari, and Nairo offered to teach Lo'a's people new tricks with a sword. It took some convincing before Lo'a and the elders agreed—more because of the rules limiting contact with outsiders than anything else; if they're going to teach people, they'll also need to talk to them.

Once they got permission, they started using the open space between the wagons to run drills and sparring matches. It was especially fun to watch when Wehlli, Miari, and Nairo show off, all three battling at once. They read each other so well, it's almost like watching a tokiansu between a sumai pair, especially since I know they *would* be soulpartners as well as bed partners if the bond wasn't so dangerous for more than two people to undergo.

Sumai or no, their display certainly impressed the hanaeuu we'la maninaio. Even I smiled when Wehli broke away from the other two, using his ryacho speed to twirl, duck, and wheel so fast his sword was nothing more than a gleaming silver blur in the air. When the three were finished, nearly every single member of Lo'a's family able to carry a sword rushed to grab their weapons and learn from their new instructors.

Now, though I watch their lesson in my peripheral vision, most of my focus is on Tsua and Chio as they prepare the leaves, roots, and oils we've gathered so far.

"How much more do we need?" Sanii asks as ey sits down next to me.

"Too much." Tsua pours the leaf dust into a pouch and rinses the mortar clean. "And I don't know how much we can find before *that* catches up to us."

She tilts her head toward the south and the black bank of clouds closing in. I don't let my eyes linger there when I ask, "What do we do if Atokoredo doesn't have what we need?"

"Find shelter fast," Chio says. "Although, even if luck and the Kaisubeh fail us, that'll have to happen anyway."

"What will we do if we can't find the last three items?" I ask Tsua as she drops new leaves into the dried-out bowl.

"Pray the Kaisubeh lead us somewhere else when the storm passes," Chio answers. "Otherwise we're going to have to spend more time than I want to think about hunting them down before…"

He looks toward the storm, but from the shadows in his eyes, I know he's thinking of more than just those clouds; that's not the only force we're racing against. Rubbing my forehead, I mutter, "I hate not knowing how much time we have left."

"What I don't understand is how a *plant* can be this hard to find." Rai looks at the interwoven branches overhead. "There are plants *everywhere*, and we found the others easily enough."

"Yes, but a long time has passed," Tyrroh says. "Do you remember the storm ten years ago?"

"I felt like the city was going to drown in that storm." I still have nightmares about it when the rains get bad.

"We lost our entire ahuri crop that year, and there weren't even any seeds to harvest. If we hadn't held some back from the last yield, we might've lost that fruit forever." Tyrroh gestures to the forest. "It could've happened here. I doubt they even know how many plants they've lost since Varan was exiled."

Tsua nods. "I don't think what we need has been wiped

out, but it's become rarer than it used to be. Mura'ina and rianjuko, especially."

"We used to be able to walk into the forest and pick enough to last us for moons." Chio sighs. "Now the supply is controlled and restricted."

"Getting caught growing mura'ina could destroy most families." Osshi shakes his head. "There are few who dare try. And rianjuko *can't* be grown most places."

"It's a good thing the hanaeuu are used to ducking the law, then." Chio's admission seems grudging, but not without respect. "I don't think you would've been able to find a potential source of either, would you?"

"Contrary to what the tyatsu now believe, I'm not actually a criminal," Osshi mutters, eyes downcast and shoulders tense. "I know *history*. I know the legends and ancient stories everyone else has forgotten. I don't know anything about…"

"How to get yourself out of the mess you're in?" Tsua gently asks.

"With*out* dying." Osshi glances up, expression unreadable. "Or hurting Ryogo."

"You're not the one trying to hurt Ryogo, Osshi," Zonna says. "And the best way out of this is to help us stop Varan."

Osshi takes a long breath. "Then listen to Lo'a. If she says we can get what we need in Atokoredo, then go there. Then, if it works, I suggest hiding on the western coast while you work out your countermeasures. It'll be far easier to escape from there."

"And easier for the tyatsu to pin us between them and the ocean." Rai flicks sparks into the fire, making it blaze brighter. "If you don't want to see Ryogans hurt, Osshi, don't suggest a plan that'll leave us no options."

She's not wrong, but I don't like the fear in Osshi's eyes. "We'll avoid killing anyone, but not if it means our lives."

"Just help us stay hidden because *most* of us are doing everything we can to keep Varan from landing here," Tessen says as he approaches. I catch the emphasis of his words and shoot him a sharp glare, but then he says, "Lo'a is ready to move. She said if we push, we can reach Atokoredo by evening." Then he looks at the andofume. "And she's ready for us to join her if you want to finish planning this."

We help Tsua and Chio clean up their work as Tyrroh calls out, "Everyone, load up."

The sword lesson breaks up and the camp is quickly broken down. As soon as our supplies are put away, Tessen, Natani, and I follow Tyrroh and the andofume to Lo'a's wagon. Inside, she's waiting with a map of Atokoredo laid out. The elders sit with her at the table. I move to the bed, Tessen and Natani joining me a moment later.

Once the door is closed, Chio taps the map. "We know what we need is so restricted that even an illegal dealer won't sell them to the hanaeuu, so Lo'a can't get it for us, and Osshi can't risk going into the city. Even if he could, it wouldn't help."

"Why not?" Natani asks.

"The people I am taking you to see do not like strangers," Lo'a says. "New faces make them nervous. It makes them think the tyatsu are closing in."

I lean closer to the table. "Tell us more about these friends of yours."

"Their names are Osota and Shideso Tarusuta, and we will find them close to where the river splits." Lo'a points to a building in the northwest section of the oblong city.

"The layout reminds me of Itagami," Natani murmurs, tracing the western edge of the city. "They just have more water."

"With the way the storm season went this year," I say, my eyes on the quadrant Lo'a indicated, "Itagami might have this much water now, too." Hopefully not, though. Atokoredo sits at the point where the Sansosi'ka River halves. Our city would drown in this much water.

"I have worked with the Tarusuta family before, carrying their goods to Jushoyen." Lo'a traces a path around the city. "I can get you in their door, but nothing I have or can do will convince them to sell me what you need."

"Nothing *we* have will convince them, either," Tsua says, frowning.

"I don't know if that's true." Zonna shrugs when we look at him. "We have the two of you, don't we? Maybe it's time to use the weight of your legend."

"Only if you plan on killing them before we leave." Chio sits straighter, sending Zonna a scolding look. "The old leaders sent nearly the entire army after us before. You're deluding yourself if you think they'll do less this time."

"And don't forget the Jindaini has whatever's left of the rock they mined from Imaku," Tsua says. "If they learn we're here, they'll try to bury us in that rot-ridden stone."

"Osshi said no one knows where the stone is." And thankfully, even if the Ryogans did find a way to bury the andofume in that rock, all touching it does is knock them unconscious. It doesn't hurt us at all, and it won't do any lasting damage to them either if we're there to dig them out again. I look between the andofume and Lo'a. "Are we sure it hasn't been lost?"

"We're not sure of anything except that that stone is the one thing we *know* can slow us down," Tsua says. "Personally, I don't want to push our luck on this particular issue."

"Exactly." Chio shivers and closes his eyes. "I've been trapped by that rock before. It's not an experience I want to repeat."

"So what do you need us to do?" Tessen speaks for the

first time, looking between the andofume and Lo'a. "Because it really seems like stealing from the Tarusutas is the safest plan for everyone."

Tsua smiles. "This time, that's exactly what we're going to do."

Atokoredo is in the foothills of the Mysora Mountains, a range long and high enough to make the one on Shiara look small. I hadn't been sure we'd be able to stay with the caravan—or that Lo'a would agree to carry us all the way to the city—but there's no talk of separating, not even when the road forces us away from the cover of the trees.

As we turn a sharp corner, Tessen calls me to the window. "Look."

Low on the horizon, almost blocked by the tops of the trees, the incoming storm is closer and denser than before. The setting sun gives the mass an undertone of red, like it's not rain but fire that'll fall when the downpour hits.

We'll beat the storm to Atokoredo, but beyond that is doubtful.

"It might be good," I say. "There should be fewer people on the streets if it's raining."

"Which means *us* being there will be noticeable." Tessen leans out the window, studying the sky. "And everyone will be inside, taking cover. There might be more people in the Tarusutas' building than we're expecting."

"You'll warn us before we go in, and we'll adjust the strategy if we can." Which we might not be able to. It isn't like we have time to try again.

Tessen shoots me a skeptical look. "Maybe I should pray

to the Kaisubeh that *you're* right this time instead of me."

"It can't hurt." I pause. "Unless they're real, they hear you, and they decide to ruin everything."

"Wow. I thought I was supposed to be the negative one," Sanii says.

I shrug. "If the Kaisubeh are real, they belong to the Ryogans, not us. They don't owe us anything."

"There's a lovely thought." Tessen shakes his head. "I hope they aren't real, then. The Ryogans and the bobasu are more than enough to handle."

"From your mouth to the Kaisubeh's ears," Rai adds, a sardonic twist to her lips.

We reach the river leading to Atokoredo minutes before sunset, and well before the incoming storm, but we stay in the wagons until the clouds block the light from the nearly full moon and the bright stars, leaving us cloaked in shadows. Only the city's lamplight gives us direction, and only the lightning that periodically cracks the sky into pieces illuminates the world.

Natani was right; the layout and feel of Atokoredo is more like Itagami than any Ryogan city we've passed. The narrow streets and closely-packed buildings are carefully laid out and easy to navigate. Almost all of it—except the roofs—is stone. Of course, I've never been this cold in Itagami. I can't imagine how bad the chill would be if my wards weren't keeping the rain off. Broad-brimmed hats help hide our faces—and our foreignness. Hopefully, since only Lo'a, Tsua, Chio, Natani, Tessen, and I are making this trip, we'll look like a family rushing to get inside.

Lo'a and Tessen lead the line, her for directions and him to watch for danger. He signals a halt more than once, urging us into the shadows to wait for someone to pass. Finally, Lo'a leads us around a large, square, windowless building. There are numerous doors along two sides. The one she leads us to has a white symbol painted on the top left corner.

Tessen steps up to the door, flattening first his palm and then his ear against the wood. "There are people inside, but not many," he murmurs.

"I can break the door," Tsua offers.

"Or we can knock." Lo'a flicks her hands at us. Once we're out of sight, she raps her knuckles against the wood in a quick, sharp pattern. A panel opens and a square of light hits her face. "It is important," Lo'a says.

"Obviously." The voice is low and gravelly. "Why else would you be out in this weather?" When the panel shuts, I strengthen my wards, making sure they'll protect against more than rain.

There's the sound of several locks unlatching, and then the door opens, spilling warmth and firelight onto the dark street. "You're lucky it's just Osota and I, Lo'a. Rumors have been spreading. They say one of your caravans is hiding the fugitive everyone in the east is looking for. You might not've gotten a pleasant greeting from some of the others."

Now I really am glad Osshi didn't come. Especially when Lo'a steps inside and says, "Shideso Tarusuta, I am afraid the rumors are true."

We burst from either side of the door, pouring into the room and forcing Lo'a and the old man back. Shideso cries out and stumbles, his arms wheeling. Lo'a catches him. A woman runs through an open door, tossing something green at us. Three balls hit in quick succession, and all of them are well-aimed—one at Lo'a's shoulder, one at the center of my chest, and one at Chio's forehead. They shatter into a cloud of dust and smoke against my wards. Sparks sizzle across the impact points, powerful enough to make me flinch.

I hold out my hand to Natani. He's a strong zoikyo mage,

and the extra energy he sends into my body boosts my protections and gives me the power to trap Shideso and Osota inside a ward of their own. Holding two is a strain; they're too different. One keeps danger out, the other encases it. Natani's touch roots me, helping to keep me from feeling split.

"I don't recommend moving." Tsua's warning is aimed at the woman; she looks ready to run. "The magic surrounding you will cause quite a bit of pain if you brush it."

"What have you done, Lo'a?" The man, Shideso, looks furious. "After everything we've trusted you with?"

"Our arrangement has benefitted both of us, and I would be sad to see it end, but if it must after this, I understand." Lo'a glances at me, uncertainty in her eyes, then she turns to him. "The goal of this journey will be worth the hardships of getting there."

"We don't have much time, so take a seat. Otherwise, you'll have to stand for however long we're here." Tsua catches my eye and tilts her head toward them. I release the ward. It feels like exhaling a long-held breath.

Quickly but gently, Tsua ties Shideso to a chair. Osota goes silently and reluctantly to the second; she's wide-eyed and watchful as she lets Tsua bind her to the second chair.

"Nothing you can do will make me give you what you want," the old man says calmly. "I'm the only one who can unlock the spell guarding the storeroom."

"I don't need keys to get past spells." Hopefully, that's as true here as it was on Shiara. Whatever magic he's using can't be as powerful as the wards guarding Imaku.

"If what we want is behind a magical protection, then it's over there," Tessen says in Itagamin, gesturing to what looks like a solid wall.

I look at Tsua. "No one's ever taught me how to walk through walls."

"Admitting there's something you can't do?" Tessen raises his eyebrows in mock surprise. "I never thought I'd see the day."

He says it with a smirk as he faces the wall to search for the storeroom with his fingertips, eyes, and ears—and Natani's hand on his shoulder to enhance his senses. While he works, I check on everyone else.

Lo'a is crouched next to Shideso, apologizing softly. Near the door, Tsua and Chio are whispering in Denhitran, their heads tilted toward each other but their eyes on our prisoners. Osota still hasn't said a word; she's watching everything, though.

Then Tessen hums in approval. I turn just as he presses a latch concealed behind a cabinet. At the touch, what had appeared to be a wall breaks. The lines of a door appear in the stone.

"Unless you want them to die, painfully, I suggest you tell your friends to step back from there," Shideso says to Lo'a.

"You make the same mistake I did at first," she says.

He huffs. "Trusting you?"

"No. Underestimating *them*." At those words, I'm glad I'm facing the wall so he won't see my smile.

"We'll see," the old man grumbles.

Just to be safe, I ease Tessen back from the door to take his place. I check everyone's wards, too, before I slip my fingers into the crack Tessen revealed and pull the thin panel of stone out. The whole thing is ingeniously hooked to a system of metal that keep it attached to the wall. Behind the stone slab is an actual door, this one locked with something far more complicated than anything I encountered on Itagami. Yorri would love to study this. I'd bring it back to Shiara for him if I could, but Shideso would probably like that even less than what we're already planning to do.

"Can you feel the buzz?" Tessen says in Itagamin as I

crouch to get a better look at the lock.

I nod. "There's something altering the desosa, I just can't tell if it's built into the door or if it's something behind it."

"Where are you from?" It's the first thing Osota has said since we walked in, so I glance back at her. Before, she was watching all of us closely. Now, her attention is fixed solely on Chio. "Your language isn't one I've heard before."

"If I told you, you still wouldn't know." Chio raises his chin toward the guarded door. "Tonight, all that matters is what you have in that room."

"Really? What is it that's turned you into a thief, Chio Heinansuto?"

Natani rubs the bridge of his broad nose. "Of all the problems I thought we'd have, Chio being this recognizable wasn't one of them."

I huff and look at Tessen. "You prayed, didn't you?"

"After what you said, I didn't dare." He shakes his head. "Maybe I should've."

Chio keeps his face impassive. "Why would you call me that?"

"Because you look so much like the pictures and statues that the artists could have used you as their model," Osota says dryly.

"And you spend enough time studying the bobasu to know their faces that well?" Chio's trying to sound skeptical. I'd believe it if I hadn't spent so many weeks with him.

Osota doesn't seem to believe him, either. "I think you're the legend we've been warned about, but you tied us to chairs instead of slitting our throats."

I should be working on breaking through the door, because nothing Osota says can change that we need what's hidden behind it, but it's so hard to tear my eyes away from this conversation.

"Do you remember the Dowakomo family?" Osota asks.

Chio shakes his head, his eyes never leaving her face. "I don't."

"Then you likely won't remember Kesori." The woman's thin lips roll between her teeth. "Kesori was a Dowakomo by marriage, and she was widowed young. She lost her son and husband in a terrible accident. For years, she lived in seclusion. Then she learned what had happened to the family she left behind and the trouble a woman named Suzu had been causing."

"Her sister," Tsua whispers in Denhitran, putting her hand on Chio's arm as though for balance. "Kesori was Suzu's older sister."

"The Chonochi ordered the bobasu bloodlines wiped out, but Kesori's seclusion protected her. It was easy for the Dowakomo elders to claim she'd died with her husband and son—no one outside their family had seen her since then." Osota takes a breath. "It worked, but it wasn't safe for Kesori to stay in the Kyo'ne Province after that, so her husband's younger brother and his family packed up to move west. They intended to head for Ejinosei."

Chio looks around the small space. "Clearly they didn't get that far."

Tsua leans in, expression intent. "What changed their plans, Osota-tan?"

The woman smiles. "They got to Atokoredo at the same time as a heavily guarded ship. Rumor said it was carrying massive slabs of night-black stone."

I hold my breath, and Chio's thin eyes widen. "The Kaijuko stone? Do you know where they took it?"

Sadly, Osota shakes her head. "Stories had already spread about the Kaisubeh-sent rock that had helped us defeat the bobasu, so Kesori knew what she was looking at. She tried to follow it, but the ship sailed north from here and there wasn't a way for Kesori to keep up without giving herself away. Instead, she and the Dowakomo settled here, and they began a search for the stone. Unfortunately, they never found it."

Tsua and Chio share a look, clearly frustrated.

Then Osota says, "My family has, however, been watching these rivers for hundreds of years, and I can tell you the stone never came south again."

"Osota? *Obyoto?*" A name and an endearment is all Shideso says. There are somehow so many questions layered in those words.

Osota meets his eyes; he sighs, shaking his head, but not otherwise arguing with whatever she's decided. She asks Chio, "Will you tell me why ghosts from my family's past have become flesh and blood again?"

"My brother is chasing revenge, and he's aiming for Ryogo," Chio answers. "We're searching for ways to stop him from obliterating your people."

"What you told us about the Kaijuko rock will help." Tsua steps closer to Osota. "What you have behind that door might help even more."

The old woman raises one straight eyebrow. "And what do you think is behind that door?"

"Hopefully? Mura'ina oil, rianjuko plants, ojoken root, and majiasu ash." Chio gives us another glance.

Osota purses her lips. "Apart from—so far—not killing us, why should we believe it's not you who's looking for revenge?"

"If you believed that, why'd you tell us about the Kaijuko stone?" Chio counters.

"To give you more of a reason not to kill us," she answers sardonically. "You don't get to be as old as we are in this line of work without learning to see when you're outmatched. The magic I'm capable of would've knocked anyone else unconscious for hours. It bounces off you all as if I'd thrown flower petals."

"If it makes you feel any better, the sting to those balls was impressive," I add. "Nothing I can't protect against, but still impressive."

"*You?*" For the first time, I see surprise on her face. "Kaisubeh bless it. I'm even more outmatched than I realized if *children* can deflect me now."

"Children of the bobasu, Osota," Shideso reminds her.

"We are *not* their children." Natani's protest shoots through the room. He glares down at the Ryogans. "Varan and Suzu are legends to you, stories most of you have forgotten, but they're more than you can imagine to us."

His words echo through me with a force that robs me of my breath.

Natani is off, words spilling out. "We lived with your bobasu, served them our whole lives. They lied to us about *everything*. Shiara is an island lost in the middle of an ocean we thought was endless. They let us believe Shiara was all there was to the world, that we were alone. And Ryogo?" He laughs grimly, throwing his arms wide. "They call themselves the gatekeepers of this place, tell us this is where we'll go when we die—*if* we serve them well."

The pain in Natani's voice intensifies until I feel dizzy with it. I extend my hand; Tessen grips it, his hold almost as shaky as mine is. I've tried so hard to brush this aside, and I knew I wasn't the only one struggling, but this... I never expected an outpouring like *this* from Natani.

"Now, Varan is about to lead everyone I love into war." Natani runs his hands over his face and then stares the Tarusutas down. "If you don't believe we want to save your people, you had better at least believe we want to save ours."

Breath coming too fast, hands clenched in fists, and

stance almost begging for a fight, Natani bears the weight of everyone's attention in silence.

Tsua swallows, looks at Osota, and simply asks, "Will you help us?"

For several long breaths, the two women stare at each other. Trembling, Natani turns away from the others and leans heavily against the wall, his hand over his eyes. I keep him in my periphery as Osota responds.

"Untie me." She looks at me and raises her eyebrows. "I'm certain you could eventually break that spell, but I'll save you the time. And save myself from having to rebuild it. If you set me free, I'll open that door and give you whatever you need. For a price."

"And what's that?" Chio asks.

"A warning," she says. "If you can't stop what's coming, I want you to find a way to give us time to leave before your brother slaughters us."

"I promise to do everything I can," Chio says carefully. "But there's no way I can guarantee we can reach you in time. No matter how powerful the legends claim we are, sending messages across the length of Ryogo is beyond me."

"Agreed. Now, let me go," Osota demands.

Tsua releases the ropes, and I move to Natani, leaning against the wall a few inches away from him. "You're not the only one dealing with it."

He doesn't move his hand from over his eyes. "With what?"

"Everything." I exhale heavily as he slowly lowers his arm. "Bellows. You're right, Natani. We've lost *everything*, and we don't know if we'll ever get a single piece of it back. But what we're doing here? This is how we'll find out what's left when we go home. We're fighting to get home, and no, it won't be the place we remember—it can't ever be that again. Doesn't mean it's gone. But it will be if we don't fight to keep the salvageable pieces."

I lean closer, until my forehead almost touches his. "I need *everyone's* help if we're going to have a chance of succeeding."

Succeeding at getting back to Shiara to find Yorri. To stop a war. To save our clan from the leaders we thought were protecting us. I try to exude confidence, but this all feels impossible. Even as we watch Osota use a key hidden at the bottom of a grain bag to open the door and hand us everything we asked for and more.

My words seem to be enough for Natani, though. Nodding, he straightens and walks to the now-open door, taking a bag from Tsua's hands and carrying it out of the way.

"That was good. You're getting better at being nyshin-pa," Tessen whispers. "Hopefully one day soon you can find a way to say it all that'll make yourself believe it, too."

"One step at a time." That's all any of us can do, face the problems—and the unexpected solutions—one at a time.

Otherwise, forget saving anyone else; I don't know how *we're* going to get through this alive.

CHAPTER EIGHT

The wind is so strong it bends the trees, swaying the massive plants closer to what must be their breaking point. Somehow, they don't snap. We might not be so lucky if we don't reach shelter soon.

We needed to see how bad the storm was getting, so I warded the door and the window to keep the weather outside. Now I'm regretting the open portals. The mountain path we've been traveling is narrow and well above the ground. I can't ward us against that drop, and not even Tsua is strong enough to catch and hold eight wagons and sixteen beasts. If we're about to face unpreventable death, I don't think I want to see it coming.

"How much farther?" Osshi asks Lo'a with his garakyu.

"In good weather? Maybe half an hour," she says. "Tonight, I do not know."

Another gust. The wagon shakes. Tips. My breath catches. I scramble for something to hold on to. Blood and rot, all four wheels *can't* be on the ground anymore.

"Etaro, help her!" Tyrroh shouts as Tsua slams her hands

against the wall.

Desosa gathers around her and the wagon shudders. With a groan and a cracking crash, the wheels reconnect with the path; it feels like the wagon is seconds away from breaking apart.

"Can you ward the caravan against the wind, Khya?" Tyrroh asks.

I shake my head, focusing on him instead of the open window. "The road curves, and I don't have wardstones in their wagons. I can't see them. I can't—"

"We better get where we're going fast, then." Tyrroh braces when another gust shakes the wagon. Even in the cold, sweat beads on his dark skin. "I don't know how much longer we'll stay on the rot-ridden ground."

"This is like running up the path to Itagami in the middle of that storm." Rai's on the bed, tucked tight against Etaro's side. Sanii, Tessen, and I take up the rest of the cushioned space.

"It's worse this time." Etaro rubs eir arm, the one ey broke the day the first unexpected storm struck back on Shiara.

Only the storm makes noise after that. What else is there to say? No magic I know will dissipate a storm, and we can't fight it. There are no battle lines or ground to gain. All we can do is head for shelter and pray to the Ryogans' Kaisubeh that we make it there alive.

An hour or so later, the wind dies. Suddenly. Completely. I strain for sound; it takes several seconds before I realize the sound isn't gone, it's simply faded into the background. And it's picked up a familiar, keening edge—the same pitch I know from Itagami when the wind blows hard enough to whine through the tunnels under the city.

Another few minutes and the wagon jerks to a halt. The hanaeuu we'la maninaio call out to each other, relief in some voices, stress in others. The sound makes Zonna stand and stride to the door. In seconds, the others are scrambling to get out. Heart pounding, I hesitantly follow.

"Bellows," I breathe when I see where we are. "This feels like home."

The stone is darker here, charcoal-gray rather than silver-gray, but the cavern is as enormous as the ones under Itagami. All the wagons and animals fit comfortably in the space with plenty of room to spare, and the roof is at least fifty feet above our heads. The floor has clearly been smoothed and leveled out by hands and tools, but the walls and roof are craggy. And adorned; symbols have been carefully and colorfully painted on the rough stone.

"Is everyone all right?" Lo'a approaches at a jog, her small white and gold ahoali'lona, which she calls Koo'a, trotting at her side.

I nod. "What is this place?"

"A secret." She gives me a rueful smile as she scoops Koo'a into her arms. "I seem to be exposing too many of those around you."

"It's only fair," I counter. "You already know all of ours."

Lo'a tilts her head in acknowledgement, her fingers tracing the gold lines on Koo'a's fur. "This cave is a hiding place we have used for centuries, usually when the Ryogans decide our presence is no longer welcome."

"That happens often?"

"Often enough that we always keep supplies hidden in the smaller caves." She gestures to the far end. "A stream runs through the mountain, and there are animals that hunt in the area. If we are careful, we can live here for quite some time. Secure if not comfortable."

"It's easy to defend." There only seems to be one entrance, so the biggest worry would be encountering a group of powerful ishiji mages, whose stone magic could turn this place into a tomb. On Shiara, that'd be a real concern. Here, the most powerful magic I've seen is the trap Varan left behind.

"It stretches beyond this, too." She nods toward the back of the cave. "When we are here long enough to bother, there are alcoves and smaller caves that can be used as bedrooms or storage."

"Useful. And well thought out." I force myself to smile. "Thank you for trusting us with this. I don't know where we'd be if not for your help."

"Honestly?" Lo'a lifts one shoulder, still stroking Koo'a. "You would likely be fine, but I have a feeling I will look back on this and be glad we did not turn you away."

"You *hope* that's how you'll feel."

"And I trust you will not prove me wrong, Khya." Then, with a smile I'd read as an invitation from an Itagamin, Lo'a turns back to her people, conferring with the elders for a moment before she begins issuing orders. Our communication with anyone but Lo'a is still limited—mostly happening only during weapons training—but they've stopped trying to hide the fact that Lo'a isn't in charge, she's simply one of the three who makes decisions for their family. It's a start, a good one considering how secretive their people obviously are.

Soon there are three large fires burning in pits. Our andofume settle near one with Osshi, Sanii, and the bag of supplies Osota and Shideso gave us. I follow and sit near Chio. "Will this work?"

"We know something worked," he says without looking up. "But it's only because of the trouble Varan went to protecting that box that I think it might be because of *this* susuji. This has to be how he pushed himself into immortality."

Hope grows in my chest, a thin tendril of it cracking through despite how hard I've tried to squash it. And despite how clear it is that Chio is trying to *make* himself believe. Hope is dangerous, and watching them work on Varan's susuji will only make it worse, so I look for something else to do. I could reread the books on Ryogan magic; I'm probably one or two readings away from having the rot-ridden things memorized. But that's exactly why I don't think I can possibly learn anything new.

So instead, I beckon Lo'a to join us and ask, "Can you tell us about the Kaisubeh?"

After the nearly unbelievable coincidence of meeting a many-times-removed blood descendant of Suzu's, I'm beginning to wonder if the Ryogan's faith may have a more solid foundation than I thought.

"That is not an easy task." She laughs and settles by my side. "There are hundreds of stories about each deity, and those are just the ones Ryogans accept. Other lands have told different tales of the gods, and there are old stories that have been all but forgotten."

"Other lands?" I glance at Tessen, but he shakes his head, eyes round. His confusion doesn't help—I feel like I should be bracing myself for what's coming but I don't know how. "What do you mean?"

There's something like disbelief in her expression as she gently says, "Khya, the world is so much more than Ryogo."

Then, shaking her head, she calls to one of her people in their language. They jog off and come back soon with a roll of paper. Lo'a spreads it on the stone. "*This* is the world as my people know it."

"I...oh." I swallow, my eyes jumping from point to point on the map, one that stretches so far beyond Ryogo and Shiara. "Wh-where are we on this?"

Her smile is sympathetic as she places her finger on a single point, the western third of a mountain range dividing

Ryogo from a place called Khylar. These mountains feel so big, endless almost, but they're really such a small part of the world, a world I've seen so little of. There's one thing I don't see at all, though. "Where is Shiara?"

"My people are travelers and traders," Lo'a says quietly. "That has allowed us to make incredibly accurate maps, but until I met you, I did not know Shiara existed. It is not included on any map I have ever seen."

"But Osshi—" I turn, finding him a few feet away. "You found us. How'd you find us?"

"I guided Kazu by stories," Osshi explains. "Old records describe where the Kaijuko rock fell and how far the ships chased the streak of light to land. It was guesswork, so it took us weeks of sailing to find Shiara. If it was ever on Ryogan maps, the leaders had it expunged a long time ago."

Lo'a nods. "You found what everyone wanted forgotten."

"What does this have to do with the Kaisubeh?" I ask tentatively.

"Each of these places have their own beliefs about those the Ryogans call Kaisubeh, but there is one thing all of us agree on." She places her hand flat on the center of the map. "Humanity may live here, but this world is *theirs*. We do not know if they created it or if they were simply the first to be born, the eldest children of land and sky. Whichever is true, we know they existed before humans found a way to preserve thoughts in words carved into stone instead of stories passed down through generations."

"Why does that matter?" Tessen asks.

"Because stone changes slower than a story," Lo'a says. "Memories are imperfect and time alters perceptions."

"What do the Ryogans believe, then?" That seems to be what will matter most to us; Varan found immortality by chasing the Kaisubeh.

"You came by boat, so you saw their Zohogasha? The statues along the coast." When I nod, Lo'a continues. "Ryogans believe in the fourteen Kaisubeh and the countless Kaimashin, the spirits who carry out orders. And they are not the only ones to make that mistake."

"How's it a mistake?" I lean closer. "Are you saying they don't exist?"

"No, the creators, the ones my people call *alua'sa liona'ano shilua'a*, are very real." Lo'a glances at Osshi, almost apologetically. His lips press together and he gets up, crossing to where the andofume and Sanii are sitting with Varan's book between them. From the look that passes between Lo'a and Osshi, I sense they've had discussions about the nature of the Kaisubeh before. And I don't think they found a way to agree on the subject.

Once he's away, Lo'a lowers her voice and explains. "The Ryogans' mistake is not in their belief, it is in their personification. They persist in seeing the creators as men and women, as people with the same faults, desires, and foibles humanity is burdened with."

"What are they, then?" Tessen scoots closer to me, his voice as quiet as ours.

"Beyond our ability to understand," Lo'a says simply. "They have proven their existence in undeniable ways—like the day the Kaijuko rock fell from the sky—but they do not walk among us. I doubt they want to. Maybe they cannot. There are stories—ones that seem to be as old as the time when the world was one piece—"

"What do you mean 'one piece'?" The map shows six expansive sections of land surrounded by water. There would be at least seven if Shiara were included.

"Look at the edges." She draws her finger along the coasts.

"They line up." The match isn't perfect, but it's consistent.

It reminds me of how a slab of stone might break if dropped. Putting it back together would be impossible, but it would still be clear where the pieces once fit. "The Kaisubeh did this?"

"The kind of power this would take is…" Tessen exhales heavily. "I can't imagine it."

"This, what Ryogans call the schism, happened thousands of years ago, when humanity was in the middle of its most devastating war," she says, suddenly serious. "You see, the Kaisubeh do act, but only when something or someone threatens not only the lives of humans but the safety and sanctity of the land itself."

"But they acted against Varan." I say it slowly, trying to grab hold of the thought rising from the depths of my mind like heatwaves. "So how could his immortality threaten the Kaisubeh or the land?"

"That I cannot tell you. The alua'sa liona'ano shilua'a have never whispered their secrets in my ear before. There is no reason why they would start now."

"Tell us stories, then, if you don't know secrets." I lean against Tessen, studying how the firelight brings out the red in Lo'a's sandstone skin.

Outside this cave, the storm pours down rain and wind and lightning. Thunder rumbles low and long, sending vibrations through the mountain. It's easy to forget it all as Lo'a begins to talk. Her voice rises and falls with the natural lilts and pauses of someone used to storytelling.

First, Lo'a gives us the creation tales she only hinted at before, both the ones that claim the Kaisubeh created the world, leaving their mark on every living thing, and the ones claiming the Kaisubeh are the first children of land and sky.

She talks about a land where it's believed the gods live in every plant, stone, stream, and animal, and she explains why another land is convinced each of the Kaisubeh lives in their own realm and watches over their most devoted worshippers.

There are stories about an afterlife in a place that reminds me of the stories Varan told about Ryogo, but then she explains that some believe we return body and soul to the land and the desosa when we die.

According to her stories, Ryogans once believed in Kaisuama, a mountain in the Mysora range where the Kaisubeh convened to observe their followers, yet today almost everyone in Ryogo insists their gods are everywhere, incorporeal only until they choose to walk the land in human disguise.

It only takes a few stories for me to see why she said explaining the Kaisubeh wouldn't be easy. No one can agree on anything except that they exist.

We listen to the stories while we eat, but everyone separates after dinner. Rai, Etaro, Sanii, and Natani get their weapons and run drills, patiently working with the students who feel like getting extra practice. Lo'a sits with Tyrroh and Osshi, watching as they talk, probably about supplies and the storm. Our three andofume are preparing what they'll need to recreate Varan's susuji. Miari leads Wehli and Nairo into our wagon, and the door closes behind them; no one who doesn't want to watch the three of them strip down and catch up on all the time alone they've missed will dare open it for the next hour or two.

They're all occupied. And we're not going anywhere for at least another full day. And there are sections of this cave that offer at least the illusion of privacy. Plus, I haven't had a calm, quiet moment since well before we left Shiara.

Standing up, I light one of the lanterns and then hold out my hand. "Come with me."

Tessen looks up, his gaze falling from my eyes to my hand to the cavern entrance.

I shake my head. "Farther in, not out."

Smiling, he grips my hand and lets me pull him to his feet. "Out of everything I miss from Itagami, it's having my own room I miss the most."

"Food. I miss the food. I think I'd kill for a well-cooked piece of teegra right now." I look over my shoulder at him, smirking. "But privacy is a close second."

I don't stop at the first small offshoot cave I find. Or the third. Or the seventh. The light from the fires in the main cavern doesn't reach this far back, but the sounds do. Picking my way carefully through the mostly even tunnel, I wait until the noise is distant and muffled before turning in to one of the hollows. I set the lantern in the center of the space, gesturing for Tessen to sit against one of the smooth walls. Once he's settled, I sit in the space between his legs, leaning back against his chest. He wraps his arms around me, pressing soft kisses against my cheek and my neck when I let my head rest on his shoulder. Now, in a quiet moment when I have a good idea of how I want the rest of the night to go for us, I remember what Zonna told me about the yugadai and the changes the hishingu mages made to us. Tonight, I'm almost thankful for it if only because those physical changes remove one more worry from my mind.

"How long do you think we have before everyone comes looking for us?" I ask.

I feel his smile against my throat. "Not long enough."

Bellows. "I'm tired, Tessen. I'm already tired and we're nowhere near finished. It all feels impossible."

"So it feels exactly like it's been for a while now?"

I smack his thigh. "Don't joke. I'm serious. What if we can't find what we need here and have to go back to Shiara with nothing? They'll be following me into danger I may not be able to protect them from."

"Do you plan on holding a sword at their throat? Or trapping them in a ward and shoving them onto whatever ship we convince to carry us back to Shiara?"

"Of course not."

"Then don't demean their choices." Tessen brushes his nose against my cheek, up the side of my face until he can kiss my temple. "We don't expect you to keep us alive no matter what, Khya. Besides, death in this battle will mean something. It's a sacrifice worth making."

"Sacrifice." I snort, unable to suppress the scorn. "For honors in Ryogo?"

"You think Varan invented the afterlife? I don't," Tessen says quietly. "You heard Lo'a's stories. It seems like a lot of what Varan taught us has been more truth than lies."

"Not Ryogo." But that isn't quite true, is it?

"It may not be the afterlife, but almost everything else is true," he says, almost chidingly. "So, yes—I think there's an afterlife, and that we can earn a place in it, I just don't know what it'll look like when we get there."

I turn to straddle his lap so I can meet his eyes. "Doesn't it scare you? Not knowing what's coming?"

So much of the future is unknown. Bellows, most of the *present* is unknown. What's happening to Yorri? Is what we found in the mountains really the key to Varan's immortality? How will we get back to Shiara? Even if we discover how to kill Varan, how do we get close enough to do it? If we somehow manage to win, what then? Will the clan kill us for destroying the leaders of Itagami, or will they let us stay? If they kill us, what comes after?

"Shh, no. Whatever you're thinking, stop." Tessen massages the knots in my shoulder with one hand while the other gently runs over my short hair. "Nothing is certain, so all we can do is make the best possible choices the moment they're presented."

"You sound like Ahdo-mas Sotra," I mutter against his tunic.

"I'll take that as a compliment. She was always annoyingly wise."

"And you're just annoying."

Tessen chuckles. "You wound me, oh deadly one."

I trace the straight line of his thick eyebrow with my thumb and then trail my fingers down the sharp slope of his jaw. His eyes close, his breathing quickens, and I smile. Tessen's skin, a few shades darker brown than mine, is paler than I'm used to seeing it without the exposure to the desert sun, but otherwise I can almost pretend we're alone in Itagami instead of hiding in a borrowed space in a strange land.

For moons now, Tessen's put everything I thought he cared about aside. Some things, like the kaigo-sei pendant marking him as a student of the councils, he literally tossed into the ocean.

It's not just now; he's been like this for years. It took me a long time to notice. I spent years taking him for granted. I still do. I count on him to simply be there, be ready to offer advice or someone to fight with or whatever else I happen to need in that moment. It's not fair.

All we can do is make the best choices in the right moment, according to him, and if I've learned anything, it's this: now is all we have.

I gently trace the line of his full bottom lip. "Do you remember what you asked me the day we found the tunnel to Imaku?"

"What?" Tessen forces his eyes open. "I, uhh…asked if you trusted me?"

"I wasn't sure then, but later, on Kazu's ship, I said I trusted you." I kiss the center of his forehead as I draw my nails over his short, black hair. "You didn't believe me."

He swallows hard. "I believed you."

"You didn't. You thought I might change my mind, which means you didn't believe me." I hold his face between my hands. "I don't blame you, not after how hard I made you fight."

His mouth opens; his words sit silent on his tongue.

"I told you all you have to do is ask when you need something. Or when you want something." I kiss the tip of his nose and then nip the lobe of his ear. "I'd hoped you were starting to believe me, but you never ask for anything, Tessen. Don't you want anything?"

Swallowing so hard all the muscles in his neck strain under his skin, Tessen nods, the motion so small it's almost unnoticeable.

"But you still don't know how to ask for it, do you?"

"I—" His eyes are wide and locked, unblinking, on mine, and his heart is beating so fast I can see his pulse pounding at the base of his throat.

Smiling, I lean in and whisper, "Maybe I should try guessing, then."

I wrap my hand around the back of his neck and pull him across the few inches separating us. At first it's just lips and hands, brushes of soft skin. Then my tongue teases the corner of his mouth.

Tessen whimpers.

My hands tighten on him, my fingers digging in and my lips sealing against his until he's not the only one sucking in sharp breaths. When he shivers, I scratch down his arms until I can slide my hands under the sleeves of his tunic and push them up, out of the way. He shudders and sits straighter, pressing his chest against mine as much as he can without dislodging my hands from his arms.

It was just supposed to be a kiss, one just like all the others we've had, but for the first time there's no ruse. No watchers. Nowhere we've got to be. For the first time since we left Shiara, we're alone, but no matter how right I *think* I am about what he wants, I'm not pushing him into this based on a guess.

"Tell me to stop." I pull back enough to whisper against his skin.

"Why?" He unties my coat. "That sounds like a *horrible* idea."

"I guessed right, then?"

"More than right." He grips my hips and tugs me closer, closing the space between us. There's an inviting darkness in his eyes. "You should've started guessing a long time ago."

"You should've asked," I whisper against his throat. But I know it isn't that simple, and I know he likely won't any time soon. There will be the mission and the squad and the war, all of it more important than what either of us wants.

Tonight, though? He gives in to me completely and in that moment, I give in to him, too.

Our boots get kicked to the other side of the cave, and our discarded clothes become a thin cushion against the hard, cold stone. He shivers and pulls me on top of him like a blanket when he lays himself back on the cloth.

I grip one of his wrists and pin it to the stone over his head, and then I lightly scratch my nails down the center of his chest, tracing the curves of his muscles and the lines of his numerous scars. He's breathing deep, and his pupils are blown wide, and yet the sight of him against the stone sparks a memory that makes my hands still. I laugh. "You know, it's several moon cycles late, but we're finally exactly where the entire city thought we were when we kept sneaking off."

"I'm glad they're finally right." He runs his free hand up my bare thigh, his touch and his voice shaky, but it's the wide-eyed disbelief on his face that makes my heart skip a beat. "I hoped, but I wasn't sure it'd ever happen."

I sit up straighter, flattening my palm against the center of his chest and watching him. "The way you're looking at me, it seems like you're still not sure it's happening."

"The good moments have been rare recently." His hand slides over my hip and presses against the center of my lower back, drawing me down until his lips brush against mine before he whispers, "And this is unbelievably good."

The tender kiss and the words and the press of his skin is so overwhelming I close my eyes. My skin tingles, the chill in the air fighting the warmth flushing my body and making me feel on fire in the best of ways. If this is what it's like for me—bellows. I'm not sure if I'm envious of what Tessen must be feeling or scared of it.

He told me once that he experiences the world so deeply he's always one lapse in concentration away from being absolutely overwhelmed. And that's on a normal day. Now, my every touch seems to shudder through Tessen's whole body. Even a breath against his skin has him shifting underneath me. When I open my eyes to meet his, they're glazed. His heart is pounding so hard and fast I can count the beats by the throbbing pulse point in his neck.

More than once, I've wanted to back Tessen up against a wall, hold him there, and see how far I could push him. I could do that now. Easily. I could grab his wrists and hold him against the stone and test him until I learned all his little quirks and reactions. It's what I've always done with my partners. I'm good at it, and the expectant tension in his eyes hints that he's waiting for exactly that.

He stiffens and then goes pliant when I press my chest against his and brush the gentlest of kisses to his lips. Everything else is a battle. We're struggling for every inch of ground and watching out for enemies from all sides, and I don't want to do that here. Not now.

I'm still in the lead, still in control so he can sink into the sensations without worrying about anything else, but I keep it slow. Soft. I draw it out and let it build slowly, taking my time because, for now, I have the time to take.

Only in the last moments do I lose my grip on slow and gentle. Tensing and tightening my hold on him, I dig my nails into his skin and cry out loud enough to hear it echo back at me. His fingers dig into my hips hard enough to leave bruises, but the only noise he makes is a long, sharp gasp.

After, when our breathing evens out and the sweat clinging to our skin becomes uncomfortably cold, I pull our clothes out from under Tessen and guide his tremoring, malleable body back into them. If I'm chilled, he must be on the edge of going numb. The layers of cloth help keep the worst of the cold off, but he'll still be too cold in here, so I straddle him and lie flat against his chest, winding my arms under his shoulders.

"We *really* should have done that moons ago," Tessen mumbles against my skin, pulling himself closer. "It wasn't nearly that good with Giryn."

"How long ago was that?" I've barely seen Giryn since our training class became citizens over a year ago. If Tessen had a relationship with him, it must've been two or three years ago. And a well-kept secret. "Did either of you even know what you were doing?"

"It's been a few years. And he did know what he was doing, but…" Shivering, he closes his eyes. "Touch like this is…intense for me. With you it's wonderfully overwhelming, but with most people it's…"

"Just overwhelming?" I was right. His senses are powerful enough to let him see for a mile and hear through thick walls of stone. Touch must be almost dangerously potent to him.

"Uncomfortably so," he admits, opening his eyes slowly.

"For a while, I thought I might be ushimo, but even when no one else appealed to me, there was always you."

"That is very good to know." I run my fingers gently up the side of his neck as I lightly scrape my teeth against the muscle connecting his neck and shoulder. "I am *definitely* looking forward to the day I get to see how far I can push you."

Tessen doesn't quite whimper, but it's close.

Later, I promise myself. When I don't have a war and a hunt and a rescue clogging my mind. So instead of stripping him again and using more teeth and nails and pressure this time around, I adjust the set of our clothes and lie down beside him, resting my head on his shoulder, my arm over his waist, and my leg across his.

"Should we go back? There's a sleep mat waiting for us back there." One I'm regretting not bringing with us.

"No. The quiet is…" He takes a long, slow breath. When he exhales, he sounds relieved. "Stay here with me?"

"Of course." I lift my chin and kiss under his jaw. "I told you, Tessen. All you have to do is ask."

He smiles drowsily, kisses the corner of my lips, and then his breathing quickly evens out as he settles into sleep.

At least we had tonight.

I try not to think about it like that, but it's hard to avoid. There are too many unknowns in our future, and too many people in the world who'd be thrilled to either capture or kill us. For now, though, I force all of that aside, close my eyes, and pretend I'll get to hold on to the comfort of this moment forever.

CHAPTER NINE

There's no way to know how late it is when I lead Tessen away from the main cavern or how long we slept, but it feels like morning when we head back toward the others. I expect either questions or snark from especially Rai and Etaro but other than a few knowing smirks and a couple of leering winks, our reappearance passes without comment. I'm not sure if I should be worried by or grateful for their silence. From the way Tessen's eyebrows rise, I think he's asking himself the same question.

"If *this* isn't proof of the Kaisubeh, I don't know what is," Tessen murmurs to me.

I laugh, and I'm still laughing as we approach the fire burning closest to our wagon. I stop when I get a whiff of something strange.

Initially, it reminds me of herbs and spices, and I think someone might be making food. Only when I get close to the central fire do I realize why it seemed off. Under the stronger smells is a floral aroma, and something else, a scent that reminds me of the air at the highest points of a mountain, crisp, sharp, and pure.

This might be what magic smells like.

Set bestride the fire is a tall metal tripod, and an iron pot hangs from the center. Tsua is standing next to the fire, hands held out on either side of the pot, well away from the heat. Next to her, Sanii is standing at attention, fully focused on Tsua's work.

"What is most important at this point is funneling the desosa in slowly but consistently," Tsua is explaining as I approach. "Like the heat of the fire, this is what will turn what would otherwise be an incredibly unappetizing meal into something that might save a life. Or take one, depending on the potion."

"I can't control the desosa like that." Sanii huffs a frustrated breath. "I'm still getting used to being able to do any magic at all."

"You can't control it *yet*," Tsua says. "But you will once we find the best way for you to handle desosa. I wouldn't be surprised if you become just as powerful as Khya."

"Hopefully stronger." I cross my arms and try to keep the smirk off my face. "Ey'll need it to keep up with my brother."

Sanii snorts. "I need it to keep up with *you*."

"How long until this is done?" The storm seems to be easing to a survivable level, but we'll have to stay. The andofume need time and quiet to work, so only Sanii is with them, watching and learning and trying to mimic what they're doing.

"Another day. At least." Tsua takes a long breath, exhaling slowly. There's a shift in the desosa surrounding her. It follows the line of her arm, pooling around her hands before the subtle motions of her fingers send the energy straight toward the brewing susuji. With the influx of power, the pot boils and thick steam rises. Purple-tinted steam.

"Do you have to keep feeding power into it the whole time?" I ask.

Tsua nods. "It's one reason so few people bother with anything beyond the most basic of potions. The complex ones take more time and power than most have." She rolls her shoulders and adjusts her stance. "And that was before Ryogo developed this ridiculous *fear*."

"They don't avoid using magic entirely," I remember. "They've got garakyus."

"They've been taught to view magic as a tool. Like a sword," Tsua explains. "It's a powerful tool in the hand of someone who knows how to use it, but it's limited. It's not easy to cut your dinner with a sword, is it?"

"Probably not. I've never been unwise enough to try," I say.

Tsua nods. "Something like this susuji is beyond anyone who views magic the same way you think about your sword. I think it's part of the reason Ryogan leaders worked so hard to push their mages away from the manipulation of desosa. From everything Osshi and Lo'a have told us, it seems like the mages who study here now only learn how to create things like garakyus and healing spells."

"They didn't want anyone even attempting what my brother accomplished." Chio comes to a stop on the opposite side of the fire from Tsua. "Their fear of him is still impossibly strong, even after all this time. More than I expected."

Then Tsua takes another long breath. "Are you ready, vanafitia?"

At his assent, she slowly twitches the fingers of her right hand. Then, inch by inch, Chio's hand replaces hers. They repeat the process on the left until Chio is the one feeding desosa into the susuji and Tsua can step back. I didn't feel the desosa flare or fade at all. It's impressive, both in their mastery of the desosa and how well they work with each other.

"So, when we finish and we have a susuji…" I lean in enough to better smell the potion, wincing at the sting. "How will we know if it works?"

Sanii lifts eir hand. "We test it."

"On who?" I gesture toward the andofume. "It's not like they can become *more* immortal."

"We test it on me."

My breath catches, fear rising like a thick plume of smoke in my chest. "And if it kills you? What am I supposed to do then? What do you think Yorri will do to me if you're not there when I free him?"

"And what do you think he'll do when I get old and he's still sixteen?" Sanii only looks more determined, eir square jaw tensing and eir nostrils flaring. "Or when I die and leave—"

Ey closes eir eyes, but I can finish the rest. They're sumai, bonded so deeply their souls have entwined. The death of one sukhai severs the connection, and it's rare for the surviving bondmate to…well, survive. The pain becomes unbearable, a constant agony that no amount of time can ease. If the pain itself doesn't kill the sukhai, they take their own lives.

Broken hearts can heal; broken souls can't.

It would be different with Yorri. If Sanii dies, he'll *have* to live with the pain and the loss and the memory of exactly how little time they had together. Even if we find a way to end immortal lives, I don't think I have it in me to hand my brother the means to destroy himself. Or watch him endlessly suffer the loss of his sukhai. Sanii becoming immortal emself is the only endurable option. For any of us.

But Tsua and Chio told us about Varan's followers who willingly drank whatever susuji Varan had created. "It didn't work on everyone who took it," she'd said. "Two weren't affected. Three died screaming."

"Say the susuji is actually capable of giving em immortality,"

I begin cautiously. "What are the chances of this killing em instead?"

Tsua and Chio share a look before she says, "Low, but not ignorable."

"I'll take low." Sanii forces a smile. "It's better odds than we've had in moons."

That I can't deny. "Fine. But you don't do it before letting us know it's ready."

"I don't think any of us are going anywhere for at least another day or two, Khya." Tsua's gaze flits toward the cavern's entrance. "It'd be hard to hide anything here."

Especially from Tessen. The reminder makes me feel a little better.

"Let me know if you need any help with this." I gesture toward the fire, but I'm already stepping back. When they don't ask me to stay, I pick up the smaller of my two bags and move beyond the perimeter of the wagons.

The firelight isn't as strong here, making reading harder than it already is. I strain my eyes, going over the lines I've studied more than once and looking for anything new. A question to ask. An experiment to try. I still can't make the cord around my wrist hold magic, but I know that's *my* failing, not a fault in the cord. This is from the same stock we found on Imaku, the same they used on their prisoners. It *must* be capable of binding something or someone.

Letting Lo'a use my wards to amplify the spell her people use to hide was hard, but possible. I was warding the caravan. It was a different kind of ward than I'd ever tried to create before, but it was still a ward. This binding spell is nothing like that. It's Ryogan magic through and through.

I keep working on it, pushing to see how far I can stretch what my training masters once told me were the limits of my ability. We can't go anywhere, so I let myself get lost in the books and my trials, attempting to wind power through the red cord so many times I lose count. Time passes, but I only know how much because Tessen appears with food every so often.

"You need to take a break, Khya," he says the third time.

I nod, absently running the cord through my fingers. "I will. When this wears me out."

"Too late. You're blinking like you can't focus." Tessen stifles a sigh and places the plate near my side. "Just because you *can* grind yourself to dust doesn't mean you should."

He leaves before I can reply, which is good; I think he might be right, but I'm not ready to admit defeat yet. Especially since I don't know when I'll next have this much uninterrupted time to work. Once the andofume finish the susuji and we test it, we'll have to move on. I don't know where yet, but it won't matter. I'll need to save my energy on those days for my wards.

I keep working, eating when I'm hungry, but skipping a lot more sleep than is probably a good idea. Some time on the second day I feel someone watching. When I look up Tessen is there, leaning against the side of a wagon, his face nearly lost in its shadow. Though I wait—for either approval or argument—he gives me nothing but a small shake of his head and a resigned smile before he walks away. It's enough to nudge me into a second nap, but even as I lay down, my head pillowed on my arm, I hope I don't sleep long.

However long I'm out, it's only a few hours after I wake up that Tsua announces, "It's ready."

I'm halfway to the bonfire before anyone else has even gotten to their feet, eyes locked on the steaming pot now sitting on the stone. At first I think it's the light from the fire, but the color is wrong. Too purple. And the light isn't reflecting off the surface of the steaming liquid, it's coming from the liquid itself.

"Are you sure I can't talk you out of this?" I'm speaking to Sanii, but I don't look away from the susuji. "I don't like this."

"There's no better plan." In my peripheral vision, Sanii seems tense. Not afraid, though. Expectant. "We know the chances of this killing me are low."

"We don't *know* anything." I tear my eyes away to look at Sanii. "Are you sure you want to take this risk, Sanii?"

"Yes." Ey kneels next to the fire and then dips a ladle into the pot, pouring the liquid into a small cup. "If you're going to argue with me about this, Khya, go somewhere else."

"I'm not going anywhere. Let's get this over with." I try not to imagine how angry or worried Yorri would be if he were here to watch Sanii raise this cup to eir lips and gulp down the glowing drink.

Ey grimaces and wipes eir mouth with the back of eir hand. "That is awful."

"It wasn't created with taste in mind." Tsua purses her lips, her gaze darting from point to point on Sanii's body. "How are you feeling?"

"The same." Sanii looks down at the empty cup. "So far."

I barely have time to build up the hope that, even if the susuji doesn't work, it also won't hurt em. Less than ten minutes pass before ey starts sweating. And shivering.

Tsua carries em into our wagon and gently lays em on the lower bed. Zonna and I are right behind her, but when Zonna moves to touch Sanii's ankle, desosa already gathering around his hand, Tsua shakes her head.

"Leave em." Tsua eases him away. "We have to let this work or fail. There's nothing we can do but make em comfortable."

Until ey becomes immortal. Or dies. Or something else entirely happens.

I kneel by the bed, holding eir hand and whispering, "Fight through this, Sanii. If you die, Yorri will never forgive me."

Breathlessly, ey laughs. "You're j-joking. He'd forg-give you anything."

It's the last coherent thing ey says for a long time.

Within an hour, ey is writhing and screaming, the sound so loud and eir voice filled with so much agony I try to create a ward to stop sound. It doesn't work.

After an hour of screaming, I send Tessen and Tyrroh away, banishing them into a wagon that one of the hanaeuu we'la maninaio drives out of the cavern entirely. Neither of them can muffle their overpowered hearing enough. It's probably painful being within a hundred yards of em, but hopefully the stone will block the worst of it. It's the best I can do.

We watch over em, waiting for the end. Whatever the end looks like. Even when the others force me to take a break, I don't go far, not beyond the main cavern. Every other moment I'm with Sanii. Waiting and worrying.

For two solid days.

The fever Sanii built up breaks as we enter day three, sweat beading on eir soft brown skin as eir shivering eases. When they're open, eir eyes look clearer and more focused than I've seen since Tsua carried em in here.

"Did it work?" is the first thing ey asks.

"We don't know yet." I brush my hand over eir forehead, pushing eir short hair off eir skin. "How do you feel?"

"Miserable," ey mutters, closing eir eyes. "But I don't think I'm about to die anymore."

My hand tightens on the edge of the bed. "You'd better not."

Ey smiles, eyes fluttering open again. "Where's your anto? We need a test."

"There's been more than enough testing already." But I reach for one of the daggers stored under the bed and ask Miari to get Zonna. Just in case Sanii can't heal this wound on eir own. Only then do I remind em, "We don't have to do this now."

"Sooner is better," ey says, almost breathless. "If it failed, we need a new plan."

Sanii's right. I should have asked about that two days ago. Blood and rot. I should've asked what our next step would be before ey ever swallowed the susuji. Hopefully Tsua, Chio, and Osshi have been working on that, because we've already spent days in this cavern. Closing in on a week. If this fails, then it's almost a full week wasted.

At least it hadn't been a waste *and* a loss. Ill as Sanii's been, ey's still with us.

When Zonna kneels next to me and nods, I take Sanii's offered arm, press it down to stop em from flinching, and cut a short line across eir upper forearm. Blood wells, leaving dark trails across eir skin. It's deep enough to cause damage, not so deep Sanii's in any real danger.

Then we watch. If the susuji worked, eir body will close the wound, healing it until only the faintest of scars is left. And even that should fade soon. But nothing happens.

We wait ten minutes before Sanii looks away from us, defeat in eir large eyes.

Zonna heals the cut ey couldn't. Disappointment wars with relief, both emotions strong enough to feel like tangible weights on my chest. When Miari and Wehli take my place at eir bedside, I leave the wagon and keep walking. I need space, so I go farther from our wagon than I have in days. Which is how I spot the smaller fire in the rear of the cavern.

The tripod is set up over the blaze, a pot hanging from the center and purple-tinted steam rising from inside. Chio and Tsua stand on either side, hands extended. Power *floods* into the susuji, so much more than they used for the first.

I've learned how to handle more desosa than I thought

was possible, but this is something else entirely. The energy crackles and sparks around them, invisble but tangible to anyone with the skill to feel it. Given that most of the hanaeuu we'la maninaio seem to be keeping to the opposite side of the cavern, I don't think I'm the only one unsettled by the work our elder andofume are doing. I also don't dare interrupt it.

Staying back about twenty feet, I sit and watch. They must've been working on this for hours. Maybe days. It'd explain why I've so rarely seen them since Sanii drank the first susuji. It would also explain why they're breathing hard and why their hands are trembling and why Chio seems seconds away from losing his balance. I don't want to think about what might happen if they're interrupted—the backlash could decimate half the cavern—so I quietly find Natani and bring him back to their bonfire. Tessen notices, of course, and follows us.

"Can you help them?" I ask Natani.

"They're already pulling more desosa than I've ever channeled." He bites the inside of his cheek. "I don't think touching either is a good idea, but I might be able to…"

Taking a deep breath, Natani steps closer to Chio, calm moving outward from him in waves. The andofume's energy doesn't lose force, but it does lose bite. Some of the lightning-like crackle in the air dissipates, and that shift seems to ease Tsua and Chio's burden. They resettle their stances. Steady their hands. Breathe deep. Keep working.

Tessen shakes his head. "I can't believe I didn't notice they were doing this. I should've felt this kind of power even from outside."

"Not even you can be aware of everything at once. You've been focused on watch shifts." Swallowing and wrapping my arms around myself, I lift my chin toward the susuji. "Can you sense anything different from the first attempt?"

"Not while they're working on it. I think I'll have to wait until they're done to know."

"Waiting." I rub the bridge of my nose. "Why is our life filled with so much waiting?"

Tessen's lips thin at my hesitation. "You've always expected too much of yourself. It was good on Shiara—pushing yourself was how you became the best in our year—"

"Second-best," I remind him. "I wasn't the one who was tapped to become a student of the kaigo, remember?"

"As if that matters now." Tessen watches me sidelong. "What I was trying to say is it's different here. Pushing yourself to accomplish everything *now* is only going to burn you out. We don't know where the end of our journey is, and we can't even see the path we're supposed to be walking on. Then you have the added pressure of a whole second project while we're stumbling our way on a first."

"What does that even mean?"

His focus shifts to the andofume and their new susuji. "That one day, probably sooner than any of us would like, you might have to choose one over the other. We may have been forced to leave Itagami behind, but that doesn't mean what we learned there isn't true anymore."

The actions of one cannot, and should not, be paid for by the suffering of many.

It's part of Itagamin law. There's more, though, and it's this other half that Tessen is probably thinking of now.

The needs of one cannot, and should not, outweigh what is best for many.

"You wanted to be a leader, Khya." Tessen's voice is low and unusually gentle. "I've always believed you could become a great one, but you have to be willing to put everything you want second."

I force myself to breathe slowly. Evenly. My heart is

beating so hard my chest hurts. "You're right, and maybe one day it'll come to that, but we got this far because I put Yorri above everything else. I've *always* done that."

"You say that as though I don't know," he says wryly. "I'm not expecting that to change, I'm just hoping you'll at least try to remember the rest of us when you have to make that choice."

Tilting my head, I watch him out the corner of my eye. "You say that as though I could forget you."

"You'd better not." He mutters the words darkly and crosses his arms over his chest, but he can't completely hide the way his lips want to curve into a smile.

An hour later the andofume shudder and lower their hands. Tessen and I get up as soon as the flow of desosa stops. I shout for Wehli. Tessen and I aren't fast enough to catch them before they sink straight to the stone, but Wehli's a ryacho—all I see is a blur of color and then he's there, catching Chio before his head connects with the stone. Tsua is farther away; not even Wehli's speed is enough to get to her in time.

"We're fine." Tsua waves off Zonna's concern despite her panting breaths and what looks like blood dripping down the side of her neck. "Tssiky'le, I haven't been this tired in ages."

"I don't know how Varan could've pulled this off by himself." Chio is curled over, resting his forehead on his knees. "Not before he had an andofume's endurance."

"Your brother was nothing if not resourceful." Tsua's eyes flutter closed and don't immediately open again. "Leave us to sleep for now. The susuji needs to settle. When we wake up, it should be ready. And hopefully it'll be *right*, too."

"From your lips to the Kaisubeh's ears," Chio mutters.

"Hush, vanafitia." Tsua lies down on the stone, using her arm as a pillow. "I doubt they want to hear anything we have to say."

Chio snorts as he settles down next to her. It seems to take less than a minute for both to fall into a deep, unmoving sleep, so I go to check on Sanii. Apparently, the susuji *did* have an effect—Sanii's various scars are all but gone, and so is the ache in eir shoulder from an old injury. Ey's healed in ways even a hishingu mage couldn't manage, but that's it. Nothing more.

So I return to watching over the andofume, waiting to see if their second attempt is any better than the first.

Four hours later, although there are bruise-like shadows under their eyes and a certain carefulness to their movements, Tsua and Chio are immediately back to work. They're also ravenous, eating out of bowls of food on their lap as they sit with the glowing pot between them.

The purple-tinted light coming from it seems brighter than the draft Sanii drank, but they're frowning as they prod the liquid with magical fingers. Before they're half finished eating, they beckon Tessen and me closer, gesturing to the susuji.

"What do you think?" Tsua asks.

Tessen will be able to read more than I can, but I still focus on the luminescent liquid, trying to remember what I felt from the first one. Far as I can tell, the sole difference is potency, and only by a little. There's nothing in it to help me pretend this one might work where the first failed.

When Tessen shakes his head, I know what he's found even before he says, "It feels like this one will do exactly what the other did."

Tsua closes her eyes and nods. "That's what I thought, too."

"I knew this wouldn't work. I *hoped* I was wrong, but when am I ever wrong about Varan's—" Growling, Chio rubs both hands over his smooth head. "This is why I never paid attention to what he was working on. None of it made sense.

None of it should've worked."

"And yet it did. Twelve times." I sit down across from him, trying to stay calm. "Your memories of Varan right before he tested this on you are the only solid lead we have to follow. Clearly what we found in the mountains didn't work, so what's next?"

"I don't know." An apology shows in his eyes. "All I know for certain is what we have won't work. Unless one of the Kaisubeh blessed the rot-ridden thing."

"Maybe Varan found Kaisuama," Tessen jokes weakly, his smile forced.

Kaisuama? It takes me a moment to remember the right story—it's a mountain the Ryogans used to believe the Kaisubeh watched them from. My smile is as weak as Tessen's joke was. "If he did, the Kaisubeh probably gave him what he wanted just to make him go away."

Tsua and Chio smile with us, distracted but listening enough to know what the expected response is. Then Tsua blinks, her eyes narrowing. "What did you say?"

"I..." Bellows. Hoping she's not going to be like Osshi and take offense at the careless remark about the Kaisubeh, I repeat what we said and then gesture toward the wagons. "It was in a story Lo'a told us. I know the belief is ancient, but I—"

"Do you remember?" Tsua faces Chio, her half-moon eyes full. "He disappeared. For three weeks. Almost four. And he was half dead when he finally stumbled back into Uraita."

"He said he'd been hunting gods," Chio responds slowly, his own eyes bulging. "And we all thought it was a joke to avoid telling us where he'd been, but what—"

"What if for once he was being *honest*?" Tsua breaks in and finishes. "You know he was obsessed with the Mysora range. It's why he hid his work in these mountains."

"And he spent years collecting every story about the

Kaisubeh he could. Who's to say he didn't hear that exact tale and decide—" Chio rubs his hand over his mouth, lines of concentration etched around his eyes. "But we don't even know where to *start*."

"In the mountains, obviously, but…" Tsua gets up and jogs toward Lo'a's wagon. She comes back with a handful of rolled maps and Lo'a in tow.

"There is only one place no one looks." Lo'a says, pointing to a section of the Mysora Mountains that's shaded gray on the map. "If Kaisuama is real and it has not been found before, where else can it be except somewhere in Nentoado?"

"Why there?" I ask, trying to get a better view of the map.

"It's impassable," Tsua explains. "Whole caravans have died trying to find a way through Nentoado."

"It's the widest part of the Mysora range." Chio traces the border of the gray-shaded area with his fingertip. "In my day, no one had found a safe path through the Nentoado range."

"But it has been a long time since you were last here," Lo'a reminds them. "And my people have the need for places to hide, places no one will bother looking for us."

"You have one within Nentoado?" Tsua asks.

Lo'a tilts her head in acknowledgement. "Kaisuama is definitely not along the path my people travel. However, we stay to the edges, never through the heart of the range."

"And if Varan found Kaisuama in these mountains," Chio says, "the heart of the range is exactly where it must be."

"We can find it." Everyone turns to me, their expressions a mix of skepticism, amusement, and resignation. "Tessen can find anything, and it's not like we don't know how to climb."

"Khya, this won't be like the mountains on Shiara," Chio says. "You think it's cold now, but this is warm compared to where we'd have to go. The peaks are so high it'll get hard to breathe, and the storms—If those catch up with us while we're in those mountains, the winds could get strong enough to knock us into thin air. And sure, no one can follow a trail better than Tessen, but we can't count on there being a trail to follow. If there were, Kaisuama would've been found centuries ago."

I can't do anything about the trail—especially since I don't know what we're looking for other than a mountain the Kaisubeh, who I'm not even sure are real, might call home. "My wards can protect us from the worst of the wind, and our magic will make the climb simpler. I'm guessing the Ryogans never tried crossing these mountains the way we will."

"Likely not," Tsua admits with a smile. "Doesn't mean it'll be easy, though."

"Of course not." I rise to find the others. "When is anything ever easy?"

CHAPTER
TEN

According to Lo'a, we can't start a journey into Nentoado from just anywhere along the Mysora range. The only path she knows of into the impossible land begins near the mouth of the Sansosi'ka River, at least three days north of where we waited out the storms.

The mountains are rocky and uneven, the massive outcroppings of dark gray stone so different from the layers of limestone and red sandstone of Shiara. Our path is narrow and curving. The tall trees clinging to the slopes make it feel even tighter, but it's good cover, hiding us from view at a distance, and it's a useful windbreak. It saves me from having to use my wards.

On the third day, we reach a point where we have to leave the wagons behind and climb the mountain on foot. The trees and growth will give us handholds to pull ourselves up the steep, sharp ridge, but the climb will still be arduous. And from the description Chio and Tsua gave us, it'll only become more exhausting the farther we get.

I think that realization is what changes Lo'a's mind about

coming with us moments before we leave. It's a smart choice. I've spent years climbing cliffs and mountains, and even I'm not looking forward to what's coming. It'll be worse when we lose the cover of the trees and the wind can come straight at us.

We leave Lo'a's caravan on a wide ledge of stone protruding from the mountain, protected from sight on three sides. They'll be safe here, hopefully. The grueling travel of the remainder of the afternoon makes me glad they stayed there. We only stop when we find a safe place to sleep for the night. We barely slow except for the moments when we have to wait for Osshi to catch up, or physically drag him up a particularly steep section of rock. In those moments, I can't help wishing he'd stayed behind, too.

Wehli acts as our scout, using his ryacho speed to dash off in different directions, checking routes for dead ends and pitfalls or, when the sun begins to set, find us a safe place to sleep. Although he does find a scattered series of ledges, there's not enough space for us all to sleep on the same one. We can cook and eat dinner on the central step while those asleep or on watch spread out along the other tiers. It's not ideal, but it's enough.

"This whole journey feels like hunting a mykyn bird at night during a new moon," Rai mutters as she lights the fire for us. "I don't like how little we know about this."

"I guess it won't make it any better to hear that we're technically not within the boundaries of Nentoado yet." Chio finishes skinning the animal Wehli caught this afternoon, and Tsua hands him a thick, straight stick to use as a spit. "This is easy compared to what we'll have to get through when we hit *those* peaks."

"But that's just it." Rai plays with the sparks, flicking them into the flames. "We're going into an area known for its dangers, and we're going not only without a map, but without a destination, a direction, or a single *clue* what we're looking for."

"We've had better plans," Etaro agrees wearily, rubbing eir sharp chin.

I rub my thumb along the red cord, absently trying to weave power into its threads. It never sticks. "We may not have a map, but that doesn't mean we don't have a destination. And Chio was right—to make the susuji work, Varan had to have used immense amounts of desosa, more than we could produce *combined*. A person or a place that powerful won't be easy to hide."

"And we have a Tessen." Rai smirks and flicks sparks in his direction.

"*A* Tessen. Does that mean there's more than one?" Sanii shudders, the motion exaggerated. "That is an *awful* thought."

Rai laughs. "Unless you're Khya."

Tessen smirks and ducks his head, rubbing the back of his neck and only looking at me out the corner of his eye. In the morning, when we move out, he's still watching me sidelong. I hold his arm, keeping him a few feet back from the rest of the group. "What?"

"Nothing. I— Well, sometimes it's easy to forget until something reminds me."

"Forget what?"

He doesn't answer immediately, and then he sighs and says, "That when someone teases us about being together, it's not a lie anymore. Or wishful thinking."

"I…" Swallowing hard, I stop walking. "It's real. I promise it's real."

"I know." He squeezes my hand and pulls me close, until the toes of our boots touch. "I do know, but with everything that's been happening, with how little time we've been able to spend alone, it can feel…"

"Far away?"

"As far away as home," Tessen says.

"Then maybe you should remind yourself more often." I grip his chin, tilting his head down until I can press a hard kiss to his lips. They're cracked the same way they were in the desert, but this time it's from the cold. When he slides his hands to frame either side of my neck, his touch is achingly gentle. My tongue swipes along his full bottom lip, but I can't do more now. The rest of the squad must be at least a hundred yards ahead of us. "Bellows, Tessen. How do you so consistently have the *worst* timing?"

"It's a talent of mine." His voice is dry, but his eyes are shining with humor. Then, whether it's to collect his thoughts or track the squad, he looks northeast. "My least favorite talent, honestly."

"Well, come on then, basaku." I pull him back, kissing him sharply one more time. Then I push him a step up the steep slope. "Go put your more useful skills to work."

"And then there are moments like this." He heaves an excessively aggrieved sigh and makes sure I see him roll his eyes before he begins climbing to catch up with the others. Catches up and then passes them all, taking a spot near Tyrroh at the front of the line, leaving me grinning at his back.

He and Tyrroh are nearly the same height, both just over six feet tall, but their builds are so dissimilar. I somehow forget how leanly built Tessen is until I see him next to Tyrroh's broad, thick frame. Tessen moves more smoothly, reminding me of a teegra cat's prowl, while Tyrroh is more solid, like a moving boulder, but they keep pace together perfectly.

Before I learned to trust Tessen, I might've been suspicious of them heading the line like this, and the easy way they pass bits of information about the road ahead back and forth. Moons ago, I might've convinced myself Tessen was trying to impress the nyshin-ma just to overshadow me; now I'm simply glad Tessen has an older riuku mage to learn from. Tessen is already more powerful than Tyrroh can ever be, but Tyrroh understands what Tessen experiences better than any of the rest of us, and that's an especially good thing here.

We don't have a map or destination, so our two riuku mages are the only guide we have. They've had to use their overpowered senses to search for anything strange, any sign of our destination. I'm still not sure how they're going to know what's strange and what's not when *everything* here is so different from what we're used to, but I'm glad we've got them to follow. Even if Tyrroh is an oraku instead of a basaku—only his sight, hearing, and smell enhanced instead of all his senses—having him and Tessen leading us into this is so much better than walking into Nentoado with nothing.

Just before midday, Tessen calls a halt, stopping as we near a rise and staying motionless.

"There's someone less than a mile up." Tessen's head is cocked like he's not sure of what he's hearing. "I don't think they're a danger."

"How can anyone who knows how to survive these mountains not be dangerous?" Sanii asks. "To people who aren't us, at least."

"Their movements are so light." He looks more confused. "It almost sounds like a child."

"If they know this area, they might be able to help," Etaro suggests.

Rai frowns. "Or they'll report us to the Ryogans, and we'll have the soldiers back on our trail. Besides, Lo'a said no one believes the old stories about the Kaisubeh anymore, so what could they possibly know?"

"They don't need to believe the stories. They only have to know Nentoado to give us something useful. A direction."

I glance at Tessen and Tyrroh, smiling. "And it's not like we won't be able to see them a long time before they see us. We can change our minds about talking to them once we see who they are."

Tyrroh smiles, a grin wide enough to part his full lips and flash white teeth bright against his dark skin. Then he nods at me as though I'm the nyshin-ma and *he's* the second. But then he faces the others, expression turning serious as he changes the order of the line and leads us out.

It doesn't take us long to find the source of the sounds. Tessen was right; the person we find can't be older than twelve. It's hard to see much about them under their thick layers of clothing, but they seem skinny to the point of starved and small, shorter even than Sanii. And they're in the middle of skinning an animal, and the animal is bigger than they are. They handle a blade well, each motion clean and practiced. And when, after Tyrroh signals approval for us to approach, the child rises to their feet with that bloody knife pointed at us, I fully believe they not only know how to use it, they're *willing* to. Even when faced with more than a dozen grown strangers.

"I like this one," Rai says in Itagamin as we descend to meet the child.

"Hopefully you'll still like them *after* we say hello." I don't take chances. My wards have been up since Tessen first told us someone was nearby; now I make them absolutely impenetrable.

"If you need food, go get your own," the child calls, stepping in front of their kill. "This mountain don't belong to no one, and I trapped this myself."

Tsua is in the lead, and I'm only a step behind her. She pitches her voice down, the tones even and low. "I promise we won't take anything you've claimed. But why are you alone all the way up here? I didn't think anyone could survive long so close to Nentoado."

"Definitely better for us here than bein' down there with the rest of them. There's dangers here, but—" They jerk their chin south, toward Ryogo. "*That* place is death."

"Oh," Osshi murmurs. "It's a hinoshowa."

The word makes the child stiffen. Tsua sends Osshi a sharp glare. "*Don't*, Osshi. I never want to hear that word from your lips again."

Osshi shrinks back, but Tsua has already shifted her focus back to the child. "You mentioned someone else. Who lives here with you?"

The child's lips thin and their stance widens, body braced and ready to fight or flee.

"Look at us." Tsua gestures to us. "Does it look like we come from Ryogo?"

"Not most of you," they grudgingly bite out. "But what's that matter?"

"Because where we come from, there's no word like the one you hate so much. The people born like you aren't treated any different."

Oh. Maybe ey's an ebet. If hinoshowa is Ryogo's word for the third sex, it isn't a kind description. Even now, the child's wary, narrowed gaze jumps from face to face. Ey backs up a step when Tsua gestures to Sanii, beckoning em closer.

"This is Sanii, and ey's like you. So is Etaro." Tsua indicates both of them as they step closer. "In our language, they're called ebets."

Our, she says. It's strangely nice to hear her claim my language as her own.

A small piece of the wariness in the child's posture fades. "Ebets? I thought you called that one Sanii."

"No. Girl," Tsua says, putting her hand on her chest. "Boy."

She touches Chio's arm. And then she points to Sanii and the child. "Ebet."

Ey relaxes a little bit more, but there's sadness in eir brown eyes when ey looks at Sanii. "Was your mama punished, too?"

"No," Sanii says gently. "Yours was?"

A hesitation, then the child nods slowly. "She can't talk no more."

"What's your name?" I ask.

"Mama can't call me by a name, but I wanted one I could say, right? So I gave myself one." Ey puffs up eir small chest, pride and defiance in eir stance. "I'm called Ahta."

"Ahta, can we meet your mother?" I'm curious to meet the woman who raised em out here.

Ahta inches away, all eir earlier wariness back. "Why you want to do that?"

"Because we're looking for something hidden in Nentoado, and you might be able to help us," Tsua says. "And because we'll do what we can to help you while we're here."

"We can't feed you," Ahta says after a stretch of silence. "We got barely enough for us."

"You don't need to," I promise. "We're carrying enough for ourselves, and we're more than capable of hunting our own food."

Ey eyes our swords for a second before ey nods. "Fine. One of you carry that and follow me."

"After all the protesting about us staying away from your kill?" I ask.

"I can run faster without it if I gotta lose you in the mountains."

Sanii laughs, and Ahta seems to relax a little at eir reaction. It doesn't last. The farther east we follow Ahta, the more often ey looks back at us, clearly conflicted.

I let the quiet settle until Tessen signals there's noise in the distance. Then I ask, "Before we meet her, what's your mother's name, Ahta?"

"Dai-Usho. She changed it after..." Ey shakes eir head. "Call her Dai-Usho."

"You said she was punished. Why?" Sanii asks before I can.

Ahta's face clouds. "Everyone knows that."

"We don't," Etaro says quietly. "Whatever happened to her isn't something that happens where we're from."

"Wish I would've been born there, then." Ey heaves a sigh that sounds too weary for someone so small and young. "The only time a hinoshowa is born is when the mother's done something horrible and angered the Kaisubeh."

"What did she do?" I ask.

"*Nothing*. She didn't do nothing. She wrote it so herself, and always told me we should never lie." Ahta crosses eir bony arms and glares. After a beat of silence, eir shoulders slump. "But there's gotta be somethin' or I wouldn't be here, and she wouldn't have been tossed out of the family, and she wouldn't have lost her voice to a knife, and she— I don't know."

It takes me a few seconds to fit those pieces into an appalling picture.

Tessen's voice is filled with all the disbelief and horror spinning through my mind. "Her family *slit her throat* because you were born an ebet?"

Ahta shrugs stiffly with poorly feigned indifference. "Her husband did it."

Husband and wife. Tsua explained the partnership like a sumai pair without the soulbond, yet Dai-Usho's *husband* drew a knife across her throat so hard it broke her voice?

"He cut her throat even though he didn't know what she'd done wrong?" Rai looks like she's bouncing back and forth between baffled and furious.

"I'm here," Ahta says scornfully. I can't tell if that scorn is directed at emself or us. "What other proof did they need?"

"How did she survive an injury like that?" A cut deep enough to keep her from talking should've killed her first.

"I wish I knew," the child mumbles. "That's a story no one's ever gotten from her."

"This place really isn't the paradise Varan said it was," I mutter in Itagamin.

"This is *nothing* like paradise. Bellows, Khya! This explains so much about Varan's crimes," Rai says in the same language. "I hate to think about what Varan would do to this place, but whoever is leading Ryogo might be worse."

"They're not worse," Etaro says before I can. "But I don't think he's any better, either. *This* is... None of them deserve to lead anyone anywhere. Except straight into Kujuko."

Ey might be right. No one in the clan went hungry except when long droughts killed too many crops and hunting grew too hard. No one was punished without evidence of a crime. No one was banished from the city...ever. It didn't happen. Either your crime was serious enough to deserve death, or you paid for it with service to the city.

Which is why Tessen, Sanii, and I wouldn't have ever been able to return to Itagami if we'd escaped with Yorri the first time we tried to rescue him—we would've been killed for our crimes. But we wouldn't have been abandoned to the wilderness. No one was *ever* abandoned the way it seems Ahta and eir mother obviously were or punished the way the citizens of Uraita have been. Unless their death or disappearance served to keep Varan's secrets or gain him something he wanted. Then, apparently, there's nothing he wouldn't do and no one he wouldn't risk.

"It's not far, but..." Ahta stops and turns sharply, facing us down with determination in eir brown eyes. "No one comes here. She's not gonna be expecting people, and definitely not so many. If you hurt her or scare her, I'll make sure you don't ever get off this mountain."

Even though I doubt the little ebet could manage to follow through on the threat, I believe ey'd die trying if we caused eir blood-mother harm. It's devotion I understand.

"We will do everything we can to avoid scaring her," Tsua promises. "And I swear to you on the Kaisubeh and the mountain you've made home, we won't hurt either of you."

Ahta watches us, eir teardrop-shaped eyes unblinking. Finally, ey sighs. "C'mon, then."

Less than a hundred yards later, we break through a thick growth of trees and see the place Ahta and Dai-Usho call home. Their small dwelling is cleverly built into the side of the mountain, a rock ledge serving as a roof, but it's the clearing in front of the house that makes my eyes widen.

Ahta and Dai-Usho cleared a broad swath of the valley, keeping enough of the trees to offer protection from wind and discovery and turning the center of the area into a carefully tended garden. It partially explains how these two have survived up here for more than a season. In the worst weather, the stone and wood building must be almost completely shielded from the elements, and if they store it well, the food they collect and grow should sustain them. It's impressive. And so incredibly lonely.

When the short door to the dwelling opens, someone who has to duck low under the top of the frame hurries out. Long black hair hides their face until they straighten. Dai-Usho's eyes widen when she sees us, and she freezes, becoming as still as the mountain behind her.

I can't keep myself from wincing. I can't keep my hand from rising to my throat. I can't keep from staring at the long-healed scar of a wound that should have killed a normal person. Ahta had told us about Dai-Usho's injury, but seeing it… It seems like only magic could've allowed someone to survive that. The scar is thick, gnarled, and pink against her beige skin, and it's an angled half circle under her chin.

"It's okay, *onyo*," Ahta calls across the garden. "They're not Ryogan, and I don't think they'll hurt us."

She gestures and signs, the motions practiced and precise even if she seems agitated. Each shape her fingers make remind me of the signals we use in Itagami, ways to communicate without speaking a word. As ey jogs toward eir mother, ey responds in words and gestures simultaneously. We approach much slower, giving Ahta time to explain, and we stop a good twenty feet away from the house. Even with Ahta's assurances, Dai-Usho doesn't begin to uncoil until Osshi and Ahta explain about Sanii and Etaro.

Osshi and Tsua lead our conversation with Dai-Usho, explaining only some of what we're doing here. There's danger headed to Ryogo, they tell her, and we believe a power hidden within Nentoado might be able to stop it.

Mother and child share a long look when the story is over. Dai-Usho seems unconvinced until the end of another hurried conversation of broken sentences and gestures. Then, she nods.

Ahta's round face is set and determined. "We've been here a long while now—more than half my life. Some years, we had to travel pretty far to find food. 'Specially before we brought up enough soil here to grow anything worth eating. We haven't been through the whole Nentoado, but we hunted up in those mountains before and…" Ey crosses eir arms and shakes eir head. "Don't care how hungry we get. I'll steal from the valley cities before I go back there."

"What did you see?" Tsua straightens.

"Found some tufts of fur and tracked the beast. We thought it was a tenrai."

"A what?" I quietly ask Osshi.

"Big cat," Osshi says. "Thick fur and sharp claws."

"Then we found prints in the snow. They were too big and the wrong shape. Don't know *what* that was. I never wanna see it." Ahta shakes eir head, the motion sharp. "We ran back down fast as we could."

"Are you sure they weren't just…big?" Sanii asks doubtfully.

"Not like this. Tenrais are about that size." Ey gestures to the beast ey'd killed, a creature that is bigger than Ahta but smaller than Tyrroh. "What left those tracks was *big*. Big as the house. Bigger. Nothing's that big."

"Could the desosa change an animal like that?" I ask in Itagamin. My understanding of what we're capable of doing with magic, and what it can do on its own, may be limited, but a power that changes the world around it without a human hand to guide them? Not even anything in Lo'a's stories hinted at that.

"I honestly don't know." Chio spreads his arms, palms up.

"If whatever's there was powerful enough to make Varan immortal, it's not too strange to think it could alter the animals, too. This is a starting point at least." Tsua responds in the same language, but then she focuses on Ahta and asks in Ryogan, "Do you remember how to get to that place? How long will it take from here?"

"You're gonna go *now*?" Ey and Dai-Usho both look at us with wide eyes. "It's too cold! The storms have been bad the past few moons, and it's just gonna get worse with the seasons."

"We don't have time to wait, and—" Tsua looks at Rai and Nairo, signing an order.

With delighted smirks, both our kasaiji snap their fingers, engulfing their hands in flames. Ahta and Dai-Usho jump back, crying out in wordless shock.

Tsua's smile stays gentle. "We're not unprotected. If you can point us to a path, we should be able to follow it."

They blink, shock slowly turning into something else. Curiosity, in Ahta's case. Ey steps closer, eir hand stretching out as though to touch the fire. "Can you all do this?"

Rai shakes her head, lifting her hand toward Ahta. "We all have different skills. This one happens to be mine. Think it'll help where we need to go?"

Ahta nods slowly, eir expression showing none of the fear I've gotten used to seeing in Ryogans, only eager interest. Zonna, I notice, is watching em with just as much curiosity as ey's showing us and a small smile. That expression grows when Ahta says, "If all of you can do tricks like that, it might actually be enough to keep you from dying."

Once Ahta and Dai-Usho agree to help, Nairo, Wehli, and Miari make food—combining our stores with some meat from Ahta's kill—and Natani, Rai, and Etaro keep watch at various points around the clearing. The rest of us sit with our new allies, our limited maps of the area spread between us. The drawings don't help Ahta—no one ever taught em to read a map—but we can use what ey tells us to give us an idea of where to go.

Even after we've eaten and gotten basic directions, it doesn't seem like either of them believe we're going to go through with this trip. Their fear of the place is fierce. When we finally convince them we're serious, Ahta insists we stay the night instead of pushing on. "The day's more than half gone already, and there's not many places to stop after this. Especially for so many people. Stay and rest. Where you're going, you're gonna need a good night of sleep. Or a week of it."

"We definitely don't have a week," I say.

"You gotta stay tonight," Ahta insists. "Won't be the same

deeper into Nentoado."

Tessen has been watching the little ebet with interest, but now he smiles at em with admiration in his eyes. "How old *are* you?"

"Not quite twelve." Ey's chin is up, but eir shoulders are curving in, like ey's not sure if ey should be defensive or defiant. "Why?"

"Because you seem older, and you have a talent for survival," Tessen says. "Your mother is lucky to have your help here."

"Yorri would like em," Sanii murmurs beside me.

I'd been thinking the same thing, my fingers finding their way automatically to the red cord hidden under layers of cloth. "Because ey would remind him of you."

Sanii blinks and an uncertain smile begins to spread across eir long face. "I'm going to pretend you mean that as a compliment."

"You go right ahead," I say with a smirk. Ey laughs, smile getting brighter, and I'm glad. Smiles have been rare from em since the day we met, but when I see a real one, it shows me a little bit more of the ebet my brother loved deeply enough to secretly bind his soul to. Of who ey was before being placed in Itagami's yonin class. And before we thought Yorri had died.

We spend the cold night piled inside their small house and don't leave until the first rays of morning creep through the cracks in the shuttered window. Moments before we're ready, Ahta asks us to wait. Ey has a hurried—and entirely silent—conversation with Dai-Usho, and ey rushes into the house. When ey comes back a minute later, ey's overburdened with a pile of cloth and furs almost as big as ey is.

"To *borrow*." Ey dumps the furs into Sanii's arms. "These took us a long time to kill and clean, and we're gonna need them when the worst of the cold hits."

"It gets *worse*?" I'm shivering almost constantly despite the warmth exertion pours into my body. "How do you live through that?"

Ey points at the furs as though the answer should've been obvious. "With those. And fires. And staying in the house when the storms hit. So, if you want to make it through Nentoado with all your limbs attached and working, you wear these." Ey's eyes narrow and ey plants eir hands on eir hips. "But you have to bring them back."

I place my hand on top of the pile, stroking the incredibly thick, soft furs. "I don't know how long it'll be, but I promise we'll return them."

"You'd better," Ahta says as we distribute the furs. "And be careful."

"As careful as we can be," Sanii promises, wrapping emself in a hooded fur tunic.

We have too much to do and too far to go to let our path end here.

Three hours after we leave Ahta and Dai-Usho, the trees grow farther apart until finally we break free of them entirely and are left facing the first peak of Nentoado.

I come to a dead stop. "What in the name of every hidden horror of Kujuko is *that*?"

"The reason Ahta gave us those furs. That, my desert-bred child, is snow." Tsua gestures to the broad expanse of pure white. It's starkly beautiful, and I wish Yorri were here to see this. Several handfuls of what looks like white sand rise into the air and float toward us at Tsua's command. "In the mountains where the air is thin and cold, can become so cold it becomes solid. Ice and snow. And when I left here, I never thought I'd see it again."

Tessen reaches out to the stuff, entranced. But as soon as he touches it he hisses and pulls back. "Blood and rot, that's cold!"

"I warned you this place would be colder than anything any of you have ever felt. Colder than it can possibly get on Shiara." Chio surveys the landscape, expression unreadable. "This is one reason no one survives Nentoado. Too much cold; too little shelter. Nonetheless, I'm almost certain this is one of the last places Varan visited before he tested what he'd created on me, and our best chance of finding a way to kill him is somewhere beyond this mountain."

He falls silent, and after a couple of breaths—which *hurt*; the air is so cold it burns—Tsua speaks. "You all have abilities that'll help us survive this, but it's still a risk for you. Decide now if it's a risk you're willing to take."

I step forward as soon as she stops speaking. The snow crunches under my boots, and without the trees' protection from the wind, the cold bites harder. Despite the layers of cloth and fur. Tessen and Sanii step into the snow less than a heartbeat after me.

"Bellows, Khya," Etaro grumbles as ey joins us. "How'd saving your brother turn into *this*?"

"Seriously," Rai agrees. "If the Kaisubeh are real, they're intent on making Khya's life as complicated as possible. And dragging the rest of us through it, too."

"You could stay here and guard our retreat." I make the suggestion without any expectation she'll take it.

She snorts, but it's Etaro who says, "You say that like you know where exactly you'll be breaking out of Nentoado if you need to retreat."

"Plus, we've stuck with you this far, Nyshin-pa." Rai

shivers and then glares at the snow-laden wind. "Not even solid, impossibly cold water is going to convince us to leave you now. It comes *close*, but…" She shrugs, but doesn't bother hiding the smile on her face.

"I'm glad you're here." I hold out my hand, palm up, and she takes it.

Then Rai tilts her head toward the snow-coated slope. "Help me do something to keep us from dying of the cold, and I'll be glad you're here, too."

"The wind will be easier." I check with everyone to make sure they're wearing at least one wardstone, and then I tweak the crystals' desosa to make sure they protect us against the wind. Keeping us warm will take a bit more work.

The andofume order us to put on every piece of clothing we have, layering them under our borrowed furs. For the first time since we left Shiara, we wrap our heads in the atakafus, this time to protect our skin from cold instead of burning heat, and we raise our hoods over our heads to keep warmth close. Those layers and my wardstones will have to be enough, because cloth alone can't possibly save us from these temperatures.

Once we set out, it only gets worse.

I never thought a place could be harsher or harder to survive than Shiara. Nentoado proves again how little I know about the world. And I can see now why the Ryogans wouldn't dare enter these mountains. There's no paths or trails most places, only sheer cliffs and sharp peaks. The wind is unpredictable, blowing strong enough to displace snow and turn the world white, to push at my wards and nearly throw us off the mountain. My wards protect from the worst of the wind's buffets, but I can't keep out the cold. It seeps through my clothes and under my skin until it feels like my bones are slowly turning to ice.

I'm used to aches and pains. How can I not be after a lifetime of training and a year of days-long hunts through the Shiaran desert? This is different. This locks up my joints and makes my limbs heavy. It slows my thoughts and my reactions. It makes me want to lie down in a bank of snow to rest, and it makes it hard to care that, if I give in, I might not wake up again.

At night, without what little heat the weak sunlight offers, we find as much shelter as we can and huddle close together. We sleep in piles, warded from the elements with Rai's and Nairo's fire warming the air trapped inside my protections with us. The air dries and cracks our skin wherever it's exposed. I would probably be bleeding if Zonna didn't heal the worst of it.

With no way of knowing how long we'll be traveling these icy, desolate ridges or how often we'll cross the trail of an animal worth hunting, we ration our food to the bare minimum we need to survive. Water, at least, isn't a problem. Even though we haven't crossed a single stream, all we need to do is fill our pot with snow and let Rai melt it.

If we'd come here without magic—especially without our two kasaiji mages—we'd likely have died by the end of the first day. The moment when Rai is so tired and numbly cold that her fire doesn't spark instantly is terrifying, but I understand. Each hour I keep my wards up makes it harder to keep them as strong as they need to be. The cold and the effort of hauling myself up the mountain and the drain of the constant wards is going to be too much. Soon.

"Either this Kujuko-cursed cold is making me lose my mind," Tessen says at the end of our second day in the snow, "or we're getting closer."

"To what?" I signal for Tyrroh and the andofume so they can hear this. Tyrroh approaches first, his steps slower and shorter than usual, and his expression is pinched, a *V* forming in the lines carved into his forehead. The andofume look just as exhausted.

Tessen gestures vaguely east, the motion sluggish and his gaze distant. "I've got no idea. It's…it's more powerful than lightning, but it doesn't flare like that. Not steady, either. It rolls like—almost like waves."

"Are we headed in the right direction?" Chio asks.

"The brightest flares seem to be east of here." Tessen rubs his forehead. "I'm starting to go numb. I don't… I can't be sure the cold isn't interfering with my—" He gestures vaguely and gracelessly, possibly trying to indicate his senses. "If this is real, it feels bright as a bonfire at midnight, and that's from *here*. Once we're within a mile of it, I think even Sanii—even *Osshi* will be able to feel this."

Relief rushes through me like warm water. This isn't for nothing. Something is out there, and we haven't wasted days.

"Kaisuama is real, then." Tsua and Chio share a heavy look, and then she smiles ruefully. "We should know by now, nothing is impossible."

"And legends have more truth in them than anyone wants to admit." Chio turns east, his shoulders rising with a deep breath. "At least this time the legends are helping us."

"Don't forget what Ahta said about the animal," I warn.

Tyrroh nods. "What do you think we'll be facing up there?"

Standing apart from the group, Chio looks east and exhales heavily. "I spent over a century trying to figure out how Varan had pulled off his tricks, and it never crossed my mind that he'd remembered a story about Kaisuama the rest of Ryogo had forgotten and then actually *found* it. Guessing what he saw when he got there is beyond my imagination."

"We'll see for ourselves soon enough," Tyrroh says, seeming resigned.

But *soon* could mean anything when we're following a feeling instead of a map. Soon isn't soon enough when each foot of ground we gain is a struggle against the ice and snow under our feet, the cold biting at our skin and lungs, and the wind doing everything it can to pound my wards into shards.

The wardstones help me stay focused, giving me something solid to hold on to when I need to be sure everyone is protected. Ever since I created them moons ago, they've been useful in ways I never guessed. A spur of the moment decision, and it's probably saved my life fifteen or twenty times over. It's still saving my life.

For two days we follow close behind Tessen, heading where he points. Sometimes, Tsua has to raise us past a ridge too smooth and icy to climb, but we try not to use her power more often than necessary. She'll recover from her exhaustion quicker than we will, but she still gets exhausted, and I'd rather save her strength for when we need it most.

The closer we get, the higher we climb. The stronger the wind. The less shelter we can find. The harder it is to breathe.

I tug the hood of Ahta's fur tunic down, burrowing into it as much as I can without losing my line of sight and missing a crucial step. My hands stopped feeling cold yesterday. Now there are moments I need to see them to be sure they're there. Even settling everyone under one ward and letting our kasaijis' fires warm the air isn't helping much anymore. Sensation is distant, like it's happening to someone else and I'm just an observer.

Is this what Tessen feels when he senses the shifts in my emotions? It's strange. It makes it hard to tell which of my body's reactions are from the cold, and which are because we're close enough to the energy source for me to be feeling it, too. I *should* be able to sense it by now, but I can't be sure. I'm so cold. Blood and rot, how can I feel anything else when it's so *cold*?

We're huddled under an overhang that's too narrow to offer much shelter, but it's enough to give us something to lean against while we try to warm our frozen limbs. Beyond my ward, the wind howls. It screams through the cracks between rocks. Between peaks. It's loud enough to bury every other sound unless I focus, force myself to concentrate.

"What's next?" Tyrroh's voice is hoarse and raw. Frost clings to the stubble that's grown on his chin, giving him a beard of bright white. Against his dark skin, it makes him look ancient.

"Up." Tessen waves his hand at an almost sheer cliff. "That's where we need to go."

I look up, trembling at the thought of forcing my tired, achingly cold body to climb *that*. "Has to be an easier way."

"Maybe, but how long would it take us to find it?" Tyrroh asks. "And how far out of our way will we have to go to get there?"

"Tessen?"

"What?" He blinks at me, confusion deepening the lines around his eyes. "You expect me to somehow *know* where another path is?"

"I…" Yes, I'd thought that. Maybe I've gotten too used to him coming up with solutions or bringing me information he shouldn't have had. In Itagami, he was so good at eavesdropping on conversations. That'll only help here if the stones can speak. So instead of asking about another path, I ask about this one. "Anything we need to be wary of on that?"

"Other than falling?" Even as he quips, his gaze roams the surface. Then he takes a long breath and points to three separate sections, the motion listless. "There's ice. Lots in places. And there's shadows. Looks like they're either deep crevices or the mouths of small caves. That's all I can tell you.

All I smell is snow. All I hear is wind."

And the wind is especially worrying.

I've learned how to do theoretically impossible things with my wards. Breaking through someone else's protections using mine. Melding my magic with something solid. Merging my power with Lo'a's to create a shield that hides us from sight. None of that prepared me for this trek.

I've *never* held my wards constant for so long. Even with stored power in the wardstones, I'm nearing the end of what I can do. I can't be sure I can even get us to the top of this cliff.

I also can't believe Tessen hasn't called me out yet, forced everyone to hole up in one of the caves we've used along the way and ordered me to sleep for twelve hours. He's been working just as hard for just as long, though. Maybe for once he's paying more attention to the world than he is to me. Which means I've got to make the call myself.

No one will argue if I ask to rest, but it's not safe here. We'll have to either retrace our steps, wasting almost another two hours, or continue north, looking for a place to rest ahead of us, which could take five minutes or five days. Neither is a great choice.

Climbing the rock wall now is the most efficient use of our waning time and energy. If I can't rest, extra food might be enough to power my wards through the climb.

When I ask, Tyrroh offers as much as I can eat. Even knowing Tsua and Etaro will try to catch us if we start to fall, no one wants to face this climb without a windbreak. The food helps; hopefully it'll be enough.

Then we begin the climb.

Miari helps where she can, going first so she can gouge handholds and footholds in the stone. Etaro and Chio are behind her, and the rest of us are scattered below with Tsua last in the long line. At first, I keep the wards in place around each person, but it's too much. Even with the wardstones, that takes more focus than I have. And the wardstones have been used too often without ever being refilled. They're almost as empty as I am.

When resources are limited, sacrifices must be made.

It was a lesson our training master drummed into our heads, one necessary for all nyshin, but especially any who wanted to command one day, and I reluctantly follow the advice. If I can't hold the individual wards, I won't. I'll focus on only one ward to keep the wind's icy claws from breaking our numb fingers' tenuous hold on the cliff.

And it's easier. It's easier to breathe and climb and focus and feel when I'm only holding one ward instead of fourteen. It's easier to keep up with Tessen's pace. It's easier to calm the quiet panic in the back of my mind that's been whispering fears of failure ever since I hauled myself up the first foot off the ground. It's easier to pull myself up the face of the mountain foot after foot. A quarter of the way up. Halfway. Three quarters.

Miari shouts. She falls. She's *falling*.

Chio reaches for her. Etaro is the one who catches her, ey's magic grabbing her out of the air and pulling her back to the rock. And then I see the small black, gray, and white birds pouring out of the cliffside caves.

They swarm and dive, screeching fury. Chio swings his arm, batting a dozen of them out of the air. Three times as many dive past. They plunge toward him with talons extended. Drops of blood fall past my eyes like red snow.

I pull my wards around us like a blanket as Etaro and Tsua shove the birds back, sending them tumbling and squawking.

"Climb!" Tyrroh bellows, fear widening his narrow eyes.

I've spent too long jumping at his commands to stop now.

My shaking, aching hands grip tighter. I drag myself

up another arm length. And another. Another. But each movement is harder to complete. My grip on the stone is getting as shaky as my hold on my wards.

The birds are still swarming, swooping and smashing themselves against my wards. Each strike sends painful rattles through my bones. I have to halt, to hold tighter to the rock. Each blow makes me flinch, almost sends me tumbling backward into open air. It's too much. I can't— I can't hold on *and* keep the wards up, but if I don't, the birds get through, attacking someone else and sending *them* falling, and what if Tsua isn't quick enough to catch them and—

I'm yanked backward, my hold on everything breaking. Screaming, I try to throw my weight forward, to reach anything solid, to keep from plummeting to the rocks below.

But I'm not falling. I'm *flying*.

All of us are rising up the last section of the cliff, shooting up arrow-quick and dropping us onto the flat, solid rock at the top. Solid, *warm* rock.

I hear the thuds of other bodies landing hard on the stone, but I can't open my eyes.

"Chio? *Chio?* Zonna, get over here!" Tsua's voice edges into panic fast.

I open my eyes as Zonna leaps over my head. He slides to a stop beside his parents. "What happened?"

"He won't open his eyes!" Tsua kneels behind Chio, his head in her lap. "The scratches— The birds— It can't be infection, but look!"

By the time I force my wards back into place and push to my knees to crawl closer, Zonna is already leaning over his father and placing his hands on Chio's forehead and chest. "Venom," he says almost immediately. "It's in his blood. The rot-ridden birds must've had it in their talons."

"But it shouldn't— *Nothing* affects us this way. Nothing's

supposed to…" She touches the scratches and gouges in his face, all of them angry and red. "I'm not supposed to be worrying about you, vanafitia."

Chio groans in pain. He's shuddering. Shivering. The longer it lasts, the thinner Zonna's mouth becomes. The harder he seems to press his hands against his father's chest. Zonna is an exceptionally strong hishingu. Chio is immortal, same as Varan, who, stories swear, once survived an arrow straight through his eye. No bird should've been able to hurt him.

"Ahta warned us, didn't ey?" Rai says, collapsing next to me. "The impossible size of the animal ey'd been tracking. Ey said things were strange up here."

"This is more than strange." This is terrifying.

An hour later, Chio shows no signs of getting better. At least it's warmer here; some heat source inside the mountain must be raising the temperature of the stone. Whatever it is, the bone-deep chill and aching numbness in my body begins to ease. It's a warm oasis in a desert of ice and rock, and one that's somehow protected from the worst of the winds. The air is still impossibly cold, and the vicious birds are still circling overhead, but the wind here isn't trying to wipe us off the peak and down the rocky cliff.

It doesn't make sense; there's nothing here. No sign of life or energy aside from the warmth and the stillness. I want to be grateful for the change, but I can't be without some sign of how this cocoon of safety exists, so I ease closer to Miari and ask, "Can you tell why it's warm here?"

"This isn't heat from a source like molten rock." She looks down at the mountain, hands pressed flat to the stone. "But it doesn't feel unsafe."

"You don't sound sure," Tessen says, his eyes on Chio.

"I'm not." Miari lies down on the stone, flat on her back like she's trying to soak up as much of the stone's heat as possible.

I do the same, turning my head so I can watch Zonna work on Chio. The stone's warmth slowly seeps into my body, but I'm still so cold I can't even properly feel fear. But there is something—a buzz coming from somewhere. I'm so tired I can't tell if I'm hearing it or feeling it, but it reminds me of...
"It might be desosa?"

"Maybe. It's stronger here, but..." Tessen shakes his head and collapses next to me on the stone. "I don't know. I can't..."

Miari waves her hand. "If it's desosa, I won't feel it even if it's right under my feet."

"I'm not sure I can feel anything right now," Tessen mutters. "I'm not convinced we're on solid ground yet. I can't feel my fingers." He raises his hands in front of his face. "Why can't I feel my fingers?"

"Because you're cold." I order Rai and Nairo to start a fire, and then I force myself to my feet, moving toward Tyrroh. "What do we do, Nyshin-ma?"

Tyrroh looks up at the birds and down at the inexplicably comfortable stone. Whatever we're looking for isn't here, but we can't do anything until Chio either recovers or...

"Make camp," Tyrroh orders wearily. "We're not going any farther tonight."

CHAPTER
ELEVEN

It takes Chio a full day to heal. I don't want to think about what might've happened if the birds had struck one of *us* instead of an andofume.

That night, we keep the birds at bay, but in the morning, Tsua and Etaro yank several down to the stone; the impact breaks the birds' necks. We don't dare eat the meat if their venom is deadly enough to hurt Chio, but Tessen and Tyrroh wanted to see the animals. They wanted to figure out how the tiny things did so much damage.

The answer is hidden at the base of their fourth toe, a small sac of venom. It's unbelievable that a liquid produced by these small birds in this remote area of Ryogo is somehow strong enough to take out an immortal. It doesn't kill them, but Chio looks shaky for hours after he wakes up. I make sure we extract all of it that we can from the birds. It might save our lives, especially if we can't come up with a better weapon before we face Varan. Before I need to shove him out of the way to get to wherever he's keeping my brother.

The question about the birds turns out to be far easier to

answer than the one about the protected oasis we're in. Even once Tessen has a chance to rest, he can't tell for certain what's protecting and warming this section of the ridge.

"I don't think we'll know for sure until we find whatever's at the end of the trail," Tessen says before we leave the site the morning after Chio is healed.

"Great. One more thing we don't know that might kill us," Rai mutters as we hike the ridge of the mountain, walking single-file along the thin trail and headed east. "That's exactly what we need when we're headed toward another thing we don't understand that could also probably kill us."

"It could, but I don't think it will." But Tessen doesn't seem sure. When I meet his eyes, a question in mine, he explains. "Anything this powerful is going to be dangerous, but it doesn't feel like an enemy, or even like a teegra. I doubt it'll attack or ambush us."

"Until we start messing with it," Rai says. "Which is exactly what we're going to do."

"We won't know until we get there, so save your breath," I order. It's enough for now that Tessen doesn't think it's malicious.

That hope is all we've got to hold on to, because the journey is only the smallest bit easier than the last two days of climbing. Whatever warmed the rock where we'd landed is still here, keeping the worst of the chill away, and the day of forced rest gave me the energy to bring my wards back up. They keep away the birds still circling overhead, and they block the wind that picked back up yesterday afternoon.

For two hours in the middle of the day, a thick, white cloud descends, enshrouding the mountaintop and making it impossible to see more than a foot ahead. Only Tessen keeps us on course. Only Tsua and Etaro keep us from dying when someone misplaces their hands or feet and begins to fall.

It's not much easier when the cloud finally burns away. The path is dangerously narrow at points. For almost a mile, it's nothing more than a ridge too sharp to balance on. Hands wrapped in strips of cloth to protect our skin, we hang off the side of the mountain, sidling along the edge.

"I can't imagine Varan doing this alone," Chio says when we find a place to stop and eat. He looks exhausted, his hand bringing small bites of food to his mouth seemingly on reflex alone as his gaze moves slowly along the horizon. There's nothing but mountains, snow, and sky for miles in any direction. Even the birds are gone; they must've given up on us at some point when we were lost in the cloud.

"He wouldn't have come the way we did, would he? Not from Uraita." Tsua shakes her head. "Although, I doubt coming from the east would've made this journey any easier. *Especially* alone, his skill with rock notwithstanding. I don't know how he did it. Or how chasing the Kaisubeh led him here. He hated those old stories when we were young, said — what was it?"

"That it'd be senseless to pray to a being you don't even believe is capable of listening, and that the old gods, if they ever existed, must have been destroyed by the Kaisubeh." Chio pops one more piece of dried fruit into his mouth and then shakes his head, almost rueful. "He wasn't willing to believe in a god he didn't also believe he could one day become."

Osshi raises his head and looks between them both, but whatever thoughts darken his eyes stay inside his head. In fact, he's been nearly silent since we started this trip into the supposedly impassable mountains. I'd thought it was energy conservation; now I wonder. After all, there's a chance we're heading to a place that will either prove or disprove some of his deepest held beliefs about his Kaisubeh.

I know what it's like to lose a cornerstone of your world. How do I approach him about it now, though? No words could've prepared me for the moment I faced each of Varan's lies, especially not the loss of Ryogo. The promise of that paradise after death was part of what made me fight for each honor I earned in Itagami. I wanted a position on the kaigo council, yes, but that only lasts for years. A decade or two at most. Earning honors in Ryogo was supposed to be forever.

So even though I understand the fear behind Osshi's eyes, and why it looks like anger sometimes, I don't say anything to him about it. Yorri would know how if he were here, but I don't have a clue where to start, and all of us have other things to focus on now.

The faint warmth coming from the mountain keeps the peaks ice-free, making hiking them easier. Everyone is worn down, none of us adapted to the cold or the thin, empty air. We *are* used to pushing through exhaustion, though, so we make miles of progress every day, pushing until it's clear Osshi can't go another step, and the rest of us are considering sleeping with our eyes open.

It isn't until three days after we started hiking the ridge that I feel more than distant flares in the desosa. I feel eddies in the air, like something is disrupting the flow. The closer we get, the stronger those eddies become and the more there are.

And then the ridge gets wider, wide enough that we can easily walk three abreast, and the stone smooths. It's as even and worn as the streets of Itagami, like thousands of feet over thousands of days have eliminated the edges. Or like an ishiji mage created this path.

"This is strange, right?" Sanii asks. "No remote mountain should have a path like this."

"No." Tessen points east of us, toward the horizon. "*That* is strange."

I don't see it right away. Or I do, but my brain refuses to believe my eyes.

There's green in the distance. It's hardly anything, a thin line peeking above gray stone, but it's the first sign of growing life we've seen since we first stepped into snow.

"That doesn't make sense. Anything growing here…" Osshi shakes his head. "We're too high, and it's too rocky here."

"Which is a good sign, isn't it?" My heart beats harder than I can explain away as exertion, hope pushing the rate higher. We didn't know what we were looking for or what to expect, but the impossible might be a good sign that we've found it.

But found what? The waves and flares in the desosa are even clearer now, and it's obvious that the power we're headed toward is not stable. At all. There's no pattern to the eruptions. The cycle isn't even as oddly rhythmic as waves. This seems more like a wounded animal randomly lashing out.

Tsua stiffens, her body leaning in toward the energy. "Chio, vanafitia, can you feel it?"

"Yes." He places his hand on her shoulder, his eyes locked on the line of green. "What the bellows did my brother find?"

"Answers, I think," she replies breathlessly. "To questions only he was foolish enough to ask."

"Should we keep going?" I glance at Tessen and Tyrroh, our two riuku. But only for a second. It's hard to keep my eyes away from that tantalizing line of green on the horizon. It's a rare color on Itagami, especially in this vibrant a shade, but now that color may be where I'll find what I need to help me save Yorri. I've never loved a color more.

"I don't sense danger," Tessen says, and Tyrroh nods agreement. "Nothing malicious."

"It's like walking into a tunnel of cobwebs." Rai shivers, looking at me with wide eyes. "Is this what the desosa feels like to you all the time? Why don't you spend every day itching?"

"This is different. This feels more like how a storm feels." I tilt my head, almost a shrug. Then I take a long breath, trying to force my heartbeat to slow. "Almost. Storms are more constant."

"Keep moving." Tyrroh rubs his hands together and then breathes warm air on his fingers. "We didn't come this far just to stare at the end."

"Then lead on, Nyshin-ten." I nudge Tessen's shoulder with mine, nodding toward the green. "We've got work to do."

After a long, deep breath, Tessen starts walking. I stay a pace behind him, wards up. We move slowly, all of us watchful and wary. It feels like the days my squad hunted Denhitran raiders through the Shiaran mountains, when we knew any moment could turn into a fight. At least then, we knew the capabilities of our enemy.

The path is cracked in places, time and nature leaving gaps we have to jump, but it's easy compared to the first two days of this journey. A mile, two, and then we're finally closing in on the line of green Tessen spotted. Large leaves growing from thick branches block our view of anything beyond the spot where the path dips with the shape of the mountain.

Cautiously, we make our way through the trees, down the path as it winds and twists. The farther we descend, the warmer it gets. Never actually *warm*, but eventually it's enough to help my tense, freezing muscles relax. I don't know if the odd balminess is why trees can grow here, or if the trees are what traps the warmer air. Whatever the cause, plants and trees have overgrown the trail in places, shrouding it in wildly thick greenery. Sometimes we must break through the brush, but we always find the road again.

"I've never seen trees this tall," Osshi says. "I thought maybe the green might be low bushes, but this... This shouldn't be here."

"There also shouldn't be a *road* in the middle of Nentoado." Chio pushes his hood back and looks up at the trees. "I think we should stop expecting anything."

He's right, but I don't know how to follow his advice. I can't keep myself from believing that every step we take is bringing us closer to answers—about Varan, about immortality, and about winning this seemingly impossible war.

As we reach flat land, apparently a long valley, and continue walking along the path, the unexpected keeps appearing. Interspersed between patches of lush, green plantlife are areas of rot and decay. Some sections have simply dried up, everything shriveled and brown, but others...

Some of the patches remind me of the day I found the body of a clansman. He'd drowned in a flash flood, had been left floating in water for days, and then baked in the sun. Parts of the valley remind me of him, all stench and wet and rot.

The sight is a disconcerting shock, and the scent nearly makes me gag. Breathing through my mouth only makes it worse. "If the Kaisubeh live here, they must not have a sense of smell."

"They don't live here." Tsua sounds as dazed as she looks. "I don't think they live anywhere—not the way we think of the word. But that doesn't mean their hands haven't been on this place. I can feel— Blood and rot. What did Varan *do* here?"

Chio simply shakes his head, his eyes unnaturally wide. It's Tessen who says, "I don't know what this is, but we're almost at its center. Another hundred yards. Maybe less."

Far less. In a way, I think we're already there.

Power is everywhere. The ground practically vibrates with it. The air is tangible in a way I've never felt before, like it's full of tiny pieces of fluff and grains of sand. I swear I can *hear* the trees growing, and the scents—stone and trees and the tangs of cold and electricity—are noticeably strong. It's nearly overwhelming, and it must be so much worse for Tessen.

The ground begins to rise again, a gentle slope that brings us away from loose ground and back to rock. With each foot we rise, the trees get farther apart until, finally, we break free of them entirely. Ahead is a rocky clearing. The surface is cracked, almost splintered like the stone was dropped, and there's a shifting white light bleeding through.

"The light's moving in time with the desosa's waves." Tessen seems mesmerized, his gaze following the light. "I've never seen anything like this. What is this place?"

"This is Kaisuama. It has to be." I take one more step into the clearing, avoiding the glowing cracks. "But what do we do now?"

Stretching her arm out, Tsua shifts her hand like she's testing something in the air. "If we're right about how Varan made this susuji powerful enough to alter us permanently, all we should need to do is rebrew it and infuse it with power from this source, but…"

"This is more energy than we expected," Chio finishes. "And it's less stable."

"Would Varan have used it if it was like this?" If he could sense the fluctuations in this desosa, and if he didn't have imminent danger forcing him into action, it's hard to imagine him—or anyone else—seeing this as an acceptable risk.

"I don't think it was like this." Tessen crouches down, hand pressed to the cracked stone, and his voice is shaking as much as his hand. "Something's wrong here. Broken. This isn't what it's supposed to feel like."

Crouching next to him, I put my hand between his shoulders. "How do you know?"

"Because it *hurts*. It's too loud and too bright and too much." He shudders, swallows, and looks up at me. "Something went wrong. It's like there was a river of desosa here once, but Varan dropped a boulder in it, and the energy has been battering against it ever since, trying to find the path it was meant to take."

"But we— We need to know how—" I bite my tongue, forcing myself to breathe before I speak again. "So what do we do?"

"Maybe we should test it on something we know first?" Etaro suggests uncertainly.

Rai looks skeptical. "Like what?"

"I don't know," Etaro admits. Just as Sanii says, "What about a wardstone?"

Most of the squad looks at Sanii, but Sanii is looking at me. "You've already proven you can handle drawing in power from a lightning storm, and we know you have more than enough skill to create a wardstone." Ey pauses, and then adds, "Plus, if doing this does enhance magic that much, it wouldn't hurt to have a bunch of overcharged wardstones."

Those would definitely come in handy. Especially when we eventually face the bobasu. "But this isn't a lightning storm. This is… I don't know how to approach this kind of power."

"Maybe that's where the road and the valley came from." Tessen looks back the way we came. "Maybe Varan realized the same thing and tested himself by reshaping the mountain. It was a skill he knew, and he could start small. Work his way up."

"It makes sense. Varan may have chased the impossible, but he wasn't reckless. Not with his life." Chio looks down at the broken, glowing stone of the clearing and then up at the trees. "That kind of testing would explain why he was so burned out when he came out of the mountains."

"Do you think you can do it, Khya?" Tsua's expression an odd combination of concern and determination.

"I have no idea." I had to hide in caves under Itagami to

create these wardstones in the first place. It had drained me dangerously low to make more than two or three in a day, but I'm stronger now. I've learned how to funnel desosa through myself better. And Natani is here to help channel the power if I need him to. I can do this. I *have* to do this. "I'll try."

I move to start now, but Tyrroh shakes his head. "Tomorrow. I doubt we have to worry about enemies or wind here, so release your wards and rest. You're not messing with whatever this is fresh off three days of travel."

Although instinct pushes me to argue, he's right. The day of rest I'd had while Chio healed wasn't enough. I'm tired, drained, aching, and still too cold. Playing with the Kaisuama's energy in this state would be dangerous. And potentially deadly.

But even when I step onto the cracked, glowing stone the next day, after two actual meals and more than twelve hours of sleep, it doesn't feel any safer. This feels like standing on the north wall of Itagami in the middle of a storm, hoping I'm strong enough to keep my feet on solid stone while the blasting wind tries to knock me into open air.

"Will you stay nearby?" I ask Natani, hoping I don't look as nervous as I feel. "I might need someone to bolster me against this."

"Of course." Natani moves to be within arm's reach of me.

Tessen is already that close, and he holds out his hand until I take it. Then, lifting my hand, he presses a kiss to the inside of my wrist and whispers, "Be careful, Khya. Please."

"I promise." No way am I dying here. Not for an over-powered wardstone.

Once I have the wardstone set in the center of the clearing and everyone but Natani pushed back to the trees circling us, I close my eyes and concentrate on the impossibly deep well of desosa undulating under our feet. I approach it cautiously, like it's a hungry teegra I'm trying not to disturb, and I only reach for the thinnest of threads. Even if I can use that to power the wardstone, it's ten times more power than what I'd been able to store inside it before.

Then the energy sparks. Tessen shouts my name.

It's too late. The spark creates another, creates another, creates another. A chain of bright lights building in seconds until the whole thing seems to *explode.*

The shockwave blows us off our feet.

I fly back, flailing for anything solid to hold on to. The ground finds me first. I land hard, my head smacking against the stone. Vision blurred and doubled, I try to move. Where's Tessen? Natani? I need to find—

A hand on my shoulder keeps me down. I can't see who it is.

"Tessen! She's here," Sanii calls. Seconds later, more hands join the first, one of them holding me down and the other moving constantly, touching my head, my arm, my chest.

"Khya? Open your eyes. Can you open your eyes?" Tessen sounds frantic. I try to do what he wants.

My eyelids won't move at first. When they do, all I can see is white, like the desosa is all that's left in the world. I blink and breathe, fighting through the haze.

The mountain slowly comes back into focus. My gaze jumps, landing on one thing barely long enough to register it before moving on to the next. Trees shaking and swaying in a wind I don't feel. Chunks of gray rock broken and scattered across the clearing. Wehli screaming, blood gushing from what's left of his arm.

"No. No!" I roll to my knees, trying to get closer. I should have been able to stop this. My wards should have been up and I should have—

"Khya, stop. Stop." Tessen wraps his arms around my waist,

holding me back. "Let Zonna work on him, and you need—Please, Khya. You're still bleeding. Stop moving. You need to stay still until Zonna can heal this."

"No, I can't— How did that—?"

"Wehli pushed Natani out of the way." Tessen inexorably draws me back down to the stone. "The wave knocked even the andofume sideways and blasted across the valley. It did a lot of damage." He holds me tighter; I'm not the only one shaking and unsteady.

"Are you hurt?" Twisting, I search what I can see of him for injuries. There's a scratch on his face and blood seeping through a cut on his shoulder where something sliced through all his layers of cloth and skin. He must know I see them, but he shakes his head and insists he's fine.

When I glare, he adds, "Nothing deadly. Nothing that won't heal on its own."

"What about the others?" I hear voices, but my vision is still foggy. Focusing on anything farther away than Tessen's face isn't easy.

"Scratches. Bruises. A few concussions. Maybe a broken leg." He closes his eyes and rests his forehead against mine, the tremor running through his muscles getting stronger. "Blood and rot, Khya. I thought— The flare hit so fast I couldn't *warn* you, and then you— It was like you just vanished. You flew back so fast, and I thought—"

"Shhh, I'll be fine." I try to massage the back of his neck to loosen the tension I feel there, but I can't get enough pressure behind my fingers. All I can do is rub soft circles on his skin. That, and the disbelieving look he shoots me, are solid signs I'm not as fine as I wish I was. Exhaling, I say, "I know, but as soon as my head stops hurting, I'll be fine. Wehli…"

I can't hear his screams anymore. Why can't I hear him?

"Zonna is with him, and the worst of the pain is gone, but

Zonna couldn't—" Lips pursed, Tessen glances across the clearing and quickly away. "Wehli's going to lose most of his arm. It was too badly crushed by the rock for even Zonna to save it."

The news is like another blast, one that sends me deeper into my own mind.

My fault. My mistake. If I had been better or faster, I could have saved him. All of us. Yorri. I'm supposed to be the strongest fykina mage in memory, but what good is that when I can't use it to protect the people I care about?

The world blurs again, and my own blood rushing through my veins drowns out Tessen's voice. I can feel him, though, and so I let myself use him as an anchor, something solid to hold me in consciousness until Zonna can leave Wehli's side and help those with less important injuries. But even after Zonna's cool, familiar magic seeps under my skin and erases the worst of my symptoms, the thoughts are still there, chasing each other in endless circles that get tighter, finally becoming one massive fear.

You're going to fail everyone who came here with you, and it won't even matter. Yorri and everyone else you abandoned is probably already lost and gone.

But no. I won't. Once I prove to Tessen and myself I'm well enough to eat something and keep it down, I check on Wehli—asleep with Miari and Nairo guarding him. Then, I head deeper into the trees. Surprisingly, though Tessen's gaze tracks my movements, he doesn't follow me. Then again, the only dangers here are ones we create. We're not even setting a watch. There's no one in these mountains to watch for.

When I reach an outcropping of rock cutting through the trees, I climb on top of a large, flat stone. I sit with my back against a tree trunk and pull my knees to my chest. Eyes closed, I tilt my head back and focus on the sound of the trees and the feel of the energy that so hated being poked at. I try *not* to listen to my growing fear. It's hard to convince myself that Varan doesn't already know how to undo the immortality he created. I can't believe whatever reason he had to keep Yorri and the other prisoners alive still matters. It's too easy to picture Varan wiping out Ryzo and the rest of my squad just on the *chance* of them knowing too much.

It's been almost two full moons since we fled Shiara. So much could have happened there, and our time in Ryogo has been fruitless at best. Far worse than that for Wehli.

Because I couldn't protect him.

"It's not like you to run away from things, Khya." Sanii's words jolt me out of my head.

I take a sharp breath, looking down at em from my perch and hoping my face doesn't give away my thoughts. "This looks like running to you?"

"A form of it." Ey climbs up, then sits across from me, eir expression placid. "Wehli woke up for a few minutes. I'm sure he'll be fine. He laughed when Miari made a joke about being glad we weren't in Itagami anymore because at least here he wouldn't be demoted—there isn't anywhere to go."

Bellows, that's true. The kind of debilitating injury he has is one of the only ways a nyshin can drop an entire class, be shoved back from the front lines and the wilds of Shiara to become an ahdo guarding the city. "He won't have that option here; there's no walled-off haven we can use to keep him safe. Unless we left him with Ahta and Dai-Usho until we were ready to leave, and I can't imagine he'd let us."

"Don't even suggest it," Sanii warns. "Realizing he wasn't going to be shunted out of the position he earned seemed like the only thing that made him smile."

"Not like it matters. I don't have the power to order anyone anywhere." I knock a small chip of stone off the side of our seat. "What do you want, Sanii?"

Ey shifts closer. The silence stretches longer and longer until I'm about to drop to the ground and leave. Then ey says, "Tessen said you're beating yourself up about Wehli and Yorri and anything else you can find to blame yourself for."

"Well, if *he* says it it must be true," I mutter sarcastically.

"When it comes to you? Probably." Sanii puts eir hand on the rock between us, palm up, an offering I don't take. "We knew the desosa here was dangerous before you touched it. Wehli knew. He's injured because he's Itagamin, not because of you. He put himself in danger to save a clansman. If Wehli hadn't acted, we would've lost Natani—the rock would've broken his neck."

"But I should've been able to—"

"Work your usual magic while flying through the air from a blast that left you with a concussion?" Sanii looks at me, affection and exasperation in eir large eyes. "You really do have an impossibly large sense of responsibility for the world, don't you?"

I swallow, looking down and tracing shapes on the rock. "Yorri always thought so."

And I should've listened to him, because look where my responsibility has gotten us.

"What do you know about the bond, Khya?" Sanii asks, almost too low to hear.

"The sumai?" It takes me a moment to remember the stories I've heard about soulbonded partners. And it was usually only stories, rumors, and general knowledge—no one teaches the full truth until you request approval for a sumai. "Mostly what everyone knows—that you're connected so deeply one can feel the loss of the other and— Oh."

"Exactly. There's so much more to it, but if you're only going to remember one thing about the bond, remember

that. As long as I'm standing and whole, Yorri is alive." Ey
smiles grimly, eir large mouth twisted. "The day I drop to the
ground and start begging you to let me die is the day you'll
know we've lost."

"But I've never— " My words trip on my tongue, the relief
of Sanii's revelation making me lightheaded. "I knew that, but
sumai pairs are always on the same squad and on the same
duty shifts, so I didn't know— You can still feel it? Even when
we're so far away?"

"I think when you're talking about souls bound by the
desosa, there's no such thing as too far." Sanii shrugs. "I
hope that's true, anyway. I'm choosing to believe it until
circumstance proves me wrong, because I can't feel much,
but I'm sure he's alive."

I close my eyes and take a long breath. "Thank you."

"You're welcome." Ey doesn't speak again until I open my
eyes, then ey gestures to my niadagu cord. "Show me what
you're doing with this. Maybe I can help figure out what's
going wrong. After we go back, though. Wehli will want to
see you when he wakes up again."

Breathing easier, I nod and follow Sanii back to the camp.
But Tessen stops us on our way back, deep furrows marring
his forehead. "You need to see something."

He leads us east through the trees, only taking us a
hundred yards or so before he points at a group of trees. I
look, but... "I don't have your senses, Tessen."

"Those were rotten and dying when we arrived. And
these..." He heads right, and the closer we get to the edge
of the valley, the fouler the air surrounding us smells. "These
were healthy and thriving yesterday."

They're definitely not now. All the trunks are cracked
open, the cores empty and rotten, and only a few yellow-
brown leaves cling to the branches above. The plants covering

the ground are decaying into putrid muck.

I cover my mouth and nose with the atakafu. It barely helps filter out the smell. "What happened?"

"The power flares, I think," Tessen slowly says. "We knew plant growth like this should be as impossible as it is on Shiara, which means it's probably able to grow because the katsujo's power is so close to the surface here, right?"

"That's what we guessed." I poke the edge of one of the tree's hollows. The wood crumbles under my finger. "You think that if the power is why there's life here, the flares are what kills parts of it? Too much or too little in certain spots?"

"Exactly. But Khya..." Tessen tilts his head back, the lines of worry on his face getting deeper. "It's no wonder trying to use the katsujo went wrong. Look at what it's capable of doing to the land in a single day."

"Bellows, Khya." Sanii rubs eir hand over eir mouth. "If that's true..."

We run back to the camp and explain what Tessen found to the others. It doesn't help us find a solution, but it does show us the kind of force we're up against and proves we might have gotten away with less loss than we should've expected. Knowing that doesn't ease any of my guilt about Wehli's injury. I need to find a way to make sure nothing happens to anyone else.

For the next several hours, we're either helping Miari and Nairo care for Wehli or we're working, and each minute is another that proves my brother's soul chose well.

Sanii, especially as the bitterness of eir placement as yonin ebbs further into the past, is insightful, determined, and incredibly quick-minded. It's so clear how ey would've both supported and challenged Yorri's intellect, even though I've never known them as a pair.

But under it all, I know we're going to have to try again.

The reason we risked the trek out here hasn't changed, and so even while I work with Sanii, I let the desosa in the clearing seep into my body, trying to adjust to the unpredictable ebb and flow of it and the way it can switch from stinging to soothing in instant-quick flashes.

Tessen was right—something is broken here. But how the bellows are we supposed to change that? The Kaisubeh, if they exist, clearly haven't fixed what Varan broke, so we might have to find a way to work with what's here. And I *will* find a way. Until then, maybe, if I can learn the pulse of Kaisuama, my next attempt to use its power won't end like the first.

CHAPTER TWELVE

"What if it's a katsujo?" Osshi's question is hesitant, like even he doesn't think he's right. But Tsua pauses and looks at him with curiosity. "I don't know what that is."

"My father… I began studying our history because of him," Osshi explains. "When I was young he told me the ancient stories, and one was about how the Kaisubeh built the world. It was said that they poured their own blood into their creation, and it fed the soil and gave life to the animals. The story claims the rivers formed from the channels the Kaisubeh's blood ran, and that traces of their power are still in all water, but nothing I've seen has ever made me think that's true. This, though," he says, gesturing to the clearing.

I turn that over in my mind, trying to fit it into the other stories Lo'a told us and what we've learned here so far as Zonna traces a glowing crack in the clearing. Nodding slowly, he says, "So they thought the rivers were the veins of the world. That's clearly wrong, but maybe they were only wrong about the leftover power being in the riverbeds. And what happened here is… Well, if the land were a person, and this is a vein, and what Varan did to it would be like leaving someone to slowly bleed to death."

"I—yes. Maybe." Osshi runs his fingers through his long hair. "*If* what my father told me has any truth to it."

"Clearly, it does," Sanii says absently, eir gaze distant.

"Only in that it exists," I protest. "It's here, but that doesn't mean it has anything to do with the Kaisubeh." Really, the only thing I've seen that makes me think they might be real is Imaku and the effect that rock has on immortals.

If Sanii hears me, ey doesn't respond. But then ey blinks, sharply focused on me. "You used your wards to pass through Suzu's. Can you do the opposite here?"

"I don't understand." What would the opposite even be?

"Don't think of it like a vein, think of it like a river." Sanii's eyes kindle with excitement, the expression so reminiscent of Yorri in a moment of epiphany it's almost painful. "The Ryogans think of the desosa like a river and a spell its banks, right? Well, it sounds like Varan blocked the flow and forced this river to flood. The banks have been crumbling, but that doesn't mean they can't be rebuilt after the barricade is removed."

"You…you think I should create a ward around this valley to seal in the desosa?" Even as I question it, my mind is spinning, trying to figure out how to make the idea work. "I don't have enough wardstones, and even if I did, we're back to the problem of removing whatever magic Varan worked that caused this. I'm *not* capable of—"

"You are. And removing the block is what we should be worried about." Tsua is looking toward the clearing and the rolling, glowing energy seeping through the cracked stone. "You're right that your wardstones won't be enough to contain this for long, so what if, instead of using them as a cage, you used them as a guide to give the katsujo's desosa a new purpose? There's enough power here to fuel anything you create for centuries or more."

And both Tsua and Lo'a have taught me enough to make me realize the crystals we mined on Shiara aren't the only material that can store energy. "This desosa didn't even like me trying to do something as small as a wardstone. You think it'll like me ordering it into an entirely new shape?"

"It's not a new shape, though," Sanii insists. "You're not trying to make it do something new, you'd be giving it a way to return to how it's supposed to be. Like removing a dam."

"That's…" I blink, looking between their faces. And everyone else's. *Everyone* is watching me expectantly. "You think I can do this? Tsua would be so much better at it."

"I can help you," she says, nodding, "but no one I've ever seen—not in centuries—has your skill shaping the desosa. You've used it in ways far beyond what we thought fykinas could do, and so yes, Khya. I *do* think you can do this."

"But…" I glance at Wehli, whose right arm now ends a few inches below his shoulder. He's physically healed, but will be mentally reeling for a long time. How can he of all people look at me without doubt? "Okay, but even if we can fix the katsujo, or whatever Osshi called it, what's next? We still need to figure out how to kill an immortal. And we won't know for sure if it works until we try it against him."

"We'll know, because we'll test whatever we create on us."

My pulse jumps. "No we will *not*."

"There isn't another option, Khya." Tsua's smiling gently. Reassuringly. But…

She can't be serious. "Putting aside the fact that this will kill you if it works, which should— No, don't put that aside. If you die, not only will we lose everything you know and your ties to the clans on Shiara, we'll lose the only people with a chance of defeating the bobasu in any kind of fight. How can you ask us to allow that?"

"Because being sure of the effectiveness of the weapon is more important," Tsua says, still gentle. "Chio, Zonna, and I might be able to stand against Varan in combat, but that's all we could do, Khya—stand against him. Long enough for the rest of you to get away, maybe, but not forever. Definitely not long enough to win. We'd simply delay defeat a while."

"And Varan has seven more bobasu on his side than we do," Zonna reminds me. As if I could forget. "We won't win unless we can make them as mortal as you are."

Zonna looks at Tsua, uncomfortable but seemingly resolute.

"All of you, though?" I swallow, making myself hold Tsua's gaze. "You're asking me to kill all three of you?"

"No," she says. "I'm asking you to accept that this is necessary. When we have something ready, we'll do it ourselves."

"But if it works you'll *die*." And since Ryogo obviously isn't the afterlife Varan told us it was, what will death send them to?

Still smiling gently, Tsua shakes her head. "We've seen so many generations come into life and leave it that we stopped counting. We watched the elements change the shape of Shiara over eons and seen the animals evolve to better survive. After more than five hundred years, we don't fear death, even if only nothingness follows."

"And you're not asking us to do this, we're offering," Chio adds. "I should've stopped Varan before he went on his mad quest for immortality. I made a mistake, and countless people have paid for it. This is a chance to help you succeed where I failed. Don't tell me I'm not allowed, child."

Sacrifice, when it's made with purpose and for the good of the clan, is a noble and honorable act. To sacrifice your life for those you're charged with protecting will earn you rewards in this life and the next.

I've heard the lesson my whole life. The part about honors in the afterlife might not be true, but the ideal is deeply buried in my heart. I can't deny someone else their choice.

Besides, there's no way I could stop them. Even if I trapped them in a warded room, what would any of us gain? Rebuilding the banks of the katsujo under our feet is asking me to knowingly take us a step closer to watching them die. Still, I know I can't—and won't—refuse.

So instead of focusing on what I can't change, I spend the next three days preparing, especially testing the reactions of the desosa at different times and at varying points in its tidal cycle. It doesn't react when I use my powers within the clearing, without drawing on the Kaisuama's latent desosa. It flares and shifts when I test the edges of the energy, not trying to use it, just touching the frayed ends. When I approach the buried desosa with *intent*, it surges.

It really is like a wounded teegra. All it wants is to stop hurting and to be left alone. Since we can't do the latter, hopefully finding a way to help with the former will be enough to keep the vein of power from extracting too much more flesh and blood from us.

Even with everything I've learned about the katsujo, we try to find a way to protect me from another energy blast. Tsua, Zonna, and Chio assure me they'll stay by my side to help, and the others promise they'll be well out of the way, but it's hard to imagine our second attempt going much better than the first.

But here I am, sitting at the edge of the clearing and wearing every wardstone we have left. The andofume are arranged behind me, and the rest of the squad is about to leave the valley, ordered by Tyrroh up to the path we used to traverse the ridge.

Tessen holds out his hand, taking mine and pulling me against his chest as soon as I close my fingers around his. "I wish I could tell you to stop getting yourself into situations like this."

"Situations like what?" I wrap my arms around his waist.

"Where the chances are too high you might not make it out." He turns his face toward my throat, almost hiding against me. "You wouldn't be you if you weren't always taking too many risks, but bellows, Khya. I hate watching you face them."

"I'll be as careful as I can be." I'm just not sure what a promise like that means today. There's only so much control I have over what's about to happen.

"You'd better be." His hold on me tightens as he lifts his head, and the kiss he plants on my lips is hard and sharp. Then he cups my face and kisses me again, this time softer, gentle and much more like a promise than a goodbye.

Tyrroh orders the squad's retreat as soon as Tessen steps away from me. Sanii, Rai, and the others nod or wave or wink as I watch them sling their packs over their shoulders and disappear into the trees. Only after they're well out of sight do I turn to the stone clearing.

"Think of it like shaping clay," Tsua advised yesterday. "You're not altering the material, you're only giving it a shape better suited to your needs. And its own."

It makes sense in theory, but this isn't clay. This is like lightning, and even those with the power to create sparks of lightning can't do more than give it fleeting shape and direction. I have to find a way to make lightning act as both thread and needle, and then use it to close a wound.

I breathe in deep cycles until my head feels airy, close my eyes, and reach for the power roiling under us. Once I'm sure the others are safely away, I begin.

I don't pull or even grab; instead, I let myself sink into

the waves of energy. They engulf me, spin me, toss me around. It's dizzying. I almost open my eyes just to give myself a point of reference, but I remember Tsua's warning. I'm in this now. There's no coming out of here until I finish my mission. Or perish attempting it.

My physical hands are pressed against the cracked gray stone of the clearing, but it's like I've been split in two—I feel the stone under my palms even as I watch myself from far below that surface. The shock at seeing *myself* is small, barely a flicker in my mind; relief is stronger. There I am. Clearly fine. Whatever's happening to my senses, *I* am fine.

I settle into this strange separation and focus on the pattern in the chaos. I find edges. Beginnings. Fissures. Ends. Eventually I find enough pieces to see the true scope of the katsujo, what it once was and where Varan broke through, splintering the power in ways it couldn't fix. But that doesn't mean it's not fixable.

An idea slowly forms, one that'll take time. And I'll have to split myself further.

Sensation gets stronger—the cold air on my face, the prickling pain of the overexcited desosa against my mind, the smooth stone under my hands, the dizzy giddiness of feeling as though I'm made entirely of magic.

Above, using only the energy from within myself, I add weight to the press of my hands against the stone, spreading a web of ward lines through the broken rock. Usually I'm careful to weave my magic into something solid—what's the point of a ward with holes in it? Now I leave spaces and hope the desosa inside the katsujo won't notice the trap closing until it's too late.

Below, I distract. Poke. Push. Prod. Pull. Move the katsujo's energy away from the surface and back toward the lines it was meant to travel. It lazily struggles at first, moving like water to flood the places I'm not guarding, and then my net reaches the opposite end of the clearing, a bandage covering the worst of the katsujo's wound. I latch the end of my ward to the opposite side of the clearing just as the katsujo's energy brushes the web.

Then it *screams*. It rails and flares, slamming me up and trapping me between the ward and the fire of the katsujo. The desosa flattens me, crushing me so tight against the webbing of my ward I feel it slicing me into pieces. I lose my physical self, lose the feel of the rock and the cold and—

Pressure on my shoulder. Holding me together, reminding me where I am outside the katsujo, and giving me space to *think*.

I absorbed the katsujo's desosa to keep it from attacking me at first, but it isn't me. The web is; I created it out of the energy that rises inside me. It *is* me, and I can always shape my own magic. Which means I can pass through without losing pieces of myself, using it like a screen to help me leave behind what I picked up inside the katsujo. Most of it, at least.

I carry a single thread of the katsujo through the gap, quickly wrapping it around and through my ward web. Give it purpose, Tsua told me, so that's what I do. The katsujo's energy latches onto the frame I created, filling in the holes and merging my magic and its own until I feel something inside me *release*. A knot tied off. A breath exhaled. A mission finished.

But the release leaves me detached and drifting. The connection to my body feels frayed, distant, unimportant, but there's a whisper telling me to fight.

Claw your way back to the world if you have to. You promised too much to too many people to fail now. Fight, *Khya.*

This time, though, a promise isn't enough. Neither is focusing on the memory of rock under my palms and cold on my skin and weight on my shoulders and voices in my ears.

They're not enough to help me find reality again. And I can't hold on to anything solid when I'm made of smoke and light.

No matter what I try to grab, my hands pass through it. And every time I miss a hold, I spin and float higher. The farther away from the top of the mountain, the thinner the connection between the two halves of myself gets. And the more remote my panic feels. The easier it becomes to forget why getting back down to the rocks below matters.

Everything is so hard down there. Above, existing is as easy as breathing. Easier. Like this, life, breath, and magic are all one, and all I have to do to join them is cut the last cord holding me to the land.

But the anchor I still have is the voices. The voices I latch on to are whispering about people, and their familiarity sparks memories. Tessen's warm hands on my thighs on the floor of those cold caves. Zonna hesitantly telling me Varan's secrets at the railing of Kazu's ship. Sanii coming to see me once the ship was away from Shiara, forgiving me for failing Yorri when I couldn't forgive myself. Rai and Etaro smirking as they corner me in Itagami, demanding details about my relationship with Tessen. Yorri sitting behind me in the crevice we'd claimed for ourselves, his fingers weaving my hair into intricate braids.

I hold onto the memories and the voices, and I drag myself back. Inch by inch. The closer I get, the darker it becomes, the world fading out at the edges to darkness barely sparked with veins of red. It gets warmer. And closer. Closer until I'm sinking into myself, realigning and resettling.

When I open my eyes, I have to blink. It's solidly dark until my eyes adjust.

Stars spill across the sky like shining shards of crystal. The moon hangs large and low on the eastern horizon, barely risen over the peaks of the mountain. Tsua is kneeling in front of me, her eyes locked on my face, and she's talking, but I don't think the words are meant for me.

"No, bringing Tessen down here won't help anything," Zonna insists. "She's physically fine. Give her another few minutes to come back to herself."

They're worried. About me? They're talking like I passed out.

I'm okay. I didn't hear the words, and they don't respond. I try again. And again. Only after I force a breath that expands my lungs until they hurt do I make sounds.

"Khya, oh thank the Kaisubeh." Tsua cups my face, tears in her eyes. "Are you hurt?"

"Hungry." My stomach is so empty it feels hollow. As soon as they hand me something, I devour it, barely chewing. Otherwise, I think I really am fine. The more I eat, the deeper I sink into my own skin, remembering what it's like to order muscle and bone to move. By the time my stomach can't hold another bite, I feel normal. My head feels clearer, and I finally remember the question I wanted to ask. "What can you sense from the katsujo?"

Chio looks at me, something like wonder in his narrow eyes. "It feels… Not quite fixed. Patched. But we haven't tried to use it. We wanted you back first."

"I wasn't gone." Between pulling the two halves of myself together and opening my eyes, it feels like only seconds elapsed.

"You seemed to be." Tsua hands me a canteen of water, and I swallow deep.

"How long did it all take?" It was maybe midmorning when we started, and it's fully night now.

"At least ten hours." Tsua glances at the center of the clearing. The stone is still cracked, but the white light shining through those spaces is steady now, no longer undulating with the chaos of the desosa underneath. "It's like you taught it how to protect itself."

"Hopefully I didn't teach it too well." I stand, my aching body protesting each motion. My first steps wobble. I quickly regain my balance and continue toward the clearing. "You've got to be able to use it to power the susuji—and whatever we come up with to kill Varan."

"Exactly, but tomorrow we can— Khya?" Zonna's voice sharpens with concern.

I step back from the wardstone I placed in the center, admiring how the glow from underneath illuminates the clear, multi-faceted stone. "Tomorrow, everyone will be back. We'll have to send them away again to test this."

"No!" Chio jumps in front of me, the lines around his eyes dug deep. "You've been working magic for hours. Rest first, Khya. This can wait."

"I don't need to sleep." His expression tightens, and he opens his mouth; I break in. "I don't know if creating the wardstones on Shiara increased my stamina, or if the katsujo refueled me as fast as it drained me, but I really am fine. I promise."

Chio looks over my shoulder, silently conversing with Tsua and Zonna.

"After everything we've been through, I wouldn't risk it all now," I remind him. "Not for this. If it seems like it won't work, I'll stop. I know the energy of this place pretty well."

Exhaling heavily and shaking his head—either in frustration or resignation—Chio backs away so I can work.

But it's barely work. The desosa jumps like a well-trained soldier, rising so fast and with so much power that it flares in my mind like a wall of fire. I guide the energy into the crystal until it's filled to bursting. The instant I release the desosa, the power drops away, sinking obediently into the ground.

Heartened and exhilarated, I remove the wardstones I'm wearing, placing them on the clearing and then quickly and easily recharging *all* of them. Simultaneously.

"Blood and rot." I laugh, picking one of the stones up and reveling in the buzz of magic inside. "It took me more than a *week* to make these the first time. This is incredible."

It took far less time, didn't drain me *at all*, and left me with wardstones far more powerful than anything I've ever created. Or anything I have ever been *capable* of creating.

"I want to try one more thing before we bring the others down," I say when Chio seems about to leave. He raises one thin eyebrow, but waves his hand, gesturing for me to carry on.

When Sanii and I worked on the niadagu spell before, ey helped me understand what I was doing wrong. Essentially, I'd been approaching the red cord the same way I did the crystals I created wardstones from, trying to force energy inside the material. Wrapping the desosa *around* it instead was the first step to mastering this spell. Now, I tie one of the niadagu cords around a small rock. With this much extra desosa under my feet, I want to see if I can take step two—giving the cord the power to bind something to a specific place. I'm starting small, trying to attach this rock to the clearing.

The desosa wraps itself around the niadagu cord as willingly as water following a path cut in stone. It winds and latches and when I whisper the spell words, "Tozaiko nitoko," it *holds*. When I take a breath and try to move the rock, nothing happens. It won't budge.

Laughing, I leave the red-wrapped stone behind and pick up one of my wardstones. With two successes after so many failures, it's easy for hope to grow wild and unchecked. Hope that recreating Varan's susuji, developing a way to undo it, getting back to Shiara, finding Yorri, and defeating the bobasu will all be as easy as this was.

I don't *believe* it, but for this moment, I do hope.

...

For two days, no one has let me do anything but rest, at least where my magic is concerned, so I've had plenty of time to watch the andofume work on the susuji. Sanii and I sit a few feet away from the fire Tsua and Chio hung the pot over. It's been simmering since I fixed the break in the katsujo, and the andofume haven't had to do more than nudge the flow of energy to keep it pouring into the susuji. And that power is amazingly strong.

Feeling them work with the katsujo's desosa, I realize something. All the energy I've ever worked with has felt a little like something else. I know when I'm drawing desosa from a storm or from the desert sun or from Natani. It's not *just* desosa, it carries some small part of the source, too. This, though…this doesn't feel like anything or anyone else. If this desosa has a source, it has to be the well of energy all desosa comes from because this is pure. It might be as close as is possible to touching the hand of the Kaisubeh. Which is exactly what Chio said we'd need to push the susuji from a powerful healing spell to a liquid capable of creating immortality.

Well before it's finished, I can feel the difference between this version and the previous. It smells more strongly of magic—that crisp, pure scent that rose from the last one—and the glow, more silver-white than purple now, is brighter.

Only Sanii and I have been entirely devoted to the susuji. Miari and Nairo have been running drills with Wehli, trying to help him learn how to regain his balance without the weight of his arm. Tessen is sitting nearby, eyes closed as he studies the katsujo; he's been fascinated with what I did to it and how it changed. Everyone else has, too, but in different ways.

Like Rai, who's been trying to see exactly how high she can shoot a flare of fire with the boost the katsujo gives her. Now, as though she can sense we're about to take the next step, Rai stops playing with her flames and comes to peer over our shoulders.

"You can still change your mind." Rai kicks a small stone toward Sanii.

"No, I can't." Legs pulled into eir chest, ey rests eir chin on eir knees. "The possibility of forever is worth the risk."

I don't look at Tessen, but I wonder what he thinks about the sumai. About the possibility of forever. I'm not going to *ask*, but I wonder. The permanence of it always frightened me; Tessen is braver than I am in a lot of ways. It's not inconceivable this might be one of them.

A few hours later, not long after dinner—and thank the katsujo for the plants growing here or we might've run out of food—Tsua calls out to Sanii. "It's ready. Are you, Sanii?"

"Ey's already the first yonin to rise out of eir class, but ey's an overachiever," Rai says. "Ey couldn't be happy with just being a nyshin. No. Miriseh or nothing for our littlest ebet."

I hold my breath. Will Sanii snap back? All ey does is roll eir eyes and mutter, "Only because it means I'll automatically outrank *you*."

Rai laughs, and she's still laughing as Tsua fills a cup with the glowing susuji. When Tsua offers that metal cup to Sanii, though, Rai stills.

The wardstones proved the katsujo was safe to use, but this is the true test. What happens after Sanii drinks this will tell us if we wasted our time coming up here or not. Maybe we're one mission closer to killing Varan. And stopping a war. And finding my brother.

Sanii closes eir eyes and downs the cup, tipping eir head back to force the liquid down eir throat. From the way ey cringes, I'm guessing it still looks and smells far better than it tastes.

The effects hit faster. Within minutes, ey's eyes are drooping. Before half an hour is gone, ey's sweating despite the cold. By the end of the hour, ey's groaning but insensate. When the sun peeks over the eastern horizon, I stop worrying the susuji won't either work or fail—I start fearing it might kill em.

Sanii suffers shaking, sweating, and absolute agony for four days. Longer. Nearly one hundred hours of watching em deteriorate makes me hate myself for letting em do this. Even though ey asked for it. And even though ey probably would've punched me if I'd tried to talk em out of it. But, blood and rot, I wish I had tried.

Eventually, it ends. Sanii subsides, unconscious but looking more like ey's sleeping than fighting off the stranglehold of death. We keep watch, rotating in shifts to make sure ey's never alone. Twelve hours after ey settled into sleep, eir large eyes flutter open.

Eir gaze immediately focuses on my face, and ey smiles as ey takes a deep breath and sits up. The motion is smooth, no signs of pain or hesitation. Without a word, I hand em an anto, hilt first. Ey doesn't lose eir smile as ey takes the dagger, adjusts eir hold on the blade, and draws it along the inside of eir forearm. Blood wells from the thin, deep cut.

By the time ey switches the anto for a piece of cloth torn from a tunic, the bleeding has slowed. By the time the blood is wiped away to see the cut itself again, the wound is half healed. By the time I laugh, relief allowing the sound to burst out, only the bloodstains on the cloth would ever prove ey'd been injured.

"It worked." Sanii's words are infused with so much *relief*.

"Of all the rot-ridden luck," Rai mutters with exaggerated

frustration. "I was hoping I could have your furs on the way back down the mountain."

Grinning wide, Sanii shakes eir head. "Not a chance."

There's more hope in eir brown eyes than I've ever seen before, the light of someone looking at forever with the one they share their soul with, and ey immediately begins asking questions. What are our next steps? What will counteract a potion this powerful?

Osshi and the andofume talk about plants I've never heard of and use words I've never been taught. I listen, only understanding half of it, but I know they're discussing how to make a potion that's essentially poison. Incredibly strong poison. Chio is the one who suggests brewing something with the venom of the birds on the cliff as its base. It's not a horrible idea, especially since we've already seen proof of its strength. Still…there's something nagging at me, a problem with the plan everyone assumes we'll be following that is only now occurring to me.

"Say we trap enough of those birds to get the amount of venom we'd need, and we manage to create a potion with that and other things that can kill all of the bobasu, *and* we make it back to Shiara alive before Varan launches his army." Everyone looks at me, waiting. Most of them just look confused, but Sanii's square jaw tenses and eir round eyes narrow. "We don't just have to come up with a weapon that will kill immortals, we have to invent something we have a real hope of getting within range of someone as powerful, protected, and paranoid as Varan. Can any of you think of a single feasible way to poison ten people who will probably be at the center of an army of thousands?"

For a few heartbeats, all I can hear is the trees.

Then Tsua sighs. "She has an incredibly valid point."

"A valid point." Sanii's voice is gravelly, and the words

gritted out through eir teeth. "You think she has a valid point *now*? After we've wasted a full moon cycle chasing a potion, now you *don't think it'll work*?"

"I—" I don't get a second word out before Sanii growls a string of vicious curses and stomps toward the trees. Tessen stands up, his gaze tracking eir path, but I put my hand on his wrist and shake my head. "I'll talk to em, just... Wait for us to come back."

He opens his mouth, but changes his mind, his lips pressing together as he sits down.

When I jog after Sanii, though, I can feel his gaze on me, following me even closer than he'd tracked em. The weight of his gaze is practically tangible, and the concern in it makes me shiver as I pull my shoulders back and follow Sanii.

Ey hasn't gone far, barely beyond the first line of trees, but ey's got eir hands braced against the trunk of a tree with eir head dropped low. Without looking back, ey says, "Go away, Khya."

"No." I walk closer, but stop beyond arm's reach. "You knew—we all knew before we landed that our plan was based on hope more than anything else."

"I *know*." Sanii slams eir hands against the tree. "I do know, okay? But there's nothing I can do to help here, and we don't have *any* plan anymore, and it feels like I'll never see him again, and we just wasted *so much time*."

And time is the one thing we don't have. "We only thought we had to bring Varan down with a potion because that's what he used to create immortality in the first place, but chasing his susuji is the reason we found the katsujo, and this kind of power is exactly what we need to create a weapon that *will* work against him."

Sanii glances at me out the corner of eir eyes, seeming to weigh each of my words. "You didn't used to be this optimistic."

"I have to be. We all do. If we don't think there's a way to win this, how can any of us keep fighting?"

"You're right, I just…" Head dropping again, ey exhales heavily. "It's already been a whole moon. I know he's alive, but that doesn't mean he's fine and it doesn't mean the rest of the clan is, either. So much can happen in one moon."

"So we have to make sure what happens before the end of the next moon is better."

Sanii turns around, leaning against the trunk and looking at me with bleak fear in eir large, dark eyes. "But if we missed something as important as seeing how hard it would be to defeat Varan with a potion, how do we know we're not missing something else, too?"

"We can't. No one can do or know everything, so we have to keep moving forward with what we have and what we can learn. So come back and help us figure out what we can do next, Sanii." I hold out my hand. "You think so much like Yorri sometimes. I don't want to have to make this decision without you."

Another long exhale and a look I don't know how to read. I almost think ey's about to walk off again, but then ey heaves emself off the tree and slips eir hand into mine. Neither of us let go until we've rejoined the others, and as soon as we're settled the conversation resumes as though Sanii's outburst never happened.

"We can use arrows," Etaro suggests. "Coat the tip in whatever we create and it could be enough to drop them."

"Only if they can get through the wall of mages ready to knock them out of the air," Rai counters.

Tyrroh nods, his expression focused, wrinkles lined up along the bridge of his wide nose. "Something that can be used at a distance isn't a bad idea, though. It's probably necessary, because Khya was right—we'll have a hard time getting close enough to force them to drink anything. A weapon with a wide range of impact would be better. Making it capable of breaking through even Suzu's wards would be best."

"Great." I pick up a small piece of rock and toss it toward the clearing. "Let me know if you find a way to do that. I've only done it with my own wards, but encasing something in my wards to get it through *their* wards will just protect them from whatever we use to kill them."

"So we need something that can get through without an extra shield." Sanii traces the arc of eir eyebrow with eir middle finger; ey looks exhausted. "Maybe we should ask the Kaisubeh to throw us another rock."

I sit up. "We don't need to. We already have one."

Tsua and Chio's eyes widen. Zonna blinks and asks wonderingly, "Why didn't we even think about that?"

"That stone can weaken wards—holding a shield against the Imaku rock exhausts mages faster than even lightning strikes." Chio speaks slowly, as though he's turning each word over. "But it's never been powerful enough to break through wards immediately."

"But what we've found here— Vanafitia, it makes sense." Tsua looks toward the clearing, her gaze sharp and focused. "The katsujo's power seems to enhance whatever effects something would naturally have. It gives a healing potion the ability to create immortality. It creates an impenetrable wardstone. I'm sure that how close the katsujo is to the surface is why there's life here—at this height, these mountains shouldn't even grow grass. If it can do all of that, what might it do to the Imaku stone? It's not impossible to think this kind of power would make it powerful enough to kill."

"Kaisubeh bless it, that might work," Tsua breathes, her eyes wide and alight.

"There's one problem, though. We don't have any. We

barely took a handful or two away from Imaku, and most of that was lost in the storm before we landed." The first time we tried to rescue Yorri, Sanii, Tessen, and I were more focused on stealing papers, cords, and boxes than rocks. "If it's going to be our weapon, we need to find more here. Or sail back to Imaku for it."

"*That* is not going to happen." Tessen shakes his head. "If we go anywhere near Shiara without a weapon, we're as good as dead."

"Then we'd better hope we can track it down," Chio says, his eyes on the clearing. "And we'd also better not waste any more time here. We'll leave at first light."

"But we don't even know if it'll work," Rai points out. "What if we're wasting time searching for something that isn't what we need?"

"Right now, this is all we have," Tyrroh says. "If anyone has a better idea, let us know."

When no one offers up another plan, we begin breaking down the camp. We've been here more than two weeks, so we've made the Kaisuama Valley as comfortable as we could. Erasing signs of our stay takes a while, but it's work I'm more than happy to do.

Finally, it feels like we're moving slowly—ever so slowly—toward Yorri.

CHAPTER
THIRTEEN

The journey that took us five days in one direction only takes three in the other. As nice as it was to be somewhere we were sure was safe, where no one would come after us, I find myself looking forward to seeing Ahta and Dai-Usho again. And reuniting with Lo'a.

But less than an hour out from Ahta's, Tessen stops. He's breathing deep, eyes closed. Then the wind shifts and even I can smell it.

Smoke.

"We need to get back to Dai-Usho and Ahta," Tessen says, the words clipped. "That's too close to their clearing."

Tyrroh orders us into formation, weapons drawn and eyes out. We move with the same swift silence we were trained to in Itagami, and the fatigue of the journey falls away as my heart pumps blood through my veins at double-speed.

It's too much of a coincidence that they would be in serious trouble so soon after we showed up at their door. We brought this down on them. I don't know what happened yet, but it doesn't matter. They helped us when there was no reason for them to. If we can, we have to do the same.

Tessen directs us along a slightly different path than the one we took before, and the smell of smoke gets thicker the closer we get. When the trail ends overlooking the clearing instead of on level with it, my stomach sinks. This is why the air burns like sulphur.

The garden, the clearing, the house, and all the trees are char and ash. I don't see fire; the flames seem to have either been stopped or burned themselves out, but thin plumes of smoke still rise from the wood.

"Where are they?" I demand just as Tyrroh asks, "Do you sense anyone nearby, Tessen?"

"There's a smell that—" Tessen shakes his head, worry creasing his forehead. "At least one person is down there, but there's no way they're still alive."

I cover my mouth with a shaking hand and close my eyes.

"I know fire. This wasn't natural. There's no way this was natural." Rai's talking too fast, her voice edged with fear. "It's too controlled. If this had been an accident, most of the mountain would've been lost. It wouldn't have stayed here. A person—a mage did this."

Tessen cleared his throat. "Well, no one's here anymore."

With his confirmation, we hurry down the steep slope, dropping the last fifteen feet with Tsua's help. This close, the smoke burns my eyes, my nose, my lungs. I feel like it's coating my skin in grime and ash. Ignoring the sting, and the too-quick thud of my heart, I run toward what's left of their small home; only the stones are left standing.

Inside is the unmistakable stench of burning flesh, and the rough shape of a body. Too big to be Ahta. Too small to be any of the Ryogan tyatsu we've seen so far.

"Dai-Usho." I exhale her name and kneel at her side, breathing through my mouth to avoid the worst of the smell.

She wasn't a warrior in the way we were trained to be; that doesn't mean she wasn't a fighter. Life had been one battle after another for this woman, and she won so many of them until she met us. "I'm so sorry. May your Kaisubeh grant you the peace you didn't know here."

"Do you see em?" Sanii asks outside. "It looked like there was only one body in there, so where's Ahta, Tessen? Where is ey?"

When I leave the wreckage of the house, Tessen is searching the edge of the clearing. At the northwesternmost point, he bolts into the trees. Sanii and I are the first to follow, but the rest of the squad is only a few steps behind us. For three hours, Tessen and Tyrroh follow days-old scents and marks in the forest. Then, finally, Tessen signals—someone is ahead.

Ahta is hiding inside what might've once been an animal's burrow, crouched deep in the shadows of the space. It takes food and several minutes of coaxing before we can get the little ebet to leave.

Ey eats silently—and fast enough that I'm certain ey's barely eaten anything in a day or two at least—and ey watches us warily with round, puffy, bloodshot eyes. We sit in a circle around em, but no one pushes em to talk. Once ey finishes eating, though, ey clears eir throat and whispers, "You saw it then?"

"We're so sorry, Ahta." I hold out another piece of dried meat, a poor offering, but all we have right now. Ey doesn't take it. "I wish we'd been back in time to prevent this."

Exhaling sharply, ey shakes eir head. "Unless you planned on stayin' a while, it would only have mattered if you'd shown up the same day those *rononi yakusoro* did. I wasn't—" Closing eir eyes, ey takes a shaky breath and tries again. "I wasn't there, either. I was coming back from hunting, and I should've been there but—"

"If you'd been there, you'd have died, too." Sanii kneels next to the child, offering a hug that ey falls into. "I'm so sorry about your mother, but I can't be sad you survived."

When Ahta seems a little calmer, I gently ask, "What are you going to do now?"

"I don't know." All the fear ey's probably felt for days bleeds into those three words.

"You can come with us."

Ahta pulls back at Sanii's words. "Come with you where?"

"Wherever we go," Sanii softly says. "It won't be safe, but you'd be welcome with us for as long as you want."

Sanii's right, it won't be safe with us, but living here with Dai-Usho was dangerous, too. Staying here alone would be worse. At least if ey's with us, there will be people to protect em. And if ey decides not to stay, Lo'a might know a safe place for em.

But Ahta looks unsure, so I shift to sit in front of em, holding eir eyes and hoping ey'll listen. "You helped us when you didn't need to. Let us help you."

"When you leave here and go back to wherever you came from, will you take me with you?" ey asks after a few seconds of silence.

"*If* we live through the battles coming for us, which I can't promise we will, then yes. We'll take you to Shiara." I try not to imagine how a child raised with trees and cold and *snow* will react to the desert, but I can't deny the little ebet's desire to be somewhere ey won't be hated for existing. "But at the very least, we'll get you safely away from here."

"I don't—" Ey closes eir eyes, lips trembling and tears streaking down eir dirt-smeared cheeks. "This was the only place I had that was home."

My chest aches. My longing for burning sunlight and

open space and endless blue skies and beautiful danger gets stronger than I've let it since I watched Shiara vanish on the horizon. I swallow, and hate the cold air freezing my throat. "I know what it's like to lose home, and to lose someone you love. I know how hard it is to have to watch everything you know slip away because nothing you can do is enough to stop it. I *know*."

Ahta raises eir eyes to mine, tears flowing faster down eir face, and there's so much exhaustion and pain in eir expression. I've never seen this much awareness in the eyes of someone so young. "Did you lose your mama?"

"My brother." The last time I saw my blood-parents, we were trying to kill each other. But ey's listening, leaning in and absorbing every word I say, so I keep talking. "What's important is you're alive. Finding a new home is hard, but not impossible. Finding people you can learn to love again isn't, either. Dai-Usho loved you, and she wouldn't want you to join her in the afterlife. Not yet. You have decades ahead of you, and the world left to see."

Unblinking, Ahta stares at me, eir expression indecipherable. Then ey bursts into motion, crawling back into the animal's den. Sanii calls em back. I press my lips thin, rolling them between my teeth to keep myself silent. We can't make em come with us, and if ey's survived this long on these mountains it's not like we'd be leaving em to die, but the thought of leaving em alone is awful. Still, it's eir life and eir choice and we shouldn't—

Ahta emerges from the burrow with several furs clutched to eir chest, a bulging bag strapped to eir back, and determination in eir eyes. Ey doesn't struggle when Sanii takes the furs from em, simply adjusts the straps of eir bag and waits.

With the child protected in the center of the line, we retrace the path to Lo'a. Life in the mountains trained Ahta well for the pace we keep; it's rare any of us need to do more than help em over a particularly high boulder.

For several hours, only Miari's and Nairo's murmured encouragement to Wehli—and his loud silence in return—overlap the breeze rustling the branches overhead. It's Ahta who breaks the quiet when we stop for food and a rest in the middle of the afternoon.

"It was soldiers. A whole squad of tyatsu. But they never come into the mountains. Not this deep." Eyes down, ey rips a piece of dried fruit in half. And doesn't eat either bit. "I wasn't there when they found our house, don't know what they wanted, but I got there when the tyatsu-lu said to— I heard the order to…" Ey closes eir eyes, small hands clenched tight. "He said to finish what her husband failed at years ago. They cut her throat open, threw her in the house, and set an asairu to burn it all down."

Sanii inches closer and offers Ahta eir hand. Ey latches on hard, and my stomach drops. I'd been right. What happened to Dai-Usho was because we led the soldiers straight to them. And I won't blame the child if ey hates us when we tell em the truth. I should do it now, but the words stick in my throat like I tried to swallow kicta thorns.

"I'm so sorry, Ahta," Tsua says, her voice full of regret. "They had to have been here looking for us."

Sanii flinches and looks down at their joined hands; other than the stiffening of Ahta's shoulders, it's the only sign the child heard a word Tsua said.

"I have no idea how they tracked us into the mountains," Chio continues, his voice low and serious. "But there's no reason for them to be here except for us."

"For *me*." Osshi knocks a small rock down the slope, his expression stormy. "Far as we know, no one in Ryogo knows you're here. If the tyatsu were here for anyone, it was me."

Ahta's chin rises, eir gaze jumps from face to face, and the muscles along eir jaw twitch. Then eir eyes drop to Sanii's hand. Frowning harder, ey pulls away, curling in on emself without a word. Eir silence holds for the rest of the day. And the night. And the next morning. However, ey doesn't leave.

As we hike down the mountain, I pray for Ahta's sake that the Kaisubeh *are* real and they grant their followers the kind of afterlife the Miriseh always promised us in Itagami. At least then the child has a hope of seeing eir mother again one day.

J ust before sunset on our second day of travel, I smell fire on the breeze again. This time it carries the scent of spices and meat. There, too, so quiet I almost miss it, the sound of conversation. Another half hour of hiking and we meet Shiu, the hanaeuu we'la maninaio standing sentry.

Grinning, Shiu calls out a signal to the others. When he's close enough to spot Ahta, there's curiosity in his eyes, but Lo'a is still the only one who talks to us. The only reason I even know Shiu's name is because I overheard the others use it. Now, when someone within the circle of wagons calls something in their language, all Shiu does is point. I assume that's the direction Lo'a is in, so that's where we go.

She's already jogging out to meet us. "We were getting worried you would not make it back at all, but you brought back more people than you started with."

There's a smile curving her lips, but her eyes are nothing but suspicion. It's slow to dissolve even after she learns why Ahta had been living out here in the first place.

Honestly, the longer I spend with the hanaeuu we'la maninaio, the more surprised I am they agreed to help us at all. They trust no one, and keep even their most public secrets shrouded in distractingly bright colors and elaborate designs. It's hard to believe even Osshi's old actions were enough to convince them to let us stay. It's also true, though, that the longer we're with them, the happier I am to have their help. Maybe *because* of how clear they make it that their trust isn't easily earned.

"I had hoped you would not cross this aspect of Ryogo while you were here," Lo'a admits sadly. "They believe in duality strongly here, and even those like Osshi who are more open to the wider world fall prey to some of the beliefs of this society."

Osshi looks down, pink rising in his cheeks and his expression conflicted.

"Duality?" Tessen asks before I can. It's a pair of something, two, but she seems to be referring to a deeper definition than that. "What do you mean?"

"Duality. To them it means night and day. Man and woman. Right and wrong. It is in their laws and their culture and their interpretation of the *alua'sa liona'ano shilua'a*—the beings they call the Kaisubeh." She lifts one shoulder, rippling the thick pink coat she's wearing. "They like to pretend that there is nothing between night and day, but there are so many beautifully distinct moments. Twilight. Sunset. Dusk. Dawn. Daybreak. Sunrise. They have words for so many moments beyond night and day, yet they ignore them, pointing to the existence of only one sun and one moon as proof that their Kaisubeh constructed the world in dichotomous pairs. Even there, they are wrong. The sun is one of a million—billion— stars, and there are hundreds of thousands of moons."

I understand the words, but I'm not sure I know what she means.

When none of us speak, Lo'a smiles sadly. "I wish they

could meet your ebets and see how wrong their treatment of their own is, but they would reject that kind of change even faced with proof. They have spent too much time making the world fit their beliefs."

"A failing of far more people than could fit in Ryogo," Tsua says.

"True." Lo'a takes a breath, quick but deep, and her smile brightens. "It is an incredible feat that you all came back from Nentoado alive and whole."

"Some of us," Wehli mutters, left hand absently rubbing his shoulder. The stump—covered in new skin and scars and as healed as it ever will be—is enclosed in layers of cloth, but the imbalance in his shape is clear. Especially since Miari and Nairo have tied the empty sleeve down to keep it from flapping free and getting caught on something.

Lo'a glances at the damaged limb, acknowledging it but thankfully not staring. "Injury like that is always hard to recover from, but you are alive, and you are young. You have time to relearn tasks you are used to doing with two hands. A friend in another family had to do the same when illness twisted one of her legs beyond use. With the help of a pair of walking sticks her brother crafted for her, she gets around almost as quickly as she ever did before. You will, too, once you learn how."

Wehli opens his mouth, then seems to change his mind. Lips pressed thin, he nods. On either side of him, his partners watch Lo'a with hope in their eyes. I can understand why.

At home, only one's partners—and sometimes not even them—would spend time helping a nyshin who'd been so severely injured get back to their old skill and speed. It's too dangerous for the other soldiers, the Miriseh and our commanding officers claimed, to have someone at our backs who wasn't at their peak. Here, we are all on the front lines, so I hope Lo'a is right and this is one more thing the bobasu lied to us about.

But that will take time, and training, so for now we finish telling the story, both what happened in Kaisuama and what we found when we left the depths of Nentoado. And why.

Frowning, Lo'a quietly offers Ahta her condolences. Though Ahta looks up and nods, ey still doesn't speak. No one prods em to.

"Especially given what you have told me, I have something for you I believe you will like." Lo'a smiles, her eyes brightening. "While you were gone, I sent messengers to other families to see if they could answer the question Osota's ancestors never could."

My heart skips a beat. I'd been thinking about suggesting we head back to Atokoredo and talk to Osota about the stones. Maybe we don't have to. "You found something?"

"I believe so." She calls out to one of the children, and they jog toward her wagon. "The black rock was taken to Mushokeiji, a prison the Ryogans built for their mages a long time ago."

After the little girl returns and hands Lo'a a map, Lo'a flattens it on the rocky ground. The map, unless I'm reading it wrong, is focused on the Soramyku Province, where Atokoredo sits. Lo'a points to a point north of that city and east of where we began our journey into Nentoado. According to the map, there's nothing there.

"I can't say I'm surprised to hear they built a mage prison, not with how their attitude toward magic has devolved since our time here." Chio leans over the map, eyebrows pulled low. "But they put it here? Suakizu seems too pretty a place for a prison."

Lo'a shakes her head. "A blight struck the area centuries ago. It never recovered. Since it is both remote and useless for agriculture, it was the perfect place for Ryogo to hide those they wanted to forget existed."

"How well guarded is it?" Tsua asks.

"Few know. Most people do not even know where Mushokeiji is let alone the details of the place," Lo'a explains. "But if you need more of your black rock, I am nearly certain this is the only place in Ryogo to find it."

"I'm worried, though." Tyrroh gestures northeast, toward Ahta's mountain. "We don't know how the soldiers followed us here. If we don't figure that out, staying ahead of them will be nearly impossible."

"Obviously they use spells for more than just to send messages," I say. "Could they be using one to follow us somehow?"

Lo'a shakes her head. "They have one spell that might do that, but it should not work while you're with us. We learned how to block it a long time ago."

"It might not be magic at all," Tessen says. "It might be people. We've stayed off the main roads, but we haven't been invisible. And we've been moving slow enough to follow."

"But could someone have been following us without *you* noticing?" I raise my eyebrows. "I'm not sure anyone in Ryogo is capable of that."

Tessen blinks and smiles ruefully. "While I really hate to shake your unquestioning faith, I'm not perfect. There's a lot here that's new. I can't be as sure of my senses as I am on Shiara."

"The point is, we don't know," Tyrroh says, cutting off my response. "And I don't like not knowing this answer."

I shift my weight, glancing at the trees hiding us from the world—and hiding the world from us. Clouds obscure the light from the stars and moon, so it feels as though our firelit camp is all there is. What magic or spy hides out there? And how the bellows do we find them?

"We have to go east to reach Mushokeiji, correct?" Tsua leans over the map. "Can we get there without using any of the roads, even the lesser traveled ones?"

"We cannot avoid them entirely—not if you want to travel with the wagons." Lo'a points to several options, explaining how long each route would take. The mountain trails would take the longest time and require leaving the hanaeuu we'la maninaio behind, but they'd take us the farthest away from any cities or settlements.

After an hour of debate—which was almost an argument at times—we decide on a path. Half of the trip will be on the less traveled roads, and we'll ride in the wagons to give us a chance to rest and time to restock our supplies. The rest we'll travel on foot to keep Lo'a's family well out of danger. At least, any danger at Mushokeiji.

"What do we do about whoever's tracking us?" I ask.

"Or *what*ever's tracking us," Rai adds.

"As much as we can. Watch for spies. Pay attention to the desosa. Anything you think even *might* be out of the ordinary here, you report it to Tsua, Chio, Osshi, or Lo'a," Tyrroh orders. "Full watch at all times, and you had better be tracking everything, down to the number of trees we pass each day. We're alone in enemy territory here, so *pay attention*. I want every one of you with me when this is all over."

I do, too. We've all lost enough already.

We travel pitted paths through thick forests for four days, hunting when we can track animals worth chasing, gathering roots and plants when we can find ones worth eating, and keeping as many eyes as possible turned outward. Watching for what, we don't know, but we're watching.

Wehli is the only one who doesn't serve shifts. He offers once, on the first day, but Tyrroh shakes his head and sends Wehli back to rest. There isn't a second offer.

I barely see him for the next several days. He spends time reading, I think, and I spot him running drills twice, the long tudo blade he used to be so proficient at wielding now awkward in his non-dominant hand. Seeing it makes me wonder if he's even tried using his power yet.

Like all mages whose power focuses on physical enhancement, ryachos like Wehli draw in desosa without thinking and use it to boost their natural speed and agility. If they're as powerful as Wehli is, they can run so quickly they're no more than a blur. It takes practice to employ that power, and balance is crucial for the skill. Balance Wehli doesn't have anymore.

I want to help him, offer comfort or advice, but I don't know how. And I don't think he's ready to hear it. He's even pushed Miari and Nairo away. Hopefully, Tyrroh will be able to reach him, or will help him regain his footing before we leave Lo'a. If he does, we'll at least be able to offer him the choice to come or stay, but it hasn't been that long since he was injured. Without his balance, he won't be able to keep up with us; forget the scouting we usually use his ryacho speed for.

And the time for a decision is looming, because Lo'a is calling a halt, and in the morning Tsua and Chio will lead us into the mountains, following trails that'll get us to Mushokeiji without being spotted. By anyone except maybe the Ryogans' Kaisubeh.

Hopefully *they're* not the ones reporting our position to the tyatsu. If so, we're in a lot more trouble than I can protect us from.

A voice shouting my name across the camp catches my

attention; Shiu beckons me toward Lo'a's wagon. Curious, I cross camp at a jog, nodding to Shiu before I pass him, jumping the three steps into the wagon. "Did you need something, Lo'a?"

She smiles and gestures to the bench along one side of the table. After I sit, she extends her hand, holding a delicate silver chain with a silver pendant.

"I would like you to have this. We do not often give these out, but there is a chance we will have to leave this place before you return if the tyatsu arrive. If that happens and you should need help, find another hanaeuu we'la maninaio family and show them this. It will get you whatever you need."

"Why?" I shouldn't ask, but I need to know. "What have I done to earn this?"

"You use the akiloshulo'e kua'ana manano in a way I have never seen before, and you taught me how to do the same. I have been trying to replicate what we did the night I borrowed your power, and if I can perfect my understanding of it, I will be better able to protect my family. It is stronger than any magic we have ever worked. You have also warned us about a danger coming for Ryogo and given us time to get messages to the families in the south. Most of them have begun evacuating already." She offers the pendant again. "The worth of all the knowledge you have brought us is incalculable. We are in your debt."

There's their fascination with debt again. It's an unsettlingly open-ended offer of aid from a culture that holds so much back, but turning away help is a terrible idea. Still, it's strange to think something I've been able to do since I was twelve could have earned me this.

I take the pendant. It's solid, heavier than I expected, and has one large, raised symbol in the center of each side with smaller marks around the edge. Like all the other symbols in the hanaeuu we'la maninaio's camp, this one brims with energy, pulling the desosa through the lines of the symbols and using what it needs before it lets the energy pass through again.

"This is a symbol of the Shuikanahe'le, my family." Lo'a runs her thumb along the symbol made of swooping curves and slashing lines. "And this one—" She flips the pendant over on my palm to display the other side. There's a strong semblance between the two symbols, but they're clearly distinct. "This indicates to other families that you are considered a friend."

I almost want to press it back into her hand, but a voice in my head that sounds a lot like Tessen's stops me: *accept the help, Khya. You don't know what's coming.* So I close my fingers around the pendant. "Thank you."

"I have a feeling that you will do great things, and an alliance with a girl on the path to greatness is never a bad idea," she says with a gentle smile.

"I hope you're right." But if she is, and we've formed an alliance, I should know more about those I'm allied with, shouldn't I? And there's something that I think I noticed… "May I ask you something else?"

She nods, and I'm not sure if it's curiosity or wariness I see in her eyes.

Exhaling slowly, I try to figure out how to word the question so that she'll choose to answer it. Or at least not be angry with me for asking. "Osshi never shortens the name of your clan. And your language, too. None of your words are short."

"Yes." Her eyes are avidly focused on my face.

The interest I see is enough to spur me on. "Yet your name is Lo'a?"

Her smile grows, delight widening her eyes. "Soanashalo'a. My full name is longer—and you have not earned that yet,

Khya—but it is a start."

I open my mouth to say it, but... No. Her name is long, and it feels like mispronouncing it would be an insult. "Would you mind repeating it?"

"Soanashalo'a," she says again. Then, she repeats it slower, breaking it into sounds. "So-a-na-sha-lo-a."

"Soanashalo'a." It doesn't sound the same shaped by my tongue, but it's recognizable.

"You really do have a talent for languages." She looks down at the patterns on her hand. "I must ask you not to tell your squad, or use my full name where anyone outside my family can hear. It is a sign of trust to share pieces of your full name." Her eyes flick up to meet mine and hold. "And you honor that when you use all the pieces of the name you have been given."

"I understand." It seems partly a sign of repect and partly a term of endearment. The latter feels especially true as I say, "Thank you, Soanashalo'a Shuikanahe'le."

Soanashalo'a watches me, her smile warm. Sometimes I feel as though she can guess at my thoughts. She and Tessen would be dangerous together. Dangerous for my peace of mind.

"If not for your mission and the obvious bond you have with Tessen, I might try to convince you to stay for a while, Khya."

"If not for my mission and Tessen, I might agree." Soanashalo'a's help is a big part of why we've made it this far. If Yorri were already with me, I wouldn't hesitate to ask if we could all stay.

"But you are heading off to infiltrate Mushokeiji, and only the alua'sa liona'ano shilua'a know what you will face after that." She approaches with a smile, and with invitation in her eyes. "Do you and Tessen share the way Miari and hers do?"

"I... Yes, but it's not the same—touch is hard to handle

for Tessen, so he's cautious choosing lovers." I smile at the memories from the caves weeks ago even as I shrug one shoulder and try to explain. "Honestly, entirely exclusive partnerships are rare in Itagami."

"It is the same with us. A little. Probably not to the same degree as Itagami. Still…" She stops in front of me, watching me with the same intensity that I'm watching her. There's a question on her face, one I've seen most recently from Tessen.

When I nod permission, she presses her lips to mine.

Her hands cup my face; mine fall to her waist. She's soft in ways almost no one in Itagami is, not unfit, but far from carved in stone, and her skin is noticeably warmer than mine. And noticeably softer, too. It's been a long time since I've been with a girl. Soanashalo'a is compelling, and I've wondered more than once what it would be like to kiss her, so I run my tongue along the seam of her lips and slide my hands under her coat to the bare skin of her back.

And then I ease away.

Soanashalo'a is lovely and skilled and kind, but I think Etaro and Rai were right weeks ago. They said I needed someone who fought with me, who challenged me, and whose edges fit with mine. Tessen is all those things, and when I'm kissing *him*, there usually isn't room in my mind for much else.

Soanashalo'a's smile is rueful. "See? I would try to convince you, but it would be a wasted effort." She brushes her hand along my short hair—which is getting longer than I like it—and then kisses me again, only a faint brush of our lips. "When this war of yours is over, you are welcome back any time. Tessen, too. The two of you are quite something to behold."

"He's been…" How do I even explain Tessen? "I misunderstood him for a long time, but he's persistent. And probably more forgiving than he should be. At least with me."

"Love makes that easy," Soanashalo'a says with a smile.

I blink, my chest warming. Love. I trust few people. I love even fewer. It's not a word I've connected to Tessen even inside my own head, but I can't say she's wrong. Somehow, Tessen snuck up on me in plain sight.

"I've never been as good at forgiving mistakes and disagreements, but I'm learning. And I'm incredibly glad to have him here." But we're leaving in the morning, and we have someone vulnerable to worry about. "You're sure you don't mind watching Ahta while we're gone?"

"Your little one has made friends with our own. I think they will be doing most of the watching for us."

The words are a relief. The hanaeuu we'la maninaio don't seem to be as strict with their secrecy around Ahta, and I'm glad. Maybe because ey's been cast out from Ryogo and orphaned—ey doesn't really belong anywhere, and ey definitely isn't loyal to Ryogo.

"Do not worry about any of us. Focus on coming back alive." She squeezes my hand and then steps back.

"I'll certainly try." We say goodbye, and then I leave the wagon, the pendant hidden under my clothing. It's likely no one but Tessen will even notice the thin chain visible at the back of my neck, something he proves less than five minutes after he finds me.

"A gift?" He murmurs the question in my ear, his finger trailing the bare skin on my neck, less than an inch above the chain.

"A promise of help from the rest of her clan if we need it."

"And not the only thing she gave you, either." He runs his thumb along my bottom lip.

"She's good, but you're better." I kiss the pad of his thumb and grin as his expression shifts from amusement to arousal. "She'd be more than happy to give you the same thing if I brought you along."

He smirks. "Is that so?"

"She's more than a little interested in you, too. Or maybe us." I lightly bite the tip of his thumb. "But somehow I don't think that'll happen anytime soon."

"I don't know. I mean, where would we find the time?" Tessen jokes, but then his expression turns rueful. "It's not an unappealing offer, but I told you—touch can be overpowering. And that's with one. Two would be…"

"You could just watch," I say with a shrug. And then start chuckling when his eyes go wide and he stops breathing for a beat. It doesn't seem like he'll be able to respond to that particular image anytime soon, so I take pity on him and look for something else to talk about. Everyone else is gathered nearby, so I nod toward their tight circle. "What's this about?"

"Tyrroh is testing Wehli," he says quietly. With a smile, surprisingly. "Our nyshin-ma is going to be astonished when he sees the progress Wehli's made already."

"What are you—" I stop short on the edge of the circle.

Wehli is sparring with Tyrroh. He's losing, and won't last much longer, but he's fighting our nyshin-ma and keeping his feet. There are bursts of his old speed, beautiful blurs of motion that slow again too soon for him to press his advantages.

"Maybe the Miriseh were wrong about this, too. Can you think of anyone who suffered this kind of injury who was even given a chance to relearn their skills?" I ask.

Rai shakes her head. "As soon as they're healed, they're placed ahdo and assigned to supervise a yonin squad. Why would anyone bother training in something no one is going to let them use?"

Yet Wehli is proving everything we've been taught wrong. There's little of his old grace and confidence in the way he wields the tudo now, but it's been less than three weeks and he's already come this far. At the end of the bout, Tyrroh announces that Wehli will come with us.

Every new bobasu lie we uncover is an echo of the first blow, the moment Sanii proved to me that they'd lied about Yorri's death. Few of their deceptions carry the same weight as the first did, but none of the others have been painless.

This is another offense against the core of what I thought it meant to be Itagamin.

What they told us, even when the story was a lie, is as revealing as what they erased or forced themselves to forget. At least, that's what I tell myself every time my chest aches with the discovery of a new lie. And anger churns my stomach when I think of the hundreds or thousands of people their lies have destroyed.

I tell myself these lies teach us what Varan and the bobasu are afraid of. I tell myself these lies are the threads that will help us unravel the control they have over Itagami and Shiara. I tell myself a lot of things.

I only hope I'm right.

CHAPTER FOURTEEN

I thought I'd seen barren. I thought I knew what a wasteland looked liked. I was wrong.

Neither the sun-baked rocks of Shiara nor the icy wilds of Nentoado felt nearly as desolate as Suakizu. It feels *empty*.

Even in Shiara's deserts, I could feel the desosa in the sun's burning rays, the rocks worn by sand and storms, and the hidden seeds of growing things that would explode with life as soon as they found water. Here, the sun feels weak and impotent. The rocks feel parched and dead. There are no plants and no hidden seeds with life left in them that I can sense. No cover from the force of the icy winds. No birds or animals calling in the distance. Nothing.

And yet, clinging to the side of one peak is a stone building, one built to practically blend in with the surroundings. The pale-gray stone is the same as the mountain, and the stepped rise of the floors mimics its natural slope. It's the evenness of the levels that first catches my attention, making me take a second look at the peak, then the periodic gleam of light through a narrow window convinces me there's something there beyond what I see at first glance.

Mushokeiji. A prison for those whose crimes involve magic, and a fortress hidden from even Ryogans.

Tsua's eyes fill with sorrow as she gazes at the pale, bare rocks. "This place used to be so beautiful."

"It feels— It's like there's no desosa here." Etaro looks down at eir hands, rubbing eir thumbs along the pads of eir fingers, like ey's trying to feel the air. "I've never felt anything like this. It's like my skin is too dry, and I feel like I have to work too hard to breathe."

"I know what you mean, but it's not the air. The air is fine. It... I think it has something to do with the katsujo." Tessen says it slowly. His hands are pressed flat against the pale gray rock, and his eyes are closed. "There's desosa here, but it's exceptionally deep, almost beyond what I can sense. I think there used to be more. The ground reminds me of the desert in the dry season. It's soaking the energy up like rain."

"Osshi, when did the blight hit Suakizu?" Chio asks.

"Fifty years or more after Varan's exile." He shakes his head. "How could that have anything to do with what Varan did in the mountains?"

"No, it makes sense," Tessen says. "Zonna described the katsujo as veins of power. Veins connect. If you cut one, you kill off the area it feeds."

"And if it's not dead, just obstructed..." Sanii nods toward the expanse of rocky wilderness. "A valley fed by a trickle of water will find a way to survive for a long time, even in the middle of a desert. Life must have held on here as long as it could."

"And the Ryogans took advantage of what was left behind when life finally gave up." Zonna looks out over the valley, expression grim.

"I don't know if we'll be able to sneak in there," Etaro

admits a few minutes later.

Rai nods. "We might have to storm the gates."

"And no way can we avoid killing some of the guards if we do that." Rai seems mostly unbothered by the realization. "Have we stopped caring about that yet?"

"No." Osshi keeps his eyes on the mountain stronghold, his expression tight.

"Fine, then what's the plan?" Rai places her elbow on the rock, resting her chin on her hand. "I could burn something in the valley and distract the guards."

"We'll keep that as a last resort." Tsua's voice is dry, and I can't tell if she's serious or not. "I'd rather save the explosive distractions for when we're on our way out, not in."

"Exactly. With no way of knowing what the inside of this place looks like, we can't begin to guess where to look for the Imaku rock." Chio pauses. "Or what they may have done with it in the last five hundred years. We don't want to be in a rush when we go in."

Wishing for half Yorri's skill with finding solutions to complex puzzles, I stare at the mountain. Only one thing is obvious. "We need to watch, for at least a few days, specifically looking for when people leave and how they approach. And, if we can…" I turn toward Tessen. "If Tsua got you closer, could you overhear the guards?"

"You know how stone walls can twist sound," he begins, "but probably. It depends on where we find a hiding spot to listen from."

"I think that should be step one then, right nyshin-ma?" I look to Tyrroh only to find him watching me with a small smile. It softens the dark planes of his oval face, and the pride in it makes my chest warm. I'm even more pleased when he nods and moves closer to Tsua, the two of them talking quietly about logistics. As though it's already a given they'll follow my advice.

"Don't look so surprised." Tessen is so close his shoulder brushes mine as he shifts. "Tyrroh's trusted your judgement for a long time. Back home, I think he would've promoted you over Ryzo if he could've done it without getting in trouble for breach of precedence."

"Don't be ridiculous." I knew Ryzo would be the squad's next nyshin-pa. Although I never admitted it, that was one reason I stopped seeing him, to avoid complicating his promotion.

Tessen looks at me, fondly exasperated. "I don't know how you can be so absolutely confident in your abilities and yet utterly ignorant of how other people see you. It's a talent, Khya." He brushes a kiss across my lips and pulls away before I can kiss him back. "Now excuse me. I was just volunteered for a mission I don't know how I'm going to finish."

"You haven't failed me yet, Nyshin-ten." I tap the end of his nose and narrow my eyes. "Don't start now."

"Never by choice, oh deadly one." Smile deepening, he brushes his fingers against mine as he walks away.

Rai is watching us with a knowing smile. Instead of the tease I expect, she asks, "So what will *we* be doing while your favorite is off with Tsua?"

"He's going to be focusing on the details, so we need to find the overview. We need to know the patterns of this place, and we need to know how to infiltrate or disrupt them."

Rai sighs and turns back to Mushokeiji. "It's like being back on the wall in Itagami. I'd hoped leaving home would at least mean no more boring wall shifts." But even as she complains, Rai settles herself to watch the prison with the same careful attention she always gave the plains surrounding Itagami. In that moment, I love her more than ever for both her sharp tongue and the unflinching loyalty she hides behind it.

"Have I said thank you yet?" I sit next to her.

"Probably not." She smiles without looking at me. "And even if you had, I could probably stand to hear it again."

"Well then, thank you." Nothing is moving in the valley below, so I watch Rai instead. "I never wanted to pull you into this, but I am so glad you're here."

"Good." She shifts, glancing at me out the corner of her eyes. "I refuse to say you're welcome until this is over and we're back in Itagami."

I roll my eyes. "I'm trying to be nice here."

"Stop." She flicks a chip of stone at me. "You being nice sounds like we're about to die."

"No one is dying." I can't let that happen, and with the wardstones I refilled from the katsujo, I almost feel as though I have the power to follow through on that promise.

"Guess that'll have to be good enough," Rai says, lifting one shoulder. "You've gotten us this far."

"Thanks. I think."

Smirking, she settles into the stone, making herself still the way I've only ever seen her on watch, all her energy and force pulled in tight and hidden away. We'll be here for hours, so I try to do the same. I refuse to let impatience ruin everything after coming this far.

And patience is necessary, because there's no easy way into this place. Three days of watching only gives us one good idea.

Tessen overheard several guards talking about the upcoming arrival of supplies. Deliveries come no more often than once a moon here—they're too far into the dead zone of Suakizu and too few people know Mushokeiji exists. Luckily, this rarity makes the arrival of each wagon of supplies a day the guards look forward to. It becomes a celebration, and that makes it a perfect day for us to sneak past them.

It also means we only have two days to find a way in before we'll have to wait a full moon cycle.

Miari is the one who offers a solution. As part of her mage training in Itagami, she worked under the ishiji mages responsible for maintaining the caves in the undercity. They taught her to detect weaknesses and cracks in the stone support pillars before they became a problem and to keep the ventilation shafts clear of debris.

No matter how secure the Ryogans tried to make Mushokeiji, a compound carved out of solid stone needs ventilation. And, since they likely don't use magic to maintain them, the shafts have to be wide enough for people to crawl through and clear by hand. Meaning *we* can use them to drop in behind their guards. As soon as we find one.

Tessen, Tsua, and Miari search, staying at a distance as much as possible, and when they're back with us, resting and eating and telling us what they've learned, we try to form some kind of plan.

"Tessen, the first thing you need to do once we're inside is find the rooms belonging to the guards," Chio says. "There'll be a map of the prison in the commanding officer's quarters."

"That won't be easy. Especially not without being seen." Tessen bites his lip, watching the empty valley below. Then he turns, eyes locking on mine. "Can you work the same magic you did with Lo'a? Just while we're on the move."

"It's hard here to even put up a ward, and this is a prison for mages, remember?" I run my fingers along the stone, wondering how the Ryogans built this place without magic. "They probably have something in there to keep everyone from using what little desosa there is."

"So you can't do it?" he asks.

"I *might* be able to, but I don't want it to be the only choice." I lean past him, peering out at Mushokeiji. "We need a solid fallback plan before we sneak in there."

"There are only two possible plans if we can't get through unseen," Chio says. "Either we create chaos by freeing the prisoners, or we kill or disable every single guard to keep them from warning the rest of Ryogo."

So, in other words, either I make Lo'a's don't-see-us magic work or someone—a lot of someones—will die. They're strangers, practically enemies. I shouldn't care one way or the other, but I do. Yorri would, too, if he were here.

"Give me some time." I take a long breath and lean against the stone. "I'll see."

Closing my eyes, I try to remember exactly how Lo'a's magic felt. It was like my wards, but thicker. They stopped sound and bent light. Lo'a explained it some, and I've learned more in the weeks we've been with her, but I haven't tried to replicate the trick yet. A mistake, clearly. I've spent most of my time on the cords or the susuji instead.

I open my eyes and search the group behind me. When my eyes meet Natani's, I beckon him closer. As soon as he sits down, I explain what I'm trying to do. "But I don't know if I have the power for it."

Natani nods even as lines appear around his eyes. "Not going to be easy here."

"I know. I'm going to have to pull from you *and* both our wardstones if this is going to work." I touch the crystal hidden under my clothes. "We might have to pull so much it drains them. Ours, at least."

"Worth it if it works, though," Sanii says.

"And we'll be heading back to Kaisuama once we have the Imaku stone, won't we?" Natani taps one of his wardstones. "You can fix these there."

It's not that, I almost say. I just hate having to pull from the wardstones at all. I hate the way this air feels in my lungs, like it's sucking something vital out of me with each breath. Can the world be so empty of desosa it steals it from any living thing reckless enough to cross into its borders? I wouldn't have thought so, but there's no other way to describe what this is like.

After resettling the wardstone hanging around my neck so it rests directly against my skin, I grip Natani's hand and close my eyes. Last time, with Lo'a, I played his part, becoming the extra power source to boost and reshape the magic she needed to work. Natani is conduit and anchor this time, but the work is all going to have to come from me.

Which means I had better know what the bellows I'm doing.

Lo'a's basic explaination of her magic has helped me understand what I sensed when a member of her family worked with those symbols. The power really *isn't* in the symbols, it's in the mage and it's in the world. Like the Ryogans' spells, the hanaeuu we'la maninaio use symbols as a visual and tangible channel for their power, an easier way for their minds to control what they want to happen. I might not need the symbols at all. But since I remember them, I sketch them on everyone's skin and clothes with the charred end of a stick. Then, I begin to try.

I start with a small ward, only around Natani and myself. Once it's in place, I focus on hiding us from sight. I remember how it felt when Lo'a took what I gave her and wound it around the protections painted onto the wagons. Repeating it, though…

Four times I open my eyes, looking up to meet Tessen's gaze. Each time, he's watching me, waiting for something to happen. On the fifth time, though, he blinks, a smile slowly spreading across his face.

"There's a blur," he says, "but it's barely there. I can't see you at all. If I wasn't me, I don't think I'd notice anything."

"I certainly don't see it," Sanii says.

Good. That's exactly as it should be.

"I don't know how long I'll be able to hold it, but I should at least be able to get us through the open places." Hopefully. Unless the whole prison is one big open space.

"At least we'll have that," Chio says on an exhale as we settle in to wait. "Kaisubeh know we won't have anything else on our side in there."

It takes Miari, Tsua, and Tessen almost too long to find what we need. The sun is rising on the morning of Mushokeiji's supply delivery before they return from one of their searches with triumphant, if tired, smiles.

We hide most of our packs and supplies where we've been camping—all we carry with us is water, weapons, and food for two days. It had better be enough.

Within half an hour of leaving camp, we're free-climbing the north face of Mushokeiji's mountain, aiming for a ledge halfway up the slope. Wehli insisted on coming with us, despite Tyrroh all but ordering him to stay behind—his persistence, and his partners' support of it, finally convinced our nyshin-ma to relent. It only takes a few minutes of climbing to prove that Wehli was right. He's slower than I've ever seen him, but he can do it. Even using footholds to launch himself up and catch the next handhold, he's a stronger climber than Osshi. Tsua and Etaro keep careful watch over our persistent Ryogan to ensure we don't lose him to gravity.

Miari leads us to a shadowy spot directly below the ledge she'd pointed out, and only when we're almost on top of it do I see why. Hidden in the natural shape of the slope is a perfectly square opening, one with thick metal bars blocking entrance. There seems to be a lock on one side and some way to open it from the inside, but Miari doesn't bother with that. She places her hand on the stone and shifts it away from the bars, making the lock irrelevant. The whole thing swings open at a light touch.

The shaft is just wide enough for us to fit through comfortably one by one. The narrow width makes it easy to brace my hands and feet against the sides and lower myself slowly instead of sliding down and crashing out the other end.

After about fifty feet, I drop onto smooth stone. The space is small, barely five feet square, so I immediately get out of the way, moving toward the doorway where Tessen is waiting, guarding the entry. I can't see much because the only light comes from the long vent cut into the mountain, but Tessen will be able to see more. Producing our own light isn't smart until we have a better idea of where we are within the prison. And who might see it.

It takes longer than usual for Tessen to tell what's ahead, and I wonder if this place is affecting him the same way it is me. It's hard to find enough desosa to power my wards in here, more so than it was in our camp. Even the very first time I purposefully created a ward wasn't this difficult. I didn't think I relied on ambient desosa this much—I'd always believed most of the fuel for a basic ward came from inside me—but here… If I didn't have the wardstones, I don't know if I'd be able to deflect more than a dozen swordblows. Hopefully, we won't have to test what the wardstones can protect us from until we're well away from this deadzone.

Leaning in close to Tessen, I hand sign, *clear?*

No. He answers in hand signals. *People. Many. Movement.*

Quick signals tell him to lead on when it's safe; several minutes pass before he moves.

We enter a narrow hall with a strangely high ceiling. It must be at least thirty feet above our heads. The lighting gets a little better as we walk, and what we find at the end of the hall must be the center of the mountain. Or at least the center of Mushokeiji. A circular ledge surrounds what looks like an open drop, and wooden doors—twelve I can see—lead… somewhere. Light comes from lamps hanging at increments from the roof of each level. From this vantage point I can see six floors above us. I can't guess how much farther up or down into the mountain the prison spreads.

"This is…big," Etaro murmurs behind me.

And ey's right. Where are we supposed to start searching in a place like this? If the doors I can see from here continue all the way around the ledge, there are at least thirty on this level. If each level I counted has the same arrangement, there are more than two hundred doors. More than two hundred rooms to search. And that's without including the offshoot tunnels and hiding places a structure like this could conceivably have and *bellows*. I hope the commanding officer has a map in their room. If not, we could be here for decades and not find what we're looking for.

Tessen waits at the alcove, staying to the shadows and listening for several minutes. We all do the same behind him to keep from making some small motion or sound to distract him.

Tessen looks back at me, catching my eye and hand signing, *ready?*

I draw power in tiny increments from my wardstones and then expand it outward, enveloping my squad one by one. Once I have a firm grip on the shape I need the desosa to hold, I straighten from the wall and issue one last warning.

"You won't be seen, and our noises will be muffled, but

if you knock into something or someone, invisibility won't matter." I remind them all. "Be careful."

They nod or simply settle in, adjusting weapons and stances and positions. No one, not even Rai, offers a smart remark. Instead, they look to Chio, Tyrroh, and Tessen, the three who will have to lead us through this labyrinth of stone.

When Tessen signals *clear ahead*, we move out. I stay securely in the middle of the group, too much of my attention tied up in keeping us hidden to trust my reaction time. Instead, I let the others guide my steps while I take in the complex structure we've found ourselves in, a place even those who belong in this land aren't supposed to see.

The floor the ventilation shaft dropped us onto seems to be near the middle of Mushokeiji. Six levels above us and four below, with bridges crossing the open center of the prison every third floor. Hanging from those bridges are iron cages, suspended in open air by long chains. The one I can see most clearly is empty, but there are more, above and below us. None of those are unoccupied, and the people inside look wasted, barely more than a pile of rags and skin and bone.

The ceiling here is only ten feet high, and I get a better look at the lamps. Globes emitting a white light a lot like Sanii's are held by metal cages and attached to the stone with iron chains. Whatever's powering them, they're spaced about ten feet apart from one another, each one centered between two of the thick wood doors in the walls. A square about the length of my hand is cut at eye-height in each door, and it's obstructed by iron bars. When we stop for Tessen to check our directions, I peer into the room.

It's a cell. There's no light inside. No mattress or sleep pad. Nothing but shadows and stone and one long-haired, blade-thin person curled up in the corner, using their arm as a pillow.

Pulling back, I look at the other doors. Thirty-six on this level. Eleven levels, at least. If all those doors are cells, and all those cells hold one or more prisoners… Bellows. A voice in the back of my head whispers, *maybe we should release them.* But no. Getting through this without anyone knowing we were here is the priority. Releasing them can't be an option unless there's no other way out.

Tessen leads us down a curving stairwell off another narrow hallway, and I drop the invisibility. I can bring it back up at a moment's notice, but it's easier to breathe without it.

At each level, Tessen pauses, listening before he continues down, down, and down again until we're at the bottom of Mushokeiji's core. There he stops longer, waving at us to be quiet. Twice. The second time, no one was even moving. All I can do to be quieter is hold my breath and stop my heartbeat. One out of two will have to be enough. I break and have to take a breath twice before he finally signals us to move ahead.

I bring my invisibility ward back up as soon as Tessen moves.

This level is obviously different from the one we came in on. None of the doors have holes or bars, and although the center is empty and open to the floors above, the rest of the level is different. There are rooms set down hallways extending from the center of Mushokeiji like the spokes of a wheel, and it feels more like the barracks of Itagami than the prison levels above us. And then there's the light. It comes not only from the globes hanging from the ceiling, but also the thin, barred windows looking out over Suakizu's empty valley.

Tessen leads us down one hallway and up another. We pass a kitchen and dining hall and a healer's workspace — but thankfully none of the people inside notice us hurry by. Twice we have to duck into an empty room and wait for a guard to pass or else risk them running into someone. Each time, I drop my wards completely, closing my eyes and leaning against the wall. I feel flushed. Overheated. The stone is blissfully cool against my skin. It's probably the first and only time I'll be grateful for Ryogo's horrible temperatures.

Maybe it's the specific magic I'm trying to work. Maybe it's this dead place. Maybe both. Whatever the cause, I don't know if I can keep us hidden long enough to get us out of here unseen. The longer this search goes on, the harder it's becoming. At first it was only a mild strain. Now, even with Natani's help and my wardstones to draw from, I feel like I'm trying to carry twice my own weight up a mountain.

I lose track of time with nothing more than my own breaths to tell me how long it's been, but eventually Tessen stops and whispers something to Chio. Then Tessen moves to the closest door, pressing his ear against the wood, and Chio turns toward us. He pulls Tsua and Tyrroh closer, whispering to them; the orders trickle down the line.

"These should be the commanding officers' rooms," Etaro murmurs to me. "If Tessen says they're empty, we'll split to search them. Don't disturb what's inside more than needed."

After Tessen gives the all-clear, Chio and Tyrroh split us into groups. Except me. When Tyrroh reaches me, he gently orders, "Let up for a while and rest, Khya. We'll need you functional once we know where we have to go next."

I nod, exhaling and releasing my wards once everyone is inside the rooms. Rubbing my eyes, I lean heavily against the wall. Someone offers me a canteen. I don't look up to see who; I take it and swallow far too much. I've been on marathon patrols in the middle of Shiara's dry season and felt less dehydrated than this.

I let my arms and head hang, eyes closed. I don't know if I'll be ready when it's time to move. Especially when my wardstones are only half as powerful now as they were when we left camp. Natani has stayed with me, so close I can grab his hand if I need the anchor; hopefully him and what's left of the wardstones will be enough to make sure we get through this alive.

Then he touches my shoulder. "They found something."

I lift my head, absently watching Wehli and Nairo flow past us. Natani and I slowly follow them toward the room at the far end of the hall. We're last to enter. Everyone is gathered around a small table, peering at something on the surface. Maps. Each shows one level of Mushokeiji with symbols and notes written on the edges. Some are numbers that don't make sense until Tyrroh adds another paper to the table, one with both numbers and names.

Cell assignments. These are the people trapped in those dark, windowless rooms.

I force the realization aside, listening to their discussion and trying to follow it, but I'm lightheaded. And hot. And exhausted. I need more time, so I let Tessen and the others decide where to go next while I find a chair and sit down.

"Unless they've turned one of the cells into storage and left it unmarked on the map," Chio says after they've gone through each level several times, "the most logical places to hide it would be on this floor or the twelfth floor."

Twelve floors? I only saw eleven. There must be a full floor above what I thought was Mushokeiji's roof.

"It had better not be in one of the cells," Tessen mutters. "If they did that, we'll definitely be spotted before we find it. Khya can't last that long."

When everyone glances at me, I just shrug. "I'd argue with him, but it's true."

"It has to be the twelfth floor." Tsua places that map on top. "I doubt the stone is common knowledge, even among the guards, and the floor we're on seems to be their shared space. There'd be too much foot traffic here to keep anything secret or safe, but they could easily restrict access to the top floor. It's also the only level not open to the rest of the prison."

"It's where I'd put something I wanted to hide," Sanii agrees.

"Then that's where we'll start." Chio looks up to meet Tsua's eyes. "Is it worth the risk to take this map with us?"

"Yes. If we put everything else back the way we found it, there's a chance the officer won't notice for a long time. Or will think they misplaced this page." Tsua rolls up the map. "It's what we'll hope for, at least."

It doesn't take much work to set it right, so we're soon moving back to the stairwell. Tessen said it was a lesser used path; that makes it the safest travel option we have.

I'm back in the middle of the group, wards up. Keeping them that way is like having a staring contest with eyes painted on a wall. Eventually I'm going to lose the fight, but for now I can do it. Even if everything else around me gets pushed to the periphery. I would probably walk straight into a wall if Natani didn't stay so close.

Hand in mine, his movements guide me. When he climbs, so do I. When he stops, it pulls me to a halt. When he turns, I follow. We stop. We backtrack. We start again. We turn. I'm barely aware of the stone walls or the symbols carved into them. I hear voices. I see flashes of light. None of it matters so long as I can keep the protections strong enough to hide us, but my wardstones are nearly empty. I'm pulling more from Natani, too. How long before I drain him?

We stop, and Tessen appears. Lines of worry ring his eyes and his mouth, but he doesn't ask if I'm okay. All he asks is, "Do you still carry lockpicks, Khya?"

"You know I do." He made sure I put them in my pack.

"I can try to do it, but you're better." He looks over his

shoulder; only then do I realize we're standing in front of a wide door.

I hold his eyes, forcing myself to focus. "If I do this, we'll lose the wards."

"I'll warn you before anyone shows up." He gets the lockpicks out of my pack and presses them into my hand. "You can do this, Nyshin-pa."

When I nod, he steps away, leaving space for me to work.

I take a long breath and release my wards on the exhale. My body aches and my fingers are so stiff that holding the lockpicks hurts. Yorri made them years ago, and he taught me how to use them. Without the weight of the wards, my head is clearing a little. Enough for me to feel steady when I kneel in front of the door and focus on the lock. Thankfully, it isn't too different from the ones we had in Itagami. A little more complicated and a lot heavier, but based on the same design. It takes several minutes to get the small pieces of iron in the right place, and longer for my fumbling fingers to keep them there, but then there's a *click*.

Tessen helps me up, his concern etched even deeper. Chio takes my place and opens the door, letting us into a long, narrow room. It only seems to be ten feet from the door to the opposite wall, but it's more than twenty feet from end to end. Raised stone platforms run in a line down the center of the room. Iron cages sit in each corner. Shackles are attached to the walls at either end of the chamber. Stains that might be dried blood are splattered across the stone. Opposite the main door is another door, but I only glance at that; my gaze is drawn by what's fixed to the stone on either side of it. Shelves of jars and books and boxes, and lots of weapons—daggers, arrows, whips, spears, and things I don't even have names for.

In a way, this room reminds me of Imaku, reminds me of the moment I found Yorri and the others trapped on black stone platforms. In a way, this room feels so much worse than Imaku.

"They were running experiments." Chio's words are infused with my own horror.

"Experiments on what?" Sanii seems to dread the answer.

"Mages. The prisoners." Tsua's hand hovers over the weapons mounted on the wall. "If I had to guess, they were trying to see if they could use a stone that brought down the bobasu against mortal mages, too."

I don't want to think about that. I don't want the meaning of her words to sink into my head because it's too much, and it's too close, and it's not impossible that Varan is using my brother and the rest of his prisoners for the same kind of torment. But it would be so much worse for Yorri and the others; they're trapped in their own minds and in life itself.

Shivering, I head across the room to the second door. It's locked, and this one isn't anything like the mechanisms I saw in Itagami. This one doesn't need a key. Instead it seems like I'll have to solve some kind of puzzle before it will open. Yorri would crack this open in minutes, but I don't have his mind for these things.

Sanii steps up beside me, eir head barely reaching high enough to catch my peripheral vision. Without turning away from the door, I ask, "I don't suppose you share Yorri's love of puzzles, do you?"

"He taught me to love them." Ey kneels to get a better look at the circular lock.

The rings are concentric, six surrounding the center solid circle—almost like it's a reflection of Mushokeiji itself. Markings line the edges of all seven circles, and each rotates, its directionality opposed to the circle preceeding it. Only the center circle doesn't move, but there are markings on it, too. Neither of us recognize the marks themselves, so we call Osshi over.

He whistles, his eyebrows rising. "These pre-date the omikia characters. These are older than the written language Varan and your andofume knew."

The translation happens slowly, and even after he tells us what each mark represents, we're still not sure what any of it really *means*. Frustration pulls Sanii's eyebrows low and makes my fists clench, but we keep working.

Ey turns the circles one by one, listening to the clicks coming from within the mechanism. In our murmured conversations, we decide the center circle will be the one that unlocks the door, but only after the outer rings are precisely aligned. And that alignment might have to happen in a specific order. The number of combinations is impossible for me to calculate.

Then Osshi remembers a scrap of paper he'd found hidden inside a book in the commander's office, something with similar symbols written on it. "I thought it might be a code to one of the pages we stole, a way to decipher a hidden message. Maybe it's for this, instead."

"It reads like a reminder," Tsua says, showing the scrap to Chio. "It sounds like clues someone might leave for themselves if they were worried they'd forget the pattern."

It's just enough to lead us in the right direction.

Several minutes later, Sanii presses hard on the center circle. It sinks. It clicks. Something inside the door grinds. I hold my breath until the massive metal door opens outward an inch. I fall back, landing on my butt and scooting out of the way as Sanii and Etaro grip the handles in the center of the heavy door and pull it open. What they reveal is worth the effort of getting here.

Shelves upon shelves of black stone.

The room is about as wide as the one we're in, and maybe

as long—I can't see either end from where I'm sitting. Boulder-sized pieces lay in the middle of the space, set in a row like the tables in the main room. The walls are full of shelves, floor to ceiling, and each shelf is packed with Imaku rock. Some are pebbles, others are as large as my head. There's more than we can possibly carry. Knowing what they're doing with it, though, I want to take it all away from them.

"Use these." Tyrroh's order makes me look up, and I watch as he tosses bags at the others. "Move quick and pack as much as you can carry."

Tsua and Chio are with Osshi, riffling through papers and books. Everyone else hurries into the vault. I try to get up to join them, but Tyrroh shakes his head and orders me to rest. Five minutes of sitting on cold stone won't do much to revive me, but I don't say that. Five minutes is the only time we have. So I sit and wait.

My squad carefully places black rocks into the bags while Osshi, Tsua, and Chio remove pages from stacks or tear them out of books and pack them away. Tessen is the only person not moving; he's near the main door, listening for incoming danger. I stand and join him. If I stay sitting much longer, I might fall asleep.

Talking to Tessen or touching him isn't a good idea when he's hyper-focused on his senses like this—it overloads and distracts him—but I lean nearby, watching his expression change minutely in reaction to whatever he's hearing on the other side of the door.

When the rest of the squad leaves the vault, closing the heavy door behind themselves and rearranging the rings of the lock, Tessen moves. "It's clear," he says, voice hoarse. "Are we ready?"

"Lead us out, basaku," Chio orders from the rear of the squad.

"Are *you* ready?" He brushes his thumb along my cheekbone. "Can we help?"

I shake my head as I straighten from the wall. "Just get us out of here."

Determination hardens his features. He reaches for the door, checking for movement one more time before leading us out.

Hallways. Staircases. Lights. Voices. We move faster this time; Tessen's already sure of the path we need to take. Soon we're back at the fifth level landing, waiting for him to make sure the last part of our route is clear.

"There's someone moving, but only one, I think," Tessen whispers, looking to Tyrroh for confirmation.

Of course the one guard we encounter is standing between us and our escape. Of course. Our luck has held too well until now. They've had enough time by now for the first wave of excitement over the fresh supplies to wane, for them to remember they have jobs to do.

"If Khya can hold the ward, we should be able to pass him. It's worth the risk to get out of here sooner," Tyrroh says.

"Sooner is better." My stomach is churning and my limbs feel heavy. If we don't finish soon, I won't be able to trust my grip on the mountain as we escape. I'm shaking and exhausted.

"When you're ready then," Tsua says.

I hold out my hand, and Natani takes it. His hand trembles—he's probably as exhausted as I am—but his grip doesn't falter. At least the desosa I'm pulling through him is from his wardstones; it should make it easier for him to bear up under the drain. Mine is empty. His is beginning to flicker. If we don't get out of here soon, I'm going to have to steal someone else's protections to keep this magic running.

We move out of the safety of the stairwell and onto the

open ledge. The guard Tessen warned us about is there, slowly approaching from the right—the direction we need to travel. I dismiss him as soon as I spot him. It's *one* guard, and he hasn't noticed the fourteen people joining him on the floor. If he becomes a problem, someone else will handle him.

Mostly because, if the guard is a problem, I'm probably unconscious.

We move slowly, and I look out over the empty center of Mushokeiji, spotting at least one guard on every level now. They weren't there the first time we walked this level, but now they're spread throughout the prison. Two dozen of them at least. And on some of the levels, pairs of guards are pushing frames on wheels suspending something that looks like a massive, round shield.

Then Sanii whispers, "What is that on his head?"

I look at the guard closest to us, but I can't begin to guess. A thick strap of something that could be either metal or hard leather rests on top of his head, holding two thick, round somethings over his ears. Those seem even more pointless than the shields hanging on frames.

He's strolling across the ledge, absently swinging a small open-sided lamp at the end of a length of rope as he peers into the cells he passes. We move closer to the open center to avoid running into him. He stops in front of one of the cells and says something to whoever's inside. I can't make out the words—they were spoken too quickly and too accented—but whatever it was makes Tessen stop.

Turning, Tessen looks at the guard. Then at the others spread throughout the prison. Then toward the framed shields.

Just as the guards standing next to those circles of metal simultaneously strike them with massive mallets.

Piercing, ringing, echoing *noise* reverberates through the prison.

Tessen collapses. Tyrroh drops against the wall. My concentration shatters, and so do my wards.

The guard is screaming, shouting a warning as he tosses his lamp toward the ledge. It lands in a groove, and something catches fire. In seconds, the fire spreads, shooting along the whole level. More shouts. Guards running in our direction.

Then Chio grabs the guard by the throat and orders, "*Run!*"

CHAPTER FIFTEEN

atani yanks me along by the hand, sprinting toward our exit. The narrow hallway is as empty as it was earlier, and we pass through it faster. Everything after is excruciating.

My body feels weighted. My lungs can't seem to find air. My reactions are slow. My joints ache. My energy is drained and my wardstones are empty, and now I've got to carry my bodyweight in stone up a ventilation shaft and down the side of a mountain.

And apparently our luck is well and truly gone.

Behind us are shouts and thudding boots, harbingers of pursuit. Miari can collapse the shaft once we're through, but the guards have other ways out of Mushokeiji, and this is their territory. No one will be better at tracking us across this wasteland than them.

I count to keep my breathing even and move faster.

By the time I reach the end of the hall, several of the squad are already clambering up the shaft, all of them moving faster than I expected. Only after Etaro lifts me the six feet to the bottom of the shaft do I see how—Miari left us handholds, all of them so deep it's practically as easy as climbing a ladder. I hope she'll do the same thing to the stone on the mountain.

Miari is waiting when I climb out of the shaft. She points down the mountain, an order implicit. There are handholds, but if she's still here, there's no way the extra help will last the whole climb; she's our only ishiji—she has to stay to collapse the vent behind us.

I descend. Steadily, not fast. My lungs burn in the cold air. My arms shake. My fingers are going numb. If I move too quickly, I might miss a grip and drop. A hundred-foot fall onto solid stone would be hard to survive even when my wards are at full power.

Hand by hand. Foot by foot. I don't look up or down or sideways. I don't look for friends or enemies. Only rock.

Hand. Hand. Foot. Foot. Right. Left. Right. Left. Down and left, inch by inch, until my next step is on solid ground and someone is pulling me away from the edge. They release me before I can flinch away at the unexpected contact. But they were right to pull me aside. No one else can fit on the narrow ledge with me standing in the way.

"Khya?" Tyrroh's dark eyes narrow as he scans my face. "Condition report, Nyshin-pa."

"I'll make it to camp, but…" I shiver and pull my hood up over my head. "Food should help. I'll eat as we go."

"But sleep will help more?" His gaze travels to the mountain, checking on the progress of the others. Then he returns his focus to me. "Hold on for me as long as you can, but you *tell someone* if you need to be carried the rest of the way. Understood?"

"Yes, Nyshin-ma." But I won't ask for that unless I can't walk another step. Especially since Chio brought the guard he grabbed with us. Everyone will have enough to worry about carrying the stones, evading pursuit, and keeping the guard from giving us away. I don't want them to be worrying about me, too.

Miari and Tsua are the last down, and Tsua is wearing an expression I don't know how to describe. Chio demands, "What happened?"

"I... We needed more time, so I opened the cells." Tsua casts one look back at the vent, her eyes troubled. "All of the cells."

"Kaisubeh save them," Chio breathes, eyes closed.

As we run toward our camp, I can barely stop myself from asking which "them" Chio means: The guards or the prisoners?

I push myself to keep up. I'm fine when we grab our stowed gear, but we can't stay there. We need to run. Problem is that hidden, defensible campsites aren't easy to find near Mushokeiji—possibly by design. We run for two hours and no one finds a safe place to rest. Two hours, though, is all I have in me.

"Tessen." My call is weak, but Tessen hears.

He turns back and slings my arm over his shoulders, his face pinched with frustration. "I thought you were better at following orders than this, Nyshin-pa. Tyrroh told you to warn us *before* you were on the edge of collapse."

"I thought we'd find somewhere to stop by now." My mouth feels dry, and my tongue sluggish, so I don't try talking again. Not even when Tessen passes me to Etaro when he has to run back to the front of the line to help find a place to stop.

The landscape becomes a blur of dark rock, and I quit

paying attention fast, pouring all my focus into keeping myself on my feet.

By the time we do stop, the sun has set. I can't see much of wherever we've ended up. It's a secure enough spot that Tessen and Tyrroh tell Rai and Nairo to light a fire. They wouldn't risk it if the light could be spotted at a distance. A couple hours ago, Etaro caught the small animal unlucky enough to cross paths with us. Now it's being cooked over the flames as everyone huddles close to the warmth. Everyone. Including the guard Chio grabbed inside Mushokeiji, who's now being closely watched by our elder andofume.

Sanii catches my eye from across the fire, a relieved smile spreading across eir face. "I don't know if I've ever seen you so happy to be sitting down, Khya."

"Me neither." I look at Rai, and when she nods permission I lean against her to rest my head on her shoulder. Then I breathe deep, testing my body and the air.

We must still be within the boundaries of Suakizu, because the desosa is thin and weak, but it's there. It's stronger than it was near Mushokeiji, and I can finally replenish some of the energy I lost. My joints still ache, but the hollowed-out nausea has ebbed. "Are we being followed?"

"Definitely, but they're about a mile east of here, and they've stopped for the night," Tessen reports. "We don't think they'll be able to follow if we keep to the mountains for a while instead of the roads. In a day or so, we'll hit the roads to pick up some distance."

"Unless the Nyshin-ma and the andofume change their mind before the sun comes up," Rai says beside me. "They didn't seem too sure about the plan an hour ago."

"Maybe because of *him*." I gesture to the sleeping guard, without lifting my head from Rai's shoulder. "What are we planning to do with our prisoner?"

"They were hoping to get details about the experiments from him," Tessen says. "And they were also thinking you might want to test your skills with the niadagu cords on him."

"What?" I sit up.

"We have a live subject for you to test yourself on, Nyshin-pa. Don't turn down the chance," Rai says.

"It's a big jump to go from binding rocks to people." And the spell comes with warnings in every book. If the mage's intentions aren't perfectly clear, and if the level of magic used isn't perfectly right, and— Essentially, if everything about a niadagu isn't perfect, it goes horribly wrong. Or it doesn't work at all. Neither risk is worth taking when it could cost a life and a lot of information.

"I'll do it if you aren't ready to try," Tsua says as she approaches. "But you know how to make the cords hold the desosa now, and you've worked the spell before."

I look down at my wrist, at the new cord tied there, a replacement for the one I left tied around the rock in Kaisuama. Binding truly is the best way to keep him here. There's too much else we need to worry about and too big a chance he'll escape from a non-magical restraint. Or his people freeing him if they find us.

"I'll do it." I look up and meet Tsua's eyes. "But not now. Tomorrow morning if I'm rested enough."

I'd prefer to wait until we're back on land that produces desosa like it should, but I have the wardstones. Natani's are too drained to be much use as protection; they'll be enough to give me the energy I need to bind the guard, though.

"Fair." Tsua looks down at the guard and shrugs. "He'll sleep the rest of the night, I'm sure. From the way he acted the last few hours, I don't think he's ever walked more than a mile in a day. He acted like he was being tortured."

"Weakling," Rai mutters, flicking a tiny pebble at him.

Near the fire, Etaro and Nairo begin slicing strips of meat off the animal and scooping cooked grain into the bowls from our packs. Then, with a single gesture, Etaro floats the first full bowl across the fire toward me.

"Eat and get some more sleep, Khya," Tsua says. "We need to leave before first light, as soon as we get our guest bound."

Since the sleep I've had wasn't nearly enough, I don't argue. I devour the food—and try not to stare at the bowl when it's empty, wishing for more.

When I wake up in the faint, gray light of pre-dawn, Tessen has curled up behind me, his arm draped over my waist and his nose pressed against the curve of my throat. Even though the fire is only embers, it's warm here, and despite the stone underneath us, I'm almost comfortable. Only when I hear others moving around the camp do I force myself to get up.

Throughout the night, some of the limited desosa here must've soaked into my body. The ache in my joints is minor now, and the gnawing hollowness inside me nearly gone. I feel almost whole. I'll still use what's left in Natani's wardstones, mostly to avoid draining myself again so soon, but I think I *could* bind the guard with my own power if I had to.

"Did he tell you anything about the experiments?" I ask Tsua over breakfast.

"Not much. Yet." Tsua turns toward the guard, a man who's steadfastly staring at the ground. "But he confirmed what I'd feared—the prison is controlled by acolytes of Masya-Mono, the goddess of both law and magic. The experiments have been going on for so long most of the guards don't know when they started. Only the commanding officers, some high-ranking staff, and selected special officials are allowed in the room."

"What makes you think he can tell you anything if he's never been inside?" I ask.

"Because in a place like Mushokeiji, where the only company they have is each other, how easy do you think it is for anyone to keep a secret?"

"They kept secrets in Itagami," I remind her. "Life-changing secrets."

Tsua shakes her head. "There were more than ten thousand citizens there, and you all had more work than you could handle keeping the clan safe and fed. Mushokeiji has less than a hundred guards and even fewer staff."

"Bellows, you're right." I rub my hand over my mouth. "Rai and Etaro acted gossip-starved even with thousands of people to spy on. I can't imagine how bad they'd be with less than a hundred."

"I'll trust your judgement on that," Tsua says with a smirk. "Are you ready, then?"

I hold up one finger, moving off to collect the diminished wardstones from Natani before I return to Tsua's side. As I settle down beside her, I see Tyrroh give most of his wardstones to Natani. I'm relieved Natani has the added protection, but I need to find something to replace the drained stones soon.

"You'll watch over it, right? In case things start to go wrong."

"Yes, but take your time, Khya." Tsua's expression becomes serious. "It's important. Once you speak the words of the spell, there's no way to go back or slow down. And definitely no chance to stop it. The magic will either succeed or fail at that point."

And that's what I'm worried about. No adjustments. No mistakes.

But how many chances will I have to feel the full use and power of this spell as it works on a *person* before I have to undo the cords on my brother and the other prisoners? None, so I'll regret it if I don't take this one.

I cross the camp and kneel next to the guard. He doesn't lift his head, but he watches me out the corner of his eye. Posture stiff, he leans away. His long hair had been tied back with a length of leather when we saw him inside Mushokeiji. Now it's loose, and when he tilts his head away, his hair conceals his face, a thick curtain of black dividing us.

His arms are restrained in front of him, wrists tied together. I move my hand toward him, but I can't make myself touch him yet. It feels wrong. In Itagami, even with our enemies, we rarely put our hands on anyone without permission. Not outside of combat. There's no chance this man is going to give me permission, though, and there's no other way to perform the spell, so I need to do this.

My murmured apology makes his head snap up, fear shining in his eyes. The look turns to confusion when I wrap the red cord I untie from my own wrist around his, above the ropes Tsua tied him up with yesterday. He struggles the instant the cord touches his skin, pulling back and trying to tip himself sideways, muttering words that must be Ryogan curses Osshi hasn't taught us. He only stops when Rai closes in on him, fire in her palm. Etaro slides into the space opposite her, making shards of rock hover in front of the guard's face.

"She is going to keep you from escaping, and you are going to let her." The threat of *or else* hovers over every one of Rai's words.

The guard's mouth opens, then his gaze jumps quickly from Rai's flames to Etaro's rocks to my red cord. His expression changes slowly, fear transforming into something else. Something calmer. Resignation, I hope. This will be so much easier if he isn't fighting me.

When I grip his right forearm to start again, he closes his eyes and holds steady. I wrap the red cord just loose enough to keep it from cutting circulation, and tie a knot he won't be able to undo with one hand. Then, touching both Natani's wardstones and the cord, I wrap energy around the fabric, shaping my intentions as I shape the desosa.

He cannot stray more than a hundred feet from my side. He cannot warn the Ryogans about us. He cannot cause us harm. He cannot sit idly by while someone or something *else* causes us harm. He cannot hurt *himself* to escape.

Layer by layer, I bind him to promises as specific as I can make them and sink them into the niadagu cord. When I feel the desosa settle, I finish the spell and say, "Tozaiko nitoko."

The guard gasps. His head snaps back. Every muscle in his body tightens, straining against his skin. Skin that's fast becoming an alarming shade of red.

"Tsua! Zonna!" I scramble back. "What is this? What'd I do?"

The man screeches, the noise barely human. Frantically, he scratches at his arm, nails digging into the skin. Like he's trying to tear the niadagu spell out of his body.

"Can you stop it?" Tsua's question makes my racing pulse stutter. Someone—Tessen, I think—wraps their arms around me. She's not talking to me.

"I'm *trying*," Zonna growls, his hands on the guard's chest. "Everything makes it worse!"

"Worse? It can't—oh. Oh no." Tsua sits back, horror widening her eyes. I lean back against Tessen; his arms tighten around me. When she speaks again, her voice is hoarse and wrecked. "Zonna, st-top. You won't… You can't save him from this."

From what? I want to demand. The words won't come. They're trapped in my throat along with my breath and my heart.

It doesn't take long. In another minute, the guard is dead.

He dies clawing at his wrists and choking on nothing. On air.

And it started the moment I activated the spell. However it happened—*why*ever it happened—I did it. His isn't the first life I've taken, but none of the others felt this wrong. They were enemies. It was in battle, in a fair fight.

This? This feels like murder.

"Khya, I'm so sorry." Tsua's words barely register, but then she kneels in front of me, and I can't see the guard. "This is my fault. I should have guessed…"

"Guessed what?" Tessen. That's Tessen's voice demanding answers.

"Here, vanafitia." Chio's voice shifts Tsua's attention, and she moves back to see what he's found. A tattoo is inked into the man's chest, the lines stark black against his beige skin.

When Tsua brushes her finger over one of the lines, she hisses and yanks her hand back. "They created the ink out of stone dust from Imaku. Bellows, it makes sense."

"What *happened*?" The words burst out of me far louder than I'd intended.

But it works. Tsua looks at me, guilt in her eyes. "It's a protection and a security measure for Mushokeiji. If I had to guess, I'd say it would stop some spells from hurting them, but would turn others into weapons that ended their lives. Spells like the niadagu, which could force them to betray the prison."

"But I… Did he *know*?" Rai demands.

"He must have." Etaro is staring at the black symbols on the dead man's chest. "Did you see his face?"

"He knew." The expression makes sense now. It *was* resignation, but not to becoming a prisoner. He was accepting his end.

Tessen makes a pained noise. "Why would they do that?"

"They were guards of a prison for mages in a land that fears magic," Chio says. "Anyone who commits a crime using magic, or breaks a law regarding the study and practice of it, gets sent here. Those people have families and partners, people willing and able to attack the prison with magic. And at least *some* of the prisoners are strong enough to break free of their cells, even with the spells they used to keep magic repressed."

"Having some measure of security in place to protect the guards or Mushokeiji as a whole makes sense," Tsua finishes. "And I should've known there'd be something. This wasn't your fault. I'm *sorry*, Khya."

It doesn't erase the guilt lodged in my chest.

And I don't even know if the binding worked before it killed him.

T sua and I arrange the guard's body under an overhang, shielding it from the elements until the other guards find him. He died protecting his land, and he deserves whatever honors the Ryogans will give him. By the time we're done, camp is packed. We're off before the sun fully rises above the eastern mountains.

The pace is grueling, the terrain is rough, and there's no good hunting along the way. Only once do we see an animal in the distance that's worth the effort, but only Wehli's enhanced speed could've gotten a blade anywhere near the beast. He tries, determination on his face, but although his left-handed skill with a sword keeps getting better, his balance when traveling at speeds the rest of us can't conceive of is still off. He tries, chasing after the creature—

—and he trips, seemingly over his own feet, before he's halfway to his target. The noise startles the animal. In seconds, it's gone.

He doesn't speak for the rest of the afternoon. Not even to Nairo and Miari. None of us push him.

Our victory is tainted by the guard's death, and by the lingering uncertainty of pursuit. Every time we think we've lost them, Tessen picks up sounds in the distance. We change direction often, sometimes going toward the wrong horizon for over a mile just to lay a false trail. If they're even tracking us by their senses.

Partially because of the hunters behind us, Tyrroh and the andofume decide to risk the more populated lowlands earlier than they'd planned in order to gain speed and distance. Speed or solitude. We can only have one, and solitude doesn't seem to be working for us now.

After Nentoado and Suakizu, the hills of northern Ryogo almost seem warm. But they're also grayer and wet—it's still raining here. From the way the ground sucks at my boots, I don't think it's *stopped* raining for days. At least the winds are gentle. It's not storming, just steadily raining.

My wards keep the water off, but the muck makes our travel slower than any of us hoped. Tsua, Etaro, and Miari help where they can, Miari firming the ground when it becomes impassable, and our two rikinhisus lifting us free of the mud when we get stuck. It makes me miss the rocky slopes of the mountains, and it forces us to stay on the roads for several miles longer than we wanted to be.

Then, near the end of the day, Tessen's head snaps north, cocked for listening, not looking. "Someone's out there."

Instantly, I check the wardstones, grateful for the normal levels of desosa in this area as I reinforce them. Everyone draws their weapons and readies their magic, most facing the same direction as Tessen. The others watch the rear.

Knowing how sensitive Tessen's hearing is when he's listening at a distance, I keep my voice so quiet I can hardly hear myself. "What is it?"

"Movement. Breathing. A lot of people—can't tell how many." His voice is barely louder than mine was. "There. They're moving parallel to this path, not approaching... They're not speaking, but there's something that sounds like..." Tessen eyes snap open. "*No!* Brace, Khya!"

A barrage of a *thwacks*. A heavy volley of flaming arrows streaks toward us. I feel a sharp impact and a flash of heat from each one. Without my ward, each arrow would've landed in flesh. And we're lucky it's been raining for so long or the trees would've caught fire.

"How long can you keep your wards up?" Zonna asks.

"Long enough," I insist through gritted teeth. "*Run.*"

Then another arrow strikes my ward.

And pierces it.

My ward shatters. I gasp, sparks of white-hot light flaring across my vision and sizzling over my skin. I stumble. The arrowhead grazes my thigh. Searing pain explodes from the wound, spreading fast as lightning.

I lose balance. As I fall, my eyes lock on something I wish I could unsee.

An arrow in Tyrroh's chest.

"No! Zonna!" My scream tears through my throat. I try to push myself back up; tremors in my muscles buckle my joints. I collapse by Tyrroh's side.

Zonna rushes toward us, hands outstretched. But there's so much blood. The front of Tyrroh's clothes are soaked, blood and rain plastering them to his chest.

"Etaro, Rai, incoming!" Tessen shouts orders because I can't. I failed. My wards *failed*, and Tyrroh is bleeding, dying, and the shocks from whatever shattered my ward are running through my body, and it's my fault because he had to give up his wardstones after I drained the ones that should've protected him and I *can't*—

Zonna shouts and jerks his hands back from the arrow shaft. He mutters curses and leaves it where it is, pressing his hands to Tyrroh's chest. I reach for the arrow; Zonna can't heal Tyrroh until it's gone. But Zonna plants his hands on my chest and shoves me back.

Another arrow smacks into the damp soil, missing Tyrroh's throat by inches. Missing my back by inches.

"Deflect what you can and *run*," Zonna shouts.

Tessen reaches over my shoulder, yanking the arrow out of the ground with one hand and forcing me to my feet with the other.

"No." I gasp, my first step sends a jolt through my chest. "Ty-Tyrroh! We can't—"

"He's gone, Khya. *Run*," Tessen orders.

But we can't leave *him!* I want to fight against em, turn around and throw Tyrroh over my shoulder to carry him home with us, but I can barely breathe. The air catches in my throat. It burns in my lungs. My skin buzzes and sparks like someone is running tiny shocks of lightning across it. I can't unstick my tongue from the roof of my mouth. My eyes won't focus.

Something is so very wrong and I can't even call for help.

And the arrows are still falling.

Then Zonna moves in on the opposite side from Tessen, reaching for my hand. His skin is noticeably warmer than mine until the cool, soothing flow of his magic rushes through me. It patches the jagged cracks it feels like the arrows left in my mind. Because they *did*. The arrow may not have struck my skin, but it broke through my wards while they were up. The impact frayed the lines of power in my mind. Much worse, and it might have broken them completely.

"Better?" Tessen casts a worried glance over his shoulder.

I take a deep breath—one that *doesn't* hurt—and nod,

lengthening my stride and forcing my wards back up. "I'm fine. Keep moving."

I keep the shield close to our skin, a last line of defense rather than the bubble of solid protection. The others have to be able to deflect the arrows blasting our direction from the archers. Their aim is straight and true, but Tessen's shouted warnings and the squad's magic and blades send most of them flying harmlessly aside.

An arrow whizzes past my head, so close it scratches my cheek. My wards crack. Fire blooms in its wake. I dodge, changing course and gritting my teeth.

Pain explodes through my chest, a double hit—lightning then blade. My ward shatters. I open my mouth to scream. I don't think I make a sound. All I can hear is the rain and the wind and my own blood rushing too fast through my veins and out the hole in my chest.

I fall, momentum bringing me down on my side. I end up twisted and staring down. At the black arrow inches away from my heart. My lungs won't fill no matter how deeply I breathe. I can barely raise my head.

Bellows, I hope the others are gone by now. Running far away from this place. I hope so, but I can't tell. My vision is blurring. It feels like my head has been shoved underwater.

Run, I want to scream at them.

I do scream when the world jerks, but there aren't words. Pain whites out my vision. The rushing in my ears becomes a roar.

Everything comes in flashes.

Flying down an empty road.

A wall of fire and stone.

Pain shooting in jagged columns through my body.

Throat closing, the muscles locked so tight not even air can get through.

Desosa rushing through my body like water dousing a fire.

Tessen's face hovering over mine is the only thing keeping the rain out of my eyes. The magic pouring into my body rolls through me in waves, making the pain ebb and rise like a stormy sea. I can breathe—barely—and my vision stops going completely white between flares, but I don't know what's happening. Or where I am. Or if everyone else got away. All I see is dark clouds and Tessen's face. His gray eyes are so dark they almost match the sky. "Etaro! Push them back!"

He's worried, but he's fine. He's fine. Even if I'm not, Tessen will be okay.

I see faces. Tessen and Zonna and someone else. They're speaking; their lips are moving and I hear tones, but I can't understand. It's like someone dumped molten rock on my chest.

Then liquid—warm, thick, and coppery—fills my mouth. Breathing goes from hard to impossible. It feels like drowning.

"Tssiky'le, I can't…fast enough." Zonna's voice. But he sounds impossibly far away and his words come in bursts, like something is missing between them. "Go get…she…only…"

"She can't breathe!" Tessen. Angry. Scared. I want to hold his hand; I can't move.

Then Zonna's voice again, but the words are lost. Energy burns through my chest. Like the desert sun, it evaporates the liquid in my throat. My lungs. I can breathe.

Blood and rot, breathing *hurts*.

Hands under my shoulders, forcing me up even though it feels like moving will kill me. Then something soft against my ear and a whisper just loud enough to hear.

"I'm sorry. I'm sorry. Khya, *please* hold on."

Sharp pressure on my jaw, forcing my mouth open. Someone is pouring fire down my throat. It burns my mouth and scalds my tongue.

And then the taste hits me.

I gag. Putrid. Rotten. Worse than foul. My stomach cramps. I double over; it's the only way to keep myself from turning inside out as pains spread, one blurring into another until I don't know anything else. My limbs are— I have them. They're there, but I can't control them. Can't move anything.

If this isn't dying, I don't ever want to know how painful death can be.

CHAPTER SIXTEEN

I gasp. My eyes fly open, and I fight my way awake. Danger. There was danger and blood and I failed but—

But I have no idea where we are. Not in the forest; there's too much stone. It's similar in color to the stone surrounding Mushokaiji, that chalky gray, so maybe the attack was only a nightmare? My breathing is fine and I couldn't survive a hit so close to my heart, but...

Tessen is sitting by my side, watching me with guarded relief. There are shadows under his eyes and his shoulders sag. It looks like he hasn't slept well in days.

"Khya. You're okay." Eyes closed, he slumps forward, his head landing on my shoulder. I move to catch his graceless fall, and when my hands land on his back, he's trembling.

"Did I—" I cut myself off, swallow, and try again. "That wasn't a nightmare, was it?"

"No. Tyrroh, he— And then *you*—" He shakes his head, the tremor in his body getting worse. When he turns his face into my neck and holds me tighter, I feel his tears against my skin. "I'm sorry, I'm sorry, but it worked and I'm so happy you're here, but I'm *sorry*."

My heart stalls, skipping a beat before doubling its pace.

Not a nightmare. Losing *Tyrroh* wasn't just a nightmare.

My stomach drops, and my eyes burn. When I close them, I can see the black arrow shaft sticking out of his chest and the blood soaked up by layers of fabric. It happened because my wards weren't strong enough. Because I took away the extra protection the wardstone would've given him.

Did we bring him with us? I want to ask. *Can we at least give him the respect of making sure his body feeds the soil like it would've in Itagami?*

But I don't ask because another memory is surfacing, and it doesn't make sense.

I was hit, too, wasn't I? I must have been. I remember the pain and an arrow sticking out of my chest. It hadn't directly pierced my heart, but it had to have sliced through a lung. Or nicked it. Zonna shouldn't have been able to save me, not in the middle of a fight like that. But I'm alive and breathing without hitch or pain, so that can only mean…

"What happened, Tessen?"

Tessen makes a noise that isn't quite a word, but he doesn't have to answer. I know as soon as I meet Sanii's eyes, and my racing pulse begins to calm.

They made me drink some of the susuji. They poured immortality down my throat to save my life, and Tessen is apologizing because… I have no idea.

Pushing away the thoughts of Tyrroh, I focus on Tessen. "Why do you think I'm going to be mad at you?"

He shakes his head; words seem beyond him. Sanii crouches on my other side. "He hates that he took away your choice. Even though I told him that you'd already considered the obvious."

"That becoming as hard to kill as Varan is probably the

only way we're going to beat him?" I run my hand down Tessen's back. "I thought about it when Sanii tested the susuji on emself. I wasn't sure if it was worth the risk for the rest of us—I can't remember how many of Varan's trials ended in death, but I know some did." I tilt my face toward Tessen, whispering the words for him. "I'm not angry. I would've eventually taken it myself, I think, and you were right to give it to me then. The only thing I regret is that we couldn't—that we couldn't force Tyrroh to drink it in time."

Tears burn in my eyes, and the tremor that's barely left Tessen's body seems to transfer to mine.

It's senseless and impossible, but I wish I could go back to the days after Sanii told me my brother *wasn't* dead. As awful as that time was, the problem and my plan to solve it had been simple—find Yorri and rescue him. At least then I felt like I knew what I was doing.

Here, I can't remember why I ever thought I wanted to lead. Or why anyone should follow.

"I know what you're thinking, and you need to stop." Sanii's voice is gentle but insistent. "You weren't shooting the arrows, and you couldn't know the tyatsu were carrying weapons created by the guards at Mushokeiji."

"Is that how they—" I shudder. I've used my ward to stop arrows before. Entire volleys of them. None of those strikes ever felt like those had.

"The weapons were spelled *and* coated with paint made from Imaku stone dust," Tessen says. "Like the tattoo on the guard. It's something they developed to fight off the bobasu, I think, but whatever magic they attach to it must make it work against *any* mages."

"Did you keep the arrow?"

"Both of them," Sanii says, nodding. "Etaro and Tsua carried you and Tyrroh with us, and all of us wanted to know about a weapon strong enough to get through *your* wards."

Eir tone makes me think ey was trying to make a joke, but I don't laugh. "Did you give him final rites yet?" Then another question occurs to me. "How long have I been out?"

Tessen glances at Sanii. "Almost six days."

"*Six?*" It can't have been that long. Sanii only slept for four, and ey spent most of that time writhing and rolling and screaming in pain. I stayed under for another two. But it doesn't make sense. If I screamed for days, my throat should be so raw and hoarse that even breathing irritates it. I'm fine. Hungry, a little shaky, and riddled with remorse, but physically fine.

"And we're sure it worked?" I don't *feel* much different, but that doesn't mean there aren't changes. Like how much better my eyes have become. I didn't notice at first, but looking at Tessen and Sanii now, I feel as though I've never really seen them before.

How have I never known there was something wrong with my eyes?

It must have been a small deficit, it had to have been for it to go overlooked for my whole life. Now it's like the world has sharpened, becoming so much clearer and brighter. Colors seem stronger somehow, and I can see details I'd never observed before. Small imperfections in Tessen's skin and minute shifts in Sanii's expressions. It's clear now that Sanii's eyes are more mottled with specks of lighter brown and Tessen's have tiny flecks of black, turning them into a beautiful reverse of the night sky.

"The odds are against you if our andofume's story was true," Sanii says. "It worked on me, and you're not dead, so…"

"So it either healed me and left me mortal, or…?" Or I've been transformed into something even more impenetrable than my wards can make me and *maybe* strong enough to stand against the bobasu a while longer.

Tessen picks up an anto and hands it to me hilt first. "Let's see."

I adjust my grip on the blade, then I draw the tip down the outside of my forearm, creating a wound that's long but only just deep enough to bleed. It stings, obvious but ignorable, and sluggishly bleeds.

Nothing unusual happens at first. Then I feel the desosa gathering under my skin, more of it than I've ever felt within myself before. Unless I called it in on purpose to power a massive ward. Without a conscious order from me, the desosa moves in clear lines, like it's following one of Soanashalo'a's symbols until it pools under the length of the wound.

First it itches, the feeling of healing skin. The itch gets worse until it's hard to keep from scratching deep. Just before I almost give in, the edges of the broken skin turn pink. Within seconds, the cut closes from both ends, like the desosa is sealing it from underneath.

"I guess that's an answer," Sanii says. "Welcome to immortality."

Immortality. Before Yorri "died," before Sanii came to me with a story about missing bodies and hidden murals, I wanted to become one of the kaigo, the Itagamin council that served our immortal leaders. Joining the Miriseh wasn't possible, so the kaigo was the next best thing.

Except, it's not impossible, but I'm still not going to join them. I'm going to destroy them. Which I had also thought was impossible. It's not; maybe nothing is.

"I'm sure you're starving—I was when I woke up. And the others will be glad to see your eyes open." Sanii taps eir own forehead. "And you won't lose those lines until every single one of them insists what happened isn't your fault, will you?"

I take a breath. I try—and fail—to get rid of the lines

and wrinkles I can now feel creasing my skin. I give up and follow Sanii toward where the others are sitting near the mouth of this cave.

Although everyone is subdued, their smiles tinged with sadness, their relief to see me is genuine. Sanii was right; none of them blame me. Knowing that eases the sharpest edges of the guilt trapped between my lungs, but that's all. It was my job to protect us. Tyrroh is dead because I failed. It may not be entirely my fault, but I'm not without blame.

"We finally figured out how the tyatsu have been following us so closely," Tessen says after we're settled. He almost sounds like he's apologizing. "I didn't even think to *look* for something like this. Not even Osshi knew about them."

"I don't understand. Them?" I look at Osshi, but his face is turned toward the ground.

"The Ryogans have started using the garakyus as spies," Sanii explains.

"They hide the spheres anywhere with a good view, like trees, and it seems like they're always active." Nairo's full lips purse, frustration and stress marring his face. "From what we can know about how they work, the Ryogans must have outposts within range so someone watches the garakyu in the area."

"And they're *everywhere*?" I can't tell if that's a brilliant idea or an absolute waste of resources.

"We're not sure, but we don't think so," Natani says.

"I found one on the road, and it helped me learn how to sense an active one. And now I know I've felt it before—so often I started purposefully ignoring them. There were several surrounding Mushokeiji, but once we left the traveled paths, I haven't found any." Tessen peers off, scanning the surrounding area. "There's no reason to watch these mountains. Or there wasn't before we started crawling all over them."

"Hopefully we'll be well gone before they think to add any more garakyus."

"We should go to Jushoyen and appeal to the Jindaini." Osshi's words are so unconnected to anything it takes me a moment to translate it. Jushoyen is... Yes. The central city of Ryogo, and the place where the Ryogan leader lives, a man who holds the title of Jindaini. Which makes what Osshi said ridiculous.

"They've been hunting you since you landed," I remind him. "Since before then."

"But I didn't think it would take this long," he argues. "It's been *three* moons and the only weapons we have are the ones they've been creating in Mushokeiji, but now you've stolen a third of their supply, so even if we do go warn the Jindaini, we won't be able to create enough of the weapons we need to defend ourselves from the bobasu!"

Rai looks at Osshi like he suggested we jump into the ocean. "Even if we warned your Jindaini, *and* he believed us, *and* we gave him back every speck of stone we took, Mushokeiji *still* wouldn't have enough of this rock to make the number of arrows they'd need to create a hole in the Itagamin army."

"And Ryogo has spent centuries villainizing the bobasu— even Chio and Tsua. They suppress magic, believe ebets are sent as retribution from the Kaisubeh, and punish an entire village of people just for the crime of being *born* in the same place as the bobasu." I gesture widely, encompassing everything with the sweep of my hand. "Yet you think the Jindaini will be fair-minded enough to listen to the very people he's been taught to fear most?"

"You forget, Osshi," Tsua begins. "You're not only expecting the other ten bobasu, you have to prepare for an army. Thousands of warrior mages just as strong as Khya and the others. If what we're attempting doesn't work, the Jindaini won't be able to save anyone."

"The only effective decision he could possibly make would be to evacuate, but that order would force Ryogans to leave everything they know behind," Chio says. "Something tells me no one is going to be any more willing to follow that order than the people I knew when I was a boy."

Osshi winces, but then nods. "Only the Kaisubeh could convince most of us to leave this land without even trying to fight for it."

"I'm certain we can convince the army itself to return to Shiara once the bobasu are dead and their lies exposed," Natani says. "But as long as Varan and his followers are alive, they're the only voices that army will listen to."

"If you want to save Ryogo, Osshi, keep helping us." I lean in, holding his gaze and hoping he's listening. "Even if we were only serving our own interests, we'd still be the only thing that can help your people, but I promise we won't abandon you. We'll do everything we can to ensure the bobasu don't cause any more damage here."

For several heartbeats, he looks at us, eyes narrow and expression uncertain. Then he drops his gaze and nods. The agreement seems too grudging for me to be comfortable with it. Tessen is watching Osshi with the same speculation.

The next morning, we leave the spot where we hid from the pursuing soldiers while I healed, and where the others gave Tyrroh a final farewell, one like he might've had if he'd died on a mission in the desert. Rai and Nairo had burned him to ash. The collected remains are now in a bag Etaro carries.

As we travel, Etaro slowly spreads the ash through the forest.

By the end of the first day, all we have left of our leader—of our friend—is his memory and the hope whatever afterlife the Kaisubeh promise the Ryogans isn't closed to us.

It's not the final rites he should've had, but it's better than anything the Ryogans would have given him if we'd left his body behind. At least now he'll feed the soil and return life to the land, performing one last service, just like he would've done in Itagami.

In the middle of the second day, with several hours to go before Osshi and the andofume expect us to reach the spot where Soanashalo'a left us, Tessen stops.

My chest clenches and I raise my wards, inwardly marveling at how much clearer the flow of the desosa feels and how much more of it I can contain. "What is it?"

"Shh." He holds up his hand. There's no tension in the gesture or his face, so I relax my posture even though I leave my wards up. Then I signal to the others to stop and wait. Tessen is looking down, so he must be sensing something on or under the wet, rocky ground. It's got to be something important to stop him in his tracks like this.

"Just because the katsujo running through the Nentoado range is the one Varan found doesn't mean it's the only one that exists. It was just an idea, but after Suakizu, it seemed more likely," Tessen says slowly, seeming distracted. "Maybe the Kaisuama vein was just the closest to the surface. I was almost positive there are others. We may not have to go back to Nentoado."

"Because what happened in Suakizu proves there's some connection at least to the survival of different areas," I murmur, working through the logic in my head. Then, "Wait. You said *was*. Why aren't you positive now?"

"No, I was almost positive until I found another one."

Tessen smirks, smug pride I haven't seen for moons shining in his eyes. "Now I'm *absolutely* positive."

A thrill buzzes through my veins, raising bumps on my arms and across the back of my neck. I used to hate that look on his face, because it always meant he was about to say something that'd make me either want to hit him or kiss him.

Now, I definitely want to kiss him. "You found a katsujo."

"What?" Tsua looks down and then into the trees. "Where?"

Everyone looks down, excited whispers rippling through the group. Miari drops to her knees, her hands pressed to the stone. I glance at them, but quickly go back to watching Tessen.

"About a half mile below where we're standing." Tessen taps the ground with the toe of his boot. If that's true, there's no way anyone else will be able to feel it. "We've been following it for a while, but I couldn't be sure what I was feeling until now. It's closer to the surface here."

Which changes so much.

Just the journey from Ahta's to Kaisuama and back took us more than a week. Returning to the section of the mountain Ahta called home from here will add more time. Traveling to wherever we need to go next—likely the coast to find or steal a ship that will take us back to Shiara—will take even longer. If we can use a different katsujo to enhance the Imaku rocks and make them powerful enough to kill the bobasu—*and yourself*, a voice in the back of my mind reminds me—then we can head straight for the coast.

No matter how hard I try, though, I can't grab hold of the desosa under our feet. I can feel it on the extreme edge of my awareness, but it's as intangible as a heatwave in the desert.

The more I consider what all of this means, the dimmer my excitement gets. "Knowing others exist won't help if we can't access them."

"True." Tessen's nose wrinkles, and he scuffs the rock with

his boot. "Lo'a knew the stories about Kaisuama. Maybe she'll have a way to track a different vein down."

I touch the pendant hidden under my clothes, and hope rises a little. She did say I could ask for help. So when we find her hours later, after filling her in on everything that happened, Tessen and I tell her about the deeply buried katsujo. "Is there anything you know of that can help track especially strong concentrations of desosa?"

Her eyes first widen and then narrow, her gaze seeming to turn inward. Then she shakes her head. "I cannot think of anything, but let me consider it. A friend from another family is better versed in the deeper, older beliefs, and she might be able to give me an answer."

As she leaves, I can't help thinking she does know *something*. I don't press, but I find myself at a loss because until we know if it's possible to track a katsujo, we can't choose a destination. Which means we can't prepare for whatever's next. After what happened with the guard from Mushokeiji, I don't even want to practice the niadagu spell. Not yet. I could train, or maybe run the perimeter of the camp, but neither holds any appeal. It wasn't my swordplay that failed Tyrroh, it was my wards. If I'm going to practice anything...

"Where are the arrows?" I ask.

"Rai has them," Tessen says. Only after the words are out do his eyebrows pull low. "Are you worried? Rai knows to keep them well away from you."

"That is the exact opposite of what I want, actually." I spot Rai near one of the bonfires, watching Sanii and Etaro teach Ahta the basics of fighting with an anto.

"Ahta, can I borrow Etaro for a while?" I ask the little ebet.

The relief on ey's face when we walked into the hanaeuu we'la maninaio camp was touching. Then ey'd unexpectedly thrown emself into Sanii's arms, which was both amusing and disconcerting. I hate to separate em from the two ebets ey seems to be especially attached to, but Etaro is the only one who can do what I need. The child agrees, only a little reluctantly, and Etaro grins as ey jogs to where Sanii is sitting with Tsua and Osshi.

"What did you need, Nyshin-pa?" Etaro asks. I'm happier than I want to admit that ey didn't call me nyshin-ma. Tyrroh is gone, but I'm not ready to take his place.

"I need you to get the arrows from Rai and shoot them as fast as you can at my wards."

"*What?*" The protest comes from four different voices in near-perfect unison.

Tessen grabs my arm and spins me to face him. "You can't be serious. Those things almost killed you *before* you were immortal, Khya. What do you think they'll do to you now?"

"I think they'll hurt, but that I won't die." I put my hand over his on my arm. "If the rock alone could kill immortals, we'd be done, wouldn't we? It won't kill me, but whatever they did to it made it capable of piercing my wards. I need to learn how to defend against them. I need to keep the rest of you safe if this is what the tyatsu are coming after us with."

"Sometimes I hate it when you make sense." Tessen's expression scrunches, his war with himself clear on his face. Then, he stills. "Compromise?"

"I'm listening."

"You ward something else. A tree or a rock or whatever you like. Ward something that won't care if an arrow strikes it, and test yourself that way."

"Not a bad idea." A grin twitches up the corners of Rai's lips. "I knew you kept him around for a reason."

"Hush, you'd miss me if I was gone, too," Tessen shoots back absently, his eyes never leaving my face. "That should still work, shouldn't it?"

"It—yes. Actually, it should." And I should've thought of it immediately. I so rarely use my wards to protect anything but people; it's like I momentarily forgot I *could.*

Once my friends believe I'm not on the edge of a dangerously ill-advised decision, it only takes a few minutes to set up a good arena for our tests away from the edge of the camp. Ahta and Sanii follow once Ahta understands what we're doing. Ey's fascination with magic is even sharper and more obvious than eir captivation with our two ebets and their weapons.

"I'll place a single flat ward in front of this tree." I point to the trunk. "Start slower than the speed it'd be from a bow, and we'll see what happens after that."

Etaro nods, warily eyeing the two black arrows in eir hands. "One at a time first, too."

"Whenever you're ready." I carefully raise a ward, still not used to how well I can feel the desosa in the air. And definitely not used to feeling as though it runs in ordered paths alongside my own veins.

The first arrow raises in front of Etaro until it's parallel to the ground and level with eir chest. Ey meets my eyes. I nod.

The arrow flies toward the tree. My ward flares bright and painful at the point of impact. I gasp, feeling an echo of that strike in my chest but managing to refill the hole punched in the ward instead of allowing it to shatter. And then—

Thunk. The arrow embeds itself in the tree.

Gritting my teeth, I shake myself out and raise my ward. It hurt, but it was okay. Better than the first strike in the forest. Maybe the susuji's enhancements weren't just physical; maybe it strengthened this, too.

"Again," I demand, keeping my voice even.

Etaro raises the second arrow, and at my nod, ey blasts it in my direction.

Thunk.

"Bellows." I rub at my chest though I know the pain is coming from my wards. "Again."

"You're gonna remind her even the high-and-mighty immortals have limits *before* she passes them, aren't you Tessen?" Rai asks wryly as Etaro magically yanks the arrows out of the wood and floats them back toward emself.

"Maybe." He lifts one shoulder, the motion dismissive but his expression proud. "But every time I think she has a limit, it moves, so I guess we'll have to see how this goes."

It goes nowhere good for the next hour. Each arrow Etaro shoots finds it's mark, and each impact echoes through my chest like it passed through me to get there.

"More power won't help." Tsua's voice surprises me. I hadn't noticed her and Zonna approaching. "Focus on the material, instead. Focus on the elements of the spell on those arrows and the feel of the stone. Adjust the layers of the ward, not the power running through them."

Layers. Could I layer the wards? I've never done that before. Maybe it's not working because I'm trying to do too much with a single ward. If I slow the arrows down with one ward, maybe I can stop them with another. And if two wards aren't enough, I can layer more behind them. Assuming I can even hold two complex wards without overloading myself. And assuming I can keep one up after the arrow pierces the first. And assuming this theory has any merit at all.

I close my eyes and try to picture what I want from the desosa, remembering the feeling of the arrows both when one struck my chest and all the times Etaro has shot them at the tree. But even after I fix the image in my mind and shape a dual layer ward in front of the tree—

Thunk.

"Blood and rot," I mutter, wincing.

Etaro pulls the arrows out of the tree and floats them back to em. Gripping them in one hand and watching me uncertainly, ey hesitantly asks, "Again?"

I nod, taking a slow breath and bringing my wards back up.

Given how this has gone so far, it's unlikely I'll make any real progress tonight, but that doesn't matter. The Ryogans have become the enemy, and this is how the enemy is armed. We've already lost one of our squad—no. *I've* already lost one, and I will do everything I can to keep from failing my friends again.

CHAPTER SEVENTEEN

On the second day traveling south, I seriously regret our decision to travel south. We've been walking straight into an ever-worsening storm, which is what made us choose land over sea. So despite the storms, we keep pushing south rather than heading straight for the western coast, all of us remembering too well how bad it had been weathering the brutal seas onboard Kazu's ship.

Seven different times in two days, the wagons get trapped in the mud; Miari, Etaro, and Tsua have to work us out again. Three times in the same period, the massive ukaiahana'lona pulling the wagons injure themselves badly; Zonna has to heal them before we can keep going. Fallen tree limbs block our passage; Etaro and Tsua push them out of the way. The wards I keep up over the caravan are all that stop falling debris from crashing through the wagons' roofs. Rai and Nairo are the only reason we have a fire at night because everything is too wet to kindle. Sanii and the andofume give us light when no torch will stay lit in the wind.

"Remind me that it'd be worse on the water." Rai grits

her teeth as the wagons bounce along the narrow, pitted road. It's the long way, but it's our only chance to avoid whoever's spying through the garakyus.

"It would be worse on the water," Etaro dutifully repeats. "Because at least here, what's underneath the mud is solid and won't try to eat us."

"And because we can't get to a katsujo while we're sailing. Unless you've learned how to breathe underwater," I add. The thickest veins of power obviously stretch far, but they're not always reachable. There's a chance on land that we can dig deep, reach it, and use it. That's not an option in the ocean. We need to find one before we leave Ryogo.

But the way conditions continue to deteriorate is seriously worrying. Because of what this weather will mean for us on a ship and what it might mean about Varan. He could be getting closer.

When we stop for the night, Tessen and I find Soanashalo'a. "Is there any word from the southern coast?"

"About invading armies?" She shakes her head. "Khya, if I had heard anything like that, you would know. The only thing anyone has mentioned about the south is the storms."

Tessen's attention sharpens. "What about them?"

"Never have so many storms followed each other like this." Soanashalo'a circles her hand, the motion like the tumbling of a wave. "One after the other after the other. This is unprecedented. It could be disastrous if it disrupts the planting season or washes fertile soil away from the farms. That is what has Ryogo worried—no one is eyeing the horizon for anything except clear skies."

Osshi joined just in time to hear her answer. He clears his throat. "What do you think, Lo'a? Shouldn't they know what's coming?"

We already told you no! I purse my lips to keep my admonition in.

Despite how often I've done it in the past six moons, questioning orders is not usually allowed in Itagami. If he were one of us, I'd be tempted to drag him in front of the andofume and report him for insubordination. As it is, I'm tempted to drag him in front of the andofume and report him for undermining our mission. Instead, I wait to see how Soanashalo'a answers.

"Nothing is harder for humanity to rise above than fear. If you tell the Jindaini that everything Ryogo has feared for centuries is about to happen, he will likely blame you for bringing it down on their heads." She pauses. "Or he will not believe a word you say, throw you in prison, and leave us all in danger."

Osshi makes a frustrated noise, and I hide a smug smile. Soanashalo'a winces sympathetically. "I know you want to believe in the equity of the Jindaini and his councils, but you have only stood in their grace before. The hanaeuu we'la maninaio have known both faces of the Ryogan leaders. I promise you do not want to meet them while in disfavor."

Osshi doesn't respond, and I can't read the expression on his face. He's known her for years, though, nearly his whole life. Hopefully he'll believe her when he clearly didn't trust us.

"Have you found anything to help us locate a katsujo?" I ask.

Soanashalo'a tilts her head, neither yes nor no. "I need to do some more digging. I should have an answer for you before we pass Atokoredo."

Tessen and I ask a few more questions about our path, and everyone else silently listens. Everyone else seems attentive, but the lines on Osshi's face speak of uncertainty. I try to ignore him. There are more important questions at hand than Osshi's loyalty.

As soon as we fill in the others, passing along everything

we learned, I turn to Chio. "Why hasn't Varan landed yet?"

"Don't question our rare good luck," Tessen mutters.

"I'm serious. It seemed like he was almost ready when we left three moons ago. Nothing's happened." I look south at the lightning flashing in the distance. "Even *walking* from Shiara, the trip shouldn't have taken them more than a few weeks."

"But we left first. All of us changed his plans," Chio says. "I can't guess what he's been doing, but he has to worry the same about us—what we're doing here, what we've found, what we're doing to defend Ryogo."

"So why didn't he launch immediately and get here as fast as he could?" I ask. "He was the one who taught us that lesson. If your enemy is preparing, don't let them."

"I'm more worried about what happened to Ryzo and the rest of the squad after we left." Etaro's long face is pinched with regret.

I've thought about that more than a few times. Etaro's pained expression makes me want to offer comfort. Even if it's probably a lie. "I'm sure they're fine."

"I don't know if that's true this time." Natani rubs the bridge of his nose, his eyes closed. "They may not have come with us, but Tyrroh told the truth to everyone he thought he could trust. Everyone who wouldn't instantly turn him over to Varan. Or tell Varan where Tyrroh planned on escaping to."

I'd known that, but everything that's happened since then pushed it out of my head. "But they didn't believe him. That's why they didn't come."

"Don't you think that might've changed after Tyrroh disappeared and Varan made it clear he really did plan to build a bridge to Ryogo?" Rai shakes her head. "You know Ryzo. He's stubborn and slow to change, but he's smart enough to see the truth. I wouldn't be surprised if he ran with as many people as he could convince."

"But to where?" I try not to picture Ryzo and the others running for their lives through the rain-flooded desert.

"Before we left, Denhitra was our only escape," Natani adds, rubbing a hand over his round face. "Anyone who left Itagami after us would've headed there."

"But they saw us leave on a ship. They had to know we weren't in Denhitra."

"Not Ryzo. The bobasu and the kaigo saw us leave on a ship," Tessen corrects. "And there's not much chance they told the clan."

He's right. Which means that if anyone fled Itagami, they're almost certainly hiding with the Denhitrans. If they're still alive.

My mind spins like a tornado, sucking in all the worries I've had since this started and spitting them out faster than I can stop. "What if Varan's plans fail and our clan drowns in the crossing? Or if they succeed and land here and realize that everything Varan told them was a lie? That will *destroy* them. And we have no idea what they've told the clan about our disappearance. What if they've punished Ryzo and the others and—"

"No. Blood and rot, Khya, *stop*." Rai shakes her head, her round face creased with worry.

I suck my lips between my teeth and bite down, but the thoughts are still spinning. Tessen puts his hand on my elbow, his touch steady.

"If any of those things do happen, and if we're all alive at the end of this, then they'll learn how to get over it in time," Sanii says. "Don't you remember? The wounds that don't kill you may leave scars, but they *will* heal."

"Will they?" Despite my new immortality, it's hard to believe anything can truly be healed; most of the time it's more like learning to live around the scars. Just because a wound isn't bleeding doesn't mean it's gone. "Varan is still chasing vengeance for wounds no one else even remembers!"

"You ridiculous overachiever. Always expecting miracles." I expected anger—Rai's almost always quick to anger—but all I see in her face is resigned amusement. "I promise, whatever happens from here, you'll walk away knowing you did every single thing it was physically possible for you to do."

If I'm able to walk away from it at all. As soon as our next mission is complete, immortality won't mean the same thing as it does now. Whatever weapon we create to kill the bobasu will work against *me*, too. Against anyone who has this magic running under their skin.

There aren't too many situations I can imagine where I fail Yorri but survive Varan's vengeance. Which maybe is a good thing. If I fail, I'll likely lose a lot more than Yorri. I might lose everything. I wouldn't *want* to live with that.

"It's not like I don't understand, Khya." Tsua smiles reassuringly as she picks up a dagger and a whetstone. "But being impatient won't make time move any faster."

"I don't—" I cut myself off and take a breath. "I'll try."

"Patience isn't one of my son's best characteristics, either." Tsua smirks as she sharpens the blade. "Zonna always moved quicker than we expected."

"He was even born early. By a full moon," Chio adds with a soft laugh, looking to where their son is checking over the massive ukaiahana'lona as one of the small ahoali'lona rubs against his leg. "We were worried he wouldn't be strong enough to survive."

"He's always surprised us." Tsua flips the dagger, catches it to sharpen the other edge.

Their devotion to Zonna makes me wonder. "Why didn't you have more children after you discovered he'd inherited the immortality?"

"Zonna was our third, not our first." Chio's lips thin, but that's all I catch of his expression before he looks at the ground. "Our eldest daughter died before we left Ryogo. Our middle daughter died of old age on Shiara. Zonna is the only one with the same Kaijuko-cursed lifespan as us. There's no way for anyone to know which children will inherit that." He looks up and gestures to me. "Just look at you and Yorri. What made him immortal, and not you? Something in our blood, maybe, or something only the Kaisubeh control."

"It wasn't worth the risk to try?" They so clearly love Zonna. Wouldn't they want more people capable of sharing the centuries with them?

"How many times would *you* be able to watch someone you love die? Would you keep bringing children into the world knowing you'd outlive them?" Tsua shakes her head, grief in her eyes. "I did it twice, and I was convinced a third would kill me. Or make me wish I could die."

I look down. I poked a wound, that much is obvious. I hadn't known it was there, but it's clear it hasn't ever healed. Apologies feel necessary, because she's right. Once would be too much to suffer something like that, and they risked it three times. What can I say, though? I can't come up with anything.

Thankfully, Tessen changes the subject. "Do you think these storms are because of Varan's work?"

The lightning on the horizon has gotten so frequent we can almost see by it, and the thunder has become a near-constant noise.

"As sure as we can be," Chio says.

Tsua scrapes the blade across the stone again. "Which is to say, not at all sure."

"What do we do if Varan gets here before we're ready?" Natani asks.

"As much as we can with whatever we have at the time." Chio looks at us with a smile on his thin lips. "If there's one thing I've learned in my annoyingly long life, it's that you can only do what you're capable of doing."

"I know that." Everyone does. What else can anyone do?

Tsua looks up from the whetstone, amusement in her eyes. "No, you don't. Not yet. I know it sounds like an obvious lesson, but it took me a *very* long time to learn it. You've only just begun, child."

And, unless Varan kills me, or I'm forced to sacrifice myself to bring him down, I'll have a lifespan as long as Tsua's to learn.

I don't know how to begin comprehending that length of time. Or what I might learn, what I might see or do or be by the end of it. I could have *centuries*. If we win this war, I could spend those centuries with Yorri and Sanii. And—I resolutely *don't* look at Tessen—anyone else who might be willing to risk death to gain that sort of life.

Getting to this point has been a series of painful revelations. Since the night Tessen told me Yorri had died, the Miriseh have been unmasked, Ryogo has been revealed, and my loyalty, once so entrenched in Itagami, has shifted. Even in Ryogo, we've revealed a truth about the Kaisubeh the Ryogans have forgotten, broken into a prison these people don't know exist, and are trying to stop an enemy from their past from rising up and crushing them.

It's all too much.

We were raised to think we were alone in the world, that our isolated island *was* the world. Now there are lands I know exist but have never seen or heard of, people with languages I can't understand, and I'm left questioning everything I once thought was undeniable.

The more I learn, too, the harder it is to believe I'll ever have a chance to go home.

It's even harder to believe Itagami will still feel like home when I do.

...

Tessen watches me with mild concern over the next three days, knowing in his usual impossible way that my mind is mired in uselessly distressing thoughts. However, he never makes me explain what has me tied me up in mental knots. Instead, he works with Soanashalo'a, Osshi, and Chio, plotting our route and helping us avoid as much danger as possible.

Twice, it's unavoidable; to get closer to where we need to be, we must risk the main roads. The watched roads. The roads where the Ryogans have hidden garakyus. To be safe, Tessen scans for signs of magic before we use any stretch of road, and we head back into the forests again as soon as we can.

Since we discovered the garakyus watching the roads, we've had to assume the tyatsu know we're traveling with the hanaeuu we'la maninaio caravan. What we don't know is if the watchers know we're with this particular caravan. And I also don't know if the hanaeuu we'la maninaio's protections and my own wards will be enough to keep us safe.

The storm hasn't let up, but for the last two days it's been a stable sort of awful. Day five of our southerly trek dawns without a dawn; the storm is so loud, dark, and strong that we never see a hint of sunlight break through the purple-black clouds. If not for the watch rotation and my internal sense of time, I'd never believe it was morning.

"I'm worried these winds will keep us on the main roads for too long." Tessen peers out of the warded wagon window at the gale.

"I can check in with Lo'a," Osshi offers. "I wanted to talk to her about a supply stop. There are some things we need at the next safe market."

Market. The word doesn't mean much at first, but then I

remember the explanation—markets are how Ryogans get necessary things like food. Even after Osshi and the andofume explained, the concept is confusing. A whole city block or more of food, clothes, and whatever else, but none of it can be taken without pieces of different metals to trade in return, according to Osshi. And if you take something without giving those metal bits, you'll be punished by the tyatsu. Even if all you took was food because you were starving.

I don't understand it, so I shrug and tell Osshi, "Whatever you think we need."

"I better go now." His gaze jumps to the door. "We'll be moving soon."

"Be careful," I remind him.

Nodding, Osshi's eyes jump to meet mine and then back to the door. Then he clears his throat. "Thank you."

As soon as I lift the ward, he picks up his small pack and jumps out of the wagon. Drops of rain and bits of debris blow through even in the few seconds it takes for him to clear the doorway. I replace the protection as soon as he's out. The caravan moves away from the camp moments later.

Throughout the day, the storm rages and swirls, battering and rocking the wagons. Trees shake and sway. We deal with stuck wagons, injured animals, and once, a box of supplies torn from where it had been strapped to a wagon. The weather is so bad we stop at what must be midday to let the ukaiahana'lona hauling the wagons rest and eat, pulling leaves from the trembling trees, but no one leaves the wagons unless they have something to fix.

By the time my stomach starts grumbling for something more sustaining than the dried meat and fruit we've been eating all day, the wagons stop and the wind quiets.

I release the ward on the door and jump down. We're in a clearing, protected on one side by the flat, rocky side of a hill and on two others by trees growing so close together they practically form a solid wall, their branches intertwining overhead to give us a roof. The protection isn't a perfect buffer, but it makes the chaos pouring out of the sky survivable.

People are climbing out of the other wagons and setting up fires. Across the small camp, Soanashalo'a is talking to one of the elders—Akia, I think his name is. He and the gray-haired woman the others call Hoku are the two who seem to be the real leaders of the family.

I head toward them and Soanashalo'a smiles when she spots me, ending her conversation with Akia after a few words and a touch to his shoulder.

It's strange to see, but gestures like that are common for her people. Slowly, my squad and I have learned how to control our instinctive reactions to it. It helps that the hanaeuu we'la maninaio have been careful not to take the same liberties with us that they take with one another.

So when Soanashalo'a holds out her hand to me, I don't hesitate taking it or letting her pull me closer to press a kiss to my cheek. I'm surprised by it—she's never done that in front of her family before—but I don't stop it from happening. It makes more sense when she looks over my shoulder and says to Tessen, "Do you even know what your face looks like when I do that? It is incredibly amusing."

"If you'd been less of a help to us, I might take offense at that," Tessen says behind me. I hadn't even known he was following.

"You mean if Khya liked me less, you might take offense at that," she counters.

I roll my eyes, suppressing a laugh. "It's harder to offend Tessen than you'd think. I've tried many times over the years."

"That is so unfortunately true," he says with an aggrieved sigh.

"But I came over to ask you about Osshi, not Tessen," I say while she laughs. "What did you two decide about the market?"

"Market? We should not need to visit one for several days." She looks confused. "Is there something special you need?"

"No, but I—" I take a breath. "Osshi left this morning because he needed to talk to you."

More confusion. "He never came. I have not seen him since last night."

"But he—" My stomach drops. "Blood and rot." I yell for Tsua.

"Osshi's gone," I say as soon as she appears, my hands clenched tight. "I don't know if he got injured by the storm and left behind or if he ran off, but he never made it to Lo'a after he left us this morning."

"This storm has been loud, but if he'd been hurt, I think one of us would've heard him calling for help," Tessen says slowly. "Why run, though?"

"We were as close to Atokoredo as we were going to get today." Tsua sounds both frustrated and resigned, as if she should've expected this.

Tessen peers northeast, toward the city. "If I'm remembering the maps right, the river that splits southeast leads directly to Jushoyen."

"It does," Soanashalo'a confirms. "Jushoyen became their central city because it sits at the junction of three major rivers. One flows into Jushoyen from Atokoredo. Passenger ships travel between the cities every day, so if Osshi was not arrested as soon as he stepped foot in Atokoredo, then he could be almost to Jushoyen by now."

"They know he's been traveling with a group," I mutter. "Breaking off on his own might've given him a chance at sneaking through the cities. I don't know if he could've come up with a better plan if he'd tried."

The squad can tell something is wrong as soon as they see our faces, and from the mix of expressions, few of them are surprised when we fill them in.

"I kind of want to hunt him down and kill him." Rai sighs. "But I also know I'd probably do the same thing if I was in his place."

Murmurs of agreement and dissent rise from the others. I keep my mouth shut, honestly not sure which side of that divide I fall on.

"We need to change our path and push faster," Chio says, his expression subdued. "If he'd left us before our trip to Mushokeiji, the Jindaini might not have believed his story, but now there's enough proof for him to point to."

"That had better not be true," Tsua says. "If they do believe his stories…"

If they do, we'll have to deal with even more trouble headed our way, and we already have more than enough.

CHAPTER EIGHTEEN

The day after Osshi leaves us—abandons us; deserts us; *betrays* us—we veer southwest and use a smaller road the hanaeuu we'la maninaioare are almost sure the Ryogans wouldn't deem worth watching. It's a risk, but it's worth it to gain as much distance as we can when our boots and the wagons' wheels get sucked into the soggy dirt whenever we leave the stone-inlaid roads.

It makes me miss the desert so much I ache with it. The missing makes me restless and anxious. The speed at which Soanashalo'a strides toward us during a brief rest only makes it worse.

I snap. "What *else* has gone wrong?"

She blinks, then she smiles. "Actually, something has gone right. Come with me."

Exhaling relief, I glance toward Tessen and back, silently asking if I should bring him along. Soanashalo'a considers it before she nods. Soon, we're inside her wagon, away from the storm and the tension as everyone waits for Miari to fill the sinkhole and free the wagon.

"When I told you I possibly had something that might help your search, I may have lied. Slightly," she begins as soon as the door is closed.

"Lied about what?" My chest clenches as I sit. If her search turned up *nothing*—

"I knew what might help you the day you asked," she admits, "but it is a guarded secret. Not something I would be able to share even with a friend of the clan unless I had permission from those far more important than my family."

"And you got it?" I lean forward, my hands trembling with excitement.

"I did. You might be able to learn how to do this magic without the symbol, but the only way I know how to teach you is to ink it into your skin." She brushes her fingers against the small symbol at the corner of her right eye.

"Yes," I agree instantly. "If it will help us find a katsujo, absolutely."

Tessen glances at me, his amusement clear. "Does it have to be on our face?"

"Not at all. Any unscarred skin will do." She bustles around the small space, picking up several items from different bags, shelves, and cabinets. "For this in particular, it might be best either on your arms or over your heart."

Tessen chooses the inside of his right wrist, but the desosa pools strongest in my chest, so I remove my layers, leaving only my breastband on top. Although her eyebrows rise and her eyes widen before she wipes the expression from her face—or tries to—Soanashalo'a doesn't comment on our choices. Instead, she asks who'd like to go first and then gestures to one of the chairs when I volunteer. She pulls her own chair up to mine, and I spread my legs to allow her to sit as close as possible.

"You really are unfairly attractive, you know," she mutters

as she cleans the skin over my heart with liquid from a white stone bottle. Tessen laughs and I smirk, but before either of us can say anything, she continues. "For this to work and hold, you cannot fight the akiloshulo'e kua'ana manano—ah no. Desosa."

"Desosa," I confirm.

"As I mark your skin, I will weave the energy into the ink. It has to sink into it until one is indistinguishable from the other and both are indistinguishable from you." She looks at both of us, her expression serious. "You cannot struggle at all or it will not work. You have to accept it." Then her golden-brown eyes lock on mine, this time filled with speculation. "And, honestly, I have no idea how the changes the susuji wrought in you will impact my magic."

"If it doesn't work on me, it should still work on Tessen, right?" It's one of the reasons I wanted to go first—I had the same concerns. Wounds heal almost instantly now. It's not impossible to think whatever process they use to deposit ink in skin will count as a wound to the magic embedded in my blood.

"There is no reason to think otherwise. Yet." She shrugs and opens a clear bottle of ink.

It'd better work, or we'll be wandering Ryogo hoping to trip over a phenomenon that has stayed hidden from the land's actual inhabitants for centuries. Or longer.

"I'll do whatever I can to make it easier on you," I promise, touching the silver pendant she gave me. Her eyes linger there, her expression fond.

"Well, even if it does not work, at least I got to do this." With a delighted grin, Soanashalo'a brushes the tips of her calloused fingers along the side of my neck before pressing her palm flat against my skin, one long edge of her hand parallel with my collarbone. The touch makes me shiver and raises bumps on my skin, ones Soanashalo'a smooths away with her thumb.

"Tell me about your home, Tessen," Soanashalo'a requests as she dips a sharp implement into the ink. "I am unbearably curious about the place that produced a family like yours."

Why didn't she ask *me* for stories? I get an answer as soon as she pokes desosa-laced ink into my skin. A tingling rush of energy bursts through my chest. It's distracting. And she was right to warn us about fighting back—this is a mental itch I want to scratch until it's gone. It'd be so easy to do it unthinkingly.

I push the urge down and focus on Tessen's description of Sagen sy Itagami and the relentless ocean our city overlooks. He talks about the dangers of the desert and elaborately details the methods we use for everything from farming to education and training.

Concentrating on Tessen helps, but the urge to itch becomes an urge to peel that section of skin off my bones to stop it from feeling like bugs have burrowed underneath. Like it has every time I've gotten even the most minor injury since the susuji, the desosa attempts to heal the irritation. I don't let it. I shove it back, down, away. *Let this wound stay. This one I want to keep.*

The energy does *not* want to comply. Soanashalo'a has to go over the lines several times, re-etching segments that the desosa wipes away. After several long minutes, I finally force it to listen to me and accept the ink as a new part of myself. I don't think I'd be able to do this with anything more dangerous than ink—the desosa's compulsion to heal is too powerful.

But it works. A looping, swirling symbol bisected by lines of various lengths is now etched into my skin. The whole design is about as tall as my middle finger and as wide as three fingers together. I like seeing it against my brown skin more than I thought I would. It's a lot nicer to look at than the scars I used to collect.

I try to explain what it felt like to Tessen, wanting to prepare my oversensitive basaku for the sensations. In the end, I do what he did, sitting nearby and telling stories about home. When he holds out his hand, the motion as stiff and tense as the look on his face, I take it gently and trace the tiny scars on his skin as I talk.

When it's finished some time later, he lets out a long, shuddering breath. "That wasn't unbearable, but I'll be very happy to never do it again."

Me, too. But I keep my agreement silent as I inspect the mark on his skin, one that should look the same as mine. The design does—they are all but identical—yet his skin is inflamed and raised and looks far more painful.

My expression must be giving me away, because he smiles and taps my newly marked, and not at all inflamed, skin and says, "Andofume."

"I knew that." And yet I forget what it means for a moment. Sighing, I squeeze his hand. "How long do you think it takes for a mind to adapt to something like this?"

"I stopped trying to predict your mind a long time ago."

"That is such a lie," I insist, rolling my eyes and smiling when Soanashalo'a laughs. No one is better at predicting me than Tessen. The reason he got involved with our hunt for Yorri in the first place was because of how good he was at it. But the more important issue now is the katsujo. "How do these work?"

Soanashalo'a's expression grows serious. "They simply work. This one is not meant to find sources of desosa like you are looking for—no one knew they were real, so I doubt any mage in the world has a spell or symbol for that. What these do is connect you more deeply to the desosa to help you use it to find something lost, or something incredibly important to you."

Tessen leans in. "Anything?"

"Any living thing or place connected to the desosa—or capable of producing it. It does not help if you have misplaced a book, for example," she says, smirking.

"How do we use it to find the katsujos, then?" I ask.

"You need to focus through the symbol with the object of your search firmly held in your mind. It should feel like a string pulling you in the direction you need to travel, faint of course, but noticable if you are paying attention. If you need to intensify the connection, touch the mark and focus on it. And on what you need to find."

"This seems pretty simple. Why is it so secret?" I ask.

"Because there is the potential for darkness in everyone, and this could easily be twisted and used for reasons a lot less noble than yours." Soanashalo'a looks down, her expression somber. "This can track almost anything or anyone, Khya. That kind of power is not for everyone."

Track any*one*. A frisson of energy shoots through me, eddying under the symbol on my chest. Could this help me find Yorri when we get back to Shiara?

This could cut hours or *days* off our search, and they're giving it to us even though it so clearly goes against all the secretiveness they've built their society on. It makes me want to grab Soanashalo'a's bright red tunic and kiss her.

Instead, I look down at the mark, wondering if I should've chosen a wrist like Tessen. Easier to access. It does work, though. Now that I know what I'm looking for, I can feel a very faint tug toward the southeast. When I meet Tessen's eyes and lift my chin in that direction, he nods absently. "Not only there. I can feel at least three lines."

"I thought it might be stronger in you because of your skills." Soanashalo'a seems pleased she was right. "Even so, it'll take time for you to learn how to feel the differences between those threads and determine which is the one you need."

"Thank you." I trace the symbol with my fingertip, wishing I knew what else I could say to explain how much her help has meant.

The smile she gives me hints she might already know. But there are shadows in her eyes. "I hope this will help you find what you need, but it is only a guide. And not guaranteed."

"That's all we need," I say as I redress to prepare for the bitterly wet cold outside her warm wagon. Hopefully, I'm right this time.

I was wrong.

Tessen's sense of the katsujos is stronger than mine, which I expected given how sharp his senses are, so we soon decide that I can probably only feel the strongest or closest of the veins. We hope that if we choose our direction based on that, it might move the search faster. It doesn't; no matter how hard we focus on the symbol, the katsujos we find are unusable.

The first, five days after the marks, was under the path of a deep river. It takes eight days to reach the second katsujo, and another four days to find the third. Both are still too far underground to be any use. It'd take days, at least, to dig us deep enough to draw power, and that's too long in the same spot.

We're still more than a hundred miles from Rido'iti which

is, according to Soanashalo'a, our best chance at a ship. It's possible to reach the city in less than a week if we travel straight there, but getting there is only part of the problem. We need a useable katsujo first.

"Your boruikku needs to give us something more useful than this," Rai mutters after our third failure.

After they learned we had a hanaeuu we'la maninaio mark, Rai and Etaro told us they'd invented a word to describe the style of magic—boruikku. Tessen and I took to using the word, too, after that; Soanashalo'a's name for the symbol is probably as closely guarded as the symbol itself.

"Maybe it would've been faster to go to Kaisuama." Sanii worries eir bottom lip between eir teeth. "At least there we knew what we'd find."

I've had the same fear since the day we found the first katsujo—but we can't change course now.

"There's another source. Southeast." Tessen's left thumb is pressed in the center of the boruikku, and his eyes are closed. "I can't tell if it's any better than the others, but it's there."

"At least it's in the direction of Rido'iti." I head back to the wagons. We got here before midday, so we can travel a while longer before the ukaiahana'lona are too worn out.

Exactly two days later, we reach the next katsujo. I want to bang my head against a wall when I see the river cutting a path through the sloping hills. The energy is closer to the surface here than it's been anywhere else, but even though I can feel it bubbling and flowing, it's more like looking down at a river from the top of a cliff than being able to wade into the water.

Then Miari kneels to touch the ground. "How far down do you need to go?"

"At least a hundred yards." Tessen runs his hand over his hair—scruffy and long now since he hasn't cut it in moons.

We're so close, standing exactly above where we need to be, and we can't get there. Worse, the only katsujo I can feel now, other than the one we left two days ago, is west of us. *Far* west by the faintness of the boruikku's tug.

"There are caves." Miari looks up, eyes alight. "This whole section of the range is riddled with caves, and if most of the digging has already been done by nature, I can probably get us at least half as far down as you need to be in a few hours. A full day at most if the caves have to be reinforced before I break from one to another."

My pulse picks up, tremulous hope kicking the pace higher. "Find us an entrance, Miari. Take Ty—" I cut myself off, pain welling up like blood from a wound. I can't send Tyrroh with her to help, because Tyrroh is gone. The excitement in Miari's eyes fades, and her gaze drops. I clear my throat and start again. "Take Nairo, Etaro, Sanii, and Tsua—if she wants to come. They'll give you light and can help move some of the stone if you need it."

She nods, expression still drawn, and stands. "I'll ask Wehli to come, too."

"Shouldn't he—" No. I've already seen that the injury isn't affecting him the way they told us it would. "Whatever you need."

"I'll go down with them," Tessen says. "I'll know better when we're getting close."

Everyone moves quickly, arranging the supplies they'll need and then setting up camp nearby. The rest of us stay aboveground, out of their way, but I don't go far. I find a grass-covered spot near the entrance and sit with a map of southern Ryogo in my lap, a ward above me to keep the pounding rain off. It doesn't take long for Sanii to join me.

Eir eyes are wide and pleading. "Are we finally close to going home, Khya?"

"No. We're close to going to war." I turn back to the map. "I'm not sure home exists."

"It can be reclaimed or rebuilt." Sanii says this with so much force it's like ey's trying to *make* emself believe it.

"Do you really think the clan will let us come back? We left. We broke almost every law that mattered and turned against the Miriseh." I shake my head, trying not to imagine the welcome we'd get. "If we defeat Varan, save Yorri, and live through both, I hope the Denhitrans or the Tsimosi let us in, because I don't see us ever being allowed inside Itagami again."

"You never know. You do keep pulling off the impossible."

I look up, raising my eyebrows. "*I* do? This coming from the yonin who managed to create a sumai bond, discovered a secret Varan has kept for centuries, and knew exactly how to convince me to go against everything I'd been taught to help you." Laughing softly, I fold the map. "Circumstance may have thrust me into command, but you're just as responsible for getting us here as I am."

Ducking eir head, ey smiles and takes the map from my hands. Ey points to where we're camped and talks about the fastest, safest way to Rido'iti. Ey's not wrong to be concerned about our route, because there are so many cities and towns here. And more roads. And more chances for us to be seen by the Ryogans' scattered network of garakyu spies.

So, while Miari and the others are below us, clearing a path down to the katsujo, I plan paths with Sanii, both of us treating it like a puzzle and trying to think like Yorri. When the group comes back, covered with stone dust but smiling broadly, I know they've succeeded before any of them speak.

"Rest well tonight," Tsua says as we head back to camp. "We'll start in the morning."

The words send a thrill of excitement through me, one

that lingers, rising and falling in my veins like a tide all night. It never falls enough to allow sleep to come easily. I lay in the wagon's bed for hours, keeping still to avoid waking Tessen, Sanii, or Ahta. When the others start getting up, I do, too, but I doubt I slept more than an hour or two. Whether because of the adrenaline or the susuji, the lack barely bothers me.

We leave the camp when Tsua decides it's morning—the storm is too thick overhead to give us much hint of the time—and everyone comes. There's no reason for it, especially since I'm positive we'll send them away once we're ready to begin, but no one orders them away.

Tsua and Etaro are leading the group, our fourteen bags of Imaku rock floating in midair between them like baby mykyns flying between their parents. Climbing down into the caves is strange, so reminiscent of descending into Itagami's undercity and yet entirely different. The air is too damp. The stone is too dirty and cold. The passages are too narrow. The desosa in the air is so strong it vibrates against my skin, infinitely more powerful than anything I ever felt on Shiara. It's different, but that's good. It helps keep my mind *here*. It helps keep the tremulous excitement building in my chest from bubbling over.

We really have found a katsujo. Finally, something is going right.

When we reach the lowest cavern, Tsua and Etaro slowly upend each bag, keeping them low to avoid shattering the rocks and making sure they're well away from our andofume. When they're done, there's a foot-wide rock line running the length of the cave. It's the only thing odd about this cave—on the surface, it's just a damp, cold bubble of air in gray stone. The immense power under the surface is invisible, but my feet buzz with it.

This looks like nowhere important, but it feels like a

place where marvels can happen, and I desperately need that to be true.

Sanii, Tsua, Chio, Zonna, and I space ourselves out along the line. I'm glad Sanii finally learned how to channel the desosa. Even with the added endurance of the immortality, the amount of desosa we're going to run through ourselves and into the stones is immense. More than I used to fix the katsujo in Kaisuama. It'd likely kill us if we were mortal. Having five of us working together on this instead of four will hopefully be enough.

"Are you ready?" Miari stands near the entrance of the cave, the rest of the squad arrayed behind her. She'll stay, with multiple wardstones to protect her from energy backlash, and she'll reinforce the caves if our work starts to degrade their structure.

Tsua nods, her eyes on the line of black stone. "Everyone but Miari, clear out."

Tessen clearly doesn't like leaving, but when he stops in front of me, he only lingers long enough to brush his fingers down my cheek and murmur, "Be careful," before following the others up to the surface.

Then the six of us are alone with rock that, according to the Ryogans, the Kaisubeh once dropped from the sky to help the Ryogans destroy people exactly like us.

"Somehow this feels like standing on the desert plain during a lightning storm." Sanii swipes eir finger through the moisture on the cave's floor.

"I've done that." I force my voice to stay light. "It's not so bad."

"Not all of us are as reckless as you." Ey rubs eir eyes, continuing before I can respond. "It might be less terrifying if I could see it as well as I can feel it."

Ey has a point. It was a little less unnerving when we were

in Kaisuama because not only could we see proof of the power under our feet in the light seeping through the cracked stone, we were in an open space. Clearly that area wasn't without its dangers, but this feels worse. We're enclosed in a small cave we had to dig our way into, and there is nothing here that hints at the power under our feet. Only mottled gray rock. As far as anyone can see, the oddest thing about the cave is our presence in it. And the line of black rocks we've brought with us.

"We're creating something that can kill us as easily as it can kill the bobasu," Sanii says after a moment. "I just want to make sure we're all aware of that."

Zonna huffs a strained laugh. "Oh, I am fully aware of that."

Chio and Tsua, their expressions more serious than their son's, share a long look. Then Chio says, "Ready, vanafitia?"

She grips his hand and nods, but says nothing else.

It's time.

As soon as I grip the katsujo's desosa, I feel like I'm falling, dropping down into the vein of energy like I had to do in Kaisuama. I'm engulfed in light that's somehow every color I've ever seen and nothing but brilliant white. I scramble upward, trying to hold on to myself, but I can't. I *can't* and that should terrify me.

It doesn't. The energy embracing me feels like feathers and niora fur. It feels like the first rays of the desert sun. There is warmth, light, and something brushing against my mind like curious fingers. And I'm not alone. Sanii, Tsua, Chio, and Zonna are here, too. Sanii looks at me with wide-eyed confusion, but the others are staring at our surroundings with nothing but awe.

I follow their gaze just as a picture forms in the light, all those colors I saw before coalescing into a landscape that looks solid enough to touch. And there's movement. Somehow, this feels like a memory, but it can't be mine because I'm looking down at myself kneeling in the center of Kaisuama and working on the broken vein of power.

Someone was watching me work. To them, a form of myself made of white light and smoke has sunk into the katsujo to work, and when that work is finished, when the katsujo is *healed*, relief crashes into me like a wave against a cliff.

White wipes everything clean and leaves the five of us standing in what feels like solid light. And then we're back in the cave, all five of us hovering over ourselves. The energy we began pulling up from the katsujo is still pouring into the black rocks, thick, bright rivers of desosa, beautifully multicolored threads of light, fill up the stones to the breaking point.

Then the color of the desosa shifts. The threads of color wind together into one thick rope of pure white light, and what I thought was the limit of the stones disappears. More energy floods into them. More.

It's like there's an extra hand on the katsujo, someone with the ability to bend the power of the entire vein to whatever purpose it wants. And right now someone seems to want to help us make a weapon more powerful than I'd even hoped was possible.

I try to get closer, wanting a better look at the flood of desosa. The energy responds. Warmth surrounds me, twining around my body like Soanashalo'a's little ahoali'lona, Koo'a, and it feels just as conscious as those creatures, but larger. And it keeps growing until it engulfs me. Warmth and a pulsing, curious touch, but it's not gentle. It scratches sharply in moments. Then soothes. It burns. And then cools.

There's a shudder in the energy, a shock.

And then everything goes black.

...

I wake up flat on my back, staring up at the rough stone of the cave's roof.

"She's awake." Zonna's worried face hovers over mine, and his hand presses to my forehead, his hishingu magic brushing through my body. "Khya? Can you hear me?"

"Of course I can hear you." I start to sit up. For a second, Zonna's hand weighs me down, but when I twitch my shoulder, he releases me. "I feel fine, I just..."

What happened? I don't know how to understand it let alone explain it.

"You all... You were unconscious." Miari speaks slowly, uneasiness laced through her words. "None of you touched the black rock, but there was a flash and then you all *dropped*."

"You and Sanii were the last to wake up," Tsua says gently.

Chio is kneeling next to Sanii, and though ey is only just sitting up, ey seems fine.

"It worked. I think it worked." Chio sounds mystified. So am I, and I was there for whatever that was. "But I have no idea what happened while we were in there."

"I think..." I rub my hand across my forehead, trying to remember everything. "We may have just found solid proof your Kaisubeh are real."

"You saw that, too?" Zonna rubs his eyes. "Tssiky'le, I thought I was imagining things."

But when we start describing what happened inside the katsujo, all of us stumbling over our words more than once, we know it's true.

"Maybe what Varan did to the katsujo really did catch and keep their attention." Chio stares at the line of black stones. "What happened in there... Maybe we have their blessing. Or

Khya does. Did you feel the way the desosa focused on her before the end?"

"I did. It makes sense. Khya did something no one else ever has," Tsua says, her voice a little stronger now. I feel a little stronger, too, knowing I didn't imagine the twining, conscious presence I felt. "She fixed what Varan broke. It must've earned their gratitude."

I never cared about gratitude, from gods or mortals; I only wanted to save Yorri.

"How... Are we sure it was the Kaisubeh?"

"No, but as soon as we touched the energy, we were sucked into it completely." Tsua gestures to the line of stones that none of us have gotten even an inch closer to. "The work was never interrupted, and it went easier than we expected. The desosa flowed into the stones almost before we asked, and it feels—" She shudders. "It feels more dangerous than anything I've ever been this close to in my life."

I concentrate on the Imaku stone for the first time—and hiss through my teeth. The energy from the stones bites. It's hot as a forge-fire and sharp as a newly sharpened blade, but the way the desosa inside those rocks swirls and coils almost feels...alive. It feels aware. Like it's waiting for me to let my guard down so it can strike.

If vengeance had a tangible feeling, it would be this.

"That's...good, right?" Sanii looks between us, lines creasing eir forehead. "I mean, we *want* them to be dangerous, don't we?"

"We do, and I'm grateful they are, but *we* didn't make them that way, and that..." Tsua pauses and takes a long breath, a look of awe sweeping over her face. "That is terrifying."

"It is, but now we have something to test." Chio's expression is unreadable as he glances at Miari. "Hopefully you'll still be able to shape this stone, Miari, because if it works, you'll have to help them find a way to use it against Varan. Khya will need your help turning a pile of rock into wieldable weapons."

Miari nods slowly. Her upturned eyes are unusually wide, and her lips are pressed thin. She opens her mouth, but footsteps and scraping rock snap our attention toward the tunnel. I bring up a ward, blocking the path instinctively. I drop it as soon as Tessen calls, "Khya?"

Wehli appears first, relief on his face when his eyes meet Miari's. "You're okay."

She relaxes a little, taking his offered hand and leaning against his chest.

Seconds later, Tessen dashes in, his eyes finding mine instantly. "Bellows, Khya. I thought I was done panicking over your survival. Why can't—oh." He stops halfway to where I'm sitting, his eyes are on the Imaku rocks. "Blood and rot. What did you *do* to them?"

"Hopefully? Created something strong enough to destroy ten people who set themselves up as gods." *I'm just not the one who did it.* I stand up and join Tessen, who's inching closer to the stones that I've kept a solid distance from since I woke up. "Everyone help load these into the bags. We need to get back to the surface, and you need to hear what happened."

He looks at me, his sword-sharp gaze scanning me, probably for injuries, but possibly because he can feel the confusion clogging my thoughts. I put my hand on his arm, silently reassuring him I'm fine, and he relaxes some. With everyone who can touch the stones without being harmed by them helping, it doesn't take long for the black line cutting the damp cave in half to be cleared away and the squad to be ready to move.

When we get back to camp, I watch Etaro, Miari, and Rai place the bags of stone in a trunk attached to the outside of our wagon, then Tsua, Sanii, and Soanashalo'a place as many protection and locking spells on it as they can. It's the only way to keep those overpowered weapons safely away from Sanii and me. Keeping them inside the cramped wagon would be too risky. I don't want to die because of an accidental brush with those stones.

Tsua, Zonna, and Chio, however, are still determined to test it on purpose.

"We should wait." I say it even as I follow the three of them toward the edge of the camp.

It's morning—as far as anyone can tell without a sunrise to mark the time—and Etaro is floating three dagger-like shards of black rock in front of em. The andofume sit on the wet ground, and Etaro lets a rock settle in front of each of them as I create a ward around us, one underneath the ward already protecting the camp. I make the shield as strong as I can. The andofume are determined to go through with this even though none of us know what to expect.

Which is exactly what makes this so ridiculous. I try one more time to get them to see reason. "Can we please wait before you do this? We don't even know what to do with this yet or how we're going to get it anywhere near the bobasu."

"The shape of the weapon won't matter if its core is flawed," Chio points out. "The bobasu will be surrounded by an army, and they must have known we'd head here when we escaped. They'll expect danger from us, so there will only be a few ways to use the stone against them—either strike from a distance or set a trap and crush him in it."

"Your group is powerful, loyal, and incredibly intelligent, Khya." Tsua smiles, affection and pride in her eyes. "Use them. Trust each other, use your strengths, and don't give up."

"We've waited a long time for people willing to help us finish this fight. It's one we should've ended centuries ago."

Too many emotions are layered into Chio's voice for me to unravel them. "I hate to leave before we see the end for ourselves—it's an end I've been looking forward to for a long time—but you've got to know you have what you'll need."

"There isn't any other way to test this?" I ask. "No one knows Varan better than you do."

"It's the *only* way to test it," Tsua insists. "And that's not true. You're the ones who've lived with Varan. We know who he was. You know who he *is*."

"But all three of you?" Rai protests. "We can't lose all of you, especially not at once!"

Chio smiles sadly. "It has to be us all. Remember? Varan's susuji didn't work on everyone. To be sure this will take out *all* the bobasu, we need to test it on all of us."

I take a long breath, holding the air in until my lungs start to hurt. "I don't want to lose you."

"Loss never comes when you're ready for it," Tsua says gently. "No amount of preparation—not even centuries—is enough."

I think of Tessen coming to me in the middle of the night, covered in sweat and desert dust, to tell me that Yorri died. I think about the day Tessen, Sanii, and I left Itagami behind, fully believing we'd never see it again. I think about hearing Daitsa and the others scream when Varan killed them. I think about sailing away from Shiara without my brother.

She's right. I knew this was coming, and yet there's no way it won't leave a hole in my chest just like all those other losses did. I can already feel it, a tight ball of sizzling fear that'll explode into a gaping wound if...*when* this works.

Tsua walks toward me and, after I nod permission, places her hands on my cheeks. I force myself to hold her gaze despite the painful churning in my stomach, and her smile softens as though she knows. "You are strong, talented, brave, and incredibly loyal to those you love. Even if you lose us, you'll be fine. The others will follow you, Sanii, and Tessen anywhere, and you're smart enough to use their skills and knowledge well. You'll succeed where Chio and I have failed. I believe that the same way I believe in the Kaisubeh."

Closing my eyes, I breathe deeply. It barely calms me. The air trembles in my lungs and my hands shake. Doesn't matter. As much as I'm arguing, I also know this needs to be done.

I can't wish them dead. If they live, we've failed. But bellows, I've never wanted so badly to succeed and fail at the same time.

"Do you remember the words to break the binding?" Chio asks when Tsua steps away.

"Ureeku-sy rii'ifu." I open my eyes. "But you said you weren't sure it'd work on Varan's spell." And after what happened with the guard at Mushokeiji, I am *not* willing to watch the spell go wrong with Yorri, too.

"We're as sure as we can be," Chio says. "The only way to be certain is to test it on a cord Varan or one of the others put in place, and…"

"I know." I touch the red cord on my wrist. Everyone trapped by that spell is on Shiara.

Biting the inside of my cheek, I listen as the others say their goodbyes. We were enemies once. Tsua, Chio, and Zonna lived in Denhitra, and we fought with that clan over territory and resources constantly. What means more now is how much more time they've spent on Shiara than anywhere else. Tsua and Chio aren't Ryogan, they're Shiaran. Zonna was born on the same solid stone and under the same scorching sun as us; he learned the reality of Ryogo at the same time as us.

Swallowing, I force words out I don't express often. To anyone. "Thank you. All of you. Just…just in case I don't get a chance to say it again."

"It was an honor, little fykina." Tsua holds out her hand, and I take it, gripping her once before I let go. "I wish I could see what you'll grow into. I have a feeling it'll be glorious."

Throat closing and eyes burning, I nod my thanks.

"Fight well, Khya, and don't give up on Itagami yet." Chio gives me a small, sad smile. "Sagen sy Itagami has survived this long. I think they can live through what's coming, too. Your clan will need someone to lead them through the aftermath of Varan's plans if anything good is going to be salvaged."

"I think Itagami will be more than happy to follow the girl who revealed the lies of the Miriseh." Zonna smiles, the expression far easier than his parents'. "I'd be willing to beg the Kaisubeh for another chance at life if it meant seeing you at the head of that city."

I can't find it in me to smile and mean it, but I can give him one truth. "If that happens, you'd be more than welcome there."

Zonna's smile turns more serious. Tsua and Chio look down at the sharp, black stones on the wet ground. Nerves they must've been hiding before seem to be rising now.

"Kaisubeh yumaryshi ware ni'te za zaini'i ware renshinai temoru suoka," Tsua whispers in Ryogan. *Kaisubeh forgive us for the crimes we may have committed.*

"Iziha anama nano'i iziha fa'ana ny boamanatra izika diosonafa," Chio responds in Denhitran. *We did what we could to fix our mistakes.*

Then, as one, they place their hands on the stone shards in front of them.

Tsua and Chio jolt, their hands clenching. Tsua's grip on the rock dagger is tight enough to draw blood where the edges cut into her palm. Zonna glances at them, his own hand tightening a second behind his parents.

Gritting her teeth, Tsua pulls her sleeve up and lifts the

stone like she's about to slice her forearm open with it. Chio grabs her wrist, his face tight with pain. He grunts. With a sharp twist, he forces her hand to turn over.

"What is that?" It looks like dirt or shadows, but when I lean in...

Her veins are turning black, and it's spreading.

My stomach turns. I hold my breath. Quick and painless. I wanted this to be quick and painless; I don't think this will be either. Their faces are twisted and their breathing sharp and there's nothing I can do to ease their pain. They're already sacrificing everything for our fight. This is too much. They don't deserve to suffer this.

Crying out, Tsua pulls back, dropping the stone and shoving her sleeve up. The lines, like charcoal marks on her beige skin, are past her elbow. Chio looks at his own hand; it's there, the same black lines mark his veins to the middle of his forearm. Shuddering, he rubs and scratches at the skin. It does nothing.

Zonna sits across from them, taut as a bowstring. His skin is unmarked.

"What can we— We need to do something," Tessen whispers. "What can we do?"

"Nothing," Sanii says, voice lifeless. "This is exactly what we wanted to happen."

No. My breathing catches. My chest hurts. I never wanted *this*. This isn't just death, this is torment.

Tsua folds over and braces herself on the ground. Her arms buckle. She falls. The black is climbing the side of her neck, creeping under her jaw, and marring her cheek. Chio's neck is unmarked, but when he drops the stone and curls himself around Tsua, he's shivering.

Zonna shoves his sleeve out of the way and drags the sharpest edge of the stone shard into his forearm, digging deep to slice a wide line.

Tsua starts screaming; tears fall from Chio's squeezed-shut eyes.

The thickest black lines in Tsua's arm are blistering, bubbling, and bursting, heavy black blood soaking into her clothes. Her cries sharpen, but only for a moment. It's like she doesn't have the energy for anything more. The dark lines have reached Chio's face, and they're moving faster now, covering his skin.

Tessen stiffens, his gaze is locked on Tsua, agonized disbelief in his eyes. I open my mouth to ask him what's wrong—and then I feel it. Desosa is flowing out of her body. It's a thin trickle at first, but it's strong, and it carries out not only the essense of Tsua's lifeforce but everything that wasn't supposed to belong to her.

That's what the Kaisubeh did to the stone; they helped us create something that would literally bleed the bobasu of the power Varan stole, leeching away everything that's kept them alive for so long.

Watching this is too much. I can't. I close my eyes, concentrating on burying the ache in my chest. I wish the Ryogans' gods could've found a faster way to do this. But it lasts.

Seconds feel like excruciating hours, but it can't be more than ten or fifteen minutes before the elder andofume drop unconscious. The only sound is their rattling breaths until even that finally falls silent. Only then do I open my eyes again.

Tsua stops moving first, and Chio soon after. Zonna watches them, so tense he's practically vibrating, but his skin is still unmarked. There's not even a wound on his forearm—the blood on his skin and clothes is the only sign he was ever injured.

This is exactly what they were testing for, exactly what they feared would occur, and yet the pain piercing through my chest proves I never believed it would happen. Not to them, not like this, and not now.

It doesn't make sense. Did Zonna survive because he's a hishingu? Was his magic healing him while the stone was trying to kill him? Maybe, but it doesn't explain why none of them were forced unconscious when they touched the black rock; that's how Yorri described what happened when he touched the stone. I don't understand how being a hishingu could've stopped that, but the how doesn't matter when I see the bleak look in Zonna's eyes.

Believing I lost Yorri hurt worse than anything I've ever felt, and we only had sixteen years to bond. Our three andofume have had centuries. How much worse must it be to lose someone after so long? After someone has become so much a part of your life, how do you learn to exist without them?

"I'm sorry, Zonna," I whisper. "We can keep trying if you want, test different things, or…" Or what? I don't know. Something. Anything to ease the agony he must be feeling, even if it's offering to keep looking for a way for him to die.

Zonna doesn't answer. Doesn't look at me. Barely seems to be breathing. After a few minutes of awful, heavy silence, he moves. He drops the stone, gets up, and tries to walk away.

Tries.

Less than three feet from us, he stops as though he's hit a wall with a jolting, full body shudder. An agonized, gasping breath. A slow collapse none of us are fast enough to stop.

When I reach him, he's on his knees, folding over until his head hits the dirt. He's gasping and sobbing, broken in a way I've never seen. Each wrecked sob stabs at my chest until it feels like all the air I breathe is gone, escaping out the holes in my lungs.

There isn't anything I can do to help or shield him from

this. I can't protect him from what's hurting him now, but we can stay with him while he breaks and try to help him collect the pieces when it's over. If it's ever over.

After an hour, I start to wonder.

What if this is the one wound our healer can't heal?

CHAPTER NINETEEN

Zonna doesn't speak for hours. For almost a day.

In near silence, he washes the blood off his parents' skin, wraps them in clean cloth, and carries them out of the camp. All our attempts to help him are refused by a single sharp motion of his head, but I encase him in a wide, domed ward whether he wants it or not—the persistent rain has become a storm again, a vicious squall that sends lightning through the sky and beats against the trees. Even with the forest as a windbreak, the gusts blowing through here would be strong enough to knock him off his feet, especially when he's unbalanced by the burdens he's carrying. If he notices my shield, he doesn't give a single sign.

Only once does he knowingly accept our help; when it's time to light the fire. When Rai, Nairo, and Etaro silently approach the site he's chosen for the burn, he relents, nodding instead of sending them away.

The blaze Rai and Nairo start is searing. It rushes out of their hands in thick ropes of orange-white flame, and it consumes the bodies, burning through flesh and bone so fast there's no smell, not even a single hint of singed hair and sulphur. Etaro works behind them, collecting what's left when the fire is through, pulling all the ash away from the pyre and into a pack we emptied for them. It's the same one that held Tyrroh not long ago.

Soon, sooner than I think any of us were ready for, there is nothing left to burn.

The impossible has happened. Two of the Miriseh are dead.

When Etaro finishes gathering the ashes, ey silently hands the bag to Zonna with a murmur of condolence. I don't even think he hears it.

We move quickly, the same pace we've been pushing ourselves to meet since Osshi left. Traveling inside the wagon, though, leaves too much time to think, for Zonna especially. He sits in the far back corner of the top bed, forehead resting on his knees. Although he responds when we ask him a direct question, he doesn't otherwise speak or move. He's not crying, he won't eat when we offer him food, and when one of the ukaiahana'lona stumbles in the mud and injures their leg, it takes far too long for him to even look up when we call his name and ask for help.

And *that* is worrying me almost as much as the way this storm feels in the sky.

This is the feeling I got in the desert sometimes, the one that made me look closer at the shadows cast by the mountains and pay extra attention to the land behind us. It's the same kind of sharp awareness that caught my attention when the first early storm dropped suddenly on Shiara, and I've learned to pay attention to it. This paranoid alertness has saved my life before.

Now, there's nothing to see. No enemy to spot. No way to change the course we're on. No way to help Zonna who looks like he's drowning inside his own head. The helplessness of it all only serves to make my skin itch. It makes me feel as though the sun—if I could see it in the sky—would be moving at twice the speed it should be, running faster through the sky and shoving us closer to the moment when we're going to have to take our next step and hope it's not too late for it to do any good.

Even with the wards over the open window and door to give us a view of the world we're passing by, I feel trapped by the storm. I want to *run*. I want something real to fight instead of this pervasive, nagging fear.

Tessen joins me at the window where I'd been watching the storm lash and rage against the world. Leaning against the wall, he watches me more than the landscape for a moment before he quietly says, "Tell me again what you saw."

"When?"

"Inside the katsujo." He reaches out, taking my hand and running his thumb along my knuckles. I glance at the others. They're close enough to listen, but most of them are either sleeping or having their own quiet conversations.

I do as he asks, closing my eyes but holding on to his hand. Even remembering the touch of the conscious energy at the end is too much, weaker but still blisteringly present. The power in it, and the strangeness of how it was painful and soothing in turns… I don't think I'll ever be able to forget a single moment.

Sighing, I open my eyes. Movement over Tessen's shoulder catches my attention—Zonna's curled up in a corner of the bed. Is his head tilted in our direction or is that wishful thinking? By all rights, *he* should be in charge now that Tyrroh and his parents are gone, but somehow it's fallen to me. And now that I have the position I always thought I wanted, I don't know what to do.

"Tessen…" I lean closer and drop my voice as low as I can. "I need to make the decisions, and I need to be right, and I'm not ready to hold the fate of so many people in my hands. How am I supposed to do that knowing the Kaisubeh or something like them are watching? What if they're expecting another miracle like the one I pulled off in Kaisuama?"

"Don't think about it like that." He brushes his fingers along my hairline and down the side of my jaw, but his eyes don't leave mine. "Think about it like— Well, from what you and the others described, it seems like they almost want to help."

"Help." I rub my eyes with my free hand; it feels like I'm only pushing the thoughts deeper into my brain. "If they wanted to help, they should've left Imaku a lot closer to Ryogo."

Tessen shakes his head. "They're not people, though, not the way you're thinking. Remember the older stories Lo'a told? From those and what you said, it sounds more like the desosa somehow gained consciousness." Then he straightens, his head snapping to stare out the window. The wagon shudders and stops, and his grip on my hand tightens. "Drop the ward, Khya. Lo'a is coming to talk to us."

I release the ward on the door, instead creating one to protect us from the cold storm. Our departure makes the others follow, all of them trailing us out. Except Zonna. His blank gaze does track us, and I almost go back in and ask him to come with us. The words stick in my throat. He looks away. I give up for the moment and trudge out the door.

Soanashalo'a is talking to the others several feet away, her skirt tied up to keep it out of the mud. As soon as I'm within range, she says, "I got a message from another family. They know the south, and they travel between Rido'iti, Po'umi, and the other southern cities often."

"Did something happen?" Tessen asks.

"Not yet, but as they were evacuating like we warned them to, they saw strange lights and night-black clouds on the horizon. The last few moons have been bad, but the way they talked about these clouds—" She shakes her head. "It sounded like a storm that would end the world."

"Maybe it's just a new storm," Etaro suggests.

"And maybe Varan will let us feed him to a teegra," Sanii mutters.

Etaro glares. "You don't know it's not!"

"And you can't assume it is!" Sanii shoots back.

Tessen cringes at the raised voices, and I cut them off. "Stop it. What else did you hear, Lo'a?"

"There have been reports of deep sea fishing vessels returning with stories of odd currents, strange clouds, and storms that rise up out of nowhere." Soanashalo'a's gaze scans the group, settling on something behind us. "Some of the ships have gone missing."

"Stolen or swallowed?" I can imagine ships being easily eaten by the angry ocean, broken up into pieces and devoured. It's what would've happened to Kazu's ship if I hadn't been there. And I doubt any of the Ryogan ships had a ward mage onboard.

It's bad news if the sea took them, because we'll have to cross that water eventually. Varan would probably laugh till he choked if we drowned before ever getting a chance to challenge him. If I can even drown now.

It's worse news if those ships were stolen. Varan with ships? The magic alone is bad enough. I don't want him getting his hands on anything that will make this invasion easier.

And if the storm *isn't* a sign of Varan's army, it could still mean trouble. I can't believe any crew will be willing to sail us into a storm that looks like the end of the world. There's even less of a chance of us being able to sail a stolen ship ourselves in something that dangerous.

"All we know is they were caught in the storms. Some believe they sank, and others insist the missing ships have been blown far off course, beyond the range of any garakyu," Soanashalo'a says.

Tessen leans in. "Is that unusual?"

"Not unheard of, but the fishing ships try to keep in contact during a storm," Soanashalo'a explains. "If only so the others can bring word back to families if a ship is lost."

"He's coming," I say, feeling the truth like a chill in my bones. "They're almost here."

"We don't know that," Zonna argues. I jump at the sound of his voice—hoarse and flat as it is—but all of us turn to listen. "Varan's never been good at seeing the negative consequences of his choices. He found a way across the ocean and so he's going to use it, but he didn't think about what this level of disruption would do to the weather patterns."

"Or, if he did, he thought it'd take more time before the damage became noticeable," Tessen adds. "And despite the number of ward mages Varan has following him, there's a good chance the storms and the journey will have exhausted them all."

I cut through the useless debate. "What it means is we need to make a decision. If they're on their way here, do we work on building our weapons now and stay to meet them, or do we find a ship and try to sail around the worst of this to reach Shiara?"

"What's the point of going home if the army is on their way here?" Rai asks.

"If we can make it to Shiara, we might be able to find more than thirty other immortals," Zonna says. "We'll have more than three times as many on our side if we free everyone

Varan trapped on Imaku."

"Sure. We can do that while they're here destroying Ryogo." Miari shakes her head. "How can we leave them here defenseless?"

"Worse than defenseless," Etaro says softly, looking back toward our wagon where Ahta is standing, watching us. "All they can do is flee, and they're not even ready for that."

"And with eleven fighters and a trunk full of overpowered rocks, we're not ready to face an army," Rai insists.

Tessen seems distracted, eyes straying toward the road ahead. I step closer, letting the debate continue behind me. "What is it?"

"I don't know," he says slowly. "There's something strange ahead, though."

I follow his gaze, but I don't see anything except trees and a solid sheet of rain. "Dangerous or different?"

"Familiarly dangerous." He looks at me, confusion creasing his face. "It feels like the Imaku rock we stole from Mushokeiji. Before you amplified it."

"What the bellows would any of that rock be doing here?" I ask. "I thought they made sure every speck of that was hidden away."

"It's a distinctive feeling, Khya." Tessen looks back toward the road. "There's nothing else it could be."

Glancing at the others, I realize they've moved closer to listen. I make a series of quick gestures and they jog back to the wagon to retrieve their weapons. Less than a minute later, we're moving forward, weapons drawn and magic ready.

There's a huge section of the road that looks different in the rain. When the thick drops strike most patches of the path, they sink and disappear. In other areas, it splashes, spraying smaller droplets into the air. Like sections of the road are dirt and some are stone.

The road is covered with black rock, from pieces the size of the slab Natani's holding to a much finer gravel Tessen is examining.

It doesn't make sense. "Where did this come from? If this from the Mushokeiji vault, I can't believe they'd use it on *this*."

"Exactly," Sanii says. "This seems like a massive waste of a very limited resource."

Etaro looks between the black stone and Sanii, eir narrow nose wrinkled. "Even if Osshi told them we were here, and they assumed we were the bobasu, did they seriously spread pieces of rock across the path and think that would be enough to take out *all* of us? Especially since we have to assume they know we're not traveling on foot."

"They had spells to make the stone capable of cracking Khya's wards," Zonna says. "We have to assume these can do more damage than the unaltered stone from Imaku. I'm guessing that walking or rolling over this isn't a good idea."

"Probably not. And there's something else," Tessen murmurs before Zonna can answer. Slowly, he stands and peers into the trees on either side of the road, searching. "Something..."

Then his head tips farther and farther back until he's looking straight up into the trees. "Oh, no. Khya, there's a garakyu up there. I didn't feel it at first because of the stone, but look."

When he points, Soanashalo'a mutters something in her language, peering up into the trees. I look, too. I can't see it, but I trust Tessen's word that it's there.

I back up, signaling the others to as well. "Have there been any others on this path?"

"Not that I've felt," he says, confidence in his voice. "I've been watching the trees since we first spotted them."

"Sanii, how far can those see?" Ey's the one who knows

the most about that magic.

"The smaller ones are usually only used to send messages between individual people," ey says. "They see whatever is directly in front of them, but those are bigger. I'd guess they were set up to be able to see the entire patch of stone they laid."

"Which means they'll know as soon as we cross it." Rai adjusts her grip on her weapon and sparks fly from her other hand, extinguishing when they meet the wet ground.

"Ambush." There's no other reason to waste this much time, energy, and stone. "They've got to have someone waiting nearby."

Everyone stills and quiets, giving Tessen the silence he needs to listen. We wait. And wait. His head tilts, multiple expressions flashing across his face.

"I can't be sure," he finally says, "but I think they're on the rise in the distance that direction. The rain and the wind make it almost impossible to hear anything else. Lo'a, is there another way out of here?"

"One possibility. If they know we are passing this direction, though, they will almost certainly have closed the paths behind us as well." She's tense, her shoulders pulled back and her hands clenched. "What I want to know is how. *How* did they anticipate our path when even we did not know where we would travel each day?"

"This is your land," Wehli challenges. "You tell us."

She pulls back a little, her shoulders curving. "I—I would say Osshi in other circumstances, but he could not have known we would be *here*."

"No, but…" I look back to the wagon, remembering the moment Osshi said goodbye. He took a bag with him, but it was his smaller pack. Some of his things are still stowed. "Tessen, you've been paying attention to garakyus outside the caravan. Did you ever search *inside*?"

"Why would—oh." He looks like a shock just ran through him. Then he curses. "It was there when I started watching for the garakyus. Bellows, Khya, I trained myself to *ignore* it. I knew it was there, so it didn't matter, and even after he left I never thought to wonder why it wasn't missing."

"And it's active?" I ask, my stomach sinking.

Tessen nods, expression harsh. "It's active."

Blood and rot. I could understand Osshi abandoning us to warn his people. There was honor in that choice, even if I thought it was wrong. This? If I ever see him again, there's a chance I might gut him for this.

"Lo'a, we need a detailed map of this area and I need to talk to whoever knows it best." I make the request as politely as possible, refusing to take my anger at Osshi out on her.

She nods and runs off, moving as quickly as the muddy ground allows. I head toward our wagon and then stop. "The garakyu. What do we do about that?"

Rai looks at me like the answer should be obvious. "Chuck it into the forest and be done with it."

"But then the Ryogans will know we've figured out how they found us," Sanii counters.

"They'll know we know as soon as we blow through whatever tyatsu are out there waiting for us," she snipes.

"Because that's worked for us so well before." Etaro gestures at me. "Khya almost died. Tyrroh *did* die."

The reminder aches. *I can block the arrows now*, I want to shout, to force them to remember I can protect them where I failed Tyrroh. But it takes three layers of wards, and it's painfully exhausting work. I can keep it up for a while, but even with the extra stamina and endurance the susuji gave me, I can't last forever.

And Etaro is talking again before I can say a word. "Ryogan soldiers may not be able to stand up against the Itagamin army, but we're not them, Rai. We're eleven runaways lost in a strange land. We're outnumbered, and they have a better position and better weapons. If they know we're preparing for them, they'll attack early and be done with it. How many more friends are you willing to lose today?"

Pain flashes across Rai's face.

"So we use it against them instead." Sanii stands with eir hands on eir hips, looking at our wagon with a speculative expression that so strongly reminds me of Yorri it hurts. This is the look he would get when he was building one of his puzzles. "If you want your enemy to be a certain place, make sure they know *you'll* be there. If you want your enemy to stop looking for one secret, let them find another."

"Give them false information." I begin to understand, and I smile. "Yes. We'll go back to the wagon and get what we need to plan the next step, and while we're inside, we're going to be talking about the news Lo'a just got—a ship on the southwestern coast is willing to take us to Shiara. It'll explain why we stopped."

"You realize we might have to head into that trap if we want to get the hanaeuu we'la maninaio out of here safely," Tessen murmurs after the others run to the wagon. "They can defend themselves, but they're not fighters. If the whole caravan turns and runs, this will happen again. They'll keep chasing them."

"I know, but honestly, I think we'll only have bad options and worse ones today." Rubbing the space between my eyes, I try to think. "The path we're on is the best way to Rido'iti, so I think we'll have to force our way straight through the worst of this."

"Hopefully someone can come up with a better plan than that."

Yet, despite Tessen's hopes, we can't. All we do is find a

way to spare Soanashalo'a and her family the danger.

"Are you sure about this, Soanashalo'a?" I ask after the others leave her wagon to prepare things in ours. "I can't ask you to leave your people behind. They need you to lead them."

"You did not ask, I offered," she corrects. "First, I helped you for Osshi's sake, and then for your own and out of gratitude, but now it is for the safety of *my* people. There are hundreds of us spread throughout Ryogo, and we will be caught in this war as much as anyone. If there is anything I can do to help you stop this before lives are lost, I will do it."

"Even if it costs your own?" It might come to that. Despite what I've learned, and even though I can't be damaged or drained quite as easily, there's no way I can promise everyone will be alive at the end of this.

She lifts one shoulder and gives me a smile that is almost believable. "What is a life when it is given in protection of family?"

"The most precious thing in the world. Don't pretend it's worth nothing."

"True, and it is my gift to give."

I can't argue with that, not when I'm doing the same thing. "All right. Be ready to leave as soon as possible, then."

We have an ambush to ruin.

M ost of the wagons backtrack a mile, and then turn east down a path almost too narrow for them to pass. They'll be armed and on guard, but we're nearly certain the Ryogans aren't watching that particular trail; the hanaeuu we'la maninaio who travel this area never use it.

Three of the wagons will continue along the road we're

on—ours, Soanashalo'a's, and one more. When she explained what she was doing and ordered her family to safety, five refused. None of us could turn them away.

As we near the stone-strewn road, I signal Miari and Natani, who are walking beside the slow-moving wagons. With Natani funneling her extra power, Miari forces the stones to sink beneath the mud and then move, breaking them into pieces and scattering them through the forest on either side of the road. When it's done, I glance at Tessen. *No change*, he signals.

Sanii came up with the second part. Because Chio's skill was with lightning, he made sure to teach em about the damage that kind of power can do to a spell. According to our andofume, a lightning strike is one of the only things that can break a spell like a garakyu without a mage's involvement. Another is to completely shatter the globe—a task that's apparently harder than it should be given how fragile the garakyus look.

None of us can create or control lightning, but there is plenty of lightning in the sky. And we have Etaro, who's more than capable of yanking that globe loose from the branches above us.

We let the first wagon slowly enter the view of the garakyu. Then, exactly as a flash of blue-white lightning streaks across the sky, Sanii shouts the spell that shuts the garakyu's magic off, and Etaro rips it out of the tree, pulling it down to the ground so fast it shatters. Hopefully the Ryogans will think a lightning strike took out their inanimate spies.

But the movement of the garakyu releases something else.

Black nets fall.

"Etaro!" I ward us, layering the magic like I would for arrows and bracing for the first touch of the black stone.

They don't land. Etaro and the wind whip the things away,

sending them flying through the air until they're wrapped around the trees, well caught.

"They're moving in." Tessen winces, trying to listen to the enemy through the noise of the storm. Then he gasps, sharp and pained. "Arrows! Incoming!"

Three dozen strike at once. Etaro knocks a dozen of them out of the sky. Only a portion of the ones that hit, thank the Kaisubeh, are spelled and tipped with Imaku stone. I'm already braced in a corner of the wagon, now I close my eyes and focus entirely on the wards.

The wagons pick up speed, jolting and jerking down the pitted path. I'm braced for another flight of arrows. It doesn't come right away, and it makes me wonder how well they can see the road from their perch. The trees are thick. The rain is, too. Without the garakyu to guide their aim, maybe they can't see we've moved. Maybe they don't know yet that their trap missed. That's what we were hoping for. The rest of the plan won't work if that part failed.

We stop, and I don't need to give anyone signals or orders. Everyone pours out of the wagons and moves into position. We've tried hard to avoid killing any of the Ryogans, and except for the one guard, we've succeeded. That streak is probably going to end today.

When we begin moving again, Rai and Nairo run alongside, eyes on the trees and hands engulfed in flames. Etaro is stationed between two of the wagons, ready to deflect the next round of arrows.

"Soldiers to the west," Tessen says from the wagson's open door. "Approaching fast."

Sanii and I, running behind the wagon, relay the warning. The desosa inside my ward shivers as every single member of my squad draws on it at once.

"Where are they, Tessen?"

"Almost in range, but spread farther than we expected."

"We knew we might not get them all." And if they're carrying the weapons from Mushokeiji, the trap won't last long without me there to reinforce it. But I can't see anything beyond the first line of trees. "Say when, Tessen."

He nods, eyes closed to listen to the incoming enemy.

Rai and Nairo shoot jets of flames into the trees, trying to force the tyatsu to change direction, keep them from spreading out too far. Shouts. Orders issued in Ryogan.

"Incoming!" I scream in Itagamin.

Another volley of arrows falls on the caravan, their aim directed by the soldiers on the ground. This time, five of them break through. I'm protecting too much space. Too many people. I can't keep the layers in place over it all.

"Khya, switch!"

I slide to a stop, eyes closed. Natani is by my side, his hand on my shoulder and an extra rush of energy flowing into my body. Using it, I activate the wardstones we hid along the road and brace myself.

Impacts. Shouts. Sparks.

The tyatsu are trapped, stuck inside a ward strong enough to stop almost anything. *Almost* anything. But the moment I bring up the trap, I lose focus. For an instant. A second. It's enough.

Arrows get through. An animal bellows in pain. Someone screams.

I bring the wards back, but whatever damage is done, is done. Ordering the others to watch the sky for another attack, I run toward the trapped tyatsu. The chances of this working aren't great—the chances of it working on my squad wouldn't be—but this is the only way out without blood.

They brandish weapons and scream insults, more than half of which I don't understand.

"Flames, Rai," I murmur in Itagamin.

As soon as the sparks surrounding her hands turn into a column of fire. The tyatsu scramble back, eyes wide with fear. One of them runs so far back he slams into the opposite wall of the ward. There are scattered mutterings of, "Akukeiji. Akukeiji."

"Evil mage," Soanashalo'a translates for us.

"Oh good," Rai intones in Itagamin. "At least they don't have the wrong idea about us."

"Listen!" I project my voice over theirs. It takes two more bellows before they shut their mouths. "I don't know what you've been told, but we're not here to hurt you."

They stir and protest. I hold my hand up and wait until they settle. "We're not here to hurt you, and we don't want to, but we will. You've been chasing us since we got here, and I *will* kill you before I let you hurt us."

"Then kill us, akukeiji," the eldest says, spitting on the ground near the edge of the ward.

Oh yes. This is going to end so well. "Return to your leader and tell him to believe Osshi's story. Danger is approaching, and when it lands, it will sweep you out to sea and then happily watch you drown."

The one who spoke goes still; the others rail, yelling threats.

"Ask your leader. He knows." I stare down the man at the center of the group, the one I think is in charge. "Your ancestors tried to exile the bobasu to a rock in the middle of the ocean. They sent a single ship and thought that'd be enough to hold the man who found a way to defy your Kaisubeh. It wasn't. Varan survived, escaped, and now he's returning with an army at his back. They could destroy an entire town in a day, raze it to the ground, and nothing you're capable of will stop them."

"We stopped the bobasu before." The leader says it, but his eyes and weight shift.

Rai raises her eyebrows. "Did you not hear her say the word 'army'?"

"There are thousands of warrior-mages crossing the southern ocean right now. Only ten of them are your bobasu." I look away from the leader to scan the faces of the others. "I don't care how powerful your stone weapons are, you don't have enough. You can't make enough, not in the time you have left. Even if you did have the time, you don't have enough stone."

"You've trapped us. You're trying to trick us."

"Why?" I want to reach through the ward and smack them with the flat of my sword. "All we're trying to do is save your lives. And the lives of every person you've ever known."

"Khya!" Tessen shouts in Itagamin from the caravan. "Time's up!"

"Call your men off." I hold the officer's gaze, hoping he'll listen. "If they attack, we'll fight. They'll die."

I don't wait for an answer. I turn and run back to the wagons.

More arrows fall, almost none of them the spelled, stone-tipped ones that rip through magic. It makes it easier to maintain my wards and it means they're conserving their most powerful weapons for when they're sure they have a shot. But it also proves they're not giving up.

One of my wards shudders, something powerful smashing against it. I look that direction as I leap into the wagon, feeding more desosa into the trap.

"Most of the soldiers on the hill are the archers," Tessen says, tension in his tone. "They're closing in from the northeast, Khya."

"Guess your rousing speech didn't work," Rai mutters.

"Time to run?"

"Miari? Natani?" I call their names out the door. "On Tessen's mark!"

They call back a confirmation and then I climb up to the roof. Tessen follows.

There's an arch to the roof, but it's gentle, and it makes it easy to crouch in the center holding on to one of the two pieces of wood running parallel down the length of the wagon. They usually hold extra cargo, giving the hanaeuu we'la maninaio a place to tie down crates and boxes, but now they keep us on the wagon as it bounces and shakes.

"I really wanted them to stop following us," I whisper.

"I know." He smiles sadly, but his eyes are on the road behind us. "But if you thought that was going to happen, we wouldn't have made this part of the plan in the first place."

It's true, and it's not the first time I've killed someone. It won't even be the first time I've killed a Ryogan. What it will be is the first time I have ever crafted a plan and given an order that will end five or a dozen or fifty lives. We won't even know. I might never know.

When Tessen shouts, "In position!" though, I don't hesitate to follow that with an order.

The road passes through a hill, a tunnel carved through dirt and rock. As soon as we're out the other side, Natani gives Miari the power she needs to collapse it behind us.

Rumbling stone from the mountain blends with the thunder overhead. Shouts echo out from inside, warnings called down their line. Screams. Then, with a rippling shudder and the sound of a rockslide, the entire hill begins to cave in.

Tessen and I watch the Ryogans die from the top of a hanaeuu we'la maninaio wagon.

Only after we lose sight of the crumbled, broken hill do I swing down from the roof and walk inside the wagon. Zonna is sitting on the bed with Nairo, and there's blood on Nairo's sleeve. My throat clenches. "Status?"

"Other than the wound Zonna's fixing, we don't know." Sanii stands by the window, arms crossed and expression pinched. "It's not over yet. Not until Lo'a says we're safe."

And that won't be for several miles. Soanashalo'a planned a route that balanced speed and secrecy. Our plans and the Ryogans' deaths will be for nothing if we let them catch up to us and have to fight our way out again.

"If Osshi wasn't in trouble with his leadership before today, he almost certainly will be now," Nairo says as he changes into clothes without bloodstains and holes. "Even if they do believe what Khya told them, I wouldn't be surprised if they think he set them up to fail."

Then Etaro clears eir throat. "How many do we think died?"

"I don't know. More than should have, considering we warned them." I'm holding on to that fact, and hoping at least one person from the squad I spoke to is left alive to remember it. That was one of the reasons we trapped them in the wards. Hopefully those traps held long enough to keep them out of the tunnel and alive.

Our trail twists and turns, but with Soanashalo'a guiding our three-wagon caravan and Tessen watching for pursuit, we make it to a clearing, safe for the moment.

When we finally stop running, when Tessen is as sure as he can be that we've lost them in the forest and that the rain will have all but erased the signs of our passage, I ease out of the wagon to see the damage for myself.

One wheel broken, but it had been quickly fixed while I talked to the Ryogan squad.

One of my people injured, Nairo bleeding through the hastily secured bandage on his arm, but Zonna healed that quickly as soon as they got back in the wagon.

One ukaiahana'lona dead, the massive beast shot twice in the moment my wards failed.

One of the hanaeuu we'la maninaio dead, shot through the throat in the same moment.

The rest of us made it through, and right now that's more than enough for me because what I told the Ryogan officer is true.

The worst is yet to come.

CHAPTER TWENTY

We almost abandon the wagons. If not for the trunk of Imaku stones, we might have.

Even with the protection of the forest and the region's small hills, the wind breaks branches and buffets my wards. Clouds thicker and darker than I've ever seen obscure the sky totally until day and night become even more meaningless. Not even Tessen has any way to sense the difference. I think it takes two and a half days to reach Rido'iti from where we were when the Ryogans ambushed us, but no one can tell.

We can't enter the city—not when every tyatsu in Ryogo is looking for us—and so we leave the wagons behind, only Soanashalo'a coming with us as we head to the western edge of the city on foot. We're only carrying weapons and enough food for a day of travel. Even the trunk of Imaku stone stays, safer here until we know we have a way home. Thankfully, the ships we're hoping to find here—ones we'll have to steal if we can't convince them to carry us to Shiara—can be reached by traveling along the rocky coast.

"Your friend really thinks we'll find a ship and crew brave enough to sail out in this?" I can't believe it. I have my wards to protect me and my brother to save, and even I don't want to get any closer to the ocean than I am right now. If it feels like the storm can obliterate us more than two miles inland, I'm not so sure I want to see the height of the waves.

And yet that's exactly where we're headed.

Turning as he walks, Tessen seems to be following something in the sky. "Do you feel it, Khya?"

"Feel what?" Whatever it is, it's beyond my senses.

"The way the desosa—" He shakes his head. "Just, concentrate. What does it feel like?"

Confused, I close my eyes and reach for the desosa and draw it in. At first, in the air immediately surrounding us, everything seems normal. Then I reach higher and—

It *burns*. It feels like trying to fill my veins with lightning.

Hissing, I flinch and yank my mental reach back. "What bobasu-cursed torment is *that*?"

I've felt the desosa powered by the hottest fires of the forge. I've felt it pouring down pure and powerful from the desert sun at high noon. I've felt the desosa electrified by lightning.

I have never felt anything like this.

It's as though each individual particle is as powerful as ten, but those small specks aren't meant to contain that much energy. The particles are breaking, and the energy each shattering spark releases burns like embers. And from the grim resignation on Tessen's face, he doesn't perceive it much differently.

"It's Varan," Rai says in Itagamin. "It has to be."

"It might be." It could be something he caused purposefully, but it could also be what Tsua feared would happen—that whatever he was doing is causing the storms to get worse and worse until they…well, until they either become one never-ending storm that will drown everything, or until they burn themselves out, like a blaze left unattended.

"Even if we somehow win, we might still lose," Sanii says softly.

Swallowing, I try to believe we won't have to face that fate. Then lightning flashes, the bolt thick at the top and splintering and splintering into hundreds of smaller pieces, spreading across the sky into one second-long, sun-bright flash. The roll of thunder is almost deafening.

What will happen to Shiara in a world of constant rain? The rocky landscape can't absorb that much water. We'll— *they'll*—either adapt or drown, but I don't know if the first can possibly happen fast enough to prevent the second.

"Maybe," I admit grudgingly. "Or maybe we can find a way to fix the damage. We can't do that until after Varan has stopped causing it, though."

"And he won't stop causing it until he's dead," Rai says.

I have to end this or he'll unmake the world, cracking it open with lightning and drowning it with ocean swells.

"He's not here yet, and we need to stick to the plan until that changes." I say it, but once Tessen made me aware of the atmosphere above our heads, I can't pull my attention away from it completely. As we slide down the muddy hill to get level with the coast, that awareness gets sharper.

I match my pace to Tessen's. "Is it getting closer?"

"Yes, and I don't like it." He looks up again, his full lips pursed and worry around his eyes. "I don't know what this is or where it's coming from or *why*, but there is nothing about this that feels like a good thing, Khya."

I pass the warning to the others, but there's nothing anyone can do. None of us can be more on guard than we already are, and unless we're about to stumble on another broken katsujo that I can fix, there's nothing we can do to alter the nature of the desosa. I don't know if even the Kaisubeh themselves can.

"Keep moving, then." I try to tell myself that the sooner we get to a ship, the sooner we can get to Shiara and stop what's coming. No matter how often those words repeat inside my head, they don't get more believable.

A mile of muddy, forested hills later, we break onto a wide, sandy beach. The waves crash fast and hard on the shore, each one rising several feet over my head. When the waves pull out, the tide is so strong the shoreline grows another twenty feet.

I've seen this before in a storm when a wave almost taller than the wall of Itagami crashed onto the shore. Before the wave, before the crash and the damage, there was this, a moment when the sea became a desert of sand and rocks.

In a way, it's a relief. The storm is vicious and brutal and it scares me to even consider getting on a boat that will take me into that, but that's all I see. Water and lightning and clouds so dark they look solid. No army. Not even within Tessen's range.

Only now do I realize how sure I was of what I would see. Only when the knot of terror in my chest loosens do I understand how far down I'd stuffed the belief that Varan would be standing on the waves.

I'm rarely this happy to be wrong.

"Khya, look."

My heart stops, fear tightening my chest, but Tessen isn't looking out to sea, he's looking up. I follow his gaze and my pulse quickens for a whole different reason.

We're standing between the feet of the Kaisubeh. The statues I saw from Kazu's ships, the Zohogasha spread along this section of the coast. Not the same ones, but they're almost identical. And so much taller than I could've imagined. They make the trees look small. They make us look like grains of sand. They tower over our heads and I can't fathom how any human hands could've made these without magic. Yes, they're useless symbols but they represent a very real power, and I can't help feeling glad that we'll be leaving under the gaze of the same stone eyes that first spotted us on the water. It feels like a good omen.

"The harbor is on the eastern side of the peninsula," Soanashalo'a says, drawing my attention back to the ground. She keeps walking, and we follow, staying close to the rocks and the treeline to keep from getting sucked in by the upsweep of the waves. "The ships here fish the deep seas, where the storms get the worst, so the crews are veterans of storms and typhoons. If anyone will be able to get you across the Arayokai Sea in something as bad as this, it will be someone there."

"I was already worried we'd have to steal a ship, but look at that." Tessen gestures out to the sea, flinching when three streaks of blue-white lightning flash across the sky. "What can we possibly offer them to make taking a risk like this worthwhile? Would any of you risk walking across the desert in a storm like this because a stranger asked you to?"

"What are we offering? You mean aside from the chance to save their homes and their families?" Sanii asks. "That should be more than enough."

"Maybe," Etaro agrees. "*If* they believe us."

"And if they don't think we caused this problem," Rai mutters.

"Stealing a ship was always an option." My words are steady, somehow. Mostly because I keep my eyes well away from the roiling ocean. "If that's what we have to do, we will."

No one says a word. They don't need to. I can feel their doubt and their fear like a chill in the already cold air. I also know they'd do it, if I told them to. They might argue with me, point out every possible way the plan would end with us lost and dying at sea, but they would still get on a stolen ship with me if that was what I ordered.

Which is why I can't order it until we don't have any other choice.

The wet sand makes traveling slow. This was the route least likely to be watched by the Ryogans, but it makes me miss the semi-solid feel of the forest paths under my feet. Even though the mud in the forest sucked in our boots and splattered over everything, it was only a few inches deep in most places. This sand isn't the packed, hard-pressed stuff I'm used to on Shiara, it's marshy and mucky and sometimes there's nothing but air under a layer of the stuff. Zonna has to fix three sprained ankles in less than two miles because even Tessen can't always predict where the ground is going to fail us.

"Just another half mile and we should be able to see the harbor." Soanashalo'a is breathing hard, her posture drooping.

The end is so close now. A quarter mile. Two hundred yards. One hundred yards.

Rounding a sharp, high outcropping of rock, we can see the broad curve of the protected harbor, but...

Soanashalo'a sucks in a sharp breath. "Oh, no."

We're too late.

The harbor is almost empty, and the ships still anchored in the middle of the bay or tied to the poles rising out of the water are lopsided and broken.

I'd guess that almost every other ship sailed away from land within the last several days, probably heading north. They likely left as soon as the ships at sea started disappearing and the storm on the horizon became this monstrous thing. And the storm was bad enough. Not one, not *one* ship, is going to be sailing toward the incoming army.

The front line stretches for at least two hundred yards, and there's a dome of calm over their heads. I can't see faces, and even separating the shape of one person distinctly from the one next to them is hard, but there are people on the ocean. They're walking toward us, supported by slabs of sandstone and surrounded by storm.

Varan's terrible vengeance is about to reach Ryogo.

The Itagamin army is almost here. They're a mile or so off, and they don't seem to be moving any faster than a slow, steady walk, but they're here.

"How long until they make landfall, Tessen?" Ideas are forming in my head, none of them very good, but I need to know how much time we have left.

Voice hoarse and eyes locked on the incoming enemy, Tessen says, "Half an hour if we're lucky."

It's enough. But before I order the squad to move, there's something else. I wind back through the group, taking just one person by the wrist and leaning down to look into her eyes. "Soanashalo'a, you have already done more than I ever expected from someone who isn't clan, but I need one more favor from you."

"Khya…" Her eyes are wide and gleaming with fear.

"I need you to run now. Go back to the wagons and head north, *far* north," I tell her. "Grab anyone you can trust not to betray your hiding place, and go to the caves where we waited out the first bad storms. Go there and *stay there*."

"I cannot leave you to this!"

"And we need to see what's happening here, but we can't afford for the black rock to be destroyed by Varan." I take her hands and hold them tight. "You'll be safe there, and you can keep what we need safe. We'll meet you. I promise."

But it's dark. And without my wards, she won't be protected from the storm. And there are about to be thousands of enemies marching onto this shore. Sending her back to the wagons alone might be more dangerous than keeping her with us, so I turn to Wehli and order, "Go with her. Carry her, and get her to the wagons as fast as possible."

"What?" His eyes go wide as he looks between his missing arm and me. "I *can't*! Khya, you know I can't. And you don't have to—"

"Don't," I cut him off and stalk closer until only inches separate us. "You've already proven us wrong more than once. Do it again. It matters more than ever now. I'm not sending you away to protect you, I'm sending you on a mission to make sure we have even a tiny chance of winning this. It won't happen without those stones, and her people need all the extra protection we can give them if they're going to guard those rocks."

Wehli bites his lip, his gaze drifting toward Miari and Nairo before snapping back to me. My first thought had been to just send him, but maybe I should let the three of them go together. They'll be able to watch each other's backs, and it won't leave Wehli alone in a sea of people who are still nearly strangers.

"Do you two want to follow him there?" I look at Miari and Nairo, asking them the question I'm almost positive they won't ask me no matter how badly they want to go with their partner; choosing the group instead of the individual is too ingrained in everyone who grew up in Itagami. "I'm ordering him to go as fast as he's capable of while carrying someone, so he'd better not wait for you, but the caravan could use the extra protection."

They look at each other, and then both turn toward Wehli. All three are the same age, and they came up in the same training class. They've been together since they were children, since before they were *together*.

"You'll follow us there soon?" Nairo glances at me,

determination in his eyes. "We're not leaving you here only to find out you tried to take on the entire Itagamin army without us."

"I'm not losing any more friends. We'll find you," I promise. "It might take us a little while to catch up, but don't wait. Push north as fast as you can."

"You can probably even use the roads in a few days." Tessen speaks quietly, and his attention is still on the sea. "The Ryogans will have something more worrying to watch for than a caravan of hanaeuu we'la maninaio."

Soanashalo'a stares at me for a long moment before she pulls me into a tight hug. "Khya, please be careful. There are so many people who need you. Come find us and we will help you fight this, but you must not be rash now. Do *not* stay here long enough to be caught."

"I won't." I hug her back, running my hand over her hair and kissing her cheek, keeping myself from adding, *not if I can help it.*

She squeezes me a little tighter, as if she can hear the words I didn't say, and then she whispers several landmarks in my ear, some I recognize from our first journey to the cave in the Mysora Mountains. I repeat them, committing the list to memory and hoping I get the chance to use it.

The goodbyes are brief, and then Wehli, with Soanashalo'a clinging to his back, runs off far faster than we made it here. His two partners follow slower, but soon they're out of sight too, around the curve of the outcropping and gone. Hopefully toward safety.

"Orders, Nyshin-ma?" Etaro asks as soon as they're gone.

"Don't call me that. That's my first order." I move closer to the water, sweeping my hand toward the sea. "The nyshins are the ones doing *this*."

"They don't know what's happening," Etaro says.

"That won't matter to Rido'iti." Tessen shakes his head and then looks at me. "What are your orders, Khya?"

"We need to see what happens," I say after a long breath. "This town isn't ready. It isn't a match for them, and there's no chance these people will fight. We need to see what Varan orders."

"And how far his army is willing to go to obey," Zonna adds.

"Exactly." Once my clan sees that Ryogo isn't what they thought, that there are people here with lives and homes and families, will they follow their Miriseh with the same unquestioning loyalty? What would I have done if I hadn't uncovered their lies? I think I would have unquestioningly followed almost every order.

My stomach twists at the realization.

The view of Rido'iti is awful from here. Only the very edges of the city. There's a rise, though, about a half mile into the forest. It's hard to be sure from here, but it looks like it'd have a perfect vantage point.

To watch a city burn.

"Can't we help them?" Etaro stands with Rai, all three of them look east toward the city. "There has to be some way to stop this. Can't we save them?"

"We don't—" I clamp my mouth shut and close my eyes. "How? The Imaku stone is back with the wagons and there are seven of us. *Seven.* Against that." I throw my arm out, eyes going wide as I glare at Etaro. "If you have a plan, great. Tell me. I'm listening. But right now, all we have is a chance to see exactly what they're planning and maybe save ourselves."

Tessen nods slowly, his eyes toward Rido'iti. "Either we die trying to save this city, or we get out of here alive and get a chance to fight back on a day when we might win."

"Exactly. So everyone shut their mouths and climb."

I follow my own order, clawing my way up the slope that's half mud and half rock. It's steep and wet and cold and my fingers would be numb if not for the extra energy of the susuji. The others likely aren't as lucky. They've had practice recently, though, and this climb is easier and shorter than the last one we had to do. It can't take us more than ten minutes to reach the top of the rise and another five to race toward a section where trees will allow us to watch without being seen.

By the time I'm hidden near the spot with the best view of Rido'iti, the army is close enough I swear I can see faces. People I once called friends. Family. Clan. They look wet and weary, more than one leaning on the shoulder of their neighbor. The group glistens with the silver of polished, honed iron, though, their blades flashing like stars in the continuous lightning.

"Whatever happens, stay here," I force myself to say, making sure the words are loud but not bothering to smother the quaver in my voice. "Do not move. Do not use the desosa. Do not do a single thing that will draw attention to where we are. We watch, we learn, we use it to prepare. That's it."

That's what I say to them, but what it all means is this:

Do not save anyone but ourselves.

I hate myself for the order. I hate Varan for putting me in this position. If this is what leadership means, standing aside and doing nothing, I don't want it.

But I have it, and I need everyone else to understand why I'm ordering this. "We were too late to stop this from reaching Ryogo, but the only way we fail completely is to die here and leave this place in Varan's hands. When it gets too hard to watch, remind yourself of the cities we saw in the north, and imagine what will happen to *those* places if we don't figure out how to stop this invasion before it gets there."

If that's even possible. If it's not already too late.

No one responds, but after Sanii climbs up to sit on a low branch of one of the trees, no one moves, either. I barely breathe, my eyes locked on the incoming army.

"The incoming army," as though I don't know exactly where they're from. As though I couldn't name so many of the soldiers and recite a list of their strongest skills. As though I'm truly not one of them anymore.

Maybe we're not. Maybe, after all that's happened, we don't belong anywhere.

The southernmost streets of Rido'iti are filling with people. Running. Screaming. Children clutched in the arms of their elders. Bags so hastily packed they leave a trail behind the runner.

The first line of Varan's army steps onto Ryogo.

Dozens of kasaiji mages throw huge balls of fire, the impacts igniting the buildings closest to the water. People fleeing their homes are cut down by the blades of the invaders. Ryogans burst out of fire-engulfed buildings, their clothes burning so hot and fast not even the pounding rain is enough to put them out. Ratoiji mages direct the constant lightning from the storm, using it to scorch streets and crush stampedes of terrified people. Entire blocks of the city crumble and disappear when the ground gives way underneath them.

Street by street it progresses as each row of soldiers enters Ryogo. The fires are spreading. The lightning strikes become more frequent.

I glance at the others, though I'm not sure what I expect to see in their faces. Tessen is standing close, but his gaze is jumping across the landscape, each new sight making him flinch. Sanii, Natani, and Zonna look as lost as I feel. Etaro and Rai are standing together, her arms wrapped around eir waist. When Rai looks away from the city, her gaze catches mine, and I can't answer any of the questions in her eyes.

The army is circling Rido'iti, and I don't have to watch to know what's going to happen, how the lines of nyshin soldiers will press forward until everything between them is crushed into blood and dust. But I do anyway.

In a spot of motionless calm in the middle of bloody chaos, are the bobasu. The Miriseh. All ten of them stand in a group, watching their war, doing nothing to pull their nyshin back even though it's clear no one is standing against them.

This is a slaughter.

Please, I beg, desperately praying to the Kaisubeh as I reach for Tessen's hand and grip hard. *You helped us once, please do it again. I'm willing to fight this war for you, but I can't win against this. Not without help. Please.* Please *help us. Help me.*

The Ryogans' gods are real, I have proof of that much, but are they listening? They'd better be, because their people need them. An entire land of people who believe in the power and the grace of the Kaisubeh will die, crushed in the path of an unstoppable force, because all I have is seven warrior-mages, three immortals, a family of hanaeuu we'la maninaio, an orphaned Ryogan ebet, and a box of desosa-charged rocks.

It's not enough, but if we can't come up with a plan, this is what Varan will do: flatten cities until there's nothing left to save.

I watch Rido'iti die.

I knew from the moment I decided to help Sanii find Yorri that I was going to lose my home, but now I know there's nothing to go back to. This waste, this brutality, this chaos, it's everything we were raised to avoid. Varan has destroyed everything I love about Itagami as completely as he's leveling Rido'iti.

Varan has so much to atone for. Somehow, I am going to find a way to make him.

Even if I have to drag him before the Kaisubeh myself.

EPILOGUE

Rain lashes the ground, creating small, quick rivers in the cracks of the red rock. Screaming wind tears across the mountain, ripping a boulder off the slopes and sending it flying into the valley below. It slams into a black stone platform, shattering a corner.

The girl trapped on that platform doesn't even scream. She's unconscious, locked to the stone as it tips off its base and slides to the valley floor. It knocks into the next platform, rattling the boy trapped on the surface.

Yorri's eyes fly open. His back arches off the black rock. He opens his mouth and screams. Thunder muffles his terror. The wind rips it away from his lips. Not one of the thirty-eight other people trapped in the valley with him hears.

One by one they wake up. Some of them struggle, fighting to break the red cords binding them to the black platforms. Some only try to hide their faces from the driving, pounding rain. Others open their mouths and drink the pouring water like they haven't tasted it in centuries.

Yorri closes his eyes and cries, his tears lost in the cold raindrops splashing on his face.

He remembers everything that's happened since Neeva

pressed a circle of black rock to the back of his neck and trapped him in unconsciousness, leaving him watching himself and everything that happened around him.

He'd thought being forced to watch others fake his death was torture. He'd been sure seeing his sister's pain as she said goodbye was the worst it could get. He'd known nothing could be more maddening than being trapped in his body and hearing only the neverending crash of the waves against the rocky edges of Imaku. He'd prayed nothing would ever hurt worse than jerking to a halt at the edge of Imaku, watching Sanii and Khya fall into the water, leaving him behind. He'd lost hope when his blood-parents came and helped carry the platforms off Imaku, hiding him in absolute darkness in a place Khya would never find.

Now this.

Time passes. Days, maybe. Weeks. Entire moons. He doesn't know. The storm continues to rage. Lightning flashes, so close it singes his skin and so bright he sees the shape of it streak across his eyelids. Yorri barely flinches. He doesn't open his eyes.

It doesn't matter anymore.

No one will ever find them here. Not even Khya. Not even Sanii. That much, at least, he knows.

No one is coming. Varan will make sure of that.

GLOSSARY

TERMS AND PHRASES (ALL LANGUAGES):

AHDO – Itagamin – Sagen sy Itagami's second citizen class; includes the following ranks (sorted highest to lowest):
Ahdo-na | Ahdo-mas | Ahdo-sa | Ahdo-po | Ahdo-li | Ahdo-va

AHOALI'LONA – HANAEUU WE'LA MANINAIO – the small, furry animals kept as companions

AKILOSHULO'E KUA'ANA MANANO – HANAEUU WE'LA MANINAIO – the universal energy of the world and the source of magic

AKUKEIJI – RYOGAN – a derogatory term that literally translates to "evil mage"

AKURINGU – ITAGAMIN – a mage with the ability to use a reflective surface to see across great distances or, rarely, a short period of time into the past or future

ALIMA'HI – HANAEUU WE'LA MANINAIO – a respectful greeting; hello

ALUA'SA LIONA'ANO SHILUA'A – HANAEUU WE'LA MANINAIO – the gods or power responsible for the creation of the world

ANDOFUME – RYOGAN – those denied death; a word Tsua and Chio invented to describe their lifespans

ANTO – ITAGAMIN – a short, slightly curved dagger used in Sagen sy Itagami

ASAIRU – RYOGAN – a fire spell to burn everything within a designated space

ATAKAFUS – ITAGAMIN – a headscarf worn on Shiara as protection from the desert winds

BASAKU – ITAGAMIN – a mage whose five senses are enhanced and who also has the ability to feel shifts in the desosa; in rare cases this includes the impact emotions have on that energy

BOBASU – RYOGAN – the exiles; a word used for the twelve immortals and numerous mortal followers who were exiled from Ryogo

BORUIKKU – ITAGAMIN – a word created by Rai and Etaro to describe magic that uses symbols to guide and control the flow of the desosa

CHONOCHI – RYOGAN – the last royal family of Ryogo; a member of this family ordered the exile of Varan and his followers

DESOSA – ITAGAMIN – the universal energy of the world and the source of magic

DYUNIJI – ITAGAMIN – a mage with the ability to use their own kinetic energy, or sometimes someone else's (for example, blows landed during battle) to augment their own strength

EBET – ITAGAMIN – the designation for one of Sagen sy Itagami's three recognized sexes

FYKINA – ITAGAMIN – a mage with the ability to shield themselves and others from both magic and the physical world

Garakyu – Ryogan – a clear, spelled globe that allows anyone to communicate across miles

Goa'wa uita – Ryogan – the spell to unseal a protection against the elements

Hanaeuu we'la maninaio – hanaeuu we'la maninaio – a group of nomadic traders who travel either by wagon caravan or by boat; the name translates to "souls carried by the wind"

Hinoshowa – Ryogan – an incredibly derogatory word for a wretch, someone lower than the peasant class; often used synonymously to mean someone who is neither male nor female

Hishingu – Itagamin – a mage with the ability to heal themselves and others

Ishjii – Itagamin – a mage with the ability to reform, lighten, move, and mold stone

Jindaini – Ryogan – the title held by the elected leader of Ryogo

Kaiboshi – Ryogan – the priests who serve the Kaisubeh, the gods Ryogans worship

Kaigo – Itagamin – the council of elders who serve the Miriseh in Sagen sy Itagami

Kaijuko – Ryogan – the place Ryogans believe souls are trapped for punishment in the afterlife; also, what Ryogans call the black rock that helped them trap and defeat the bobasu

Kaimashin – Ryogan – the spirits who carry out the orders of the Kaisubeh, according to an ancient belief

Kaisuama – Ryogan – a mountain in the Mysora range where the Kaisubeh convened to observe their followers, according to an old legend

Kaisubeh – Ryogan – as a whole, the gods and goddesses that the Ryogans believe created and control the world

Kasaiji – Itagamin – a mage with the ability to create and control sparks and/or fire

Katsujo – Ryogan – a vein of concentrated power and energy

Kujuko – Itagamin – where Itagamins believe souls are trapped for punishment in the afterlife; Varan introduced this to his city, a twisted version of Ryogo's belief in Kaijuko

Kynacho – Itagamin – a mage with enhanced speed, agility, strength, stamina, and endurance

Kyneeda – Itagamin – a mage with enhanced strength, stamina, and endurance

Kyshiji – Itagamin – a mage with the ability to find, cleanse, and sometimes manipulate water

Limahi – hanaeuu we'la maninaio – an unwelcome stranger

Miriseh – Itagamin – the title Varan gave himself and the other immortals after he built Sagen sy Itagami

Mura'ina – Ryogan – a purple flower with healing properties that only grows in specific climates within Ryogo

MYIJI – ITAGAMIN – a mage with an extremely rare ability to manipulate wind and detect or, sometimes, call up storms

MYKYN – ITAGAMIN – a large, predatory bird that lives on Shiara

NIADAGU – RYOGAN – a powerful binding spell using specially made red cords

NYSHIN – ITAGAMIN – the first and highest of the citizen classes within Sagen sy Itagami; includes the following ranks (sorted highest to lowest): Nyshin-lu | Nyshin-ri | Nyshin-co | Nyshin-ma | Nyshin-pa | Nyshin-ten

OBYOTO – RYOGAN – a deeply personal term of endearment

OJOKEN – RYOGAN – a plant whose stem and roots are used for powerful healing potions

OMIKIA – RYOGAN – the old, now unused written language of Ryogo

ONYO – RYOGAN – mother

ORAKU – ITAGAMIN – a mage with three enhanced senses: sight, smell, and hearing

OSUKIGA – RYOGAN – a portrait to which a family continuously adds famous, powerful, or influential ancestors; usually includes a shrine where people pray for advice and guidance

RATOIJI – ITAGAMIN – a mage with the ability to create lightning

Rianjuko – Ryogan – A rare flowering plant used in a variety of ways depending on which part of the plant is used; powerful when added to magic work

Rikinhisu – Itagamin – a mage with the ability to move physical objects without touching them

Riuku – Itagamin – the class of mage that includes enhanced senses: uniku, oraku, and basaku

Rononi yakusoro – Ryogan – a strong expletive, its meaning close to "cursed bastard"

Rusosa – Itagamin – a mage with the ability to create illusions in other people's minds

Ryacho – Itagamin – a mage with enhanced speed and agility

Ryiji – Itagamin – a mage with an affinity for plants and soil who can help plants grow

Shuikanahe'le – hanaeuu we'la maninaio – a family name of the hanaeuu we'la maninaio

Shunkyus – Ryogan – the title held by the leader of Ryogo when the position was earned by birth instead of by election; emperor

Sukhai – Itagamin – a bondmate or one partner in a sumai soulbond; often used as a term of endearment between bonded pairs

Sumai – Itagamin – a magical bond that ties two souls together beyond death

Susuji – Ryogan – a potion used to heal

Sykina – Itagamin – a mage with the ability to shield themselves from other magic

Tenrai – Ryogan – a large mountain cat with thick white fur and sharp claws

Tokiansu – Itagamin – the warriors' dance, performed once a moon cycle in Sagen sy Itagami during their celebrations

Tozaiko nitoko – Ryogan – the spell used to activate the niadagu binding

Tssiky'le – Denhitran – a curse close in meaning to dammit

Tudo – Itagamin – a long, slightly curved sword used in Sagen sy Itagami

Tyatsu – Ryogan – the Ryogan army

Ukaiahana'lona – hanaeuu we'la maninaio – horned herbivorous beasts with tough, mottled gray hides that the hanaeuu we'la maninaio use to pull their wagons or cargo loads

Uniku – Itagamin – a mage with a single enhanced sense, usually either vision or hearing

Ureeku-sy rii'ifu – Ryogan – the spell Tsua and Chio think might break the magic binding Yorri and the other prisoners to the stone platforms

Ushimo – Itagamin – describes those on the asexual spectrum; someone who feels little to no sexual desire for anyone, regardless of gender, appearance, or personality

Vanafitia – Denhitran – a term of endearment meaning beloved one

YONIN – ITAGAMIN – the third and lowest of Sagen sy Itagami's social classes; includes the following ranks (sorted highest to lowest): Yonin-na | Yonin-mas | Yonin-sa | Yonin-po | Yonin-li | Yonin-va

YUGADAI – RYOGAN – describes the system Varan enforced in Itagami requiring approval for all births and lifetime partnerships

ZOHOGASHA – RYOGAN – the massive statues guarding the Ryogan coastline; each set contains fourteen statues

ZOIKYO – ITAGAMIN – a mage with the ability to boost other people's powers

SENTENCE TRANSLATIONS:

Ou'a ka lea'i imloa ka'i ia okopo'ono aloshaki ana'anahou. – hanaeuu we'la maninaio – It is good to see you again.

Aloshaki naho olea'o wa'heekohu shahala'kai. O'kaoo malohakama ka lea'i le'anohu – hanaeuu we'la maninaio – You were not lying. Your friends are many.

Shomaihopa'a sha opai'hoa. – hanaeuu we'la maninaio – Bless this fate.

CITIES AND PLACES:

ARAYOKAI SEA – the stretch of water between Shiara and Ryogo

ATOKOREDO – a city in northwestern Ryogo within the Soramyku Province

DENHITRA – the city in the southern mountains of Shiara

EJINOSEI – a city on the western coast of Ryogo within the Soramyku Province

IMAKU – the black-rock island off the north-eastern coast of Shiara

JUSHOYEN – the capitol city of Ryogo, located in the center of the country

KANAGA'AKO – a city in southeastern Ryogo within the Namimi Province and Osshi's hometown

KHYLAR – the country directly to the north of Ryogo, separated by the Mysora Mountains

MUSHOKEIJI – a prison for mages located within the Soramyku Province in northwestern Ryogo, specifically the Suakizu region

MYSORA MOUNTAINS – the northern-most range of mountains that separates Ryogo from Khylar

MYSORA'KA RIVER – the river that runs from the eastern half of the Mysora Mountains to the eastern coast of Ryogo

NENTOADO – the section of the Mysora Mountains known for being harsh and impassable

PO'UMI – a port city on the southeastern coast of Ryogo within the Namimi Province

RIDO'ITI – a port city on the southern coast of Ryogo within the Namimi Province

RYOGO – the country north of Shiara where Varan, Chio, and the other immortals are from

RYOGAN PROVINCES – (clockwise from the southwest)

> **MINOWA** – southwestern-most coastal region

> **AZUKYO** – central western coastal region

> **SORAMYKU** – northwestern-most mountains

> **KYO'NE** – northeastern-most peninsula

> **OKASUTO** – northwestern coastal region

> **HYNOCHI** – central plains

> **TOMI'ISHI** – central eastern coastal region

> **NAMIMI** – southeastern-most coastal region

SAGEN SY ITAGAMI – the city in northeastern Shiara; often simply called Itagami

SANSOSI'KA RIVER – the river running from the western side of the Mysora Mountains to the city of Atokoredo where it splits

SHIARA – the island nation south of Ryogo

SUAKIZU – the region within the Soramyku Province where the prison Mushokeiji is located

TIRODO – a city in northeastern Ryogo, near Uraita, within the Kyo'ne Province

TSIMO – a city on the western peninsula of Shiara

URAITA – a village in northeastern Ryogo within the Kyo'ne Province and the hometown of Varan and Chio

ZUNOATO – a city in the Okasuto Province that sits just north of the Mysora'ka River

ACKNOWLEDGMENTS

Writing is always more marathon than sprint, but that was especially true with *Sea of Strangers*. The book contained in these pages is a cleaned-up version of the third story I wrote—because my editress, Kate Brauning is a perfectionist. And I adore her for that. Kate, this book is almost as much yours as it is mine at this point. Thank you for pushing me past what I thought this story was and making it what it needed to be instead.

Innumerable thanks are also due to the entire Entangled team, all of whom have supported this series and me with all their hearts, but special love goes to Ashley Hearn, Bethany Robison, and Melissa Montovani.

Keeping myself centered and sane is a full-time job on its own, and my friends pull it off so well. Thank you to Cait Greer, Katrina Kerr, Lani Woodland, Olivia Falk, and Tristina Wright for being a constant support.

Publishing can be a tough industry to survive in. A professional support system (and venting arena) is necessary, and my #TeamRocks agent siblings are mine: Laurel Amberdine, Samira Ahmed, Jill Baguchinsky, Mike Chen, Lizzie Cooke, Dave Connis, Julia Ember, Rebecca Enzor,

Kati Gardner, Anna Hecker, Bassey Ipki, Elizabeth Keenan, Sangu Mandanna, Alan Orloff, Rebecca Phillips, Tom Ryan, Lindsey Smith, and Diana Urban. My love for you flows in all its waterfall glory forever and ever.

I owe so much gratitude to my sisters, Haley and Colleen, and my mom, Corey. Mom, you're absolutely amazing, and I am so grateful for everything you do for me. It's because of your support that I can chase the dream of writing full time. Thank you, thank you, thank you.

And finally, THANK YOU to everyone who gave *Island of Exiles* a chance. Thank you to everyone who talked about it and posted reviews and shared pictures. Thank you to everyone who loved *Island* enough to follow me to book two. I sincerely hope I didn't disappoint.

Grab the Entangled Teen releases readers are talking about!

27 Hours
by Tristina Wright

Rumor Mora fears two things: hellhounds too strong for him to kill, and failure. Jude Welton has two dreams: for humans to stop killing monsters, and for his strange abilities to vanish.

But in no reality should a boy raised to love monsters fall for a boy raised to kill them.

During one twenty-seven-hour night, if they can't stop the war between the colonies and the monsters from becoming a war of extinction, the things they wish for will never come true, and the things they fear will be all that's left.

The November Girl
By Lydia Kang

I'm Anda, and the lake is my mother. I am the November storms that terrify sailors, and with their deaths, I keep the island alive.

Hector has come to Isle Royale to hide. My little island on Lake Superior is shut down for the winter, and there's no one here but me. And now him.

Hector is running from the violence in his life, but violence runs through my veins. I should send him away. But I'm half-human, too, and Hector makes me want to listen to my foolish, half-human heart. And if do, I can't protect him from the storms coming for us.

HAVEN
BY MARY LINDSEY

Rain Ryland has never belonged anywhere. He's used to people judging him for his rough background, his intimidating size, and now, his orphan status. He's always been on the outside, looking in, and he's fine with that. Until he moves to New Wurzburg and meets Friederike Burkhart.

Freddie isn't like normal teen girls, though. And someone wants her dead for it. Freddie warns he'd better stay far away if he wants to stay alive, but Rain's never been good at running from trouble. For the first time, Rain has something worth fighting for, worth living for. Worth dying for.

BLACK BIRD OF THE GALLOWS
BY MEG KASSEL

A simple but forgotten truth: where harbingers of death appear, the morgues will soon be full.

Angie Dovage can tell there's more to Reece Fernandez than just the tall, brooding athlete who has her classmates swooning, but she can't imagine his presence signals a tragedy that will devastate her small town. When something supernatural tries to attack her, Angie is thrown into a battle between good and evil she never saw coming. Right in the center of it is Reece—and he's not human.

What's more, she knows something most don't. That the secrets her town holds could kill them all. But that's only half as dangerous as falling in love with a harbinger of death.

entangled teen

an imprint of Entangled Publishing LLC